Books by Mariah Stewart

MOMENTS IN TIME

A DIFFERENT LIGHT

CAROLINA MIST

DEVLIN'S LIGHT

WONDERFUL YOU

MOON DANCE

PRICELESS

BROWN-EYED GIRL

VOICES CARRY

Published by Pocket Books

MARIAH STEWART

Priceless

POCKET BOOKS
New York London Toronto Sydney

This book is a work of fiction. Names, characters, places and incidents are products of the author's imagination or are used fictitiously. Any resemblance to actual events or locales or persons, living or dead, is entirely coincidental.

 POCKET BOOKS, a division of Simon & Schuster, Inc.
1230 Avenue of the Americas, New York, NY 10020

Copyright © 1999 by Marti Robb

ISBN-13: 978-0-671-02625-7
ISBN-10:   0-671-02625-9

First Pocket Books printing June 1999

10 9 8 7 6 5 4

POCKET and colophon are registered trademarks of Simon & Schuster, Inc.

Cover design by Jae Song

Manufactured in the United States of America

For information regarding special discounts for bulk purchases, please contact Simon & Schuster Special Sales at 1-800-456-6798 or business@simonandschuster.com.

To Jo Ellen,
for all the years
of love and friendship

Grateful acknowledgments to:

"Underwater Bob" Decker, Olympus Diving Center, Morehead City, North Carolina, for his patience with my most elementary questions and his prompt and cheerful responses to my e-mails. I can honestly say that he taught me everything I know about wreck diving. It goes without saying that any errors are mine, not his.

Chery Griffin, whose encouragement, friendship, and twice weekly phone calls went a long way in helping me to finish this book.

Joan Galvin, for "loaning" her family's farm, Pumpkin Hill, for my last book, and for helping me to keep my head above water.

Helen Egner, for honest opinions on those first drafts.

Loretta Barrett, my agent, for keeping the faith.

Lauren McKenna, for all she does.

1

GORDON CHANDLER stood on the deck of the *Albemarle* and leaned over the railing. His head and shoulders cast an elongated shadow across the blue-green ocean below, where his children frolicked in the late afternoon sun, and he closed his eyes, impressing the scene upon his memory. Over the past several weeks, it had become painfully obvious to him that his vast stash of memories contained far more images of sunken hulls than of his son and his daughter at play, and he was stunned as well as saddened by the realization. Somehow, during all those years he'd spent carefully locating and digging artifacts from the ocean's floor, both Jared and Rachel had managed to grow into adults with precious little assistance from him.

Gordon was at a loss to explain how it had all happened so quickly.

After all, hadn't it been just yesterday that he'd bought Jared his first wet suit and taken him on that trip to the Florida Keys? And how long ago could it have been that he'd gifted Rachel with that small conch shell that she, even now, wore about her neck on a thin silver chain?

Gordon sighed and shook his head imperceptibly. The years had drifted past as stealthily as a sailboat on a calm sea, gently and without fanfare. Water through his fingers.

Jared had been nine years old the year that his father had taken him out of school for three weeks to spend most of the month of April tracking a Spanish galleon that had centuries ago gone down in a fierce hurricane off the coast of Florida. Gordon had wanted his son to be standing on the deck with him on the day that the remains of the *Santa Maria Elena de Cordoba* would see the light of day for the first time in four hundred years. He'd wanted Jared to understand that what kept his father away from his family for weeks, often months, at a time was not so much the hint of finding lost treasure as the chance to touch other times, other lives.

Jared was now thirty-two years old, Rachel, twenty-eight, and Gordon was still not certain of how much of their lives he had touched, beyond, of course, their choice of profession.

It never failed to humble Gordon to realize that both his children had chosen to follow in his footsteps, as he had followed in his father's, and his father had before him. Jared was the fourth generation of Chandler men to seek to uncover the mysteries hidden beneath the sea, Rachel the first woman. Both had joined Chandler and Associates upon graduating from college. Both had worked various operations, sometimes with their father, sometimes with each other, but the three Chandlers had never worked the same job at the same time. This latest venture, the salvaging of the *True Wind*, with all its legendary pirate treasure aboard, would mark the first time father, son, and daughter had worked together.

Somehow, despite his shortcomings as a father, both of his children had seemed to understand that the countless hours Gordon spent researching the location of each vessel was a journey toward fulfilling the legacy of every one of the men on board those doomed ships. That each salvaged ship brought to light the stories of a hundred or more men who had perished on an angry sea, and in the remains left on the ocean's floor, Gordon often learned just what it was that those men had believed was worth dying for.

For some, it had been gold.

The act of finding the treasures that Gordon had resurrected over the years had satisfied him in much the same way another might be pleased at having solved a particularly vexatious puzzle. True, the financial rewards he reaped were a means of supporting his family as well as his next salvage operation, but it was his respect for the past that drove him. Over the years, his strict honesty and his meticulous efforts to preserve his finds had earned him a reputation as a man who could be trusted equally with the treasure and with the integrity of the site. Gordon Chandler's name was always on the top of the list of men to call when there was an important salvage operation to be planned.

Gordon watched his son and his daughter as they

swam through the gentle swells like true children of the sea. They were beautiful, as had been their mother, Amelia, who had died when Rachel was eight, Jared twelve. The death of one's wife might be expected to bring one home from the sea, and it had, though only briefly. Amelia, a concert pianist, having been away from home nearly as much as Gordon himself had been, had long since sweet-talked her Aunt Bess into moving in with her children. As soon as Gordon had been assured that Bess would stay on with them after Amelia's death, he had set off to research a ship—suspected to be Sumerian—that had been located off the coast of a small island in the Aegean.

And somehow, between that job and the next, and the one after that, his children had grown up without him. Somehow Jared had shot up to well over six feet tall, had grown broad shouldered and trim and handsome enough to catch the eyes of the young ladies wherever he went. And somehow, Rachel, who had always seemed to skip through her father's heart, a perpetual little girl made of spun glass, had grown into a strikingly beautiful woman, one who was not the least bit hesitant to let it be known that she was now made of much sterner stuff. A few short years out of college, Rachel was more competent a salvager than many of the men Gordon had worked with over the years. Smart and savvy, Rachel was as accurate in locating a ship, as sensitive and exacting in preserving all of the site's artifacts, as was Gordon himself.

A small school of dolphin approached, passing close enough to the swimmers for Rachel to be splashed in the face by a lively youngster. From his position on the *Albemarle*—the retired tug he'd bought and refitted years ago—Gordon heard his daughter's laughter float above the waves, watched his son race gamely to keep up with the pod before dropping back as the animals sped out to sea, and was struck almost numb by the depth of his love for them both.

And yet Gordon knew with certainty that before the day ended, one of them would be fiercely disappointed and painfully angry, and he, Gordon, would be the cause.

Well, Gordon sighed, it couldn't be helped. If he'd passed up the unexpected offer from the Foundation for the Preservation of Eden's End, the job of bringing up the *Melrose* would have gone to another salvage firm, perhaps one who might not be as concerned with preserving the details of the historic vessel. And wasn't that the Foundation's primary purpose in wanting to salvage the *Melrose*, to find and preserve as many of the personal belongings of that ship's venerable captain as possible?

Of course, the fact that this particular operation would stand him in exceptionally good graces with the state of North Carolina—with which Gordon was currently negotiating the rights to another ship he'd spent years tracking off Kitty Hawk—had not been lost on Gordon.

Besides, it was a done deal. He and Norman Winter, the head of the Foundation, had shaken hands on it just a few hours earlier. Now Gordon would have to break the news to his children that one of them would have to leave the *True Wind*, and the certain joy of discovering its pirate treasures, to salvage Civil War artifacts from a sunken blockade runner that might, at best, yield arms and ammunition that had been intended to bolster the Confederate cause, but had, alas, lain untouched on the ocean floor for the past one hundred thirty-five years.

Noticing his father standing alone on deck, Jared paused to tread water and call, "Hey, Dad! You up for a race to the sandbar?"

Gordon laughed, the sandbar being a good quarter mile from the tug. "Another time, maybe. Actually, I was just about to ask you and your sister to come aboard. There's something I need to discuss with you."

"Ooh, that sounds ominous!" Rachel swam toward the ladder that was suspended from the side of the boat and hoisted herself up the rungs.

"How was your meeting in Wilmington?" she asked as she climbed aboard and paused briefly to squeeze the water out of her long auburn hair.

"Interesting. *Most* interesting. Actually, that's what I need to discuss with you and Jared."

"Who was the meeting with?" Jared followed his sister over the side of the boat.

"A man named Norman Winter."

"Norman Winter," Rachel repeated softly. "That name is familiar."

"Oh, I would expect that it would be. He's quite the philanthropist. Heads up the Foundation for the Preservation of Eden's End."

"Of course. I remember. He's a real Civil War buff. Gives lots of money to historical preservation groups in North Carolina."

"Didn't he recently endow a chair at Pamlico State?" Jared pulled a worn Duke sweatshirt over his head.

"Yes. And he's financed a number of historic preservation projects over the past few years."

"I read a magazine article about him not too long ago," Jared recalled. "He's apparently restoring an old plantation he bought outside of Wilmington."

"That would be Eden's End. Once the home of Captain Samuel Lawrence McGowan." Gordon nodded and opened the door leading to the small cabin he used as an office, motioning for his children to follow him inside. "McGowan was a hero of the War between the States, a loyal and venerated son of Dixie."

"Shed his life's blood for the cause, did he?" Rachel eased into a chair that stood near the worn rectangular table.

"Actually, McGowan never saw battle. At least, not on land, anyway. He was a blockade runner, kept Lee's troops in food and guns, and kept the ladies of Wilmington in parasols and hoop skirts. Wilmington was the last of the Southern ports to remain open during the Union blockade."

"He sounds like Rhett Butler." Rachel grinned.

"A real-life Rhett Butler." Gordon nodded.

Jared opened the small refrigerator and took out a beer. He held it up, wordlessly offering it first to his father, then to his sister, both of whom declined.

"I'll take a bottle of springwater if there's any left," Rachel told him.

"I brought some back with me this afternoon,"

Gordon said as he took a seat at the long wooden table that served as his desk.

"Great. I'll have one." With one hand, Rachel caught the small plastic bottle that was tossed in her direction by her brother, then turned her attention back to her father. "So, what's up with this Winter guy? I'm assuming there's a story here."

"Quite an interesting one." Gordon leaned back in his chair, tapping his fingers on the wooden arms. He'd have to make the story *really* interesting if he had any hope that either of his children would agree to join Winter on his quest for McGowan's vessel. "Were you aware that he funds the Foundation himself?"

"Wow. That's impressive." Jared popped the lid off the beer can and took a swig. "Where does his money come from?"

"He gave me the impression that he's a self-made man," Gordon told them.

"He must have made a lot," Rachel mused. "Foundations like that are hungry buggers. And it takes truckloads of cash to restore a plantation."

"He didn't go into detail, but he did allude to having made a lot of money in construction when he was younger, then invested well. Lucky in the market, I guess. He's doing a marvelous job restoring Eden's End, by the way."

"You've been there?" Rachel asked.

"This morning. That's where I met with Winter. He told me that he first became interested in historic preservation when he was in his early twenties and was working at Eden's End with the contractor who had been called in by the McGowan family to do some work on the old house."

"And he ended up buying it?" Jared leaned back in his seat, tilting the chair onto its two back legs.

"Years later, yes, when William McGowan passed away and the family put the house on the market."

"The house had remained in the same family since the Civil War?"

Gordon nodded. "Until just a few years ago, Rachel. Apparently William McGowan's widow was unable to keep up with the property, and agreed to sell it to Winter, who is supervising the restoration himself, by the way. He's meticulous about detail, and was dedicated to salvaging as much as he could of all the original structures."

"Commendable." Rachel took a long pull on the bottle of water.

"Yes, it is. And in the process of restoring the property, Winter has become somewhat of an expert on old Sam McGowan."

"There's a marine archaeologist named Sam McGowan. Dr. Sam McGowan," Jared said. "I worked with him on the *Esmeralda* off the Keys a few years back. Smart. Hard worker. Good diver. Great instincts. He taught graduate courses at East Carolina State for a while."

"Old Sam's great-great-grandson," Gordon told him. "And I heartily agree. Sam is all of those things. Our paths have crossed several times. As a matter of fact, I've been trying to talk him into joining Chandler and Associates for the past several years—I think we're more than ready to hire our own resident archaeologist—but so far, I haven't had much luck.

Sam likes his independence, I suppose." Gordon smiled. "I'm glad you like him, son, since it appears that you may very well have a chance to work with him again."

"I'd welcome it. McGowan's a great guy. He's a man you can trust and respect. We got along really well."

"I can't tell you how happy I am to hear you say that, Jared, since Sam will be the archaeologist on the job that Winter has contracted Chandler and Associates to run."

"Terrific." Jared grinned. "You just let me know where and when."

"Next Tuesday." Gordon met his son's eyes across the table. "Bowan Island Marina."

Eyes flickered, son to father, brother to sister, daughter to father.

Finally, Jared cleared his throat and said, "I think you must have left out part of your little story, Dad."

"I was getting to it, son. You know that Sam McGowan—the first Sam—was a blockade runner. In September of 1864—the twenty-first, actually—McGowan's paddleboat was caught in a squall and sank. Winter is convinced he's found the wreck. He's struck a deal with the state of North Carolina for salvage rights, since he's planning to open part of the old McGowan plantation as a sort of Civil War museum."

"Okay, so he knows where the ship is and he's managed to get the rights to some of the booty." Jared tapped out his impatience on the tabletop, much as his father had earlier tapped on the arms of his chair. "What's the big hurry?"

"He wants to open the exhibit on September twenty-first."

"Of this year?" Rachel's jaw dropped. "Dad, that's only five months from now."

"I'm aware of that," Gordon said calmly, preparing himself for the storm that was yet to come.

"Dad, this is crazy. How could you possibly carry out an operation like that in five months?"

"Not so very crazy, Jared, considering that the trickiest part has been done. Winter found the ship, all we have to do is figure out how to salvage it between now and September," Gordon said, only half tongue in cheek.

"Are you telling us that you have already committed to this?" Rachel pushed her chair back from the table.

"Yes. Yes, I did."

"Dad, how could you possibly get a crew together . . . the divers, the equipment . . ."

"Winter has a boat outfitted and ready to go."

"How could he do that so quickly?" Jared asked.

"He's been planning this for a long time, Jared. He's prepared." Gordon lifted a leather folder from an adjacent chair and set it on the table between his son and his daughter. Neither reached for it. "Winter has researched this very thoroughly. He has maps, historical documentation, and recently he came across accounts of the residents of Bowan Island who saw the boat go down. All he needs is someone to run the project, a few divers . . ."

"How can you run two jobs at the same time, Dad?" Jared asked pointedly.

"Obviously, I can't. One of you will take the lead on the *Melrose* project."

The silence was overwhelming.

"I was hoping that one of you would volunteer to take it," Gordon said levelly, looking from his son to his daughter. "Apparently I was overly optimistic."

"Dad, with all respect, I have waited ten years for a shot at the *True Wind.*"

"Jared, you don't need to remind me that you were the one who tracked her down."

"Then you will understand why I'm not going to volunteer to give her up. If you tell me to go, I will, but I'm not going to walk away willingly." Jared turned in his chair to gaze at his sister. "Now, sweet cheeks here is always after you to give her a project of her own to run. I think this little gun runner might be just the thing to let her cut her teeth on."

"Oh, no!" Rachel stood up, shaking her head adamantly. "No, you don't, Jared. I've waited forever to dive on an undisturbed pirate ship. You've done it before—several times, as I recall. Dad, Jared was the one who said he'd be happy to work with this McGowan guy anytime."

"You're the one who's always whining that she isn't taken seriously enough."

"I don't whine, Jared. And for the record . . ."

Gordon held up both hands, imploring his sparring children to cease.

"I was afraid this would happen." He sighed. "There's only one way to resolve this."

"Call Norman Winter and cancel?" Rachel asked ruefully, knowing full well that her father would never go back on his word. "Put him off until *next* September?"

"Winter wants to open his exhibit this September . . .

the one hundred thirty-fifth anniversary of the sinking of the *Melrose*. Which just happens to be Sam McGowan's one hundred ninetieth birthday."

"McGowan was born and died on the same date?"

"Yes. He died on his fifty-fifth birthday. Which is also, coincidentally, Norman Winter's birthday."

"Oh, I get it," Jared said dryly. "Winter wants to bring the good captain up as a sort of birthday present. Dad, I don't know that that's a good enough reason to take one of us off the *True Wind* to go after this wreck. What does he expect to find, anyway, besides a few old guns and maybe McGowan's pocket watch?"

"Probably not much more than that. Which was one of the reasons I agreed to this job."

"Sorry, Dad, but I'm not following that bit of logic." Rachel shook her head.

"Winter has shown me exactly where the ship is resting. Sonar has backed him up. It will be a quick in and out. There might be, as Jared noted, some guns intended for the Confederate army, maybe some cargo meant for the civilians. Whether or not any of that survived all these years, well, that will depend on what the cargo was packed in and how deeply it's been buried. As you both know, some wooden trunks have remained intact for centuries. What Winter really appears to be most interested in is McGowan's personal items, cuff links, perhaps a sword, maybe some porcelain. The ship's log—he mentioned that specifically—if McGowan was wise enough to keep it in a watertight box."

"Seems like a lot of trouble to go to to recover so

few items, none of which may be particularly valuable."

"It means a lot to Winter. McGowan was a genuine Civil War hero."

"I hope he's paying you a lot of money for this job," Rachel grumbled.

"Twice the going rate."

Rachel's eyebrows arched.

"Twice?"

"If we bring up the box with the ship's log and whatever else we find in time for Winter to open his exhibit at Eden's End by September twenty-first."

"No sweat," Jared said. "As you said, Dad, it should be a quick in and out."

"Good." Rachel smiled sweetly. "Then you won't miss much of what's happening on the *True Wind* while you're gone."

"I didn't say I'd go. I just meant that it sounds like a relatively easy job. Take it, Rach. Just think, your first solo job, a guaranteed success . . ."

"Thank you, but no. With your vastly greater experience—of which you remind me at every possible opportunity—you should be able to take the *Melrose* in record time." Rachel tossed her empty water bottle across the room and it somersaulted neatly into the recycling bin in the corner.

"I was hoping it wouldn't come to this, but you're not leaving me a choice." Gordon stood up, his right hand rustling in his pocket for change. He held up a quarter. "You're going to have to flip for it."

Sister and brother glared at each other. Reluctantly, they both nodded their agreement.

"Go 'head, Rach." Jared gestured. "Call it."

Gordon tossed the coin into the air and caught it smartly, slapping it onto the back of his hand. He looked up at Rachel expectantly.

"Heads," she said.

Holding out his hand, Gordon uncovered the coin as both Jared and Rachel leaned forward anxiously.

Tails it was.

"Rachel, you have won the right to lead the expedition to salvage the *Melrose*." Gordon eyed her levelly.

"Thanks, Dad." Rachel couldn't meet his eyes. She just couldn't. Nor could she look at her brother, who would surely, while not gloating, be relieved that he had escaped what seemed at that moment to be the most burdensome of missions.

"If you'd like to take one of our divers, I believe I can arrange it with Winter."

"Can I pick Jared?" She batted her eyelashes in mock coyness, feigning innocence.

Gordon hesitated. Jared glowered.

"Just kidding." Rachel sighed heavily. "You won, fair and square, Jared. You stay. I go."

She went to the cabin door and pushed it open. She would have a lot of preparation if she was to meet Norman Winter on Tuesday.

"Rach, I'm sorry, sweetheart." Gordon reached for her hand. "The next one, I promise, is yours."

Rachel tried to force a smile but her mouth tightened into a thin, tense line. She hoisted the leather portfolio that her father had earlier placed on the table.

"Thanks, Dad. Now, if you'll excuse me, it looks as if I have a lot of reading to do."

*   *   *

It took all of Rachel's self-control to not slam the door of her cabin behind her. Tossing the leather folder on her narrow bunk, she crossed her arms over her chest and blew out the hot air of exasperation she'd been holding. Her right foot began to tap, and she forced the hot tears that welled in the corners of her eyes not to fall. Angry, disappointed, frustrated she might be, but she would not cry, any more than Jared would have cried had he lost the toss. Rachel had spent most of her life trying to live up to her father and her big brother. She would not do less than either of them would do now.

For several minutes she tried pacing off her warring emotions, but the small cabin was too tiny for her to walk far enough to work it out. She stood in the center of the small space and closed her eyes, imagining herself beneath a canopy of blue-green water, diving deeper and deeper into the darkness below, where she could lose herself, if only for a while, in the only true escape she'd ever found, and wished she could be there, on the bottom of the ocean, right at that minute. In her mind's eye, she watched herself head down toward the remains of the *True Wind*, seeking its form below her and dodging a sand shark along the way. Closer, closer, she swam through the cool water, eyeing the cracked hull of the ship, her heart beating excitedly as she drew nearer, her legs rhythmically propelling her onward, alone in a deep blue sea with a treasure unwittingly left behind by the pirate captain and his hapless crew over two hundred fifty years ago.

Of course in real life, she'd never make such a dive without a partner, but at this particular moment, company—even if only imaginary—was about the last thing she wanted.

Rachel sighed and reluctantly let the vision pass. Diving on the *True Wind* would have to wait for another day. Her father had given his word, and she had given hers. Dwelling on her loss would only make her bitter, and there was work to be done.

That Rachel felt absolutely no enthusiasm for the project at hand would not influence her total committment to its success. It would never occur to her to give any job—even one she didn't want—less than her best. She was Gordon Chandler's daughter, and she knew that much was expected of her. She would die before she'd disappoint.

Leaning over to retrieve the portfolio she'd earlier tossed aside, she slid its contents onto the mattress. A stack of marine charts, colored to show, among other navigational information, water depth and shoals, accompanied historical data relative to the ship, and a sketchy biography of Samuel L. McGowan himself. There was little about the Foundation and its director, Norman Winter, though the omission wasn't particularly unusual. Many philanthropists preferred to keep a low profile.

Rachel sat in the scaled-down chair at the small desk built into the narrow corner and shuffled through the charts. She was no stranger to the North Carolina waters, having cut her wreck-diving teeth on several of the sunken vessels off the area known as the Crystal Coast. As a college student, she'd spent summers with a classmate, Jill Simmons, on Emerald Isle, where they'd worked as waitresses at night and spent the days diving. Five years ago, Jill had married a businessman and moved to London. She now had a house in the Nottingham section of the city, two children, and a booming career as a sought-after interior decorator, but she had clung to her love of diving. Once every year, Rachel and Jill would meet at an agreed-upon location and they would spend a week diving, shopping, and catching up on each other's lives. This year they had gone to Curaçao. Next year would find them in Australia.

And the next few months would find Rachel off the coast of North Carolina tracking down a ship laden, not with pirate gold, but a cargo of guns that hadn't seen the light of day in almost one hundred thirty-five years.

She turned on the desk lamp and began to read.

She was still studying water depths around the vessel when she heard a light tap on her cabin door.

"Rach?" Jared called softly.

"It's unlocked."

For such a big man, Jared could move quietly when he wanted to. Rachel barely heard him enter the cabin.

"I brought you a sandwich. Turkey on whole wheat. A little mayo, a little lettuce. Three pickles on the side. Just the way you like it."

"Is it dinnertime already?" She turned to look up at him.

Jared filled the space of the small doorway. He wore cutoff shorts and an old tee, and held the plastic plate out to her as a peace offering. Rachel smiled in spite of herself. It would take a stronger soul than hers to remain angry with Jared for too long.

"Dinner's long past, Rach. It's almost nine."

"Oh. I didn't realize it was so late." She rubbed her hand on the back of her neck, which was stiff from being hunched over the desk for several hours. She pointed to the charts and said, "I've been doing a little light reading . . ."

"Mind if I take a look?"

"Help yourself." She lifted a stack of charts and said, "We'll trade. I get the food, you get the charts."

"Deal." He handed over the plate, took the sheaf of papers from her hand, and sat on the edge of the bunk.

"Hey, I know this area." He frowned. "I wonder why I never heard of the *Melrose*."

"I was wondering that myself," she said after she swallowed a bite of sandwich. "I've been diving in those waters a dozen or more times."

"Remember the first time we dove together in North Carolina?"

Rachel nodded. "You took me to the wreck of the *Papoose*, off Cape Lookout. Ninety feet underwater, and surrounded by sand tiger sharks. Not the type of thing a girl forgets. I thought Dad was going to kill you when he found out where you'd taken me." Rachel took another bite. "Great sandwich, by the way."

"Thanks." Jared grinned. "And you're right, Dad had a fit. But I never doubted for a minute that you could make that dive, and that you'd love it."

"I did love it, Jared, once I realized that the sharks weren't going to eat me. I must confess that I had a few antsy minutes there at first. Sitting on the ocean floor surrounded by a school of mean-looking carnivores was a whole new experience for me."

"And you did great, like I knew you would. Convincing Dad that you were ready hadn't been as easy."

"Dad always thought of me as this helpless little girl who needed someone watching after her. Sometimes I think he still does." She looked him squarely in the eyes and added, "Sometimes I think you do, too."

"No." Jared shook his head. "No, I know better. And in his heart, Dad does, too."

"You know, I think he was really torn today. On the one hand, I think he was afraid that you'd lose the toss. On the other, I think he was afraid you wouldn't."

"What's that supposed to mean?"

"That Dad really wants you with him on the *True Wind*. He knows that's what's right. It's your ship. On the other hand, he isn't so sure that I can handle the *Melrose* alone." Ire tinged her cheeks with a hint of color.

"Well, then, this is your chance to prove otherwise, isn't it?"

"As good a chance as I'll ever get."

"If there's anything I can do to help out . . ." Jared stood, his hands shoved into the pockets of his cutoff jeans.

"Yeah, I know where to find you." She nodded and smiled weakly.

"Have you decided if you'll take someone from our crew?"

"I really hate to do that, Jared. All of Dad's men are psyched for the *True Wind*. I'd hate to take any one of them off the job. And I don't know that

I'll need an extra diver. Dad said that Winter already has a couple of divers, and you said the archaeologist . . ."

"Sam McGowan."

"Yes. You said he was a good diver."

"He's excellent."

"Well, that makes four, counting me. Enough for two sets of partners. I don't see where we'll need more than that for this job, judging from the information I've read tonight. I think the *True Wind* is more likely to need the rest of the crew."

"If you change your mind, you can always holler. We'll send someone out if need be." Jared grinned again. "Hell, if things get slow around here, I'll come for a day or two myself."

"I may just take you up on that." Rachel stood and handed her brother the empty plate. "Thanks for dinner, Jared. I appreciate the gesture as well as the food."

"Well, I can't have you skipping meals and fading away to nothing. You're the only sister I have. Besides, I needed to make sure that you were all right with this. If you weren't, Rach, I'd go."

"I appreciate that, but in all honesty, even if I'd won the toss, I'd probably have offered to go, in the end. It wouldn't have been fair otherwise, Jared. You were the first one to find out about the *True Wind*, you did all the research. Dad might never have even heard of it, if not for you." Rachel shook her head again. "The *True Wind* is yours, bucko."

Jared leaned over and kissed the top of his sister's head, a rare and unexpected gesture.

"Thanks, sis. That really means a lot to me."

"You'd do the same for me."

"Probably," he conceded, as he pushed open the cabin door. "I probably would have. But don't forget what I said, Rach. If you think of anything you need, anything you want . . ."

"Well, there is one thing." Rachel leaned against the doorjamb.

"Name it."

"Could you save me just one tiny little piece of the *True Wind*? Just one little square that no one touches, that I can sift through when I get back?"

"You're on, kid. One tiny square on the grid will remain untouched." Jared laughed as he ducked and went through the doorway. "Looks like you'll have the best of both worlds, Rach. By the end of the summer, you'll have a successful operation under your belt, and your chance for pirate gold. And who knows what you'll find on the *Melrose*."

Rachel wrinkled her nose.

"A bunch of old rusty guns, that's what I'll find on the *Melrose*."

"Well, even that should be interesting. You know what Dad always says."

" 'Every wreck tells a story. A good salvor listens well.' " Rachel laughed as she repeated her father's favorite phrase. "Some stories are just more interesting than others."

She closed the door and went back to her desk, lamenting the certainty that any tale told by the *Melrose* would surely pale next to the *True Wind*'s, and there was nothing she could do about it.

2

---◆◇◆---

THE STIFF April breeze fought the ferry every inch of the way from Ocracoke to Cedar Island. Even the gulls that followed along behind, begging tidbits from willing passengers as they crossed the sound, seemed to be blown off course from time to time. Rachel stood atop the upper deck, watching the water below change from blue to gray-green as they threaded their way through the restless shoals, and unconsciously spread her feet apart just enough to ensure her balance as the ferry rode the twenty-two miles of choppy waves from the Outer Banks to the mainland.

In spite of her father's assurances, Rachel still wasn't wholly convinced that Norman Winter was happy to have *any* Chandler willing to work with him at such late notice. She'd believe that when she saw it. Who in their right mind would be as happy with Rachel in charge of their expedition as they would have been with Gordon—or even Jared, for that matter? She wrestled with edgy nerves, willing herself to exhibit a confidence that she did not feel. By the time the boat reached the shore, she would have total control. More importantly, Norman Winter would believe she had total control.

A gull landed on the railing and eyed her hopefully.

"Sorry, pal. Nothing today." Rachel held her empty hands toward the bird, which, apparently understanding what an empty palm meant, took itself down to the first level of the boat, where it clearly hoped to find a better reception and a few good handouts.

Up ahead, through the fog that clutched at the shore, Rachel could see Cedar Island. As the ferry docked, she took the map from the side pocket of her dark green jacket and unfolded it to check her directions yet again. Route 12 south to where it meets Route 70, then south to Bowan Island, midway down the coast between Morehead City and Wilmington. Bowan Island, where she'd meet with Winter himself, and get her first look at the boat that would serve as her home for the next several months.

At least I'll be in relatively familiar waters, she reminded herself as she drove her old red compact off the ferry and past the rambling white visitors center. *And it could be worse, all things considered. I could have been bumped off the* True Wind *and sent elsewhere. Under any other circumstances, I'd be begging for a chance to work here. And if I can work fast enough, efficiently enough, I'll be back on the* Albemarle *just about the time the* True Wind *is giving up her gold.*

Rachel rolled the window down and let the breeze

blow through, hustling out the stale air that had been locked for the past two hours inside the small car and searched the radio for a station that offered some good solid rock and roll and no static. She settled for the country station with the strongest signal, and eased back to enjoy the ride. She was to meet Winter around four on Bowan Island. She had plenty of time, and so had the luxury of driving leisurely through one small town after another, each with the inevitable white spired churches, gas stations, and coffee shops. Rachel smiled to herself. Her father always said if you want to feel the beat of a town, take its pulse in its coffee shop.

Rounding a curve that showed on the map as a mere curl, she discovered that the road branched out into three prongs—left, right, and the narrow access road straight ahead leading to a drawbridge standing open like giant jaws reaching to snap at some unseen prey. A sign on her right assured her that Bowan Island lay just on the other side of the bridge. She hesitated, peered over her steering wheel, and searched the waters beyond for the passing ship for which the bridge had opened. Within seconds of her stopping, the span began to lower, and the safety arm began to rise.

Crossing onto Bowan Island, Rachel passed from the familiarity of the last of the small towns to what appeared to be a narrow stretch of uninhabited land. While the road was two-laned and well paved, it seemed to lead nowhere but deeper into the marshes that spread out on either side of the car. Rachel was just beginning to think that perhaps she'd made a wrong turn somewhere along the way when the mac-

adam came to a sudden end. Having nowhere else
to go, Rachel got out of the car and climbed to the
top of the dune, her steps cautious, knowing that the
quiet marshes teemed with life. Loggerhead and
green sea turtles, both protected species, made stops
on islands just like this one every year to lay their
eggs. Alligators crept through the still waters and
were not above making a meal out of the nesting
turtles, government-protected or otherwise. Not
wishing to surprise or be surprised by either, Rachel
tread with keen awareness of her surroundings.

Once at the top of the dune, she raised a hand to
her eyes to block the sun that danced in sharpe-
edged shards upon a clear, calm ocean. A man
dressed all in white, from his brimmed hat to his
deck shoes, stood looking out to sea as if searching
for something. Rachel paused, wondering if this was
Norman Winter, and if so, where they were to go
from here. There was no boat, and she hadn't seen a
living soul since arriving on the island. She was just
about to return to her car to call her father on her cell
phone, when the man turned around. He appeared to
study her for a long moment, then waved one hand
over his head and called, "Rachel? You are Rachel
Chandler, aren't you?"

"Yes," she called back. "Are you Mr. Winter?"

"Norman to you."

He approached her swiftly across the sand and the
marsh grass, moving on land as smoothly as she herself moved through water, and was midway up the
dune before Rachel could react.

"Now, I do hope you had a pleasant trip?" he

asked in a slow drawl as he extended his right hand and removed his hat with the left.

His hair, Rachel discovered, was as white as his jacket, and her mind conjured up a photograph she had seen of Andy Warhol, years ago. Dark glasses shielded Winter's eyes, and she wondered unwittingly if they, too, were white.

"Yes, I . . ."

"Good. Good. I'm afraid we'll have to walk a ways down to the cove. It appears that Saturday's storm destroyed the dock I had here—it built up that sandbar, too"—he pointed offshore—"so I had to leave the boat that will take us to the *Annie G.* on the other side of the island. I hope you don't mind the inconvenience."

"Not at all. But my car . . ." She gestured toward the dune behind her.

"Not to worry. I'll have one of my men bring your things to the ship and drive your car to Eden's End. You can leave it there while you're at sea. Now, if you're ready . . ."

He reached for her hand again. His dark glasses covered one-third of his face, and Rachel wished that she could see his eyes.

"I just need to get a few things." She turned toward the car. "Just my purse and a bag. I'll be right back."

Rachel returned to her car, uneasy with Winter's suggestion that she leave it here on this deserted dead-end road, filled as it was with several thousands of dollars' worth of diving equipment. What if someone else found the car before Winter's men did? She reached in through the open window and pulled out her purse, then grabbed a big nylon bag containing her clothes and personal items from the backseat. The least she should do would be to roll up the windows, maybe grab a few things from the trunk. How much could she carry? How far down the beach would they have to walk?

As if reading her mind, Winter appeared at the top of the dune and called down to her.

"It's all right. Really. Just leave your keys in the ignition. Someone will come for your things. You don't need to load yourself down. I promise, all of your things will be aboard the ship by the time you are."

Winter smiled, exhibiting an almost jaunty air, and removed a small phone from the inside of his tidy linen jacket. Seconds later he was giving instructions to have her car picked up, its contents delivered to the ship, and the car itself to be driven to Eden's End.

"Satisfied?" he asked as he slipped the phone back inside his jacket.

"Yes, thank you." Rachel nodded.

With a bow toward her uncertainty, Winter added, "It may make you feel better to know that Bowan Island is privately owned, and that access is restricted."

"Privately owned? By you?"

"Yes, of course." He smiled again, showing a row of teeth too white and perfect and even to be natural. "I bought the island with the intention of building a small resort community, but never got further than building the marina. Which is, alas, empty except for my own vessels right now."

Rachel swung her bag over her shoulder, anxious now to get the project under way. "Which way?"

"Right along the beach here"—Winter motioned toward the ocean—"then around a bend or two and we'll be at the marina. I had hoped to be able to just hop aboard the boat here, without making you walk halfway around the island, but . . ." He held both hands out in front of him and shrugged.

Rachel nodded, understanding well the vagaries of the sea. Today's beach was yesterday's inlet. Yesterday's inlet is tomorrow's shoal. And so it went, coastlines changing—sometimes subtly, sometimes dramatically—with every storm.

The walk along the beach was pleasant, the sand littered with shells tossed up by those same waves that had devoured Winter's dock and blocked the cove with the newly formed sandbar. On another day, Rachel would have picked up this shell or that, to study its shape and its coloration, but today, her mind bent on business, she passed them by without a second thought. This man walking beside her was their client, and he deserved her full attention.

She just wished she could see his eyes.

"My father said that you and Sam McGowan share the same birthday," she said, hoping to draw him into conversation.

Winter tilted his head, as if considering the question, then said, "I've no idea when his birthday is."

"I could have sworn that my father told me that you both were born on the same day in September."

"Oh, you mean *Captain* McGowan. I never think of him as *Sam*. Sam is the young archaeologist. A descendant of the Captain's." Winter nodded. "Yes, the Captain and I were both born on September twenty-first. Years apart, of course." He grinned, as if to show that he could—did—make a joke, and looked to her as one who was used to having his jokes appreciated might do.

Rachel smiled weakly.

"Have you always been a Civil War buff?"

"I don't know that I consider myself a Civil War buff as much as an admirer of Captain McGowan. He's recognized as quite the hero, you know."

"As a blockade runner."

"Oh, and a bit more, I suspect, than just one who outran the damn Yankees. No offense." He smiled in deference to the hint of New England in her voice. "But blockading the Southern ports took a terrible toll on the general populace, not to mention the effect on Lee's troops. If not for the brave men willing to take on the Northern Navy, more people would have suffered from hunger, from lack of medical supplies and clothing."

"Ah, yes." She nodded. "Not to mention the ladies' deprivation of hoop skirts and fine silks."

Winter laughed.

"Who could deny a Southern lady her right to the latest fashions? Don't women, even today, joke about going shopping when they need a little morale boost?"

His voice was coated by a slight accent. Rachel, who had attended college for a time in North Carolina, could usually recognize the subtleties that differentiated a coastal Carolina accent from the drawl of the deep South. She was, however, having difficulty placing his.

"For some it's less of a joke than for others." Rachel smiled, thinking of her Great Aunt Bess, who was notorious for making a beeline to the nearest mall in times of stress.

"Well, then, you see, some things never change. But it was the arms, the guns and the ammunition, that the South was most desperate for. With the ports blockaded, the Southern army was cut off from supplies. When the ammunition was gone, it was gone. If not for the blockade runners, the war would have ended a lot sooner."

"And that would have been a bad thing? Considering the loss of life, wouldn't ending the war sooner have been a better option?"

He looked at her through his dark lenses for a long moment, then said somewhat stiffly, "It's not for us to judge what others should or should not have done. It was their lives, their culture, their homes, that were at stake. We are just observers of the past. We can learn from them, but we should never pass judgment."

Feeling oddly chastised, Rachel merely nodded.

They walked in silence for a few moments, then rounded another bend in the beach, beyond which lay a long dock that reached like a thin arm into the sea. At the end of the dock, a handsome cruiser lay tied and waiting.

"Ah, I see that we're just in time. That's the boat that will take us to the *Annie G.*," Winter said. "And there's Calvin. See, just as I promised, he has your things."

Rachel peered up ahead and in the distance, and could see a tall man tossing several items into the arms of another man who stood on board the boat. She had started to ask how they had managed that feat so quickly when she saw her little red car parked just on the far side of the dune next to a dark blue Jeep Wrangler.

Satisfied, she touched Winter's arm, and said, "Thank you. I couldn't dive, you know, without my gear."

"I assure you that the *Annie G.* is fully equipped with all the latest equipment. Including extra suits—wet and dry—and everything from fully loaded tanks to masks to regulators and fins. Whatever you might need, you'll find. However, if you prefer your own . . ."

"I appreciate the gesture, but I do like the comfort of the familiar," she said. "I have everything broken in just the way I like it."

"Well, then, in that case, I'm glad we were able to accommodate you." He placed a hand on the small of her back and gestured toward the boat that waited at the other end of the dock. "Shall we?"

She smiled and walked the wooden path that stretched out over the water on stilts that raised it above the tide. As they approached the boat, she could see that it, like the dock, appeared new. *Winter's Quest* was written across the back of the boat in bold black script. Aptly named, she thought, as she accepted a hand from Winter and jumped lightly aboard.

The boat was immaculate, its deck was gleaming, its ropes and rigging bleached and white in the late afternoon sun.

"Have you had lunch?" Winter was asking as her eyes scanned the boat.

"No, actually, I haven't. I wasn't sure how long it would take me to drive to the island, and I didn't want to run late and make you wait for me."

"Well, then, your diligence should be rewarded." Winter motioned to a member of the crew who had appeared out of nowhere.

Within minutes, a small table and two folding chairs were set up on deck, a white linen cloth spread, upon which white china was placed.

"I thought perhaps we'd have a bite while on our way." Winter guided Rachel to the table and held a chair for her. "I had an expanded galley built down-stairs—built to my cook's specifications, actually—so that I can eat as well at sea as I do back at Eden's End."

"Then you must spend a lot of time on the boat." For some reason, Winter did not strike Rachel as much of a seaman. Perhaps she'd been wrong.

"On and off over the past few years, yes, I have. However, now that the *Melrose* has been found, I expect to be spending less and less time out here"—his arm swept to indicate the ocean—"and more time at Eden's End. My boats—this one as well as the *Annie G.*—are really just a means to an end to me."

"The end being finding the *Melrose*."

"Yes. Of course. And now that I've found it, I can hardly contain myself, waiting to see what's aboard."

"Are you a gun collector?" Rachel asked as a crystal goblet was filled with water from a pitcher, and topped with a paper-thin slice of lime.

"No, why do you ask?"

"You're going to considerable trouble to recover a ship that probably holds little more than some old weapons. If anything has survived the passage of time, that is."

"There are likely to be other things on board that might interest me." He seemed to be forcing a tight smile. "Some personal mementos of the Captain's, one might suspect. And if we can recover them and return them to Eden's End, why, local history would be enriched, don't you agree?"

"Well, certainly, but . . ."

"You were a student at East Carolina University at one time, if I recall correctly."

"I took several summer field courses there."

"Have you ever been to Eden's End?"

"No. But I understand it's lovely."

"The loveliest spot you could imagine. Oh, the house is grand, with its great white pillars rising from the front porch and wrapping around both sides. Inside, a sweeping stairwell . . ."

"It sounds like Tara, in *Gone with the Wind*."

"Eden's End makes Tara look like a tenement," Winter snapped.

Ooo-kay.

Rachel smiled faintly as a fruit salad was placed before her.

"I didn't mean to imply . . ."

"Of course you did not. You simply don't know. You'll see it soon enough. I promise."

"I'd like that."

At least, I think I will, she thought as she studied Winter out of the corner of her eye. Winter was signaling to an attendant, who disappeared below deck like a shadow slipping through fog.

The moment she had completed her salad, the plate was whisked away and a second appeared, this one holding a rare petite filet mignon and a tidy stack of julienne vegetables. Rachel's stomach lurched at the sight of the red pool that was starting to form under her vegetables. Biting her bottom lip, she eased the thin strips of carrots closer to the edge of the plate, hoping to rescue at least this much of her meal. Oblivious to her distress at the sight of the bloody meat, and apparently having no problem with un-cooked steak, Winter had attacked his lunch with gusto. Rachel nibbled on what vegetables she could salvage.

Finally, Winter looked up, and after staring mean-ingfully at her plate, observed, "You're not eating."

"I . . . I'm not really that hungry." Feeling as if she was being accused of something illegal, she heard her stammered response.

"What is it that you don't care for?" He leaned forward far enough to notice that her steak had not been touched.

"You're a vegetarian?" he asked, as if terribly sur-prised by the prospect. "I had no idea that you were a vegetarian."

"I'm not. I just don't . . ." she grappled with words, unable to tell her host—her employer—that the thought of eating cow flesh made her physically ill. "I just don't eat beef. Or lamb. I don't eat furry animals."

The words sounded foolish, even to her, but that was exactly the truth. Until her mother's death, she had spent summers at her grandparents' home in the country, where she'd had playmates named Betsy and Tillie, big round-eyed heifers and soft young lambs. She'd been unable to eat red meat once she'd realized where it came from. Eating poultry didn't bother her—she'd never known a chicken or a turkey that had much personality—nor did pork, her grandparents' neighboring farm being stocked with cows, goats, and sheep, but no pigs.

"I see." Winter frowned. At least, Rachel thought that was a frown behind those dark glasses. "I don't know why I didn't know that," he repeated.

"Mr. Winter—Norman—there's no reason why you would know that."

"I make it my business to know everything I can about all my employees before I hire them," he said somewhat stiffly.

The faintest cool breeze kissed the back of Rachel's neck.

"And what," she asked as she quietly laid her fork across her plate, "do you know about me?"

"I know that you graduated from the University of North Carolina with honors seven years ago, earned a master's in marine biology. I know that you have assisted your father—and on several occasions, your brother—on a number of projects. I know that you are considered to be one of the top women in your field, and I know that you have the reputation of being a perfectionist when it comes to identifying and cataloguing your finds. Your father's influence, no doubt, all the way around."

There was more—so much more—that he could have added . . .

"That's all public knowledge." A sense of uneasiness slipped around her. "But my taste in foods would not appear on my résumé."

"And is germane only if a man is ordering your dinner, or in my case, stocking a boat with foods that you might enjoy," he said with deliberate softness, the tone meant to reassure. "Had I know that you have an aversion to red meat, I would have had the cook order less."

"You needn't go to any special trouble on my account," Rachel said warily.

"Now, now, I've alarmed you, and I assure you, there's no reason to be. I simply want you to be comfortable so that you can concentrate on the job at hand, and not be bothered worrying about whether or not there's anything on board that suits your palate. Now, is seafood to your liking?"

"Absolutely." Rachel nodded.

"Good." Winter signaled to the tall dark-haired man who stood by seemingly existing only to await orders. "Please remove Miss Chandler's plate and ask Tom if there are some scallops he could grill."

"Oh, no," Rachel protested. "The salad that I had is fine. There's no need for you to go to any trouble . . ."

"It's no trouble, I assure you. It's important to me that you are comfortable." Winter smiled and patted her hand. "Now, let's talk about the *Melrose* while we await your lunch. You've had time to look over the information I gave your father last week?"

"I've memorized most of it," Rachel told him. "I know the general area, by the way. My brother and I used to dive not far from the *Melrose*."

"Really?" He leaned forward, as if he was about to hear something that he didn't already know.

"Yes. My first real wreck dive, as a matter of fact, was with my brother, off Morehead City. About two hours offshore, there's a sunken World War Two tanker, the *Papoose*. It's one of the most popular diving spots on the East Coast." She paused and then asked, "Do you dive, Mr. Winter?"

"Me?" He appeared mildly amused by the inquiry. "No. No, I don't. And please, it's Norman."

"You might want to consider some instruction. There's an excellent diving center in Morehead City, Olympus . . ."

"Why would I want to do that?"

"Well, it just seems that you're so interested in the *Melrose*, that you'd want to see the wreck before it's disturbed . . ."

He dismissed her with the wave of a hand.

"I've been tracking this ship for years. I had an underwater photographer down there for several weeks, shooting her from every conceivable angle. I know exactly what she looks like, Rachel. I have no need to see it firsthand. For my purposes, I have seen it firsthand." He shook his head. "I have no more interest in diving than you might have in a desk job in an office."

Rachel laughed and reached for her drink.

"Well, you might want to take a look as we start uncovering the wreck."

"My photographer will be with you at all times," he told her. "He will videotape every dive. I will not miss a thing, I assure you."

Rachel's glass stopped in midair.

"You're not serious."

"Of course I'm serious. Ah, here's your lunch. I hope this is more suitable."

The attendant placed a plate of perfectly grilled scallops resting on a bed of shredded red cabbage.

"This looks wonderful. Thank you." Rachel smiled at the attendant, who smiled back mechanically and somehow managed to maintain his stoic expression.

To Winter, she said, "Are you planning on making a documentary, then?"

"What?" He appeared not to understand.

"You said you were filming the entire operation. I'm assuming that you're making a documentary."

"Why would I do that?" Winter's shoulders straightened, his jaw tightened.

Confused, Rachel stammered slightly, "Well, it would just seem that if you're spending so much money filming the salvage of what is, after all, not a particularly significant wreck, that you'd . . ."

Winter sat stock-still, his fork stalled somewhere between his plate and his mouth, as if uncertain he'd heard correctly.

"Rachel, while the *Melrose* may not be the *Titanic*, to me, it is more than significant. It is the end of a quest. I've dreamed about this ship for more than twenty years. Now that I've found her, I want to see it all. I want to be watching *every minute* that someone is down there with her, I want to see every artifact as it's forced free from the sand. I don't want to miss a thing. I've waited too long." Winter's voice dropped with each sentence.

"All the more reason why I'd think you'd want to dive yourself."

"I have a heart condition." He leaned forward to confide. "I cannot dive."

"Oh, I'm so sorry," Rachel told him, feeling sheepish, as if she had forced him to tell something about himself that he would just as soon have kept private. "I didn't mean to pry. I'm sorry if I offended you."

"You weren't, and you haven't. It was a logical assumption, that someone who is clearly as obsessed with a wreck as I am with the *Melrose* would want to see her in her virgin state." He patted her arm. "I'm afraid I'll just have to rely upon my photographer, and on you, of course, to help me experience her. It's the best I can hope for."

"Yes, of course, I understand." Rachel speared a scallop and raised it to her lips and added, "But you might want to consider showing the film to civic groups or local schools. After all, you never know what we'll find down there."

Winter merely smiled and sipped his wine. He had a damned good idea of what they were going to find, and there wasn't a snowball's chance in hell that he'd share it with a group of schoolkids or anyone else.

3

⎯⎯⎯⎯⎯⎯⎯❦⎯⎯⎯⎯⎯⎯⎯

Sam McGowan leaned into the dual throttles of the forty-one-foot Bayliner the *Shearwater*, cleared the "No Wake" buoy at the head of the marina at Wrightshead Beach, and headed out to sea. Punching through the waves, the cruiser crisscrossed the wake of a larger boat, the twin four-blade props solidly holding its position. Sam stood at the helm on the flybridge and looked over his shoulder as the coast of North Carolina receded into a blur behind him, before settling into the single swivel chair. He'd be another few hours at the wheel before he met up with the *Annie G.* and Norman Winter, his employer for the next few months. Might as well settle in for the ride.

Of course, right off the bat, Winter had made it clear that he himself would be little more than the signature on the paycheck. The real boss would be the salvager, which suited Sam just fine, since Winter had mentioned that Chandler and Associates had hired on in that capacity. Having worked on several occasions with the legendary Gordon Chandler, and once or twice with his son, Sam was thrilled to have been selected as the marine archaeologist on this job. It had pleased him inordinately when Winter told him that his name had appeared on a short list of archaeologists that Chandler specifically recommended. While the *Melrose* was not the type of wreck that would normally interest Sam, the opportunity to work with Gordon Chandler was simply too good to pass up.

Then, too, there was the other unusual but not wholly unappealing aspect of this job. There was something, Sam figured, almost fateful about being there when the sand was nudged from atop the ship upon which his great-great-grandfather had met his fate. Somewhere beneath the wreck of the *Melrose* rested whatever might be left of the bones of the first Sam McGowan, perhaps even the ship's log written in his own hand, and very likely, some personal items belonging to the Captain.

Though he'd been named for the man, Sam couldn't say he'd ever had any particular affinity for his predessessor. Everything the former had ever heard about the latter gave Sam reason to suspect that his ancestor, despite his war hero's reputation, was a shrewd opportunist with a shady past, a man who thought nothing of buying and selling slaves. Stories passed down through the family hinted that Old Sam—as his descendants referred to him—had married Trinity Prescott, the homely only child of a very wealthy family, only because he'd had an itch to own a plantation. However, having given the Prescotts their obligatory heirs, Sam found that he was unable to enjoy the sedentary plantation life as the husband of the dour and quiet Trinity, who was four years his senior in chronological age but was closer to her parents in demeanor. It wasn't long before Sam had taken a trip back to Texas and had returned with a pretty dark-haired woman and a boy whom many said was Sam's son from an earlier alliance with this same woman. Trinity had appeared not to notice that Sam built a house for his other family at the farthest end of Eden's End, and for years, Sam had been content to play lord of the manor, visit his mistress several nights a week, and play cards on the others. Once the war broke out, all his gambling and drinking cronies joined up with Robert E. Lee. Trinity had become increasingly distant, his mistress more demanding, and his sons had all left home, the Prescott boys enlisting in the Confederate Army and his mistress's son, never comfortable at Eden's End, having gone back to Texas. Now in his mid-fifties, Sam decided it was high time he had some adventure in his life again. Having spent a sufficient number of his younger days in the employ of the U.S. Army, and not fancying a repeat performance at his age, Sam recruited a bunch of old army cronies, outfitted a ship, and headed for the high seas.

More than once it had occurred to Sam that perhaps Old Sam's hero persona had been born more from a desire to remove himself from the boredom of life on a backwoods plantation than from any desire to serve the South, an opinion young Sam frequently voiced at family gatherings for the sole purpose of seeing his cousin Larry bristle. Larry had a stronger sense of genealogy than did Sam, who, while devoted to his living family, had never thought too much about those who had come before him. Sam had been one of the few McGowans who hadn't screamed bloody murder when Judith, his grandfather's second wife, had, upon her husband's death, promptly placed the old family homestead on the market and accepted the first good offer. It was, Sam had pointed out, Judith's property to sell. And since none of the present generation could afford to buy it from her—let alone pay to have the place renovated—it had seemed to Sam that if Norman Winter could purchase the place and restore it, he was welcome to it.

Sam didn't often dwell on the past, at least, not his personal past, which he felt was pretty insignificant in comparison to the past that he investigated for a living. His family history had never interested him as much as did that which was hidden beneath the sea.

Sam cruised toward the horizon at twenty knots, and watched the day unfold, feeling, as he always did, that he was as close to being at home as he'd ever be. Flying across the waves without another boat in sight, Sam relished his solo run. Soon enough he'd meet up with the *Annie G.* and her crew. For now, he reveled in his solitude as only a man who'd grown up in a large family could do. He checked his position and found that he was right on target according to the coordinates he'd received via radio just that morning. Slowing the twin diesel engines, he swung himself down to the deck below to grab a second cup of coffee.

Sam paused at the lower helm station as he passed, leaning over to check the digital depthsounder. All was as it should be. Sam proceeded to the galley and poured a mug of coffee, pausing for a moment to pull the cover off the cage of Hound Dog, the parrot on loan from his sister Daria. Sam figured that in the six years that Daria had had the parrot, she had must have listened to a hell of a lot of Elvis. Somehow, Hound Dog had managed to learn scraps of just about every song The King had ever recorded, a fact that Daria had neglected to mention when she dropped the bird off into her brother's safekeeping on her way out of the country for a two-year archaeological stint in central Asia tracking the legendary griffin.

Hound Dog made Sam crazy.

"Awk! Blue suedes! Don't step on 'em! Don't step on 'em!" the bird screeched as Sam passed the cage.

"You're lucky no one's stepped on you," Sam muttered as he went back up the narrow steps and seated himself on the double bench seat at the lower helm, where he sipped his coffee and watched the ocean's color change from green to blue, indicating that he'd moved into deeper waters. Soon, he knew, it would change again to indigo, as he moved farther out into the sea.

Sam set his mug into the cup holder and went back into the starboard lounge to open Hound Dog's cage.

"You can come out for a while, H.D., but you have to stay down here. We're moving fast enough to blow you clear off the railing. You'd make some pretty sorry meal for a passing shark."

Hound Dog squawked and tiptoed out of his cage, looking around as if scanning for predators.

"Nope. No cats. The coast is clear."

"Don't be cruel! Don't be cruel!"

Sam laughed and eased the throttles forward.

"Hold on to your tail feathers, H.D."

"Kiss me quick! Kiss me quick!"

"Thanks, Daria. I owe you one," Sam muttered as he headed toward the sun and the *Annie G.*

It was a little past two when Sam first spotted the *Annie G.* At first he wasn't sure it was she, but he'd approached her from the side and with his binoculars read the name in fancy red scroll. That was the *Annie G.*, all right. He cut the Bayliner's engine and just drifted for a few minutes. Sam wasn't certain just what he'd expected her to look like, but it sure hadn't been the yacht that rested comfortably and confidently upon the blue swells.

The *Annie G.* was long and sleek and looked more posh than any boat Sam had seen outside the boat shows, certainly nothing like a working vessel that was supposed to be home to a crew of divers. As Sam drifted closer, he noticed the diving platform off the back of the boat, which, on a yacht that cost an easy half a million dollars or better, appeared slightly out of place. Sam raised the glasses to his eyes again and took her in. Her deck sparkled and her wood gleamed in the afternoon sun. Even from this distance, Sam would have bet it was all teak. Clearly built to order, built to impress, the *Annie G.* rode the waves like a haughty queen.

Sam wondered what Gordon Chandler, the bulk of whose boats were reconditioned trawlers or tugs, must think of the *Annie G.* He figured he'd find out soon enough.

Eager to see the salvager again, Sam ducked into his stateroom below and changed from shorts to a swimsuit and pulled the blue tee over his head. He'd swim over to the *Annie G.* once he got a little closer.

"Come on, H.D.," Sam called to the parrot, who was sitting on the back of an upholstered chair and picking at the rivets in a nearby window.

"Return to sender! Awk!"

"Oh, don't you worry. The minute Daria hits U.S. soil, you're on your way back," Sam said as he closed the cage. "You can bet your birdseed on it."

Back at the helm, Sam started the engine and eased closer to the yacht, maneuvering the cruiser slowly. He'd barely gotten within three hundred feet when several men appeared on the starboard deck and watched his approach through binoculars. A man dressed in white strode up to the rail and waved. Sam waved back, and after coming to within a hundred feet of the *Annie G.*, he cut his engine, dropped anchor, and dove overboard.

Sam swam strongly through the mild swells straight toward the diving platform. He'd no sooner hoisted himself up when the man in white appeared at the top of the ladder that lead up to the deck.

"Welcome, Sam McGowan," the man in white called jauntily. "I've been waiting for you!"

"Mr. Winter?" Sam raised a hand to shield his eyes from the sun.

"Norman, please. Now climb on up here so that I can shake your hand!"

Sam did as he was told, and once atop the ladder,

swung his legs over and hopped down the short distance to the deck.

It was, as he had suspected, teak.

"Norman." Sam extended a hand. "I'm pleased to finally meet you."

"As am I. Sorry we weren't able to get together sooner, but once I had confirmation from Chandler, well, I wanted to waste no time in getting the operation going."

"Well, I'm pleased to be part of this team, I assure you." Sam looked beyond Winter to the small crew that had gathered on deck. Gordon Chandler was not among them. Perhaps the salvor had not yet arrived. "Anytime the Chandler name is put to a project, you know that it will be done right."

"My thoughts exactly. Now, let me introduce you to some of my crew." Winter ushered Sam toward the small crowd. "Our skipper, Ward. Next to him, going down the line, is Richmond, Noah, Renny, and Ernie. Scully and Turk there on the end, they're my divers."

Each man waved or touched the brim of his hat, if he was wearing one, but none of them spoke, except for Renny, who mumbled, "Hi. How are you?" from one side of his mouth.

Sam was about to ask when Gordon Chandler was expected to arrive, when a wet-suited figure appeared at the top of the ladder and swung over. The diver was followed by a second who hauled an expensive piece of underwater video equipment.

"So! You're back! Did you see her?" Winter called to the first diver, who was, Sam was just realizing, most definitely a woman.

"Oh, we saw her all right! She's lying slightly on her side, just like in the photographs. I think this should be a piece of cake, Norman. A few days with an airlift and we'll have enough sand removed to see our way clearly around her. I think we'll have a very clean shot at whatever's on her."

The diver had pulled off her hood and a tumble of soft auburn fell out, the curls picking up gold from the sun and dazzling Sam with their brilliance. The woman unzipped the wet suit and began to peel it off, unconscious of her audience.

"Excellent!" Winter dismissed the crew with a wave of one hand. "And, Hugh, I take it you took more film while you were down there?"

"Another cassette's worth," the second diver responded.

"Wonderful! When can I see it?"

"You can see it right now." The photographer handed over the camera.

"I'll take a quick look now," Winter said eagerly, "then we'll all take a look after the four o'clock meeting. Hugh, have you met Sam McGowan?"

"No, but I'm pleased to. Welcome aboard."

"Thanks," Sam returned the greeting.

The female diver continued to peel off the wet suit. Was Sam the only one who noticed?

"And, Rachel, I don't believe you've met Sam."

"No. No, I haven't. But I've heard great things about him." The diver flashed a million-watt smile as she slipped out of the wet suit. The conservative black maillot swimsuit beneath wasn't worth a damn at hiding what the wet suit had covered up.

Sam's throat went dry and there was a humming sound behind his ears.

Venus had risen from the sea, not in a shell, but in neon yellow and black neoprene.

Green eyes seemed to assess him, as he stepped forward to take the hand she offered. Winter and the photographer faded away entirely.

Please, please, please, he silently begged, *don't be Winter's wife.*

"Both my father and my brother spoke highly of you," Venus was saying.

"Do I know your family?" Sam managed to say.

Winter's daughter, perhaps?

"Oh, Sam, this is Rachel Chandler," Winter interjected.

"Rachel Chandler?" Sam asked, then took a deep breath, relieved. "Gordon is your father?"

"Yes."

"I'm a great admirer of his. I've really been looking forward to seeing him again. Is he already here?"

"No, my father's not working this job. He's tied up with another project right now."

"I don't understand." Sam turned to his employer. "I thought you said that Gordon Chandler agreed to work this operation."

"No," Winter said slowly, "I believe that what I said was that Chandler and Associates would run the operation. Which they are doing. Rachel is the salvager on this project, Sam."

"Rachel?" Sam said more abruptly than he'd intended, making it perfectly clear that he was less than thrilled with this unexpected bit of news.

"I assure you that I'm well qualified," Rachel said, piqued.

"I'm sure you are," the archaeologist was saying. "It's just that, well, I rearranged my schedule for the opportunity to work with Gordon again."

"And now you're sorry that you did?" Rachel took a step back and assessed the man who stood before her. With his dark hair, deep blue eyes, and muscular physique, he'd been appealing up until now.

"Look, it's nothing personal . . ."

"Oh, but it is, Mr. McGowan. It's very personal. I take a lot of pride in my work." Rachel drew herself up to her full height of five feet four inches, one bare foot tapping out an agitated rhythm on the wooden deck. "I am every bit as good as any salvor you'll ever meet—with the exception of my father, but he'd assure you that I learned everything I know from him, and that I'm very good at what I do. I'm as good as my brother, and probably better than anyone else you've ever worked with outside the Chandler operation."

"I'm sure you are, it's just that . . ."

"It's just that I'm not my father. I'm not even my brother." She stared him down with those green eyes that began to smolder with cold fire. "I'm so very sorry to have disappointed you."

Her tone made it crystal clear that she wasn't sorry in the least.

Before he could reply, she had turned to Winter and asked, "Will the meeting be here on deck?"

"Yes."

"Fine. I'll be back in twenty minutes."

Rachel gathered her wet suit, and without a backward glance, disappeared down the steps to the cabin area below.

"Oh, now, it appears that you've insulted her." Norman Winter shook his head slowly, as if concerned.

"I didn't mean to do that. I just assumed that Gordon would be here."

"Perhaps that's my fault. Perhaps I should have been more explicit. It really never occurred to me to mention it. Gordon assured me that he has total confidence in his daughter. That was good enough for me."

The implied, *And it should be good enough for you*, was not spoken, but hung between them.

Sam merely nodded, not willing to concede a thing at this point. Of course Gordon would say that, Rachel was his *daughter*. The old blood-is-thicker-than-water thing could influence even a man like Gordon Chandler.

As far as Sam was concerned, it remained to be seen just how good she was.

Rachel declined the folding deck chair offered by one of the crew, opting to lean back against the railing of the *Annie G.* where she could best avoid eye contact with Sam McGowan. In spite of her outer confidence, Sam's reaction had been exactly as she had feared it might be—disappointment that he would have to work with her, rather than her father. She'd seen it in his face even before he'd spoken a word. Even Jared would have been a more welcome partner. McGowan obviously thought she got the job only because Gordon was her father.

Well, okay, she *had*, but that didn't mean she wasn't qualified to do what had to be done, as the arrogant Sam McGowan would soon find out.

Too bad he's such a handsome cuss, she grimaced, watching as Sam finished up a lively conversation with Hugh and took one of the swivel chairs along the port side. To her annoyance, he swiveled it around so that he was looking right at her. He smiled and saluted her with his right hand before swiveling back to face Winter, who was just about to officially launch the salvage of the *Melrose*.

"It's my pleasure to have you all here today," Winter said, his arms reaching forward slightly as if to embrace them all. "I cannot tell you how much this operation means to me. I've dreamed about finding the *Melrose* for most of my adult life. To be standing here, sixty-five feet above her, and knowing that soon we'll be able to touch her secrets . . . it overwhelms me. And to have such an illustrious team assembled! Each of you has been hired for your expertise in your field. Hugh Callahan, some of you may recall, made the documentary of the salvaging of the *Ellen Crenshaw* two years ago and has on occasion filmed for the National Underwater Society. Rachel Chandler has been diving for—hard to believe, though her father swears it's true—eighteen years. Can that be true, Rachel?"

"I made my first dive when I was ten years old." Rachel smiled. "I didn't go very deep, and I didn't stay down very long, but yes, I was ten."

"And you trained with your father for the past several years," Winter said, then addressed the crew collectively, adding, "And you should know, if you don't already, that Rachel's father is the esteemed Gordon Chandler."

The crew mostly nodded acknowledgment. Rachel forced the smile to remain on her face. Rachel's diving hadn't exactly been Gordon's idea. It had been hers, and it was only through bribing Jared with her allowance that he—not her father—had taught her to dive. It hadn't been until Gordon had seen her diving off the Florida Keys with her brother that Gordon finally broke down and bought her equipment of her own. But early on, he had discounted her, and that had rankled most of all. Not that he hadn't taught her to dive, but that apparently he hadn't thought her capable, or worthy, to learn.

Rachel's jaw tightened with the memory of all the times her father had come home from expeditions, how he would address Jared directly as he told his stories, as if only Jared would be interested, only Jared could understand. And all the times that Gordon had taken Jared along on operations during vacations and breaks from school, leaving Rachel home with Great Aunt Bess, well, that still hurt, too, if she dwelled on it. Which, generally, she did not. Those days were behind her now. Her father had come to understand that her love of diving, her commitment to unlocking the secrets held beneath the sea, was as deep as his, as deep as Jared's, and he had, after all, offered her a position with Chandler and Associates.

Rachel just wished it hadn't taken him so long.

And she wished that Sam McGowan hadn't somehow managed to dredge up all those feelings of inadequacy that she'd spent years trying to overcome through hard work and a single-minded determination to be one of the best women divers in the business.

She forced her attention back to Winter, vowing that she would not let McGowan get under her skin.

". . . and of course, to have a direct descendant of Captain McGowan as part of the team, well, that just adds a special dimension to the operation, I think you'll all agree."

Oh, he's added a special dimension, all right, Rachel thought sourly, refusing to look at the archaeologist, who had grabbed a beer from the cooler and was popping the tab off the top.

Rachel glanced across the water to where McGowan's own boat was tied at anchor. She was a pretty nifty cruiser, there was no denying that. She looked relatively new and would be well equipped, Rachel was certain. Pricey, too, she knew, and wondered why McGowan would have brought out such a boat instead of meeting up with Winter back on land, as she herself had done.

". . . determined to find her," Winter was saying. "I was absolutely certain, from reading the documentation available—letters, diaries, newspaper articles—that she had gone down somewhere off Lookout Shoals, but there was no mention of her on any of the wreck maps. There was no mention of the *Melrose* ever having been found."

"How did you find her?" Rachel asked.

Winter turned to her and smiled as if grateful that someone had asked so that he could continue his story.

"After passing over every inch of water between here and Cape Lookout a dozen times without success, we came out one last time in February, after a horrendous storm. I thought perhaps the winds might have rearranged things a bit, and I was right. My patience was rewarded. With the aid of a magnetometer and side-scan sonar, we found her hull, in just sixty-five feet of water. I sent several divers down, and they confirmed it was the *Melrose*. Hugh went down to take some preliminary photographs, and it was obvious that she's in better condition than I could have hoped, given all the years she lay buried in sand."

"Which that last storm cleared away for you," McGowan spoke up.

"Yes. A sign, I thought, that she was waiting for the right time to be discovered. And certainly, that time would be now. Whatever items are brought up will go into the Samuel L. McGowan Museum at Eden's End, the Captain's old home, which I am restoring for that purpose. It all seems to fit, don't you think?"

"Sure sounds like it's meant to be, sir." One of the men nodded.

"My thoughts precisely, Noah." Winter nodded back. "So. There we are. Are there any questions?" Winter looked around.

"When do we start?" Sam asked.

"First thing in the morning. Rachel, you've already made your first dive. Why not tell Sam what you found?" Winter leaned back against the doorway of the cabin, a white figure against the white-painted frame.

Rachel stared straight ahead to Winter rather than to her left, where Sam sat sipping his beer, three feet away from the cooler. She would have loved one, but she'd have had to ask him to pass it, and wasn't about to ask him for anything.

"The *Melrose* is lying just barely on her starboard side, the bow facing east. The wreck is totally pristine. She's never been touched, which is nothing short of a miracle. There's still a great deal of sand covering her, but I think with an airlift, we should be able to clean her up enough to get into the cabin and see what's there."

"Is there an airlift on board?" Sam asked.

"Yes," Rachel replied.

"Are there any DPVs available?"

"I don't know," Rachel said, still not looking at him. "Norman . . . ?"

"DPVs?" Winter frowned.

"Diver propulsion vehicles," Rachel told him.

"Ah, the underwater scooters." Winter nodded. "Yes, we have several of them. You'll find we're well equipped—extremely well equipped—and you'll find everything you need. Gordon kindly gave me a list of equipment that we should have on board. Any other questions?"

"Rachel," Sam addressed her directly across the deck.

She bristled at the sound of her name as spoken in his slow, Southern drawl, which he had, she felt certain, exaggerated somewhat just to annoy her further, but she could not avoid turning toward him.

"Yes?" she answered coolly.

"You seem to feel certain that this is a completely untouched wreck. What makes you so certain that someone, over the years, hasn't poked around, taken what they wanted, and just not bothered to mention it to anyone?"

"Have you ever known a diver who could keep his—or her—mouth shut when they found a wreck that isn't mentioned on any of the maps?"

Most of the crew chuckled.

Sam shrugged. "Wouldn't have to be a professional. Lots of amateurs dive in these waters. You don't know how long it was covered by sand. Could have been right there out in the open till just a few years ago, could have been covered up as recently as five years or so."

"No," Winter said sharply, as if offended by the very suggestion. "Rachel is right. The ship hasn't been touched."

"How do you know that for certain?" Sam asked.

"Because I've been looking for it for a lot longer than five years, Sam. And if she'd been found before, there'd be record of it. *I'd have known*. Besides, I've been over these waters with a fine-tooth comb—or, in any event, the most sophisticated equipment available—and there's been nothing until now."

There was something in Winter's face that told Sam he'd hit upon a touchy subject, so he backed off. He'd know soon enough if Rachel was right. Maybe as soon as tomorrow.

"Now, if there are no more questions, cook has prepared a lovely buffet for our first night at sea. Please join me in the lounge, after which we'll view the video that Hugh took today." Winter dismissed the group to dinner with the wave of a hand.

"Rachel." Sam caught up with her as she was about to descend the steps.

"Yes?" She raised an unfriendly eyebrow in his direction.

"What time do you want to start tomorrow?"

"Seven would be fine."

"Fine." He nodded. "Seven sounds fine."

"Good." She started past him, and her perfume, the lightest, most delicate citrusy scent, drifted on the sea breeze.

"Have you ever mapped a wreck before?"

Rachel rolled her eyes. "No. We at Chandler and Associates practice the snatch and grab method of salvaging."

"That wasn't meant as an insult. Most salvors don't think like archaeologists."

"Most salvors never worked for my father."

"I'll start again," he muttered. "How would you propose we map this site?"

"Well, since you've asked. I'd use an azimuth circle and plot the site out that way." She paused in the doorway, unable to resist adding, "But you'll probably want to use the grid system. It'll take ten times longer, but you'll get to show off all of your archaeological skills."

To her surprise, Sam laughed.

"Well, we'll take a look tomorrow and get a handle on the ship's position."

"Fine. Now, if you'll excuse me." She resumed her descent, as regal in old faded denim shorts and a short-sleeved sweatshirt as she might have been in a ball gown.

Sam watched her disappear below, turning to ask Hugh as he passed, "Did you feel a chill?"

The photographer smiled and followed Rachel down the steps.

Well, Sam thought, as he, too, went below deck, he'd been snubbed by women before, though never by one as intriguing nor as pretty as Rachel Chandler. It was clear she didn't care for him, and Sam knew he could thank himself for that. Well, she didn't have to like him, but if they were going to dive together, she'd have to trust him. And he would have to trust her. Their lives could depend on it.

Sam spent a long night wide awake, walking the deck of the *Shearwater*, wishing he could take back those words that had opened a rift between them, and wondering if there was a way to make it right.

4

———◆◆◆———

THERE WAS something almost sinfully pleasurable in sipping that first cup of morning coffee on the fly-bridge of a handsome yacht, while overhead the sea-birds swooped and soared and shrieked and the early sun scattered handfuls of glitter upon the waters. Rachel turned her face into the breeze, letting it muss her just-brushed hair and tease her nostrils with the scents of the sea. The ocean was a placid blue, the swells gentle, and Rachel couldn't wait to dive.

The *Annie G.* was already alive with activity, and had been since six. Breakfast was long past and the crew was busily assembling the equipment required for the dive. Several tanks, filled with mixed air, sat waiting on the platform below. Two scooters and an airlift, its long aluminum tube lying in pieces length-wise across the deck, had been brought up from below in case they were needed. Norman Winter was a very anxious man. He would not be pleased to learn that his divers might not be using such equipment today.

A glance at her watch told Rachel it was almost seven A.M. She went down to her cabin to change into her bathing suit and ready herself for the dive.

Within twenty minutes she was standing on the diving platform, zipping up her wet suit and pulling on her fins. A sound from above drew her attention, and she looked up to see Hugh swing a leg over the ladder and start to climb down.

"Any sign of the professor?" Hugh pointed across the water to the *Shearwater*.

"Not yet. I was thinking perhaps I'd swim over and bang on his hull," Rachel replied.

During the night, the two vessels had drifted at anchor until the were closer than they had been the day before. From the flybridge of the *Annie G.*, Rachel had had a good view of the *Shearwater*. The cruiser appeared new, expensive and well equipped. Teaching at the college level, even part-time, apparently paid quite well.

Sam appeared on deck, and began to pull on his wet suit. He'd gotten both legs and both arms into the one-piece and looked across the water as he began to zip it up. Caught staring, watching him dress, Rachel's cheeks stung with color. Sam grinned broadly.

The flush began to spread down Rachel's neck. She peered sideways at Hugh, who, oblivious to everything else, was loading his camera.

Sam hopped down to the platform level of the *Shearwater* and strapped on his tank. Leaving his mask hanging around his neck, he slipped on his fins and slid into the water from the back of his boat.

"Looks like the eagle has landed," Rachel told Hugh as she dropped into the warm blue sea.

"Ready, all?" a voice from above called.

Rachel looked up to see Winter standing on deck, the ever present dark glasses shielding his eyes.

"We're ready," she called back.

"Aren't you taking the equipment down with you?"

"Not yet." Rachel craned her neck to look up at him. The impeccable white sleeves of his jacket hung slightly over the railing like two little surrender flags. "I'm still not sure if we want to go in initially with the scooters or the airlift. I want another look, and I thought that Sam should be given the opportunity to voice his opinion."

"That's big of you." Sam surfaced behind her.

Rachel looked over her shoulder to where Sam was treading water.

"I'm trying to keep the fact that you wish you didn't have to work with me from interfering with the way I handle this job. You're the archaeologist, you have the right to see the site, untouched. I have an obligation to Winter to make certain that every *i* is dotted and every *t* crossed before we remove one grain of sand. I resent the fact that you're apparently sexist but I . . ."

"Sexist?" Sam's eyebrows raised slightly. "No one has ever accused me of being sexist . . ."

". . . won't let my personal feelings toward you influence one aspect of this job. Now, if you can be a big enough man to look beyond your prejudices,

I'll be a big enough woman to overlook the fact that you have them."

"What prejudices?" Sam swam closer to her, his eyes narrowing.

Rachel instinctively moved backwards in the water. Sam continued to close in, until they were circling each other warily.

"You think that I'm prejudiced against you because you're a woman?" Sam said between clenched teeth. "Because I wasn't overjoyed to find that a man I revered and admired and looked forward to working with had been replaced on this job by his daughter, who is probably younger than I am and who probably has less experience with this type of operation than I have, that makes me sexist? Prejudiced? Sweetheart, you don't know who you're talking to. You just don't have a clue. Now, if you're finished with your little tantrum, I'd like to get to work."

Rachel stared at him coldly. Before she could respond, Hugh jumped off the platform and called to them, "Showtime, boys and girls."

Still eyeing Sam, Rachel slid her mask over her face, put her regulator into her mouth, and rolled herself over and under the surface of the water. Side by side, they made their descent into the quiet world beneath the water.

He's not going to spoil this for me, Rachel repeated over and over as she dropped lower and lower. *He can be as big an idiot as he wants to be, but he's not going to spoil this for me.*

With customary control, Rachel forced the rancor from her mind. Once back on deck, she'd deal with it. Here, under the sea, there was no place for discord.

Hostility between divers could prove deadly. If she'd learned nothing else from her father, she'd learned to leave certain things behind when she dove. Today would certainly be a test of just how well she'd learned that lesson.

Sam spotted the clearly visible wreck below, and increased his pace downward, eager to see her close-up, eager to get to work, and eager to put aside the indignation he'd earlier felt when Rachel had suggested that he might not want to work with her because she was a woman. He, Sam McGowan, whose anthropologist mother had dragged him and his siblings from Alaska and the Australian Outback to Zanzibar and just about everwhere in between and had written the definitive book on family dynamics—whose one sister was the only woman to have been invited to join the highly esteemed Dr. Elwood Allen in his trek across the Gobi Desert in search of proof that griffins actually existed, and whose other sister had single-handedly put together a successful import business. He, Sam McGowan, having been raised in a house where women were expected to achieve, had had any potential sexist inclination beaten out of him by his oldest sister long ago. He put Rachel's words behind him, and focused wholly on the ship. To do otherwise would be counterproductive. There was no place for animosty—or distraction—at sixty-five feet below the surface of the water.

Rachel followed close behind Sam, knowing that the safety in numbers adage was nowhere as true as in the depths of the ocean. She turned and looked for Hugh, who was right behind her, his camera already running.

Apparently when Norman Winter said he wanted every minute on film, he wasn't joking.

Twenty feet above the wreck, Sam paused, treading water slowly to take in the entire scene below. The *Melrose* lay embedded in sand from just slightly above her cabin back to her stern, one of her twin stacks half-hidden in silt. The other would be under her. She looked to be about one hundred sixty feet in length, petite as many of the Confederate ships went. Somewhere beneath the silt and sand lay one of the big paddles that would have propelled her. Sam guessed that the paddle wheel lay on her starboard side, and that she was resting on it.

He swam slowly toward the bow, which stuck partially from the sand. The wood was partially rotted but the wide planking that had hugged the underside of the hull were still visible. That she'd been built well was readily apparent. The light from Sam's flashlight bathed the silent remains in a faint, ghostly glow.

Rachel followed Sam downward and waited as he inspected the wreck. With the flat palm of one hand, he brushed away enough sand to read the letters "elro" on her side. Sam looked back up to Rachel and pointed to the letters, and she nodded, then ducked downward as a dark form suddenly darted past and over her. Sam pointed to the back of the wreck, where several sand tiger sharks had appeared. No threat to divers and often seen in the waters off North Carolina, the sharks passed by casually as if out for a stroll in the country.

There being no danger, Rachel dropped down to the ocean floor, and knelt upon the sand, watching as Sam continued to swim around the sunken ship, touching it here, prodding the sand there. The *Melrose* was in better shape than he'd thought she'd be, and absolutely intact. Winter had been dead right about that.

A tickle of anticipation began to build inside Sam. He loved this part of his job, loved removing the outer layers to see what lay within, then putting it all together like an exotic puzzle to learn its story. Even though the *Melrose* would be a quick operation and wasn't likely to give up much more than small cannonballs, some guns, perhaps some dinnerware and a piece of silver flatware or two, the joy was clearly in the hunt. Sam glanced upward. Rachel hovered above him, her eyes glowing.

She feels it, too, the realization crossed Sam's mind.

While Sam inspected the wreck, Rachel held back, grudgingly admiring the manner in which he would stop to touch the hull here and there almost reverently, much as she herself had done the day before on her first dive. Finally, he looked up and signaled to Rachel that he was ready to surface. She nodded, and began a gradual ascent along the anchor line toward the light above.

Surfacing about fifteen feet from the *Annie G.*, Rachel tread water until Sam appeared through the crest of a swell, Hugh following close behind. Rachel had been so absorbed in the *Melrose*, and in following Sam's inspection of the wreck, that she had forgotten that Hugh had been with them. It was not a good thing to have forgotten the presence of another diver. Under other circumstances, it could have proved dangerous, and Rachel silently berated herself, wondering how she could have done such a thing.

Somehow, it had almost seemed as if she and Sam were the only inhabitants of that silent world they had just left behind.

"Did you get all the film you needed today?" Rachel asked the photographer.

"I shot the whole time, just like the boss told me to do," Hugh told her. "But oh, man, did you see those sharks? God, I hate sharks."

"Hugh, you act like you've never seen a sand tiger shark before," Rachel said.

"Sand tiger shark, great white shark, they're all the same to me. Man-eaters." He grimaced. "It was all I could do to keep the camera steady."

"Almost seems like a waste of film," Sam said. "There really isn't much to see at this point."

Hugh shrugged and headed toward the platform. "Mr. Winter wanted the entire operation on tape. He's buying the film and he's paying me well to shoot it. Maybe he wants to live vicariously through you two."

"Or maybe he's afraid of missing something," Sam murmured aloud.

Rachel turned to look at him quizzically. She'd had exactly the same thought at the same time.

Rather than admit it, she asked, "How would you like to proceed?"

"Well, you were right. I will want to map, but as you pointed out earlier, the traditional means—gridding the area—would take too long. The azimuth circle might make the most sense, though I would also like to scan some of Hugh's photos into my computer to get an image. Then we can mark off our finds on the computer."

"That could work well, certainly less time-consuming than all that plotting. You surprise me, McGowan," Rachel said over her shoulder as she swam toward the diving platform.

"How's that?"

"I've never met an archaeologist who took the short way home."

Sam laughed out loud and followed her to the back of the *Annie G.*

"So? You think the airlift first?" she said, all business as she peeled back her close-fitting hood and shook out her hair.

"Definitely. There are tons of sand to be moved. Let's get it out of the way as soon as possible so that we can establish a starting point." *If she can maintain her professionalism, I can maintain mine.*

"You approach a wreck the same way my father does," she told him as they hauled themselves onto the back of the platform.

"Thank you," he told her, surprised but pleased by the unexpected compliment. As he eased out of his tank, he added, "So do you."

"Well, Dr. McGowan?" Norman Winter leaned over the back. "What do you think of the *Melrose?*"

"I think it's a remarkable find, a wreck so obviously untouched after well over one hundred years, particularly in waters that are as popular as these are. It's exciting just to look at her. How have you managed to keep her location a secret? I'm surprised that there aren't a dozen other divers down there with us."

If possible, Norman Winter turned a shade paler.

"I have been granted exclusive rights by the state of North Carolina," Winter said archly. "No one has permission to dive on this wreck other than the members of this crew."

"I don't know that that alone would stop anyone who got wind of it. We could end up with an audience out here," Sam told him, only half joking.

"Why, then, Dr. McGowan, I guess we'll just have to shoot them." Winter smiled, showing even white teeth, then laughed to assure that it was only a joke. "Now, come up and let's talk about what you'll do first."

Once up on deck, Winter said, "Tell me what equipment you'll need."

"Nothing that you don't already have," Sam said. Then, remembering that Rachel was officially the salvager, he turned to her and said somewhat gallantly, "Unless of course there's something you want, Rachel."

She shook her head and tried not to stare at the broad expanse of his chest as it emerged from the top of his wet suit as he drew the zipper down.

"I think we're fine."

"Well, then. What's the next step?" Winter asked eagerly. "Will you take the airlift down now?"

"Not yet," Sam told him. "First, we have to map the site . . ."

"Map the site?" Winter frowned. "Why do you need a map? We have all those photographs from Hugh."

"And we will use them, I assure you. But an archaeological excavation is done stratigraphically, that is, layer by layer, so that the depth of each find can be recorded."

"What is the purpose of that?" Winter demanded.

"Under other circumstances, mapping is invaluable in providing a step-by-step record of the operation. Ordinarily, we're looking for historical information—how and out of what materials was the ship constructed? What type of rigging and armaments were on board? What was the cargo and where was it stored? What caused the ship to sink? What efforts were made to keep her afloat?"

"We know most of that already," Winter pointed out. "You know how old the ship is, there's no question of when she went down."

"You're right. We do know that the *Melrose* was a wooden-hulled paddle steamer. I would have expected to find that she was an ironclad, like so many of the blockade runners were. But the fact that she is a wooden hull leads me to believe that she may have been older, may have served another purpose before being used to run guns. She might even have started her career under another flag and another name. And certainly we can expect to find armaments aboard—that was her purpose—but it will be interesting to see exactly what else she carried."

"I still don't understand why you can't just remove all the sand and bring up what you find."

"With all due respect." Sam folded his arms over his chest. "If all you wanted was an extra diver, you probably should not have hired an archaeologist. We're devils when it comes to details, and not likely to opt for speed when accuracy is at stake."

Norman glanced at Rachel, who nodded and said,

"Sam is absolutely right. My father would never touch a wreck until he had mapped the site."

"I don't understand what it will prove."

"It's simply a means of preserving the record. And if nothing else, it will show us what happened to her. Why she sank. Where was Captain McGowan when she went down? Where was the crew? Had she taken water? Had an attempt been made to bail her out? And besides, didn't you tell me that once your salvage operation has been completed, that you are turning the wreck itself over to the state archaeolocial society?"

"Yes. They have reserved the option to bring her up in her entirety, depending, of course, on her condition."

"Then you'll want a perfect record the first time. You won't be able to go back down and re-create the site, once she's been moved."

"How long will your little mapping exercise take?" Defeated, Winter sighed.

"Not as long as you think. Rachel suggested that we use an azimuth circle . . ."

"What the devil is that?"

"It's a brass circle marked with the degrees of a compass, which is mounted on a brass rod that is driven into the bottom near the center of the wreck site and becomes the datum point. We use an underwater compass to line up the circle with magnetic north. We connect a chain to the center of the circle, and distances are marked on the whole length of the chain. When the chain is stretched to an object—say, a cannon—the diver notes the compass bearing on the azimuth circle to the object and the distance from the datum point. All the information is marked on a chart."

"How long will this take?" Winter repeated.

"We can probably set everything up this afternoon, then we'll be mapping as we go along," Sam told Norman. "That is, assuming that you have an azimuth circle and some chain on board."

"If we don't, I'll have one brought out here by this afternoon." Winter turned and signaled to one of his crew. After giving directions in a low voice, which Rachel, still on the diving platform below, could not decipher, Winter leaned over the railing and asked, "Can you still use the airlift?"

"Yes, of course." Sam nodded. "There are tons of sand to be moved."

"When do you expect to be able to do that?" Winter persisted.

"Depends on when we can start mapping."

The crew member—Rachel could see now that it was Richmond, the one she thought of as tall and burly—returned and spoke briefly with Winter.

"We're in luck. Your azimuth circle is on board. Thank Gordon Chandler when you see him, Sam. It was on the list of items he'd suggested."

"Excellent. I'll need two of your other divers to take the equipment down and help set up. Rachel and I should be ready to dive in another hour or so."

"I'll let them know," Winter told them before disappearing above them on deck.

It was almost noon when Sam hoisted his air tank onto his back and prepared for his dive.

Turk and Scully, the two divers hired independently by Winter, made their way down the ladder, and without fanfare, strapped into their gear. From above, the azimuth circle was lowered, along with the lengths of chain.

"All set?" Sam asked.

The four divers, equipment in tow, slipped into the ocean and headed for the bottom. Following the anchor line from the *Annie G.*, they dropped the full sixty-five feet, careful not to go too quickly.

Once below, Sam directed the two divers, and with their assistance, set up the post as close to dead center of the wreck as he could determine. Using his underwater compass, Sam found magnetic north on the azimuth circle, which he then set upon the post. After attaching the chain to the center of the circle, he motioned toward the surface. He had told Winter that the process would not take long, and he wanted to return to the ship as soon as possible. Which appeared to be fine with Turk and Scully, who, oddly enough, exhibited little curiosity about the wreck that had totally obsessed their employer.

"That was remarkably fast." Winter smiled broadly, clearly delighted by their unexpectedly prompt return.

"Setting up the equipment takes no time at all," Sam said, "but it will require some documentation following each find."

"I feel certain you'll manage to take care of that in record time, too, Dr. McGowan. And now, come up and take a look at the airlift. I know how it works, in theory, but I'd like you to walk me through the components."

"He's a persistent bugger, isn't he?" Sam grinned at one of the crew, who turned a dour, unsmiling face in Sam's direction before reaching for the ladder and heading up to the deck.

"Well, then." Sam turned to Rachel. "Am I the only one who thinks that Norman Winter is obsessed with the airlift?"

It was Rachel's turn to laugh, the sound melting through Sam like snow in the afternoon sun, warming him, the feeling staying with him for the rest of the day.

"Norman," Rachel called from the deck, "did I hear you say that you do have a basket on board?"

"Yes. It's below. I'll have it brought up right away." Winter signaled to Richmond and Noah, who immediately went below deck.

While she waited for the mesh basket to be brought up, Rachel sat down on one of the benches that ran along part of the back of the boat and watched the crew members assemble the aluminum tubes that made up the hose that would be used to "vacuum" the sand from the wreck.

Renny, one of the crew, came up next to her and sat down.

"What does that do, that hose thing?" he asked with all the openness of a child.

"Well, it will suck the sand off the *Melrose* just about the same way that a vacuum cleaner sucks dirt off a carpet."

"We don't have any carpets on the *Annie G.*," he told her earnestly. "We just have wood. It's my job to keep the wood polished and looking nice. This wood is special wood called teak. It takes a lot of work to keep it nice. You have to clean it carefully.

You wear rubber gloves on your hands to keep the special cleaner off your skin. Then when it dries you use special oil called teak oil. You rub that in"—he made a rubbing motion with his right hand—"and it makes the wood look just like new."

"Well, if you're the one in charge of the wood, Renny, you're doing one heck of a job. It does look just like new," Rachel assured him.

Renny beamed.

"Renny, don't bother Miss Chandler," Winter called to him.

"He's not bothering me, Norman. He's just sharing the secrets of how he keeps the teak looking so beautiful."

Renny ran his hand proudly over the teak railing.

"Yes, Renny does a wonderful job. Now, Renny, go help Richmond and Noah bring up that basket from down below. It will need to be mounted on the side of the boat, and we don't want the wood scratched."

Concerned over the possibility that such a thing could happen, Renny hustled across the deck.

"Renny," Norman said softly to Rachel, "is . . . slow. He suffered a head injury as a young boy and his development stopped at that point. He's thirty-six, but he'll always be an eight-year-old."

"He seems to be totally competent on board."

"Renny loves the ocean, he loves the *Annie G*. It's the best thing that ever happened to him. He's totally different at sea. If I'd known that, I'd have bought a boat years ago."

Rachel's puzzled expression caused Norman to confide, "Renny is my younger brother."

"Oh, I see." That would explain what had seemed to be an inordinate concern for a hired crew member. "It's wonderful of you to take care of him so."

"Rachel, he's my *brother*," Winter repeated, as if she hadn't heard him the first time. "My only living relative."

"Of course." Rachel drew back, feeling as if she'd been chastised but not fully understanding why. Not for the first time, she wished she could yank those glasses from his face to see what, if anything, showed in his eyes. "I'll see if Sam is about ready to go back down."

Excusing herself, she met Sam halfway across the deck.

"Do you need help fitting the sections of hosing together?" she asked.

"I'm just about through. Who will man the basket?"

She paused to consider the possibilities when the three crew members emerged from below, carrying the mesh basket into which sand, after having traveled the distance from the airlift on the bottom of the sea through the entire length of the tubing, would be dumped. As the sand spilled out through the top, it would be directed into the basket and fall through to be carried away by the current. The only things that remained in the basket would be those things too large to fit through the mesh. Someone would have to be watching the basket, and retrieving the items that were trapped there. Once, in Key West, Rachel had picked an emerald ring out of the basket. On other occasions, she had found gold coins and a length of gold chain that had once been part of a necklace. While no such treasure was anticipated here, there were other things that could be expected, from brass buttons to pocket watches, wedding rings, and coins.

"Renny." Rachel almost smiled at Sam, the thought pleased her so. "I'll ask Renny to watch the basket."

She called to the short, dark-haired man, marveling at the fact that he and Norman—always a study in white—were even related, no less brothers.

"Renny, we have an important job to be done, and we think you're just the right person for it," she told him. "We are going back underwater and we're taking the hose with us. The sand will come back up here and must be directed into the basket."

Renny thought about this a moment, then said, "The sand will fall through the basket, Rachel. It has holes in it."

"That's right, it does. But we're looking for things that are too big to go through those small holes."

"Like treasure?" A young boy's hopes were reflected in the eyes of the man.

"Exactly. Now, we don't know that there is treasure down there, not what you normally think of as being treasure. But we're hoping to find some interesting things just the same."

"Things for Norman's museum."

"Exactly. What do you say, do you want the job?"

Renny hesitated. "I have to ask Norman. He's the boss."

"By all means, ask Norman." Rachel nodded solemnly.

Renny took off after his brother.

"That was good of you to think of him," Sam said.

"I'm certain that he'll do an excellent job."

"You ready to go back down, or would you rather wait until later in the afternoon?"

"Are you worried that I don't have the stamina to dive three times in the same day?" Rachel's jaw tightened.

"Don't put words into my mouth, Rachel." Sam bristled and grabbed her by the arm. "I meant nothing of the sort. It was a courtesy, okay? Just a courtesy."

He let her go and turned his back. Rachel watched him walk briskly to the other side of the deck, where he checked the air in his tank.

Rachel blew out a long breath she hadn't even realized she'd been holding. Unconsciously the fingers of her right hand gravitated to her left elbow, where he'd held her. He'd applied little pressure, but her skin still felt his touch.

"Rachel, Norman said I could watch the basket," Renny had returned to announce proudly.

Rachel turned to him. "That's wonderful. I'm so glad. That makes you officially a member of the team, even if you're not diving with us."

"Show me what to do," Renny said excitedly.

"Okay. We'll set the basket up right here." Rachel pointed to the railing. "We need to set it up in a place where the wind won't toss it back on deck."

Renny looked horrified at the thought of sand being dumped on his hand-scrubbed floor.

"Go ask Richmond to bring it over," Rachel told him, "and we'll set it up right now."

Rachel glanced at Sam, who, having topped off his own air tank, was now filling hers.

The thought crossed her mind that maybe she should be filling her own tank.

Feeling her eyes on him, Sam looked across the deck.

"Ready?" he called to her, and she nodded.

"Yes. In a minute."

Renny returned with Richmond and the basket, and Rachel showed him just how to arrange it on the side of the boat. By the time she had reached the other side of the deck, Sam had strapped his tank on and was holding hers out to her.

"Thank you," she said as she slipped her arms through the straps. "And thanks for filling it for me."

"Are you sure you trust me?"

"Yes," she told him levelly. "Yes, I trust you. I may not like you very much, Sam, but if my father trusts you enough to work one of his jobs, I have to trust you, too. On a professional level, that is."

Sam nodded, pleased but not about to show it. Whatever else she might think of him, she trusted him with her air tank. Which meant that she trusted him with her life. Which was more than he had expected. For now, it would do.

evacuated. As Turk approached, Sam took the tube and slowly sank to his knees on the sand-covered hull and turned on the valve that would begin the process. Judging the depth of sand to be close to eight feet at this location, he turned the lift on to full power. Using the tube like a giant vacuum cleaner, he began to clear away the sand and silt.

Rachel swam to one side, watching as massive amounts of sand made its way up the long tubing, which both Turk and Scully were, at intervals of twenty feet, maintaining in position, while Hugh recorded the scene below. Aware that the noise from the equipment would tend to scare away sharks and barracudas, Rachel knew there was little danger from large predators. However, she knew as well that sea worms and other marine life that had taken up residence in the wreck would be dispersed, providing an irresistible buffet for small fish, some of which might mistake a diver's fingers for something else. Gloves were a necessity at such times, and she was especially glad to have hers on when the first of the trigger fish, always aggressive, arrived to dine.

While Sam operated the controls, Rachel kept a keen eye out for any artifacts that might have been lodged close to the surface. After nearly an hour, she tapped Sam on the shoulder and motioned for him to give her the airlift. Surely he must be getting tired from remaining in much the same position for so long. He nodded and allowed himself to float upwards slightly, stretching his legs after having been on his knees for more than forty-five minutes. Rachel took over and Sam swam closer to the exposed hull to inspect the decking he had uncovered.

The deck, which appeared to be made of pine, was in better condition than any he'd ever seen, a result, he knew, of having been buried beneath the sand for so many years. Typically, wood under the sand is preserved, having not been destroyed by sea worms and other sea creatures. The storm that had taken her must have pretty much covered her, Sam thought. So far, he saw no sign of rot. The possibility that the *Melrose* could be this well preserved excited him. He tapped on Rachel's tank and motioned for her to turn off the airlift, which she did, puzzled. With his index and middle fingers, he pointed first to his own eyes, then to the wood that they had exposed that afternoon.

Look at this.

Rachel's eyes widened appreciably. She understood exactly the significance of the vessel's condition. As far as she knew, no wooden Confederate blockade runner had been found in such solid condition.

Rachel gave Sam the thumbs-up sign and went back to work.

An hour later, on the deck of the *Annie G.*, she tried to explain the importance of their find to Norman Winter, who was, to her amazement, not as impressed as she had expected him to be.

"Norman, wait till you see Hugh's film from today!" she had called to him as she hopped over the rail and onto the deck.

"You found something already!" he said excitedly. "What did you find? Tell me!"

"The *Melrose* is in incredible condition! I've never

seen a ship this old so well preserved!" she told him, her eyes shining.

"Yes, yes, that's wonderful, but what did you *find*?"

"That's what we found, Norman. We found that the deck of the *Melrose*—at least the bow section—is in beautiful shape. The hull at that section shows very little sign of rot."

Norman's head tilted slightly to one side. This was clearly not what he had wanted to hear.

"I think the state team should be called in now so that they can participate in—" Sam began.

"No!" Norman stepped back as if he'd been struck. "No! This is mine, Sam. When I'm finished with her, the state's people can do whatever they want with her, but for now, she's mine."

"But, Norman, this is a highly significant find . . ."

"And it will be no less significant when our phase of the operation has been completed. But until then, no one dives on the *Melrose* except the four of you, do you understand?"

Rachel and Sam exchanged a long look, then both nodded. They understood.

Off to one side, Turk and Scully stood with their hands folded across their chests like twin statues. It was pretty clear that they, too, understood perfectly.

"And there is to be no mention of this to anyone, do you hear? The last thing I want is the bunch of photographers and who knows what all we'd end up with. Hugh will continue to record every dive, and the four of you will continue with your jobs. But until such time as I have decided that our work here is done, not a word leaves the *Annie G.*" He looked

at Sam and added, "Or the *Shearwater*. I apologize,
Dr. McGowan, if this offends your scholarly inclina-
tions, but that's how it has to be. I need this job done
as quickly as possible, and if we are to be overrun
by outsiders, we'll have chaos. Not to mention how
much more difficult it will be for you to carefully
map and record each detail, as you are so intent
upon doing."

Sam hesitated. Winter was right about the site
being overrun with other divers and photographers
should news of the *Melrose* leak out. Reluctantly, he
agreed.

"The only thing I ask is that, if we get into a situation with the ship that we cannot handle, you permit
us to bring in help," Sam said.

"What kind of situation do you think we cannot
handle, Dr. McGowan?"

"Well, there's always the possibility that the hull
farther along the ship may not be in as good condition as that near the bow. Moving the sand out rapidly could cause a section to collapse."

"And what would have to be done, should that
occur?" Winter stood stock-still, his arms bent at the
elbows, held waist level, the fingers of both hands
touching at the tips.

"You'd most likely need engineers, some heavier
equipment . . ."

"I promise you, anything that we need, we will
have. I will tend to it. Without bringing in the state
or anyone else. Gordon Chandler has his own engineers, I believe?" Winter looked to Rachel to confirm.

"Yes. Yes, he has several."

Winter turned back to Sam and said, "There you

have it. Chandler and Associates, as the salvor, will have that responsibility should the need arise. Of course, I'm hoping that it does not. It's important to me to open my museum in September. I'll be more than disappointed if that doesn't happen."

With that, Norman Winter turned heel and disappeared into the cabin.

"Well, then." Sam leaned back against the railing. "I guess we have our orders."

"I guess we do," Rachel murmured. "Odd, that he's more interested in keeping the site a secret than he is in the historical significance of the wreck."

"He's right about the site being at risk, though. Right now, we can excavate this ship very carefully, we can record every inch of her. I shudder to think of what would happen if another team or two—or three—of divers descended on the *Melrose*. Historians or not, they'll make a mess of her. It's a case of the more most definitely not being the merrier."

"I know that's true, but somehow I didn't get the feeling that the integrity of the site was his concern."

"Rachel!" Renny had spotted her and was waving for her to come look in the basket.

"What did you find, Renny?" she asked as she crossed the deck.

"Nothing! I stood here all that time and I watched all that sand go right through the basket and I didn't find *anything!* Some shells and stuff, but they're nothing!"

"Well, then, that really makes you a member of the team. Some days, that's exactly how it goes. You find nothing. It can be a long, tedious process, Renny. Sometimes you can look for days and find nothing.

And other times"—Rachel peered into the basket and grinned, lifted out a starfish—"you find priceless treasure. Now here, we have a wishing star, Renny. Why not make a wish then throw him back?"

"Wish upon a starfish?" he asked skeptically.

"I always do." She nodded.

"If you wish on it, can I still?"

"There's no limit to the number of people who can wish," she told him, "but I believe we only get one wish each per starfish."

"Okay." Renny squeezed his eyes tightly. "I wish we could find a wonderful treasure."

"Ooh, don't tell your wish."

"It's okay. It doesn't mean it won't come true," Renny assured her. "What are you wishing for, Rachel?"

Rachel watched Sam unzip his wet suit.

"Ummm, I'm not quite sure yet, Renny." Rachel smiled. "Anyway, throw the starfish overboard and we'll bring the basket back on deck till tomorrow."

"My wish will come true, Rachel. I know it will," Renny said with solemn conviction.

"Well, just remember what I told you, Renny. The *Melrose* wasn't a treasure ship. We don't really expect to find treasure."

"We will, though," he told her.

"We'll just have to wait and see what comes out of the sand tomorrow, then. In any event, you did a great job today. Thank you." Rachel patted Renny on the back as she made her way toward the cabin where Sam stood in the doorway, in the midst of discussion with Hugh.

"I want to scan them into my computer, and use

them to make a digital imaging of the ship," Sam was saying.

"You'll have to take that up with Norman." Hugh shook his head. "The photos belong to him."

"Fine. I'll do that." Sam stepped around Hugh and went through the open door.

"Have you been taking still shots along with the videos?" Rachel asked Hugh.

"Yes. I took a series of shots from about twenty feet above the wreck, from the bow to the stern. Pieced together like a mosaic, you can see the entire length of the wreck. The professor wants to feed them into his computer to get an overview of the entire site."

"That's an excellent idea. What's the problem? Why not just hand them over?"

"The problem is that I don't have them to hand over. Winter has them all."

"You don't have any of your own photos?"

"Not a one."

"What's Norman doing with them?"

"Who knows?" The photographer shrugged. "They're his to do with as he pleases. He's bought and paid for them. Now, if you'll excuse me, I need to get today's film developed."

"There's a darkroom on board?"

"Of course." Hugh grinned. "In case you hadn't noticed, our employer is long on cash and short on patience. I develop every roll as I take it, and Norman sifts through the photos over his afternoon tea."

I shouldn't be surprised, Rachel thought as she headed for her stateroom to shower, *since Norman is keeping everything connected with the* Melrose *as close to his vest as he possibly can . . .*

Rachel rounded a tight corner and collided with Sam McGowan, who had fire in his eyes.

"Oh. Sorry." She stepped back to allow him to pass her in the narrow hallway.

Sam appeared to barely notice.

"Sam . . . ?"

"He won't give me the photos," Sam said, incredulously.

"What?"

"I asked Norman to lend me the photos that Hugh took of the wreck before we started airlifting today. I thought I'd scan them into my laptop, then I'd make a digital image from it."

"That's a wonderful idea, Sam, and it would certainly make it easier to record where artifacts are found."

"That's the whole idea. And he said no."

"What reason did he give?"

"What reason didn't he give? The photos might get wet. They might get damaged. They might get stolen." Sam sighed with exasperation. "I told him I'd place them in a watertight pouch to take them over to the *Shearwater.* Hell, I offered to bring my laptop over here. What does he think I'm going to do with his pictures? Sell them to *National Geographic?*"

"Look, we're really early into this operation, Sam. It's all new to Norman. He's waited a long time for this, and he probably feels very protective of the wreck right now."

"Protective?" Sam snorted. "It's more like obsessed. What does he think is down there?"

"The remains of his hero."

"Listen, if Old Sam is still down there, there's precious little of him left."

"I think he's just waited for this for so long that he doesn't want to give up any of it. And I think he'll come around as the days go by and he becomes accustomed to the routine."

Sam stared hard at Rachel.

"You're the salvor, Rachel. Technically, you're in charge of this operation. You can suggest that the photos be used to create a computerized record of the site."

"Yes, I probably could."

"Are you going to?"

"No. No, I'm not. At least, not right now. I really think that Norman will loosen up on his own after a few more days."

"How many are a few days, Rachel?"

"I don't know." She tried not to let her annoyance show.

"How much time do you think your father would give him?"

As soon as the words left Sam's mouth, he regretted them.

Rachel's jaw set squarely, as if responding to a slap.

"I don't know what my father would do. I suspect he'd simply go back to his cabin and manually sketch out the wreck, just like he used to do before there were computers." She spoke coolly, and pushed against his chest to get him out of her way. "And if you'll excuse me, that's just what I'm going to do."

"Rachel, I didn't mean . . ." Sam put an arm out to block her path.

"Oh, but you did. You've made it clear from the first day that you consider me a poor substitute for my father." She stared straight ahead, her face white and taut. "Please just get out of my way and let me pass, Sam. I really have nothing more to say to you."

The damage done, and fearful that anything he said at that moment would only make things worse, a reluctant Sam stepped aside and watched her walk, head high and with total dignity, to her stateroom and open the door, leaving him to ponder the possibility that perhaps Daria had been right all along, and he had in fact been born with both feet in his mouth.

He had no way of knowing that once she had stepped inside and closed the door behind her, tears born of anger and frustration, evidence of the delicacy of her self-confidence, began to stream down her face.

Rachel sat in the vague glow of the anchor light, lit when darkness fell to warn other vessels that someone lay at anchor, and watched the gentle rise and fall of the *Shearwater* as it drifted on its line fifty feet away. So far that day, she'd worked side by side with Sam McGowan, sided with him against their employer, and cursed his very existence.

It was an ominous start to what should have been an easy operation.

If only Sam hadn't been so clearly disappointed to find her instead of Gordon aboard the *Annie G.* If only he hadn't embarrassed her by saying so. If only she could have pretended that it didn't matter.

If only she could have ignored those blue eyes, or pretended not to notice how strong his arms were when he'd blocked her way in the hall earlier. If only she could accept the fact that, in this business, she would always be Gordon Chandler's daughter first, and Rachel Chandler second.

But it seemed she couldn't do any of those things. And wasn't that the story of her life?

As hard as she tried to stand on her own, once having chosen to follow in Gordon's footsteps, she would always be compared to her father. It was inevitable. Maybe she should just learn to accept that as a fact of her life and let it be, the same way she had had to accept that Jared had been the favored child and she an afterthought as far as her father had been concerned. It wasn't until Gordon realized that she could hold her own as a diver, had solid instincts when it came to approaching a wreck and nerves of steel underwater, that he had begun to see her, not as his fragile girl-child, but as a person in her own right.

He just wasn't there, she reminded herself. *It's not as if he set out to ignore one child and dote on the other. He just didn't know how to relate to me. He just didn't know what to do with a little girl. And so he had done nothing . . .*

The cabin lights on the *Shearwater* radiated atop the water and cast soft shadows on the ocean. Somewhere down below, someone had a radio playing, and the sweet sound of a saxophone floated up to the flybridge. The sea glistened with moonlight, and the swells struck the wooden hull gently, more a lover's tap than a slap. Overhead, the sky was endless and clear, the stars spread out like a giant quilt sewn with sparkles and twinkling lights. It was, Rachel sighed, a most romantic evening.

Raising her small field glasses to her face, she focused her attention on the *Shearwater*. Through her lenses, she could see Sam as he hunched over the table in his cabin, a light trained down on the surface. She watched for a few long minutes, and knew exactly what he was doing. He was sketching the *Melrose*, as she herself had earlier done, trying to decide where her captain's cabin lay, where the mess would have been, where the cargo would likely be stashed. She wondered if Sam had laid out the ship in the same fashion in which she had, if his instincts had been the same as hers.

She lowered the glasses and bit her bottom lip, wishing things were different between them, wishing she could have been there to watch Sam sketch the bones of the ship, rather than here, on the flybridge alone, on this very beautiful late-spring evening.

She sighed and slipped the glasses back into the pocket of her fleece jacket.

Sam's sketches would be neat and precise, she told herself. *I'll bet that's a mechanical pencil he's using, and I'll bet he has a whole supply of lead refills. I'll bet he measures out everything to one-eighth of an inch. I'll bet he even . . .*

"Hi, Rachel." Renny stood at the top of the ladder, a cup in his hand. "I brought you your coffee. It's decaffeinated, just like you like it. One sweetener and a little bit of cream. And I know it's fresh. I made cook brew a new pot, just for you."

"Why, Renny, that's so thoughtful." Rachel stood, touched by the gesture.

"You didn't have any after dinner tonight, so I thought maybe you forgot." Renny climbed the last step carefully, and held out the cup to her. Rachel took it with both hands.

"I'm so flattered that you did this for me," she said sincerely. She sipped at the coffee and told him. "And it is exactly the way I like it. How did you know?"

"I like to watch people," Renny said shyly. "You can learn a lot about people just from watching. And you never know when it will come in handy. Like now. I watched you fix your coffee this morning and after dinner last night, so I knew how to fix it for you tonight."

"You are very resourceful. Thank you."

"I like to learn about people. Sometimes I learn about them from their names."

Rachel looked at him blankly.

"People's names *mean* things. Like me, Renny." He sat back against the railing. "Renny means small and mighty. And I am small, but I am strong."

"Well, you are certainly right about that." Rachel smiled. "I watched you with the diving equipment this afternoon. You are very strong."

"Yes. I am. And there's Ernest, see him down there?" Renny pointed down on deck where one of the crew members had gone to smoke a cigarette. "Ernest means sincere. And he is a very sincere person. And you know what else? The cook's name is Mr. Cook. Isn't that funny?"

His smile was so genuine, so unaffected, that Rachel had no choice but to smile back.

"And your name, Rachel, I looked it up in my name book," he told her. "It means *ewe*."

"Yes, Rachel means me, all right."

"No." Renny frowned. "Not *you*. Ewe. A female sheep."

Rachel laughed softly.

"What does that tell you about me? How am I like a female sheep?"

"Your hair is soft, just like I think a woolly baby sheep would be. I touched it, when you were helping me set up the basket for the airlift." He hesitated, uncertain. "Was that a bad thing to have done, to touch your hair?"

"Well, I think it was okay, because we're friends. But I think with other ladies, you should probably ask first," Rachel told him, considering how strangers might react to having a strange man stroke the back of their head.

"I didn't mean anything bad, Rachel. It just looked so shiny in the sun."

"It's okay. Now at least we know how Rachel is like a female sheep." She grinned.

Just then, Sam appeared on the deck of the *Shearwater* and stood, hands on his hips, looking across the distance to the *Annie G.* Rachel wondered what he was thinking.

Probably trying to figure out how to get those photos from Norman and scan them into his laptop . . .

"What does Sam mean?" Rachel asked Renny.

"I don't know." He shook his head. "Want me to go look it up?"

"No," she told him. "It's not that important."

Rachel drained her coffee cup and glanced at her watch.

"Renny, I think it's time for me to turn in. I have to get up early tomorrow morning."

"Are we going to use the airlift again?"

"Yes."

"Do I get to man the basket again?"

"Yes, of course. That's your job, Renny."

"I think I'd like it more if interesting things came up through that tube."

"I'm sure something will, soon enough. Maybe buttons, for instance . . ."

"Buttons are not very interesting," he told her flatly.

"Well, these buttons could be. They'd be old, and maybe ornate . . ."

"What does that mean, ornate?"

"Fancy. The buttons could be from uniforms, maybe brass, maybe with different designs on them. And then you get to think about the man who wore the coat or the shirt or the pants that the button came from." Her voice dropped low, and she sounded, she realized, exactly like her father.

"Like maybe was he the captain or the first mate?"

"And maybe was he from North Carolina, was he a farmer, a young man or a seasoned sailor? Did he leave behind a wife and children, or parents or siblings? Did he like to read or hunt, did he have a dog or . . ." She glanced at Renny out of the corner of one eye. His mouth hung open. "Well, you get the picture."

"So many questions from one little button," he exclaimed.

"That's history, Renny."

"I never did too good in history when I was in school."

"Well, as you start to pull things out of that basket, Renny, you'll be helping to write history, what do you think of that?"

He nodded. "I think that would be fine."

"Well, get a good night's sleep, because we're going down early again in the morning." Rachel stood and stretched.

"I think we'll find some treasure, Rachel," Renny said as she started down the steps.

"I was thinking earlier, that maybe you would find some coins." She paused at the top of the steps. "Maybe some of the crew members had some money in their pockets when the ship went down. Or maybe, just maybe, there might be some gold in the paymaster's cabin."

"What does that mean?"

"It means that the crew member who was responsible for paying the others their wages might have had some coins in his cabin, money that he would have used to pay the crew. But mostly, we'll find guns, I think."

"I don't think they'll come up through that tube into my basket," Renny said glumly.

"Probably not. But something interesting will, sooner or later," Rachel told him. "Good night, Renny. And thanks for the coffee."

Rachel hopped down the ladder, leaving Renny to dream about just what might come up that tube, sooner or later.

6

---◆◇◆◇◆---

SURROUNDED BY the steady hum of the airlift and the light swirl of sand that accompanied it, Sam used a gloved hand to shoo away a curious grouper who'd been attracted by the teredo released as the excavation continued for the second weekday. From the corner of one eye, he watched Rachel attempt to juggle three sand dollars she'd lifted from the ocean floor. She looked up at Hugh and waved, grinning, as she tossed the white disks into the air to break the monotony. Sam wished she'd smile at him like that. It had been days since they had exchanged a civil word, and it was bothering him more than he'd ever imagined it could.

Sam felt like kicking himself. It was obvious to anyone with a brain that Rachel was sensitive about being compared to her father, and yet he'd thoughtlessly—though not intentionally—done it anyway, on more than one occasion, questioning her judgment and wondering aloud how Gordon might handle the same situation. He hadn't meant it as an insult, but as the middle child, Sam, of all people, knew how it could sting when others compared a child to his or her older siblings. How much more so to be compared to your father, who was widely recognized as one of the best in your shared profession?

And it wasn't as if Rachel was a total initiate as a salvor. He'd watched her carefully since the first dive. She was not only a strong and able swimmer, but she handled herself competently at the wreck site. More than competently, Sam acknowledged.

Well, he was just going to have to find a way to apologize, and he'd have to do it soon. He'd lost enough sleep the past few nights on her account, his thoughts progressing from how those green eyes had clouded as his careless words struck home to how the sun played off the glint of red in her hair to how that black swimsuit clung to her well-proportioned body.

Motion from his right caught his attention. Rachel swam toward him, waving to him with both hands. Sam turned off the airlift and dropped the tube to the ground. She looked above him to where Hugh floated with his ever present camera, and waved for him to drop down. Following her to the far side of the hull, Sam saw immediately the cause of her excitement. Using her underwater light to illumine the area for Hugh, Rachel pointed downward to the wooden boxes spilled out below.

Sam swam closer, then with his hand swept away the clinging bits of sand from one of the boxes.

ENFIELD.

In the boxes marked with the name of the manufacturer of Civil War–era bullets, they'd found their first bit of cargo.

Rachel pointed to the azimuth circle, and Sam nodded, then swam for the chain, which he used to measure and chart the location of their first artifacts.

With her thumb, Rachel motioned upward. Sam nodded, gesturing for her to grab one of the boxes of bullets to take topside to give to Winter. Surely he would be pleased to see the first of the real cargo artifacts surface.

While Winter appeared only mildly interested in the recovery of the bullets in their original containers, he had been much more enthusiastic over Renny's find in the basket.

"Rachel!" Renny had called as soon as she had surfaced. "Come look! Come see!"

"I'll be right there, Renny," she called back before turning to Norman. "It seems that the *Melrose* has given up the first of her gifts."

She held out the wooden box and said, "Bullets. In the same boxes they left the factory in. And they're in excellent condition."

Winter glanced at the boxes that Rachel and Sam had set upon the deck.

"Bullets. Yes. Well, she was a gun runner, wasn't she?" He nodded, then opened his hand to show his divers what he held in his palm. "Renny retrieved this from the basket about an hour ago."

Rachel leaned forward and turned Winter's hand into the light, where a glint of sunlight struck the object and cast sparkles before her eyes.

"What a lovely watch!" she exclaimed. "Much too

small and delicate to be a man's, though. This must have been a gift for a special lady back home."

"It was perfectly clear of debris," Winter said as if surprised. "It came up through the tube and fell into the basket just this clean."

"That's because it's gold," Rachel told him. "Gold doesn't suffer from immersion in seawater. It can remain underwater for hundreds of years and look as good when it's recovered as it did on the day it was struck."

She turned the watch over.

"There's an inscription," she said, "but I'll need my glasses to read print that small."

"Here, let me take a look," Sam reached out and she placed the watch in his hand. It was as close as he'd been to her in two days, and catching the scent of the sea in her hair made his breath catch in his throat.

" 'To my beloved.' "

"How romantic." Rachel smiled. "And the stones on the face are beautiful. Definitely sapphires."

"May I?" Winter reached out a white-clad arm and took the watch, reading the inscription under his breath as if suddenly fascinated. " 'To my beloved.' "

"Norman?" Rachel asked, touching his arm.

"It's lovely, don't you agree? So romantic a sentiment." He removed the white handkerchief from his breast pocket and wrapped the watch carefully in the pristine linen, then slipped the watch gently into his pocket. "Now, come see what Renny has in his basket. He's quite excited."

Winter took Rachel by the elbow and said, "That was a great idea, to have Renny assist in this way.

He's thrilled to be a part of the treasure hunting team and it's doing him a world of good, giving him the responsibility. Thank you for thinking to ask him."

"You don't have to thank me. I thought he'd enjoy the experience, but I also thought he'd be very conscientious. But, Norman, this isn't a treasure hunting team. I've tried to explain that to Renny, that we're not likely to find treasure on board the *Melrose*. At least, not treasure in the traditional sense. We're looking for historical artifacts, items that will give us an idea of what life was like on this ship, who the men were who served on her, what cargo she carried . . ."

"Of course." Winter's murmur was a dismissal if she'd ever heard one. He dropped her arm and headed to the place where his brother stood waving something in his hand.

"I found stuff, Norman! Rachel, Sam, I found treasure." Renny all but jumped up and down.

"Let's see what you have there." Rachel leaned over the basket. Some small, calcified objects lay upon the mesh.

"Here, here." Renny held out his hand excitedly and opened his palm, where several gold coins lay. "I found gold! Rachel, do you think it belonged to pirates?"

"No, I'm afraid not." She shook her head. "I think they belonged to a member of the *Melrose*'s crew. Now, see here, in the basket?" She lifted the pebblelike objects, and with a fingernail, picked off bits of deposit. "Buttons, Renny, just like we talked about the other day. The buttons could have been on the shirt, and maybe the coins were in the pockets of the same man. Now, Norman said they came up about an hour ago. That could have placed them right around the area where we found the bullets."

"Which means that we should start looking in that area specifically for armaments." Sam picked at one of the indeterminable objects that Rachel had pronounced buttons, and picked away at the calcareous growth that covered it. "There should be guns mounted on either side. We can expect to find iron shot stacked in racks along with the swabbing rods and gunpowder. The *Melrose* would have had significant armaments on board to defend herself from Union ships, but remember that she also would have carried weapons to be delivered to the city of Wilmington, which was the closest port to where she went down, and the only city that hadn't been completely closed off by the Union Navy."

"I'm all for going back down and using the airlift strictly on the deck this afternoon," Rachel said.

"Excellent idea." Norman nodded enthusiastically.

"Rachel, will you find more coins?" Renny asked.

"Most likely." She smiled and patted him on the back, then walked toward the ladder that would return her to the diving platform.

"Will I be able to keep some?"

"That will be up to Norman."

Renny looked expectantly at his older brother.

"I'm certain the museum will be able to spare a coin or two for the finder. Now, let's not keep Rachel and Sam. They're going back down to see what else they can find."

Rachel slid into the water, and knowing the dangers of diving alone, waited for Sam.

Catching up with her, Sam said, "It would appear that old Norman is catching treasure fever from his brother. I thought for a minute there he was going to toss us both over the side to get us back down there faster."

Rachel shrugged, not interested in getting into social discussion with Sam about their employer. Or anything else. For the past two weeks, she had made a painstaking effort to restrict her conversations with Sam to the *Melrose* and the operation at hand only. After all, once bitten . . .

"Oh, come on, Rachel. Admit that you were surprised that he was totally disinterested in the bullets."

"I would have expected Norman, of all people, to understand what we're dealing with here," she conceded.

Sam continued to tread water, in no particular hurry to dive. Not when she was this close, close enough for him to see the slight sprinkling of freckles that danced across the bridge of her nose.

"I thought that recovering objects from the ship that were directly related to Old Sam's war efforts was Norman's first order of business," he said. "You know how it is, when you first see that gleam of gold. I'm sure you remember the first gold you recovered from a wreck, and how exciting that was."

Sam nodded, inching closer to her. Water slid down the side of her face, and he had to fight the urge to reach out and trace its path down that smooth, lightly tanned skin with his fingers.

"I haven't had much experience in recovering treasure. Most of my dives have been commercial."

"I'm sorry to hear that. I remember mine as if it was yesterday," he told her. "It was in the Mediterranean, off of Cyprus. I was nineteen years old and had been selected as one of five students who would accompany Dr. Grossman on the expedition to locate the legendary *Cosima*."

"Dr. Grossman?" Rachel's jaw dropped. "You don't mean Josephina Grossman?"

"You know her?" Sam said casually. Of course, she would know Josephina Grossman. Grossman was one of their generation's leading underwater archaeologists.

"I don't know her personally, but certainly, I know of her reputation." Rachel couldn't help herself, and for a moment forgot that she and Sam were only to talk about the wreck. She was, truth be told, every bit as awed as she appeared to be. "She's a legend. Only the very best students were selected to work with her. You must have been very good."

"I like to think that I still am, Rachel."

"Yes. Well." She backed away slowly in the water, drawing her mask down over her face. "I think it's time we got back to see what else we can find for our employer. He's watching us from the deck and probably wondering why we're still up here."

Sam looked back over his shoulder to see Norman Winter watching them through his dark lenses. Sam waved, and turning to Rachel, said, "After you."

She rolled under, and he followed.

Reaching the bottom, they found that Scully had turned the airlift back on, and that Turk was combing through the silt in the area where the bullets had been found. He waved them forward, indicating he'd found something that they should see.

Excitedly, the two divers joined him on the wreck to see that he had uncovered one of the big guns that would have inflicted immeasurable damage on enemy vessels. Nearby, as Sam had predicted, sat a pile of shot, now encrusted with iron oxide. Overhead, Hugh's camera continued to roll, filming every artifact from every angle.

During the course of the afternoon, the divers recovered several muskets, pistols, and cutlasses. Once the positions of the artifacts had been duly charted, they loaded the portables onto a lift that was brought down by Scully and hauled the day's find to the surface.

"Hopefully Winter is equipped to treat the iron," Sam said to Rachel once they were back on the *Annie G.*

"I'm sure he is."

"What comes next?" Norman called down over the railing.

"We'll need to clean the items we brought up today." Rachel lifted a hand to shield her eyes from the warm afternoon sun. "We'll need to keep the artifacts in seawater to preserve them until they've been treated."

"Then you'll need buckets . . . ?" Norman asked.

"Buckets will be fine for the smaller objects, but I'm afraid that the muskets and the longer items won't fit."

"What would you suggest?"

"A couple of kiddie wading pools would work just

fine, though I don't suppose you have any of those on board."

"We can get them. I'll have someone bring them out." Winter disappeared.

"Want to spend some time this afternoon cleaning the iron?" Sam asked.

Rachel nodded. "I think I'll run down to the galley and grab some lunch first. I'm starving."

"Mind if I join you?"

Rachel's disparaging look would have paralyzed a lesser man.

Sam chose to ignore it.

"That's what I thought. Well," he said, falling into step with her, "hopefully, Norman hasn't become so enthralled with the morning's find that he's forgotten about eating."

"I doubt it. He's quite the gourmand." She glanced at her watch and frowned. "I didn't realize it was this late. I'm sure everyone else has already eaten. We may have to beg leftovers from Cook."

"His leftovers are worth begging for, I'm certain. He's an amazing cook. Lead on to the galley, and let's see what we can scrounge."

Leftovers were tuna salad made from freshly caught fish and greens brought in just that morning by the supply boat.

"I saved you some lemon squares," the beefy Cook, who looked more like a longshoreman than a cook, told Rachel. "And some iced tea with a little fresh mint."

"Norman certainly does like his comforts, doesn't he?" Sam leaned back against the leather seat of the banquette that ran along one side of the spacious lounge area in the downstairs cabin.

"That goes without saying. My father would just about die if he knew how well appointed the *Annie G.* is. We Chandlers aren't used to such luxury while at sea. As a matter of fact, right now, as we speak, Jared and my dad are aboard an old refitted tug, and are dining on much less sumptuous fare than we're enjoying."

"I've worked with your brother, did I tell you?" Sam said.

"He did."

"What are they working on these days, your dad and your brother?" Sam was as curious about the operation that had kept Gordon from joining them on the *Melrose* expedition as he was anxious to draw Rachel into conversation.

"The *True Wind*. Ever hear of her?"

Sam shook his head no, he had not.

"Och, laddie, the *True Wind* was the pride of Ian Christie's small fleet of privateering sloops." Rachel lowered her voice to a rasp. "Terrorized the Southern coast, she did, for many a year. The governor of South Carolina put a bounty on Christie's head, so feared was he."

When Sam laughed, she smiled in spite of herself. Sam McGowan had a great laugh.

"The *True Wind* was Christie's pilot ship, and for years, it was thought that he went down in a hurricane near Assateague Island off the coast of Virginia. However, my brother came across a reference to Christie in some letters he'd found in a small country library when he was doing research for his master's thesis. The letters were written by a woman to her sister, and spoke of how they had watched a ship toss onto the shoals and crack apart in a storm. She told her sister that her husband had been among the party of local men who had set out to try to save the men who had been tossed into the sea, but the ocean was too rough. One survivor had washed ashore, and before he died of pneumonia a few days later, had babbled on about the *True Wind* and his share of the prize having gone down with her. Knowing only the name of the woman who wrote the letter, Jared tracked her through one small town historic society to another. He finally found her in Bishop's Cove."

"How long ago was this?"

"Oh, maybe ten years. The *True Wind* was Jared's dream ship. That's why it wouldn't have been fair if . . ." She paused, the words *if Jared had lost the toss* sticking in her throat. Rachel found herself not wanting Sam to know that the *Melrose* had been, in her estimation, a poor substitute for the *True Wind*.

"If what?" Sam leaned forward to ask.

"If anything had happened that would have prevented him from bringing her up."

"Is that what he's intending? Bringing her up?"

"If he can. The jury's still out on that. They'll have to see what condition she's in, how stable the wood is."

"So your father is helping Jared there, and you were sent here to work for Winter." Sam nodded slowly, understanding her presence on the *Annie G.*

"I think I'll go upstairs and see if Norman has found the nitric acid. I told Renny I'd show him how to clean the calcareous deposits off the brass buttons." Rachel pushed her chair back abruptly.

Sam's hand shot out to encircle her wrist.

"I don't blame you," he said.

"For what?"

"For wishing you were there instead of here."

"I never said that I'd rather . . ."

"You don't have to. Why would you want to be here, digging cannons out of the sand, when you could be diving for pirate treasure? Why would anyone?"

"Well, then, I guess it's safe to say that neither of us got what we wanted this time around." She shook her hand free and pushed the chair under the table. "I got the *Melrose* instead of the *True Wind*. You got me instead of my father. It's just one of life's little disappointments that we all have to live with from time to time. But we're professionals, so we move past it and get on with the job at hand and do the best we can with what we have to work with."

"Rachel, about that . . ."

Rachel stepped back from the table and held up one hand. "Please. We've done this one. I don't want to have this conversation again."

She was halfway through the door when he said, "Rachel, how would you feel if you had a chance to work with Josephina Grossman?"

The light that flashed in her eyes was her unspoken answer.

"That's what I figured. She is, hands down, the best. As you said, a legend. You get a chance like that, you lay awake at night, just dreaming about it. Just the stories she could tell, all you could learn from watching her. Well, then, suppose you had that chance, but when you showed up at the site, you found me, instead of her. How would you feel? Wouldn't you just be as disappointed as all hell? Wouldn't you be wishing—at least at first—that I was Grossman?"

Rachel stood in the doorway for a long quiet moment, the light fading around her, before turning to take the steps two at a time.

Sam tapped out a tune on the table with his knife in one hand and his unused spoon in the other. He'd thought it had been a good analogy. Obviously, she hadn't.

With a sigh, he returned their plates to the galley, and followed Rachel up the steps.

". . . so we need to clean off the chemical deposits so that we can see what's underneath," Rachel was telling Renny as Sam came up on deck.

"Will it be shiny?" Renny asked, watching as she lined up two glass bowls on the deck and filled them each with water.

"I think so." She nodded. "I think it's brass, but we'll just have to see. Now, these things have been underwater for a long time. That's why the buttons are a little green. But we'll put them into this special bath—a combination of fresh water and ten percent nitric acid. We'll leave them in there for a little while, then we'll wash them with clean fresh water, and they'll be as good as new."

"I can do that," Renny said confidently.

Rachel added measured amounts of nitric acid into one of the bowls.

"Okay, pal, I'm putting you in charge of buttons. Just try real hard not to get any of the liquid on the deck. It might mar your lovely finish. When the buttons are clean, then you drop them into the bowl of clear water."

"What are you going to do, Rachel?" Renny asked.

"I'm going to see about getting the deposit off that cannon that Turk and Scully brought on board a while ago."

Renny frowned. "I don't think it will fit in the bucket, Rachel."

"No." She smiled. "It won't. I'll be using something else to clean off the cannon."

"Have a mallet." Sam walked up behind her and casually handed her a small hammer with a rubber head.

"You're prepared for just about everything, aren't you?" She took the tool he offered. "And what will you be doing?"

"I'll be working right alongside you." He pulled a second mallet from his belt. "I always carry a spare."

"Fine." Rachel nodded. "Let's get started."

She paused and pointed to the cannon that lay perpendicular across the deck on a thick canvas tarp.

"I'll start at this end, and you start at that," she told him.

"I think we should both work on the same section at the same time," he told her, "and we'll just work our way back together."

Rachel's hands found her hips as she watched him kneel down alongside the long rusted shaft and begin to hammer away at the corrosive crust that had formed on the iron.

"On second thought, I don't think this is a good idea," she said. "I think the cannon should be sent to a lab to be treated. We don't have anything large enough to hold a sufficient amount of water to bathe it."

"True enough." Sam nodded without looking up at her. "But then, I wasn't planning on trying to bathe it, just to knock the worst of the deposit off."

"Are you saying, Sam, that we are not equipped to deal with the cannon?" Norman approached them.

"That's what I'm saying, Norman." Sam tapped away at a clump of dark sediment.

"Tell me what you need."

"We need long troughs that we can fill—and keep filled—first with nitric acid, then a wash of sodium hydroxide and water. It will have to soak for several weeks."

"Why can't you do that here?"

"Because there are about a dozen more cannon down there, and it will add too much weight to the ship if we bring them all up at once. Some of them, by the way, are likely to be permanently affixed to the ship, and will have to stay down there until the state's engineers figure out how to get the entire ship up."

"What do you suggest?"

"I suggest that we send the guns we bring up to a lab to be treated. They're going to have to be kept wet anyway, and we can't do that here, so we might as well send them out now, as soon as we can get them ashore."

"I'll have a boat pick them up first thing tomorrow morning," Winter told him. "Is that soon enough?"

"Should be." Sam stood up and slipped the small mallet into the waistband of his swim trunks. "There aren't many facilities equipped to handle this much material at one time, though. You may have to take it to Virginia. Would you like me to call a few places I've dealt with and see if I can find an available lab?"

"That won't be necessary." Winter smiled. "Though I appreciate your offer."

"Where will you send the cannon, then?" Sam stood up, concerned that the artifacts would be properly treated and preserved.

"To Eden's End, of course."

Rachel and Sam exchanged a puzzled look.

"Oh. Have I forgotten to mention that I purchased some equipment for just this purpose? Several large ultrasonic baths, and an electrolytic bath, I believe they're called," Winter told them. "I asked Gordon to order whatever equipment he felt we might need, and have it shipped to Eden's End. There's a barn that's just the perfect size for this type of thing."

"But someone needs to know the process, how long to submerse different items, how much of which chemicals to use . . ." Rachel frowned.

"All taken care of, I assure you." Norman waved away her fears with the flutter of a few fingers. "I've contacted the local university, and arranged for several graduate students to work this part of the operation for us. The students are eager for the experience, and you won't have to be pulled off the wreck to do that portion of the work. All I have to do is call the school, and the first of the students will be on their way to Eden's End. So you see," Norman turned to Sam, "that you needn't be concerned. The cannons—

indeed, all of the salvaged items—will be in very good hands. You probably don't even need to waste your time chipping away here"—he pointed to the cannon that Sam and Rachel had set upon—"since it can all probably be bathed away."

"That's a wonderful idea, bringing students in, but the worst of the concretions need to be manually removed," Sam told him. "Besides, I want to see if there's a name on the cannon."

"You mean a manufacturer's name?" Winter asked.

"That, yes, but I'm really looking to discover the name of the ship."

"We know the name of the ship, Sam." Winter looked puzzled.

"We know that *Melrose* is written on her side, and we know that that's what McGowan called her. But I'd bet a bucket of gold coins that she was christened otherwise."

"You think she was a British ship, reincarnated?" Rachel raised an eyebrow.

"Absolutely." Sam nodded. "She's just too small and trim to have been built as a gun runner. Most of the ships built by the Confederacy were bigger, brawnier, and were ironclads. She's sleek, slender, and she's solid wood. I'm betting she was dropped off in Bermuda or Nassau and refitted, renamed, and handed over to her new captain. So it's important to take our time and see if there's a history here that we should know about."

"Is this relevant?" Winter asked coolly.

"Relevant?" Sam wasn't certain he'd heard correctly. "Forgive me, but isn't your plan to establish a museum at Eden's End?"

Winter nodded.

"I would think that there would be a certain amount of accuracy required for the displays. If you're going to exhibit the cannon from the *Melrose*—and, eventually, the *Melrose* herself—I would think you'd want to know—need to know—where she came from and how she came under Old Sam's command. If she started out life as another vessel, I would think that you'd be eager to know that. I think it's as important to know as much about the vessel as you do about her captain."

"Of course." Winter nodded. "But we can't very well stop the operation while you personally clean every cannon, Dr. McGowan. Do I need to remind you that time is, after all, a serious consideration, if my museum is to open on schedule? Frankly, I would think that your time is better spent down at the wreck, uncovering whatever is down there."

"Norman, everything has to be properly identified, cleaned, and catalogued if you're going to display them in your museum."

"May I remind you that if the artifacts are not recovered and brought up—which is, after all, your primary responsibility—there will be nothing to identify, clean, and catalogue, and therefore nothing to exhibit?"

The two men faced each other from ten feet away. Rachel felt an urge to hold her breath. Standing behind Sam, Rachel could not see his face, nor could she read what was in Winter's eyes, shielded, as they always were, by dark glasses. In another day, a duel might have been called out, such was their stance.

"Mr. Winter, you have a call from Eden's End." Richmond approached from behind.

"Yes. I'll be right there." Winter nodded to his crewman, then turned back to Sam. "Now. Will you be diving again this afternoon?"

Sam appeared to consider the sky before responding. "Yes. There's time for another hour or so below before it begins to rain."

"Good. Be sure to take Hugh back down with you. I want every minute on film. Every minute." Winter nodded first to Rachel, then to Sam, before turning and heading across the deck to the cabin, leaving the two puzzled divers to contemplate their employer's behavior.

7

---◆◇◆---

"THAT'S EXCELLENT, Rachel. Excellent."

Rachel could almost see her father nodding slowly as he digested the information she gave him. She leaned over the ship's railing with the portable phone pressed close to her ear and watched a dark school of something pass about twenty feet off the bow of the *Annie G.*

"See, sweetheart? I was right. You'll have this operation completed in no time at all. And before you know it, you'll be back here in Maryland, having successfully completed your first solo job, and having found a lifelong friend in Norman Winter."

Rachel mulled that over for a moment, not sure that she wanted to be lifelong friends with Norman, though not exactly certain why.

"Rach? Are you there?"

"Yes, Dad. I'm here."

"You haven't said what you think of Sam McGowan."

Rachel sought the right words to sum up just how she felt about the archaeologist.

"He's one hell of a diver, isn't he?" Gordon said, as if to prod her.

"Yes. Yes, Dad, he is."

"And very knowledgeable."

"He seems to be. Keep in mind that we've only been working together for a few weeks."

"So?"

"So it's hard to form an opinion of someone that you've only known for a short time."

"I see."

Rachel doubted that he did, but she let it pass.

"Norman told me that you've arranged for a lab to be set up at Eden's End." She decided to change the subject.

"Yes. He thought it would be advantageous to have all the artifacts cleaned and restored right there. And of course, he's willing to let other salvors use his equipment once he's done with the *Melrose,* which is very generous of him. It's often difficult to find baths large enough for the big cannons and such. It's good to know we'll have access to them if we need them. It's also difficult for students to gain hands-on experience, so Norman's really providing an exceptional opportunity for them as well."

"Yes. Yes, he is."

"Well, I was just calling to see how things were going, and to ask you to let Norman know that his equipment is on its way to Eden's End."

"As is Norman."

"Oh?"

"There was some accident . . . part of a chimney fell onto a section of roof and the roof collapsed in one of the outbuildings. Norman was quite concerned. He had a boat pick him up. I expect he'll be back soon enough," Rachel said dryly.

God forbid Norman should miss a minute of our underwater adventure.

"He's an interesting fellow, wouldn't you say?"

Rachel took her time with this one.

"Interesting?" Rachel frowned. It wasn't exactly the word she'd choose.

Gordon hesitated, then asked, "Rachel, is something wrong?"

"No, not really."

"Is there a problem with Norman?" Rachel could hear the catch in his voice. "He isn't . . . *bothering* you, is he?"

"Bothering . . . ? Oh, no. No, nothing like that." Rachel laughed out loud at the thought of Norman, who seemed so prim, *bothering* anyone.

"Then, what?"

"I don't know, Dad. It's nothing I can put my finger on. It's probably nothing at all."

"Well, obviously, something is on your mind," Gordon persisted.

"It's just that I find him . . . odd. Maybe that's all it is."

"Odd in what way?"

"You mean other than the obvious, that he always dresses in white clothes and dark glasses that he never takes off?"

"Rachel, I've never known you to base your opinion of anyone solely on the way they look or dress. There has to be more to it than that."

Rachel sighed. What was it, exactly, about Norman Winter that pricked at her so?

"I guess it's his attitude toward this whole operation. He wants this done in record time . . ."

"You already knew that," her father reminded her.

"You can be in a hurry and still not be willing to compromise the job."

"What do you mean? What's been compromised?" Gordon's voice held more than mild concern. Compromise was not something he understood.

"Well, nothing yet. Not really." She thought of Sam's efforts to locate the name of the ship on the old cannon the previous afternoon. "Though yesterday we brought up the first of the big guns. Sam wanted to remove the concretions right here on the *Annie G.* because he believes the cannon might bear the name of a different ship. He thinks the *Melrose* started out its seagoing life as a British ship and was sold, probably illegally, to be used to aid the Confederacy. Norman insisted it would take too long to chip away the debris by hand and he sent the gun back to Eden's End on the same boat that took him."

Gordon was silent.

"Dad?"

"I'm listening. What else?"

"We can't dive unless the photographer is with us. He films every minute we're underwater."

"You used to dream of being a movie star, Rach. This could be your big break."

"Very funny. How 'bout this, though? Norman had Hugh, the photographer, shoot a lot of still shots. Sam wanted to scan them into his computer, to make a grid, have the wreck site on the screen so he could chart the location of every artifact."

"That's a great idea. It's an excellent way of recording and preserving what you've found and where you've found it."

"I agree. Norman, however, did not. He wouldn't give Sam the photos."

"You're kidding?"

"Nope. We both ended up sketching out the wreck the old-fashioned way, with pencil, on graph paper."

"Nothing wrong with that. I still use that method myself. But it is strange about the photos. Has Sam given Norman any reason to not trust him?"

"Not that I know of."

"Maybe Norman is afraid that someone will be able to get into Sam's computer and lift the photos of the wreck," Gordon speculated.

"Dad, Norman's been so secretive, I doubt if anyone, other than the crew here, and you and Jared, even knows that we're out here. Norman is almost obsessed that someone else will find out about the *Melrose* and try to join us."

"That's not necessarily unusual, Rachel. Especially when one has searched for a particular wreck for a long time. Why, I've known salvors who have set out buoys on dummy sites to draw attention away from where they were really working. I remember one time in the Florida Keys . . . ah, you've heard that story."

"The one about you and Mel Fisher trying to camouflage your sites so that neither of you would know what the other was doing?" Rachel laughed. "Yes, I've heard that one many times."

"It's not often that you come that close to a legend."

"And I'm certain that Fisher felt the same way about you."

"Ah, you're sweet, Rachel." Gordon paused, then asked, "Why aren't you working together?"

"Who?"

"You and Sam. You said you each sketched the wreck site. Why didn't you work on one comprehensive sketch?"

The silence was a little longer than Rachel had wanted it to be.

"Sam is staying on his own boat, Dad. He isn't staying on the *Annie G.*"

"So?"

"So, we're kind of busy during the day, and not getting time to sketch and record data till after dinner, so I've been doing it by myself."

"How do you know that you're not missing something? You trust your memory that much?" Rachel could almost see the furrow in her father's brow deepen. "And how far away is Sam's boat? Too far for a dinghy? Too far to swim?"

"He's anchored close enough," she conceded, then couldn't resist adding, "But I haven't been invited."

"Invited? Since when do you have to be invited to collaborate on something you're supposed to be working on together?"

"Maybe you're right," Rachel said, uncomfortable with the thought, but knowing that her father had a point. It was easy to overlook something on a sketch that one made from memory.

"Of course, I'm right. You're going to end up with two different versions of the same site. You'll recall things that Sam will have overlooked, and vice versa. If I were you, I'd consolidate the two now, before things become more complicated, and work from one set of sketches in the future."

"Okay," she said tersely, annoyed with herself that it had taken her father to point out the obvious to her.

"And I'd suggest that you make overlays on clear plastic or tracing paper so that you can sketch out the changes as you progress from day to day."

"I've been doing that, Dad."

"Of course, you would have. Sorry, sweetheart. I wasn't questioning you, it's just an old habit of mine to sort of think out loud." Gordon's voice softened. "It's a habit I'm trying to break. It's driving Delia crazy."

Rachel laughed.

"How is Delia?" She asked.

"Charming and delightful, as always," Gordon told her.

"Please give her my best. And tell her that when I'm finished here, we'll spend a day shopping." Rachel had become quite fond of her father's lady friend, the well-known mystery author, Delia Enright. "And tell Jared and everyone I said hi."

"Will do. Now, call me if you need anything."

"I will, Dad. You take care."

"You too, sweetie. Watch the currents there where the Gulf Stream meets . . ."

"I know, Dad. It's not been a problem. I'll keep in touch. Bye." She disconnected the call before she said something she'd regret later, wondering when her father had last felt compelled to remind Jared to watch the currents.

Rachel took the steps down to the lower level two

at a time. Once inside her cabin, she tucked the phone away and drew out the packet of sketches she had worked on earlier and looked them over. Tapping a foot lightly on the carpet of her small home away from home, she debated her options. She could ignore her father's advice and sketch today's finds alone, as she had the others, or she could swim over to the *Shearwater* and suggest to Sam that they begin to collaborate on one set. She peeked out her porthole. There would be another hour or so of daylight. Surely she could swim across the forty feet or so that separated the *Annie G.* from the *Shearwater* and back again before it got too late.

Digging out a waterproof travel pack from the suitcase that she'd stashed under her bunk, Rachel slid in the folder of sketches, then added a sweatshirt. For some reason, the idea of working closely with Sam while dressed only in a bathing suit made her nervous. She zipped the pack snugly and strapped it around her waist. Before she could change her mind, she headed back up the steps and across the deck.

"Rachel!" Renny called to her. "If you wanna have your coffee now, I'll get it for you."

"I'm going to have to skip the coffee tonight, Renny, but I appreciate the offer." She paused at the top of the ladder. "I have to go over some paperwork with Sam."

"You want me to get the dinghy?" he offered. "I could row you over. Scully taught me how to row. I am very good at it."

Rachel considered it, then shook her head. "I'm sure that you are, and thank you, Renny, but no, I think I'll swim. But thanks anyway."

"Don't be long, Rachel. It will get dark. You don't want to swim in the dark."

"It's okay, Renny. I've done lots of nighttime dives."

"You have?" His eyes widened at the thought.

"Sure."

"Aren't you afraid of . . . things?"

"No. No more than I am in the daytime. Besides," she assured him, "you take lots of lights down with you, and you never go alone."

"You're going alone now, Rachel."

"So I am. But I don't have far to go." She pointed at the short expanse that separated the two boats. "And there are lights from both boats."

"Still . . ." Renny looked worried.

"Why don't you watch me swim over," Rachel suggested, "and I'll make sure that Sam watches me swim back."

"That's a good idea," Renny said solemnly. "Scully always says you *never* go in the water by yourself."

"And Scully is right, it's always best to have a buddy."

"I'll be your buddy, Rachel. I can be your buddy from right here. I'll watch, and if you need help, I'll row out to get you in the dinghy. Unless there's a shark. Then I'll run and get Scully."

"Thanks, Renny." She smiled, touched by his sincerity and his concern. "I'm going to swim over now, and when I reach the platform on the back of the *Shearwater*, I'll wave to let you know that all is well."

"Want me to watch for you to come back?"

"No, I might be a while. And remember, Sam will watch me come back."

"Okay." Renny nodded. "I'm ready to watch you swim, Rachel."

"Okay, Renny, here I go."

Rachel entered the water softly, a mere slice in the surface of the dark ocean. A strong swimmer, she reached the *Shearwater* in minutes. Pulling herself to the platform, she turned back to the *Annie G.* and waved to Renny, who waved back. Opening her pack, she eased the sweatshirt over her wet body and repinned her hair atop her head where it had begun to slide down.

Taking a deep breath, she started up the ladder. At the top, she paused.

Someone was singing a mighty off-key version of the chorus from "Viva Las Vegas."

"Sam?" she called from the back of the boat. Now that she was here, she felt awkward. Maybe Sam wouldn't want her here. Maybe he was sleeping. Maybe he was . . .

"Awk! Blue suedes! Don't step on 'em!"

Rachel laughed out loud and took a few steps forward. "Sam?"

"Wear my ring! Wear my ring!"

Still laughing, Rachel followed the sound through a doorway into the cabin. Windows all around brought the sea and the sky together from every side. A comfortable-looking lounge, deeply cushioned, wrapped around the right side to form a banquette, with a rectangular table directly in front to provide dining space. To the left, an entertainment center boasting a TV and stereo system sat behind partially closed mahogany doors. The galley lay immediately beyond, with a small sink and three-burner stove with an oven below, a microwave oven, and a refrig-

erator-freezer combination that stood against the wall
that partitioned the galley from the helm, which was
two steps up. Three steps down, a door stood open,
and through it, Rachel could see the bed that was at
the center of the stateroom below.

"Sam?" she called again. He had to be there. It
wasn't as if he could have stepped out for a newspaper.

"I'm a hunk of love! I'm a hunk of love!" the parrot crooned from its perch behind the helm.

"I'll just bet you are," Rachel said as she stepped
closer to the gaily colored bird.

"I'm a handsome devil," the parrot tilted his head
and announced. "I'm Daria's handsome boy!"

Rachel laughed about the same time she realized
that the sound she just heard was the sound of water
being turned off. Probably the shower. Probably
Sam . . .

Before she could utter an *uh-oh*, a door had
opened below.

"Sam!" she called to him, to let him know that she
was there. "It's Rachel."

"Why, so it is." He stood at the foot of the steps,
holding a white towel in front of him, grinning and
taking his time to wrap it around his tanned waist.
"I guess you just stopped by to say 'hey.' "

"No, actually, I brought my sketches over." Rachel
eyed him steadily, as if oblivious to the fact that the
only thing that prevented her from getting a glimpse
of Sam in all his glory was a bit of terrycloth. Feeling
a flush spread from her neck to her hairline, she
turned her back and made a show of casually un-
zipping the backpack and sliding the sketches onto
the table.

"Oh? What sketches are they?" He still stood in the doorway at the bottom of the steps, his arms folded across his considerable chest, as if in no hurry to do anything about the fact that he was wearing nothing more than a towel and a few errant drops of water.

"My sketches of the *Melrose*."

"You want to show me your sketches?" The hint of amusement in his voice was unmistakable. "I'm flattered, Rachel, I truly am. And here all this time I thought you didn't like me."

"I didn't." She looked up a bit too sharply. "I don't. But we have a job to do. And it would make much more sense if there was one set of sketches. After all, we don't want to end up with two versions of the wreck site. You'll forget things, I'll forget things . . ."

Sam nodded and started up the steps.

"I couldn't agree more. I'm all for collaboration."

"Sam. Aren't you forgetting something?"

"What's that?" He crossed the cabin in three slow strides and was within inches of her before she knew it.

"Your clothes."

"Oh. The towel thing bothers you? I'm surprised, Rachel, you being a scientist of sorts." He stretched an arm out toward her and she ducked. Sam laughed and reached behind her to open one of the overhead storage cabinets. He withdrew a stack of papers and tossed them onto the table.

"My sketches," he told her. "You can look them over while I get dressed."

"I'm such a handsome boy," the parrot crowed.

"Nice bird," Rachel said to Sam's back as he reached the steps.

Sam laughed softly as he closed the stateroom door behind him.

He emerged five minutes later, wearing khaki shorts and a dark blue T-shirt. Rachel willed herself not to stare. To be professional. To be mindful that this was a job, and that he was a member of the crew. That she didn't really like him all that much.

Oh, hell.

"Are you aware that this bird can sing the entire chorus of 'Jailhouse Rock'?" Rachel asked. Casual, she reminded herself. Just keep it casual . . .

"And you're wondering if he knows the verses?"

"No, I was wondering why anyone would teach their parrot to sing Elvis. Fractured as it is."

"You'd have to ask Daria. H.D. is her bird. He does a really mean 'Crying in the Chapel,' by the way."

"Preeetty Daria. Be-u-ti-ful Daria," H.D. chortled.

"Who's Daria?" Rachel asked.

"My sister. She's out of the country right now. She dropped H.D. off on her way out of the country."

"H.D.?"

"Hound Dog."

"I see."

"You would if you knew Daria." He grinned. "Can I get you a beer?"

"No, thank you," she answered primly, still trying to banish the vision of Sam wearing nothing but a towel.

"Soda, water . . ." he offered as he took one out of the refrigerator for himself.

"No. Let's just get to work."

"Fine. Let's take a look at your sketches."

Rachel, seated on one of the built-in sofas, pushed her folder across the table. Sam leaned down on one elbow, studying each page carefully. He turned his own sketches around and compared them, side by side.

"What's this, right here?" He pointed to the left of the wreck.

"That's that outcropping of rock off the port side."

"The ones you were sitting on this morning?"

"Yes."

"And this is what?"

Both of Rachel's elbows rested on the table. She slid forward, resting her chin in the palm of one hand, to see what he was looking at.

"That's that large mass of seaweed."

"Near where you found the sand dollars?"

"Yes." Rachel withdrew back across the table, wondering how he could have been watching her if he'd been watching where he'd been going with the airlift.

"You caught more of the surrounding detail than I did, that's for sure." He looked down on her and smiled, deep grooves punctuating each side of his mouth.

Rachel sighed. Why did he have to have dimples? And was it her imagination, or were his eyes really the same shade of cobalt as those lapis beads she'd bought in Turkey years ago?

"That wasn't a sigh of boredom, was it?"

"What? Oh, no. No." She'd had no idea she'd been audible. "No. It was a sigh of . . . relief. That between the two of us, we seemed to have pretty much captured everything."

"Well, you're right. I have a little more of the ship's detailing than you do . . . the cannon mount here, for example." His index finger tapped on his sketch.

"I don't know how I missed that." Rachel frowned.

"Probably the same way I missed the pile of iron shot that you have on yours. How do you want to go about doing this? Want to add mine to yours, yours to mine, or do completely new sketches?"

Rachel hesitated, then looked over the two piles of drawings.

"Maybe we'll use mine—not because they're mine, but because I've included so much more of the surrounding area. It will be easier and faster to add the elements that I missed onto the ship than to try to squeeze the rest of it onto yours." She held up his sketch. "See, your rendering of the ship takes up almost the entire page."

"You're right. I totally agree. Let's just add these few things here . . ." He reached into a drawer built into the edge of the counter behind him and removed a pencil.

Rachel smiled to herself. She'd been right. It was mechanical. Blue.

She carefully penciled in the cannon mount and several other items she had overlooked.

"Starting tomorrow, we can do our subsequent sketches on transparent plastic sheets. That way we can make overlays," Rachel said as she worked.

"Let's see that sketch. You must be finished."

She pushed it to him and leaned back away from him.

"This is really good, you know?" He studied the drawing carefully. "Much more artistic than mine."

"I minored in art," she told him.

"I can almost see the seaweed moving," he said, "and the sand shifting over here where the main cabin is still covered. At least, that's where I think the cabin is."

"I think so, too. And I think that the cargo hold is back here." Rachel tapped the sketch a little farther back, toward the stern.

"Right. And I think the captain's cabin will be here, and the crew's quarters over here."

"That's how I see it, too." She nodded. "When do you think we'll get below board?"

"Within a day or so, I would guess. I'm concerned a bit about the weather forecast, though. They're calling for rain tomorrow." Sam frowned. "I'm praying there are no high winds or undue wave activity that would cover up what we've cleaned off."

"Well, that can work both ways." Rachel started to pack her sketches into her waterproof pack. "The water can move the sand in any direction. It can move the sand away from the ship as easily as it can cover it up again. But I agree, I would hate to see any delays."

"Why don't you leave those here?" Sam placed a hand over hers as she reached for the sketches. "I'll scan them into the computer. It'll just take me a few minutes to set everything up. I have a laptop downstairs . . ."

Rachel pulled her hand out from under his.

"Rachel." Sam reached for her hand again, and this time when she tried to pull away, he refused to let her. "We got off on the wrong foot, you and I. It was my fault, I admit it, and I'm sorry. I never meant to insult you or to hurt you or to make you feel bad. I've watched you over the past few weeks, and I can honestly say that I don't know any other salvor who would have done one thing differently, or better. You are, as you tried to tell me, very good at what you do. I'm proud to be working with you."

"Well, thank you, Sam." Rachel was stunned by the unexpected praise. "Thank you so much for telling me that. It means a lot to me."

"Good. I don't want there to be bad feelings between us, Rachel."

"You mean, maybe we could be friends?"

"Oh, at the very least, yes. Friends. That's a start."

"Okay. We can be friends." Rachel handed Sam the sketches. "You can return these tomorrow. I think I'd like to go back to the *Annie G.* now. It's dark and I have to swim."

"No, you don't. I'll row you back."

"That's okay. It's only forty feet or so."

"Not anymore." Sam nodded to the *Annie G.*, which had drifted at anchor to a good hundred feet or more.

"You have a dinghy?" she asked.

"An inflatable."

"Fine. Thank you." Rachel stood and buckled the pouch around her waist. "Can we go now?"

"Sure." Sam nodded. "Right this way . . ."

He stepped past her to open the cabin door, and caught that whiff of citrus again. That light combination of orange blossoms and lemons seemed to follow her right out onto the deck.

"How long will it take to inflate it?" she asked, as if suddenly in a very big hurry.

Sam laughed. "Rachel, if I didn't know better, I'd think you were afraid of me."

"That's silly. Why would I be afraid of . . ."

He hadn't made the decision to kiss her until she had stepped back into the moonlight and it softened her with pale shadows and silvery light. It was, Sam thought, a moment that might never come again. He caught her face in his hands and tilted it upward, at first just brushing her lips with his own before kissing her for real, tasting the faintest of salt water. Her breath caught, and he deepened the kiss, probing the corners of her mouth with his tongue. She was soft and warm and sweeter than anything he'd ever known. His thumbs traveled down the side of her face, tracing the outline of her jaw. And then, for good measure, he kissed her again.

"That," he said, leaning back to look into her eyes, "is what you were afraid of."

"That's ridiculous," she said, pushing him away with both hands.

Sam laughed.

"Whatever you say, Rachel." He stepped behind her and pulled a pair of short wooden paddles from their place along the side of the boat, then opened a built-in bench and removed a casing. Dumping the small blue and white object onto the deck, he activated the self-inflating device.

"Your chariot, madam."

"Look, I'll row myself over. You can pick up the dinghy tomorrow . . ."

"And what happens if my boat decides to sink tonight? I'd be dinghyless."

She nodded. The odds were against it, but still, you never know.

Sam dropped the dinghy off the back of the *Shearwater*.

"After you." He stood on the platform at the back of the boat and held on to the dinghy by the rope while Rachel climbed inside. Handing her the paddles, Sam stepped into the small craft and, on his knees, pushed off the back of the larger boat.

"Ever look at the ocean at night, at that fathomless darkness, and wonder what's under there?" he asked.

"Same thing that's under it in the daytime." Rachel shrugged.

Sam laughed. "I see there's no scaring you into moving a little closer to me for safety."

"Not likely." She leaned back against the side of the boat, one arm stretched along the upper side of the pontoon.

He rowed in silence for a moment, the paddles making a lapping sound as they dipped in and out of the water. The swells were slightly larger than they had been when Rachel had set out earlier.

Clouds drifted across the face of the moon momentarily. Rachel looked upward just as they passed, and the gentle light cast a glow about her face.

As they approached the *Annie G.*, Sam said softly, "Moonlight becomes you, Rachel."

Taken off-guard, she replied, "That's a song."

"So it is." He raised one paddle out of the water slightly and leaned forward. "Johnny Mathis. It was an old favorite of my dad's. He used to sing it to my mother and they'd dance in the front parlor when they thought none of us were looking."

"Your parents did that?" Rachel appeared surprised, as if never having considered that parents would do such a thing.

"Oh, all the time. He's a romantic old coot."

As hard as she tried, Rachel could not in her wildest dreams imagine her father singing a love song to her mother, or the two of them dancing anywhere, least of all in the parlor of their house. Neither of them had really lived in that house, and the times when they were both home at the same time were few and far between. She wondered if there had ever been a time when her parents had lived together happily, when neither of them had been looking forward to leaving for the next concert, the next ship . . .

"Well, here you are," Sam said as they reached the *Annie G.* He pulled the paddles in and reached a hand out to her.

"Sam, I've been around boats since I was ten years old. I don't need help getting out of a dinghy."

"I didn't ask you if you needed help, Rachel. I offered you a hand." Sam rested the paddles across his lap and before she could open her mouth, said, "And no, I don't think you need help. I don't think you're weak, and I don't think you're incompetent. I just wanted to offer, okay? So save your little insult, Rachel. It wasn't a commentary on your physical strength or your ability to get out of a boat all by yourself. Everything isn't a challange to your competency. I've found you to be *very* competent. As a matter of fact, I'd say that you are every bit as good as you said you are. I merely offered you a hand because I wanted to."

Rachel had slid her bottom onto the platform across the back of the *Annie G.* and had just swung her legs over. She sat there for a long moment, trying to remember the last time such chivalry had been extended on her behalf. In the dusky light, she could just make out Sam's face, and the slow beginnings of a smile that were starting to tug at the corners of his mouth.

"Now, I'm surprised at you, Rachel." Sam turned the dinghy around in the swells and pushed off in the direction of the *Shearwater.* "I would have thought you'd have something to say."

She stood up on the platform and watched the dinghy rise and fall, so small a craft in so great a sea. She did have something to say, but for the first time in a very long time, words failed her, so she simply stood there, on the back of the *Annie G.*, her arms wrapped around her midsection.

"Sam," she called out to him when he had crossed from the ship's lights into the darkness.

"What?" he called back, a disembodied voice.

"Sam, I was thinking." She took a deep breath and called to him across the water. "If I'd signed on to work with Dr. Grossman and showed up and found you instead of her, I think I'd probably have been thoroughly pissed off." It was the only thing she knew for certain he'd understand. "In fact, I know I'd be . . ."

He didn't answer, but Rachel knew he'd heard. The whistled tune—"Moonlight Becomes You"— drifted across the moonlit sea. She leaned against the railing and listened until the song faded away into the night.

8

────── ∞ ──────

High above the *Shearwater*, clouds swirled slowly as if just waking up and taking that first early morning stretch. Sam stood atop the flybridge and watched the waves below billow and foam. Far off in the distance, dark clouds massed and multiplied. Norman had been right to call the boats in. The coming storm could be a demon.

That he had also summoned Sam and Rachel to Eden's End, well, that could turn out to be a good call, too, Sam thought, as he watched her below on the deck, tightening this and tying down that. The woman knew her way around a boat, that much was evident. That she knew exactly what to do to ready the boat for rough seas had not come as a surprise. What had been unexpected was the way in which she simply did things, without waiting to be asked. She quietly and efficiently did her part and then some, leaving Sam to navigate the boat. It also afforded him a few minutes to admire Rachel and the way she moved, matter of factly and without giving thought to anything other than getting the job done.

Sam had never met a woman more seemingly unconscious of the way she looked, more unaware of her beauty, than Rachel Chandler.

Right now she braced her legs to roll with the choppy sea, stood easily astride the pitching deck with the same grace she exhibited when diving. In gray sweatpants and hooded sweatshirt, she all but blended in with the mist that shrouded the bow. Errant strands of auburn hair escaped to twist in the wind like flags on a mast to mark the spot where she stood. She was a creature of both sea and land, perhaps, he mused, the only true mermaid he'd ever met.

Watching her struggle with a tangled bit of rigging gave him the chance he'd waited for to bring her in from the storm—Lord forbid he should suggest to Rachel that she let him do the toughest work. He whistled at her to get her attention over the wind, then pointed down below, motioning her inside, and followed her into the cabin.

"I'll take over the rigging, you take the wheel." He pointed to the helm station, trying to ignore the fact that her clothes, saturated with rain, clung to her body like a second skin.

"I was doing okay."

"You were doing more than okay. You were doing the job of two men. But I like certain things stashed in specific places, and it's just easier for me to do it myself." Sam pulled up the hood of his windbreaker. "Besides, you're soaking wet. As soon as I come back, you can run downstairs and dry off, but for now, you can take over the wheel."

"You'd let me steer your boat?"

Sam grinned and pointed out over the port-side bow.

"Land is that way. You can't miss it. Just head due west."

"And straight on till morning," she muttered.

Sam laughed and went out into the rain.

The wind was brisker, the rain colder, than he'd thought. Within minutes, his face and hands stung, and again he marveled at how long Rachel had withstood the storm without complaint. He completed his tasks as quickly as he could and returned to the cabin.

It cheered him to have her there, at the helm of his boat, looking just like she belonged there. Still dressed in wet sweatpants and sweatshirt, her wet hair brushed straight back from her face and held in the back with some sort of clip, she looked every bit the sailor, albeit the most beautiful sailor Sam had ever seen.

"I think the wind is really starting to pick up now," Sam told her as he shook out of his windbreaker.

"I can feel it in the wheel. She's a tight craft, though. She's holding her own," Rachel said admiringly.

"Home, sweet home." Sam grinned.

"My dad feels that way about the *Albemarle*. It's his second home." She tossed a towel in his direction. "Here. I thought you might need this."

"Thanks." He pressed the towel to his face. "In my case, it's my first and only home."

"You live on the *Shearwater* all year round?" Her eyebrows raised.

He nodded.

"You don't have an apartment someplace?"

"Nope."

"Where do you keep your stuff?"

"What stuff?"

"You know, personal belongings. Clothes, things you've collected over the years . . ."

He shook his head. "I don't really have any stuff. As for clothes, I have two suits—one for summer, one for winter—three actually, if you count the tux, but I keep that at my parents'—and one sport jacket, two dress shirts, all of which are hanging in the closet downstairs. A couple pairs of khakis, some shorts, a couple of T-shirts, sweatshirts. Other than that, what do I need? A few pairs of socks—which I hardly ever wear—underwear, and something to wear into the water." Sam rubbed his hands together to warm them. "I don't collect anything, the books that I have are on shelves downstairs, and my music is in there"—he pointed behind her to the lounge. "I can't think of anything that I need that I can't fit onto this boat."

"How do you get your mail?"

"I have a post office box in whatever town I'm closest to. Right now, for example, I'm having things forwarded to a box in Morehead City. When I move on to the next job, I'll have it forwarded someplace else. I'll take over the wheel—why don't you go change into something dry."

Rachel grabbed the bag containing her clothes and went down the steps to his stateroom, quietly closing the door behind her. She went into the small bathroom and stripped off her wet sweat suit and hung it over the shower rail to dry. Next she ran the water in the sink until it was warm enough to thaw her hands. She hadn't wanted to complain to Sam, but she was chilled through to the bone.

She held a steaming washcloth to her face for a long moment just to inhale the steam, then took a towel from the rack and dried her hair as best she could before pulling it back with an elastic. Having traded the wet sweatpants for dry leggings, she gratefully pulled a navy fleece shirt over her head. She couldn't remember the last time that warm and dry had felt this good.

"Your turn," she told Sam. "I'll take the wheel now while you change, but only because you promised me coffee."

"Cream? Sugar? How do you like it?" he asked.

"Real cream, artificial sweetener, if you have them."

"You're in luck. I'll be right back."

He returned ten minutes later with two steaming mugs bearing the image of the black and white candy-striped Hatteras lighthouse. He passed a mug to her, and she sipped at it, then unconsciously made a face. It was the worst coffee she'd ever tasted. She watched out of the corner of her eye, thinking that perhaps it was a joke. But no, there was Sam, sipping away at his.

"Sam," she asked, "what's in your cup?"

"Same stuff that's in yours," he told her.

"Oh." So much for the *Ha ha, he gave me something vile as a joke and now I'll get the real stuff* theory.

"It's pretty bad, isn't it?" he said calmly. "The coffee, I mean."

"Hands down, the worst I've ever had, Sam," she agreed.

"I should have warned you. I don't seem to have the knack for it. Would you rather have tea?"

"No, Sam, I'd rather have a good cup of coffee." She got up and motioned for him to move, so that she could get out of the bench seat. "Want some?"

"I'd love it." He sighed.

He handed over the mug and took the wheel. "Aren't you going to make some wise remark about not signing on to make coffee?"

"Not as long as you make coffee that tastes that bad."

Sam smiled to himself as she went back to the galley. He could hear her talking to H.D., though he couldn't make out the words. There was something so natural about having her there on board, something so right about sharing the helm and a cup of coffee with her on a stormy morning with the wind hissing through the cabin and the waves crashing against the bow.

So natural, so right, that it almost scared him.

Almost, but not quite.

"Here, now, try this." She gave him a mug and he held it under his nose.

"Mmmm. This smells great."

"By the way, how long has it been since you cleaned that coffeepot?"

He looked at her blankly.

"I wash it out every time I use it."

"Well, I would hope so. No, I mean clean out the insides."

"You're supposed to clean it inside, too?"

Rachel grimaced. "I guess that answers the question. I won't ask how old the machine is. I don't think I really want to know."

Sam laughed. "Would it make you feel better to know it was a Christmas present this past year?"

"Better than wondering if you've had sediment building in there for the past two or three years? Yes, yes it does make me feel better, Sam." Rachel sat on the edge of the seat. "But I'd feel better still if I could clean that sucker out before the return trip to the wreck site."

"Feel free." He grinned. "My galley is your galley."

"Maybe next trip," she said, leaning back a little. "You really live on the *Shearwater* all year round?"

"Yes. Oh, sometimes I dock her and spend some time with my parents."

"Where do they live?"

"On St. Swithin's Island, off the coast of South Carolina."

"I know the area," she told him. "Is that where you grew up?"

"No. When I was younger, we lived in Florida, but then both of my parents joined the faculty at Princeton, so they hauled us to New Jersey along with them."

"You and your sister?"

"Sisters. Daria and Iona. And we had a brother."

"Had?"

"We lost him two years ago. Literally. He was lost in South America while on an expedition."

"I'm so sorry." She touched his arm. "Was he an archaeologist, too?"

"Thank you. We're all sorry, Rachel. Every day. And yes, we're all in the field, in one way or another. It's sort of the family calling."

"Both parents, too?"

"My mother has her Ph.D. in anthropology, my father in biblical archaeology. Daria specialized in Middle Eastern studies, and Iona has a master's in ancient cultures. Then she turned around and got a second degree in business and surprised everyone by opening a little shop in some trendy neighborhood in Philadelphia where she sells reproductions of jewelry and pottery and textiles from developing nations, along with her own jewelry and fabric designs. It's quite a mixed bag. My father calls it Iona's International Flea Market."

"What does she call it?"

"She calls it Miletus."

"Wasn't that a city . . . ?" Rachel frowned, trying to remember.

"Miletus was an ancient Greek city at the mouth of the Meander River in southwest Turkey. It was one of the first sites that Iona ever visited—she was young, maybe five or so. She heard someone refer to the city as Ionian, and thought that they meant the city was *hers*. We still tease her about that from time to time."

"That must have been some trip, for a five-year-old," Rachel mused.

"Oh, we all went. Dad had a grant for something at the time and we were there for six months."

"He took you all with him?" Rachel, whose parents had routinely left them behind, could not fathom such a thing.

"Yes, of course. Always. We went everywhere with them. My father would not go without my mother, and my mother wouldn't go without her children."

Rachel shook her head.

"My father never would have taken us on board ship, that really wasn't a place for small children. And I simply cannot imagine having accompanied my mother anywhere." She was almost numb at the very thought. "She didn't like us that much when she was home. She certainly wouldn't have taken us with her."

"Did your mother travel with your father?"

"No. She was a concert pianist. She went on long tours and only came back home when she didn't have anyplace else to go."

"That must have been very hard on you and Jared."

Rachel shrugged. "She died in a hotel fire in Switzerland when I was eight. I barely remember her."

"Rachel, I'm so sorry." He put an arm around her shoulders. "I'm really so sorry."

"It's okay. I never really knew her. I don't remember what her voice sounded like, or what color her eyes were. She never sang to us, never rocked us to sleep, never played games or told us stories." Rachel's voice caught and Sam could tell it was only sheer willpower that kept it from breaking. "She never cared much for either of us, Sam. The only mothering we ever got—such as it was—was from Aunt Bess, my mother's aunt, who lived with us. The funny thing is that Aunt Bess never approved of my father because of what he did for a living. She thought it wasn't very respectable. At least he came home whenever he could. At least he remembered our birthdays, knew where we went to school and what our middle names were."

"What is it?" Sam asked, hoping to move away from an area that obviously caused her great pain.

"What is what?"

"Your middle name?"

Rachel leaned back and announced with all due drama, "Evangeline." She rolled her eyes. "When was the last time you heard that one?"

"Oh, probably not so long as you might suspect."

She turned to look up at him. "Didn't your mama ever tell you it wasn't nice to make fun of people's names?"

"I wouldn't think of making fun of it, Rachel. That was my grandmother's name."

"Your grandmother's name was Evangeline?"

He nodded.

"I don't believe it. You're just saying that to make me feel better."

"No, I'm not. That was her name. Evangeline Mason."

"How 'bout that?" Rachel mused. "I've never heard of anyone else named Evangeline. For years I thought it was something my mother made up just to torture me with."

"It's a beautiful name."

"It's an odd name. I had enough other things setting me apart from the other kids when I was growing up. I didn't need an odd name to make me different."

"Like what other things?"

"Like the fact that I had red hair. And I was tall

and thin—tall for my age, anyway. Till seventh grade when I stopped growing and everyone else seemed to take off. And I was the only girl in my class whose parents never came to parents' night, teachers' conferences, or school plays. Everyone thought I was an orphan, and that Aunt Bess was my guardian."

"Did you tell them that, or did they come up with that on their own?"

"Might have dropped a hint or two. It was just easier than explaining."

"I would have thought that it would have been more exciting to tell the other kids that your father was a treasure hunter."

"I never really understood all that when I was little. I only knew that he wasn't there, and when he did come back . . ." She paused. "Well, he was always closer to Jared. I just think he didn't know what to do with a small girl."

Off to the starboard side a jagged line of light split the sky, and Rachel jumped.

"Sorry," she mumbled. "I didn't expect that."

"Good."

"What's that supposed to mean?"

"It means that for once, you just sat back, relaxed, had a normal conversation, and forgot to hang on."

"Hang on to what?"

"To your control button."

"What control button?" Rachel's eyes narrowed.

"The one you always have your finger on so that you can direct the course of every conversation. Do you realize this is the first normal conversation I've ever had with you?"

"My conversations are all normal."

"I've never had a conversation with you that wasn't about work."

"Oh, and I've known you roughly a month? A month during which, may I point out, we have been working nearly every waking hour."

"My point exactly."

"You had a point? Somehow I missed it, Sam."

"Rachel, I have this feeling that outside of your work, you have no life. You need to just kick back once in a while and . . ."

"What do you mean, I have no life? I have a life." Rachel's eyes narrowed. "I happen to have a great life. I'm doing exactly what I always dreamed of doing."

"And precious little else, I'd venture to guess."

"I do lots of other things. I . . . I read. And I knit."

"You knit," he repeated.

"It's a very good thing to know how to do. It's portable, the supplies don't take up all that much room on board ship . . ."

"Knitting doesn't sound like it would add much to your social life. And what do you get out of it, in the end?"

"Sweaters. I get sweaters," she told him firmly.

"Ummm-hmm. How many sweaters did you make last year, may I ask?"

"What difference does it make?"

"Work with me, Rachel, I'm trying to prove a point here. How many sweaters did you knit last year?"

"Seven."

"Seven sweaters. You knitted seven sweaters?"

"Yes. They were gifts. Except for this Aryan knit cardigan that I made for myself . . ."

"And what else did you did you do? For example, how many times did you go out to dinner last year?"

"Lots. I go out to dinner a lot," she said with emphasis on the last two words. "Why, every time we're in port, we . . ."

"With a man."

He saw her hesitate.

"A man who wasn't your brother, father, or a member of your crew."

When she didn't answer, he asked her again, more gently this time.

"How many, Rachel?"

"One. But I was working steadily last year, Sam. The only men I came into contact with were members of the crew. I never date crew, Sam."

"Why not?"

"Besides the fact that it could have serious repercussions, should things not go well, I always feel that . . . well, that I'm being asked out because someone wants my father to hire them on."

"You think the only reason why a man would ask you out is because he wants your father to hire him? Are you serious?"

She nodded.

"Rachel, have you looked in a mirror lately?" Sam took her face in his hands. "Apparently not. So let me tell you what you'd see. You'd see sea green eyes with long dark lashes that curl just on the end. A straight nose that has just enough freckles to be interesting. A mouth that a man wants to taste. More than once."

Sam stood and reached for her. "And I know about this, Rachel. I tasted. And once wasn't enough."

He kissed her gently, moving onto her mouth slowly at first, as if not sure whether she'd object.

"And just for the record, your father already tried to hire me, Rachel," Sam whispered before he kissed her again. "I turned him down."

It was, Sam thought, quite fitting that the storm outside the cruiser's cabin chose that moment to kick up. He felt perfectly in tune with the elements, felt the current flow to her and back again as surely as he'd heard the thunder off the bow. It rose within him, drawing his nerves taut. He slid his hands down her arms, from her shoulders to her hands, laced his fingers with hers, then kissed her again, slowly, deliberately. She tasted of coffee and salt spray and was, to Sam's way of thinking, a most irresistible combination.

The sound of something slamming into the windshield reminded them that they were at sea, in a storm that had been gathering momentum.

"What was that?" Rachel jumped.

"I don't know. I'll be right back. You steer."

He stepped past her to open the door, then all but disappeared into the rain beyond the cabin.

Her hands shaking, Rachel took the wheel, keenly aware of two things. One was that she couldn't see a thing beyond the cabin door. The second was that no one, but no one, had ever kissed her the way Sam McGowan did. She'd felt it clear down to her toes, just as she had the night before. It left her weak and breathless, and yes, just slightly out of control.

Inexplicably, she liked the feeling. And worse, it left her wanting more. Sam came back inside before she could decide if she was afraid that he would kiss her again, or more afraid that he would not.

9

———— ❧ ————

"It just occurred to me that we have no car." Rachel frowned as Sam worked with the wind to guide the *Shearwater* into a slip at the Bayhead Marina in Dickson's Beach on the Carolina coast. "How are we going to get from here to Eden's End?"

"Norman said he's reserved a car for us at Petersen's. They have rentals. It's just a block or two over." Stepping onto the bow, Sam tossed a length of polyester rope and lassoed a cleat on the dock, then proceeded to tie up the *Shearwater* in a four-point suspension, two lines on the bow, two on the stern.

"Do you have your things?" Sam asked when he had finished.

"Yes." Rachel nodded. "Though I didn't bring all that much with me. I don't expect that we'll be here that long."

"Who knows what Norman has in mind?" Sam gave a look around the cabin. After securing anything of value—stereo, TV, microwave—behind locked cupboards, he swung his bag over his shoulder and said, "Ready?"

"I'm a hunk of love! Awk!"

"Oh. H.D. I almost forgot you." Sam peered into the bird's cage. "I fed you this morning, so you don't need food. And you still have plenty of fresh water. You should be fine." Sam pulled the curtains closed around the cabin, shutting out the light.

"I'm locking the cabin so that no one can steal you, though I'm tempted to leave it open and take my chances," Sam told the parrot.

"I'm Daria's be-u-ti-ful boy!" H.D. reminded him.

"And that's the only thing that keeps me from opening the door and letting you take your chances on the high seas, believe me."

"Ha! And you think that I don't have a life?" Rachel grinned as she walked past Sam to the cabin door. "At least my companions are human."

"Right. Norman Winter and Hugh the photographer. I'm not so certain that H.D. isn't better company sometimes."

"Putting the subject of our employer and his idiosyncrasies aside for the time being, what's wrong with Hugh?" Rachel asked as she stepped from the bow onto the dock.

"For one thing, he isn't much of a diver, is he? I mean, he doesn't even seem to enjoy the water. And haven't you ever watched him shoot that video? It's like he's on a pulley. Back and forth across the site. All morning, all afternoon. Unless you've found something—then he's right on your back."

"He's been hired to document the entire operation," Rachel reminded him. "That's what he's being paid to do."

"And don't you find that a bit odd? Don't you feel as if Big Brother is watching you?"

"Big Brother is watching us," she conceded. "I admit it's a bit creepy."

Sam fell into step next to Rachel. "I've never worked a job where I've had someone watching, literally, every move I make."

"I just have to keep reminding myself that since Norman can't dive with us, he must want to feel like he's right there with us."

"Oh, he's right there with us, all right. And why can't he dive?"

"He mentioned something about having a heart condition of some sort. I didn't ask him to go into detail, but it apparently keeps him from diving."

"Well, it's weird to know that every moment of your working day is being recorded on film."

The sidewalk running from the marina led out onto a somewhat short but wide street. Trailers with boats lined both sides, and at the end of the street was a broad intersection. The office for the marina and boatyard stood on one corner, the others being occupied by a newsstand, a small restaurant, and a gas station, respectively.

"Where to?" Rachel paused at the corner.

"Norman said that Petersen's was about two blocks down Bay Avenue. And there it is. I can see the sign from here." Sam nodded in the direction of the intersecting street. "Look, why don't you run over to that little café on the corner and scope out the lunch menu while I check in here at the marina. I won't be long."

"Okay."

Rachel tossed her bag over her shoulder and walked across the street, picking her way around the puddles left from the earlier storm that had started inland and moved out to sea. The *Shearwater* had passed through the worst of it about a mile out. Rachel and Sam were equally happy to find clearing skies as they approached land.

The one and only luncheonette in Dickson's Beach was nearly empty, the hour being midway between the lunch and dinner crowds. Rachel peered inside at a row of chrome and Formica tables nestled into booths with red leather seats. All was neat and tidy, the tables looking newly wiped down, the salt and pepper shakers freshly filled. She smiled at the gray-haired waitress who sat at the counter on the end stool, and scanned the menu that was posted on the window.

"What looks good?" Sam said as he came up behind her.

"Are you kidding? This is North Carolina, bucko." She grinned and opened the door. "Barbecue country."

"Sounds good to me."

Sam held the door to permit Rachel to enter first. He half expected her to protest that she could open the door herself, and was pleased when she did not. Sam found that he liked this new, more relaxed Rachel. He liked her a lot.

"Is any table all right?" Rachel asked the waitress, whose name tag identified her as Mary Rose.

"Any table is fine, folks." The waitress swung

around on her stool, reluctantly, it seemed, her rest apparently having been all too brief. "Now, the cook just went over to the post office, so if you want something from the grill, that might be a few minutes. Otherwise, the owner is in the back."

"You have barbecue on the menu," Rachel noted.

"Sure do. It's our specialty."

"We'll have that. Some coleslaw. Hush puppies." Rachel looked across the table at Sam. "What are you drinking?"

"Iced tea is fine."

"Two iced teas," Rachel told the waitress, then said to Sam as the woman went into the kitchen, "I haven't had eastern Carolina barbecue in more years than I can remember. Not since I took summer courses at East Carolina State when I was in college. I lived on the stuff. I gained a ton that summer, but boy, I was well fed and *real* happy."

"Now, is eastern Carolina barbecue different from western Carolina barbecue?"

"Oh, bite your tongue." A bit of a drawl colored her speech. "Honey, there are only two kinds of barbecue down here. Eastern and western. Eastern is made with lots of vinegar and crushed red pepper. They use the entire pig—you do know that it's always pork, don't you?—and it's lean and sometimes just a touch on the dry side. They serve it chopped, with lots of sauce on the side. Western, on the other hand, is generally made from pork shoulders, and the meat is marbled, so it's moister, and usually chunkier. The sauce is sweeter and has a bit of tomato, which you rarely see in eastern barbecue. Both are served with coleslaw, by the way, and hush puppies, and sometimes, easterners will have a little Brunswick stew."

"Which is better, eastern or western?"

Rachel appeared to consider the question carefully.

"Depends on which you are eating at that particular moment. And at that moment, it's the best food in the world."

"My grandmother used to make Brunswick stew." Sam rested both arms on the gray and white Formica table. "Tomatoes, corn, sometimes okra, fish or chicken, sometimes both. Hush puppies, of course. Sweet potato pie. Banana pudding. Grandma McGowan was one fine cook." Sam grinned. "My poor father went from a home where fine, traditional Southern cooking ruled to marrying my mother, who could make two styles of eggs, cream puffs, and vegetable soup. And precious little else."

"You look as if you fared well, in spite of it."

"We had a cook. My father liked to eat."

"What's your father's name?"

"Samuel the third."

"Ah, that explains it." She nodded, leaning back to permit the waitress to serve their iced tea.

"Explains what?"

"How someone who has sisters named Daria and Iona could come to be named Sam. Not that there's anything wrong with Sam, mind you. But Daria and Iona are a bit unusual." She sipped at her tea. "What was your brother's name?"

"Jackson. Jack. He and Iona were twins." Sam stirred a packet of sugar into his glass. "After Jackson Prescott McGowan. My father's great-uncle. My mother, as you noticed, favored somewhat exotic

names for her daughters, but went with traditional
family names for her sons."

"She sounds like a really interesting woman."

"Interesting?" Sam raised an eyebrow and looked
amused. "Oh, at the very least, she is that. Mom
is . . . different. You're like her, in some ways."

"Oh?" Rachel took her plate of barbecue from the
waitress's hands. "Oh, smell that vinegar? Yum!"

"Here's some extra sauce for you." The waitress
set a white pitcher between them.

"Thank you." Rachel dug in, then sighed. "This
is wonderful."

"It is good," Sam told her after a bite or two. "And
it does remind me of my grandmother's. I haven't
thought about that in a long time. She's been dead
for almost fifteen years now, so it's been a while."

They ate in silence for a few minutes, then Rachel
asked, "How am I like your mother?"

"Oh." He put his fork down. "Well, you're both
strong women with that don't-get-in-my-way attitude when you have a job to do. And she always
had the ability to turn off everything around her and
focus on the job at hand, sort of the way I've seen
you do underwater. She is always prepared before
she tackles something. Never waits for anyone to ask
for help before she pitches in. And she's as impatient
as the devil when she wants something done, and
she always takes the part of the underdog. You do
the same type of thing. I've watched you with Renny.
You're very kind to him."

Rachel's fork hung between her mouth and her plate.

"All that in just a little over a month?"

"It's been a pretty busy month. Nothing to do but

watch the sand go up the tube and watch you swim around. Not a whole lot of variety down there."

"Dessert, folks? Coffee?"

"I could not eat another bite," Rachel exclaimed. "I don't even know if I can walk after that meal."

"Well, if worse comes to worst, I'll roll you down the street like a beach ball until we get to the car rental place."

"Oh," the waitress said. "That would be Petersen's. Right on up the block this way." She pointed to the left with a long fingernail painted red, the tip decorated with a tiny white painted rosebud.

Sam paid the bill and Rachel tucked the tip under her plate. They stepped outside into a bright afternoon, a dramatic contrast to the morning's storm.

"Cleared up nicely," Sam noted. "Of course, out at sea there will be some current activity and sand movement for a day or so due to the storm, but it should be fine for diving by Thursday."

Rachel rustled in her shoulder bag searching for her sunglasses as they walked along, their hips occasionally touching.

"How far do you suppose we are from Eden's End?" Rachel asked.

"About an hour and a half or so."

"How long has it been since you visited?"

"My grandfather died three years ago. I've only been back twice since then. The first was for his funeral. The second was for the reading of his will. His widow sold the property to Norman immediately upon my grandfather's death. We all suspect that she had made an agreement prior to his passing. The deal had gone through too quickly for it to have been otherwise. I don't think Granddad was in the ground for more than two weeks before Judith—my grandfather's wife—announced that the property was for sale and did any of us want to buy it."

"And no one did?"

"No one in the family could afford to buy it, let alone restore it, too. We all had to turn it down, and the next thing we knew, we all got letters from Judith telling us that Eden's End had been purchased by one Norman Winter and that all of the grandchildren would receive a portion of the proceeds from the sale."

"That was good of her."

"Yes, it was. She didn't have to do that. We all recognized that." Sam grinned. "That's where the down payment on the *Shearwater* came from."

"Does it bother you that Norman owns and lives in your family home?"

"No. I can honestly say it does not. It's *his* family home now. He bought it, and I understand that he's spending a not so small fortune to restore it to its former glory. And he's even willing to open it to the public. In spite of the fact that I think he's odd in a lot of ways, I have to admire anyone who is willing to do that. To spend his money restoring a way of life that has passed so that we can all remember, and maybe learn a little from it."

They had reached Petersen's, and paused outside its white clapboard office. The car lot contained an eclectic mix of sedans, pickups, and minivans.

"That was some storm that passed through, wasn't it?" a middle-aged man in a yellow short-sleeved sport shirt called to them from the porch.

"It certainly was," Sam agreed.

"Can't remember the last time I saw the wind pick up that fast. My wife just called and said it blew the shutters right off the next-door neighbor's garage. How 'bout that?"

"Yup. That was some strong wind," Sam replied.

"You folks looking for a car?" The man in the yellow shirt came off the steps.

"Yes. A rental. Our employer called . . ."

"Oh, Mr. Winter. Yes, sir, he sure did. And I got your car all ready for you. Just come on in here and sign the papers and you can just go right on about your business."

"I wonder which one is reserved for us?" Rachel whispered from the side of her mouth.

"I'm putting my money on that mustard-colored Escort."

"My bet would be the pea green pickup with the rust on the wheel wells."

They were both wrong. Norman had reserved a newer model four by four, easily the best vehicle on the lot, for their use. Relieved, they threw their bags into the back and climbed in.

"You know how to drive a stick?" she asked.

"Do I know how to drive a stick?" Sam repeated, passing a scowl in her direction.

"A lot of people these days don't." Rachel feigned innocence. "I was just checking."

"Exactly like my mother," he muttered, trying to appear put out, but the twinkle in his eyes gave him away, and Rachel laughed. Sam found he was enjoying the sound of it more and more.

The town of Dickson's Beach was four blocks in each direction, and each block sported its share of neat, trim clapboard houses with wide front porches. Front yard gardens, defined by budding azaleas, sported tulips of every color and variety, and spilled pink and lavender phlox onto well-worn sidewalks. Just outside of town, an ancient windmill, it's paddles long rotted, stood lonely and forgotten in a sandy field. A mile down the highway, the road narrowed. Dilapidated houses here and there appeared to be abandoned.

"Are you sure you know where you're going?" Rachel asked.

"Sure. Wilmington is that way." He pointed left at a Y in the road, heading to the right past a low-lying pond upon which ducks gathered for an afternoon nap. "Which means that Eden's End is this way."

Rachel covered a yawn with her hand. It would appear that the ducks had a pretty good idea. She leaned back and reached under the seat, searching for the lever that would tilt the seat to a more comfortable position. Easing back, she sighed with contentment and watched the scenery go by.

Bald cypress, moss draping like shawls over the shoulders of tired matrons, rose from a dark swamp that stretched endlessly to her right. Overhead a hawk spun circles in the sky as it drifted downward, enticed, no doubt, by the newly hatched ducklings that swam clustered near their mothers, who sought the safety of the rushes and fallen logs. It was a lonely stretch of road, and it seemed they drove forever before they passed another car.

"Rachel, see if you can find something good on the radio," Sam said after they'd passed another quiet mile.

She sat up and pushed the button to turn it on, asking, "What do you consider good?"

"Some blues might be nice right about now." Sam nodded to himself. Blues would be perfect as he cruised the back roads through the swamp, a beautiful woman at his side, on his way to his family's homestead.

Former family homestead, he corrected himself.

"Are you sure you know where you're going?"

"Positive. Just relax and keep turning that dial till you find something."

Rachel leaned forward to hear through the static. "Ah, yes." She smiled up at him happily. "The Dixie Chicks."

Sam smiled back weakly. He'd been hoping for B.B. King. Or Buddy Guy. Or Muddy Waters.

Rachel started singing along with the radio, and Sam scratched his head and looked out the window to keep from smiling too broadly. Rachel's singing was every bit as bad as his coffee. Maybe worse.

It was somehow endearing.

Sam settled back to enjoy the ride to Eden's End.

The slowing of the car, the slight whine of the engine as Sam downshifted, roused Rachel from a light nap just as they made a sharp right turn. Before her eyes, white dogwoods stretched to line a narrow lane as far as she could see.

"Where are we?" she asked.

"Eden's End," he replied.

Rachel sat up and to get a better look.

"Where is it?"

"This is it. This is the road leading up to the house."

"Wow. Just like in the movies. And look, there's my car, safe and sound."

Rachel rolled the window down and the sweet scent of wisteria seeped in.

"Oh, that's lovely!" she exclaimed. "I love wisteria!"

"Then you will love Eden's End." Sam smiled. "It grows like weeds down here. It's all through the woods and it's all around the porches. At least, it used to be."

As they approached the house, it was apparent that the wisteria had maintained its hold on Eden's End. Great thick vines twisted around the classic white pillars that stood across the front porch, giving them the appearance of soldiers trying to maintain their dignity while wearing feather boas. It was charming, a perfect contrast to the solid redbrick, white-shuttered mansion that graced the top of a very gentle rise.

"Oh, it's beautiful," Rachel murmured. "Just beautiful. Exactly what an old Southern plantation house should look like. Oh, how could your family part with it?"

Sam laughed. "Well, there was the matter of the roof over the kitchen that was falling in . . . the barns that were caving in, the chimneys that were falling down. I'm afraid this generation of McGowans are scholars, not gentleman farmers or philanthropic preservationists. We leave that to the Norman Winters of the world."

As if on cue, the new owner of Eden's End stepped through the oversized front doors and stood on the top step, his hands in his pockets. Even in the shade of the porch, his dark glasses shielded his eyes.

"Rachel, Sam." He stepped forward to greet them as they exited the car. "I trust the seas weren't too rough this morning."

"It got a little dicey right before it broke," Sam told him. "Nothing that the *Shearwater* couldn't handle, though."

"Good. Good." Norman held his arms slightly open, his palms up, and asked, "So. Is it as you remember?"

"Better than I remember," Sam told him. "The last time I was here, a few of the shutters were hanging slightly cockeyed, and every inch of wood needed to be scraped and repainted. You've doing an incredible job, Norman. You're to be commended."

Norman looked inordinately pleased. Clapping his hands together, he smiled broadly. "I'm so glad to hear you say so, Sam. It's been a tough job, but a labor of love. It's important to me to know that the Captain's descendants approve of what I'm doing here."

"Well, this descendant does. I'm sure the others would, too, if they could see what you've done here."

"I'm hoping they'll all have the opportunity to come for the opening of the museum."

"That would be a lot of fun for everyone," Sam told him sincerely. "I think the entire family would come for that."

"I would hope that they would. Now, if you'd like to bring your bags inside, I'll arrange for you to have a bite, then we'll take a tour of the grounds so that you can see what else we've worked on."

"We had lunch in Dickson's Beach," Rachel told him. "I'd just as soon go right to the tour, anyway. I can't wait to see everything. I'm enchanted!"

"Well, then, perhaps we'll start with a walk around

the grounds, then have tea when we come back to the house. Let's start with the side gardens . . ."

He motioned to their right, and they followed him across the grass and around the side of the house, where handsome hedges formed a natural fence. A wooden gate led to a somewhat modified maze, at the center of which was a small, neatly pruned rose garden.

"Lovely." Rachel reached out to touch glossy dark green leaves and apricot-colored buds.

"It will be quite striking when the roses bloom. Those right there will be pale peach, and the ones next to it are a deep violet. Not a traditional pairing, to be sure, but it pleases me," Norman told them.

"We used to play in here when we were kids," Sam said. "Of course, it was all overgrown back then, my grandfather rarely remembered to keep it trimmed. And the roses were red, I think."

"They were." Norman nodded and paused to light a cigar. He offered one to Sam, who declined with a shake of his head. "The journals kept by the old gardeners led me to believe that those same roses were originally behind the house, so I had them moved. And I was lucky to find someone who knew how to reconstruct the flower gardens. Some of the plants were, it would seem, original to the property, including several varieties of vegetables from the old kitchen garden. A historical horticulturist has been taking cuttings and gathering seeds over the past year."

"It must be exciting to be part of living history," Rachel said, "and to be in a position to perpetuate the older species to ensure that they survive."

Norman waved a hand magnanimously. "My predecessors here did all that. Sam's people were the stewards for the past hundred and fifty years, my dear. I'm merely carrying on where they left off."

Sam laughed. "You give my family far too much credit, Norman. If anything survived, it was in spite of us. Except for my grandmother, there hasn't been a gardener under this roof since the days when they could afford to hire one. And that's been a long time."

"It's more important that they did no harm." Norman patted Sam on the back as they walked toward the garage. "Whether by accident or design, the old varieties were saved. And that's what matters. Take those apples, for example."

Norman pointed to an orchard that spread out to their right.

"And in my youth, I did," Sam told them. "We climbed those trees. Picked the apples. Ate some and gave some to the horses. My grandmother made apple pies and applesauce and apple everything you could possibly think of."

Sam stood as if momentarily stuck in time. He could almost see his sister Daria as she raced him to the third tree in, the one they climbed to peer into the robins' nests in late spring.

"Hey, wait for me," Iona would call, her legs churning to catch up.

"Sammy, Daria, Jackson! Wait for Iona," their grandmother would appear from nowhere to scold.

"Sam?" Rachel touched his arm.

"Oh. Sorry. For a minute, I could have sworn I heard my grandmother calling me."

Norman moved on as if he hadn't heard and

pointed to the red clapboard barn. "That's where the museum will be."

"I sure hope you can get the smell out. That barn has been home to countless generations of horses, cows, and goats."

"I've read that the Captain had some very impressive horses. Fastest in the county, according to one report of a race that was held one summer." Norman nodded to the open field. "It seems Thomas Norton, a neighboring farmer, owned a section of land between Eden's End and the river that the Captain coveted. Well, they said that Norton prided himself on breeding the fastest horses on the coastal plain. He had his eye on one of the Captain's mares—one that he'd brought back with him from Texas. Norton kept asking to buy the mare, and the Captain was looking for a way to get that piece of land. Finally he challenged Norton to race. If Norton won, he got the mare. If the Captain won, he got the land." Norman took a puff on his cigar. "The Captain won."

"I've heard a lot of stories about Old Sam, but I'd never heard that one before. Where did you say you read that?"

"I didn't say." Norman flicked an ash. "I suppose it must have been in an old newspaper."

"What's down this path?" Rachel asked.

"Oh, there used to be an old, burned-out house about a quarter mile away," Sam told her.

"The Captain's mistress lived there with their son," Norman announced quietly.

"So Old Sam did have an illegitimate son," Sam said. "I seem to remember some story that hinted that he might have. And you're certain?"

"Oh, quite certain." Norman nodded. "There's plenty of documentation. And the Captain never denied that they boy was his."

"I don't recall having heard any of the details when I was a child."

"I doubt if it's a story that would have been told to the children," Norman said. "But it's true enough, I assure you."

"Well, how 'bout that? Somewhere there's a branch of the family running around that the rest of us never heard of." Sam turned back to the path that led through the dense wood. "I wonder whatever happened to her."

"Your great-great-grandmother killed her," Norman stated, as matter of factly as if commenting on the weather. "Trinity McGowan burned the house down with Anjelica—that was the woman's name, Anjelica—inside."

"Norman, did you just say that my great-great-grandmother was a murderer?" Sam was wide-eyed.

"Yes. Sorry, Sam, but I have it on the very best authority." Norman shrugged his white-clad shoulders. "Trinity's diary. Perhaps you'd like to read it later on?"

Sam nodded.

"Ironic, don't you think, that you know more about my family history than I do?"

Norman glanced at his watch. "I believe that our tea is ready to be served. Come along, Sam, and I'll see if I can find that diary for you."

A curious Sam followed Norman across the once-familiar stretch of grass that led to the sprawling house his Prescott ancestors had built generations ago.

10

—❦—

"Sam, are you all right?" Rachel asked after Norman had disappeared into the house in search of his cook.

"About as well as anyone would be after having just learned that their great-great-grandmother was an arsonist and a murderer."

Sam stood at the edge of the wide veranda that stretched across the entire back of the house, his hands in his pants pockets, looking out over the property much as the first Sam McGowan must have done.

"You know," he said, "I always thought there was something just a tad shady about Old Sam."

"Building a home for his mistress and their child on the property that belonged to his wife's family qualifies as shady in my book." Rachel paused to inspect the tea table, which, dressed as frilly as a preschooler at a wedding in pale blue and white, had been set for three.

"But of course, by then, the property had been transferred to the Captain." Norman joined them via French doors that stood open to the spring air. "So, technically, it no longer belonged to the Prescotts."

"In a sense, Eden's End will always be Prescott land," Sam told him. "Prescott brothers, John and Ethan, claimed and cleared it at the turn of the century. The eighteenth century, that is. They fought Indians, mosquitoes, malaria, alligators, and pirates to keep it. The house, as you now see it, is the third to have stood here. As a matter of fact, I believe that the room off the back of the kitchen—my grandmother used it as a summer kitchen—was actually part of the original cabin that the first Prescotts built here in 1704. On the back wall, you can see the marks in the wood where they kept track of the number of days they were under siege from the Tuscarora until help arrived. But I'm sure that you know all that."

"Unfortunately, I had to have it taken down," Norman told him almost apologetically. "I'm afraid it was overrun by carpenter ants. Oh, here's Mrs. Thurston with our tea. Please join me . . ."

Norman turned his back and smiled at Mrs. Thurston, his cook and housekeeper, who at that moment was wheeling a wooden tea cart upon which rode several covered trays, along with a silver tea service.

"Sam, Rachel." Norman gestured to the table. "Mrs. Thurston has prepared a lovely tea for us. I see scones and jam here, and some tea sandwiches. Nothing too heavy, of course, Mrs. Thurston will have a wonderful dinner for us later. No red meat, of course, Rachel." Norman paused for a moment, then said, "Sam?"

Sam had walked to the opposite end of the veranda and seemed to be inspecting the rounded, glass-walled room that jutted off the back of the house. Made of redbrick that exactly matched the old, no one would suspect that it had just been added the previous fall. No one but a McGowan.

"Sam?" Rachel went to him, touching his arm gently.

"You know, Norman, I'm surprised that you weren't able to find a way to preserve the original section of the house. With all the contractors you must know, all the people you must have had out here, I'm really surprised that none of them were able to restore that room." Sam appeared to be doing a slow burn.

Norman shrugged. "I was told that the damage was too extensive. Had I known it would mean so much to anyone . . ."

Sam turned to Rachel. "The first school in the county was held in that room. The first Jackson Prescott went all the way to New Jersey to go to college. While he waited for a permanent teaching assignment, he gave instruction in reading and mathematics right there in his mother's kitchen. It was a historic structure. I'm just baffled that you didn't go to greater effort to preserve it."

"As I said, the experts told me it couldn't be saved. I'm sorry it's upset you. There was simply nothing to be done. Now, if you please, Sam, before your tea gets cold . . ."

Sam ambled back to the table, his hands still shoved into the pockets of his dark green Dockers's, a look of discomfiture still on his face.

"So tell me, Norman, what else have you uncovered about my great-great-grandfather that I don't know?"

"Probably a lot, Sam. Sit down, and we'll talk about it." Norman held a chair for Rachel, and she sat slowly, watching Sam's eyes fade from indigo to blue ice.

Norman poured tea into a fragile china cup and handed it to Rachel, saying, "The scones are Mrs. Thurston's own recipe. You'll want to try them with the raspberry jam. Sam, may I pour a cup for you?"

"Yes, thank you." Sam took his seat.

"Now, why don't you tell me what you know about Captain McGowan, and I'll tell you what I've learned," Norman said, hoping to pacify Sam.

Sam took a sip of excellent tea and fought the ire that had risen inside when he realized that what he'd considered the most historically significant section of Eden's End had been destroyed. Surely his annoyance with Norman was misplaced—the old story of shooting the messenger, he reminded himself. As conscientious as Norman was about preserving the past, he'd certainly have made every effort to save the old summer kitchen. It wasn't fair, Sam told himself, to be angry with Norman because his contractors had failed.

"I know that my great-great-grandfather was born in the Ohio Territory. As a young man, he traveled the Mississippi River and at some point joined the army. He was assigned to Colonel Prescott's division and sent to Texas to support Sam Houston at the battle of San Jacinto. Later, on an army post in Mis-

souri, he met Prescott's daughter, Trinity. Shortly
after that they were married."

Sam paused for a bite of a watercress sandwich,
then said to Norman, "Feel free to add whatever you
know at any point."

Norman, looking amused, carefully placed his cup
upon his saucer.

"Well, perhaps we should start by saying that apparently Trinity Prescott was . . ." Norman paused,
as if considering, "would *homely* be too strong a
word?"

Sam shook his head.

"No, probably not. It's no secret within the family
that Trinity was not blessed with physical beauty."
Sam turned to Rachel and added, "And that's being
kind. There used to be a portrait of her in the front
hall. As kids, we were afraid of her."

"That's a terrible way to speak about your ancestor," Rachel protested.

"It's sad, but true. Apparently, Trinity's most appealing characteristic was that, as an only child, she
was the only heir to the Prescott holdings, which
were considerable," Sam explained. "In addition to
Eden's End, which was a profitable plantation, there
was a textile mill in Pennsylvania and land in both
Maryland and Georgia. Trinity was quite the catch."

"If they were so wealthy, why was her father in
the army?" Rachel asked.

"As I understand it, Trinity was the image of her
mother, in both looks and temperament. Which, as
the story goes, was less than gracious," Sam told her.
"It would seem that Colonel Prescott found it prefer-

able to spend as much time as possible away from home."

"So he joined the army?" Rachel raised a curious eyebrow. "Isn't that a bit extreme?"

Sam shrugged. "Hey, it was adventure of a kind he wouldn't have seen at Eden's End. And it gave him some respite from his wife's reputed sharp tongue."

"Who ran the plantation while he was gone?" Rachel asked.

"She did. His wife. Temperance Delicia Prescott."

"And might we assume that she taught her daughter everything she knew?"

"It would appear so." Sam's good humor was beginning to return. "Strong willed, both of them. Trinity had turned down dozens of proposals before meeting Sam. She was smart enough to know that none of her suitors were attracted by her looks."

"How did she meet Sam?"

"Well, remember that he was under her father's command. When the Colonel first returned from leave following his wife's death from a fever, Trinity accompanied her father. The Colonel was not oblivious to the fact that his daughter was obviously attracted to Sam. Anxious to see her married, he threw them together as often as possible. Trinity, apparently, liked the way Sam looked. Sam liked the fact that Trinity was a very wealthy young woman. He liked the idea of being a plantation owner, and it goes without saying that he certainly wasn't above marrying her for her money. Before leaving to return to Eden's End three weeks later, Trinity asked Sam to marry her."

"She asked him? That was so bold of her. Such behavior must have been unheard of back then!" Rachel exclaimed.

"Trinity was apparently a woman who knew what she wanted. Sam, however, shrewdly balked at a marriage where everything would be in his wife's name, and sent Trinity back to Eden's End to ponder her options. Fortunately for Sam, the Colonel had the good grace to succumb to the fever he'd caught when he'd gone to Eden's End to bury his wife. Trinity promptly returned to the fort to attend the memorial service for her father—he'd already been buried, it being August at the time—and promised Sam that she'd have everything transferred into his name if he would marry her right then and there. Recognizing that such offers don't come every day, Sam married her the following week, and even before the ceremony, she had the family lawyer working on putting everything in Sam McGowan's name. Sam quit the army and settled in here at Eden's End with his bride."

"Leaving behind a very pregnant young Mexican girl," Norman added pointedly.

"Now, that's a part of the story I've never heard," Sam said.

"Oh, I don't doubt it." Norman dabbed at his lips with a napkin of snow white linen. "But it's true. Of course, he may not have known the girl was pregnant when he married Trinity. But all the same, he left behind a lover. For a time, anyway."

"For a time?" Rachel repeated his words. "Would this be the woman Sam built the house for at the end of that lane?"

"Yes. Anjelica. According to all reports, she was quite the beauty. But we're getting ahead of ourselves. Let's take things as they happened." Norman leaned back in the sturdy wicker chair, obviously relishing his role as storyteller. "Sam and Trinity set up housekeeping, as it were, here at the plantation, and for a time, I suppose things were tolerable as far as Sam was concerned. They had three sons, each a year apart, and Sam enjoyed being the lord of so fine a manor. He had his nights out with his friends—fellow plantation owners like himself who met several times a week to drink and play cards and visit the bawdy house outside of Wilmington. Not so bad a life, for a while."

"How did you find out all this information?" Rachel asked.

"Again, Trinity's diaries. She noted that her husband seemed to become bored with her, and mentioned that he was taking more and more frequent trips back to Texas."

"Back to Anjelica?"

"Yes. It was after one of these trips that he began to build the house for her and their son. Although the child was born after he had left with Trinity for Eden's End, the Captain never disputed that the boy was his."

"I can't believe that he would bring them here."

"Keep in mind that it was not uncommon for a man to have a mistress back then, Rachel. Nor was it unusual for a man to have children by more than one woman."

"I'll bet it made Trinity crazy, just the same. For him to have brought this woman to Trinity's family home, to build a house for her on Trinity's land . . ." Rachel shivered. "It's not an arrangement I'd sit for, believe me."

"It apparently took a while for Trinity to catch on, though perhaps not as long as the Captain had hoped. Trinity's diary suggests that even after she found out, she did not acknowledge Anjelica's existence."

"But you said she burned her house down."

"That was much later, after Sam had died at sea. Once Sam was gone, of course, the property passed on to Sam and Trinity's oldest son, who was the second Samuel McGowan. Trinity lived on with her son and his family until her death in 1885 at a very ripe old age."

"How long had Anjelica been living on Eden's End before Trinity ended it?"

"Oh, it must have been years. The boy was already grown and gone when the war broke out and the Captain went to sea."

"I wonder what happened to him?" Rachel frowned. "Did he take McGowan's name?"

"No. I don't believe he did," Norman told them, his cup to his lips.

"Without knowing his last name, you'd never be able to trace him. It would be interesting, don't you think, Sam, to find a missing branch of your family?"

"It would be." Sam nodded, wondering how much the rest of the McGowan clan knew of this stray branch and how they might react to the news. "And, Norman, you are absolutely certain that this story is true?"

"Absolutely. I have read this in Trinity's own

words. Which I will be happy to share with you later." Norman poured himself another cup of tea, after offering first to his guests. "Actually, I called you here for another reason."

In the midst of the unfolding drama, both Rachel and Sam had nearly forgotten that they'd been summoned by Norman.

"Which is?"

"There's something in the barn I'd like you to see. If you've finished your tea, we can go take a look."

Rachel and Sam rose, Sam especially intrigued by what else the day might offer.

"Lead the way, gentlemen." Rachel fell in step with Sam and Norman.

Well to the back of the property stood the old barn, proudly sporting a new coat of paint and new windows. Shiny new brass locks protected the building from intruders on all three doors, though who there might be out here to steal, Rachel couldn't imagine, the house and outbuildings being far from the nearest road. Norman released the lock on the wide wooden door with a key, and pushed it open. Turning on overhead lights from a switch just inside, Norman illuminated the wide expanse of work space. Once the home of Sam McGowan's prized horseflesh, the barn had been totally renovated, with a new roof and walls, and a new wooden floor, upon which stretched metal vats of various sizes.

"Oh! You've already started work with the ultrasonic baths!" Rachel beamed and went immediately to the nearest vat. "I see you've already started working on the cannon."

"Yes. It's amazingly easy to remove the concretions

in this manner. I came out to watch Harley, one of our graduate student helpers, and was truly surprised at just how easy it is. Though I admit that this first one probably cleaned up more quickly for having undergone Sam's mallet the other day."

Norman stepped closer and motioned to Sam and Rachel.

"This is what I wanted you to see. It appears that Sam was absolutely correct in thinking that perhaps the *Melrose* had been obtained in, shall we say, a questionable manner?"

Sam and Rachel leaned forward to peer into the vat. On the shaft of the cannon, where the name of the ship would be engraved, were the letters WINDE-MERE. While the name of the city where she'd been built was obscured by concretions, the clearly visible letters . . . NGLA . . . supported Sam's theory that she was English in origin.

"Well, then." Sam touched the letters reverently and smiled.

"One has to wonder how Sam McGowan, former U.S. Cavalry, came to be commissioned in the Confederate Navy and then came into possession of such a ship," Rachel said.

"If he was commissioned. We know that many of the blockade runners were mercenaries who bought their own ships and then volunteered to serve the Confederacy," Sam said.

"With no experience as a sailor?" Rachel raised a skeptical eyebrow. "He must have paid a lot for a ship like the *Melrose*, Sam."

"Who said he was inexperienced?" Sam looked up from his methodical inspection of the cannon. "He'd spent years on a paddleboat on the Mississippi, we know that much. While it's not known exactly what his job might have been, chances are that an opportunist like Old Sam took good advantage of his time. My guess is that he knew his way around a ship pretty well. Nothing that I know of the man would lead me to believe that he was a fool. If he put out the money to buy himself a ship like this, you can damn well assume he knew exactly what to do with it."

"But there's a big difference between a riverboat and a cruiser like the *Melrose*."

"Depending on the age of the ships, they could have been powered pretty much the same way, Rachel. And keep in mind that there are years of his life that are unaccounted for. We really don't know what experience Sam may have had. We do know that he'd tried his hand at a number of things between the time he left home and the time he arrived at Eden's End." Sam ran one hand along the side of the cannon.

"This does, of course, raise all sorts of new questions, though. How did he arrange for her purchase?" Sam murmured. "Where did he take possession? How did he assemble his crew?"

"Frankly, I'm still trying to figure out how he talked Jefferson Davis into letting him captain a ship."

"By 1862, the South was so beleaguered by the Union blockade, they would have accepted Blackbeard himself, if he'd been able to get guns and supplies through. And frankly, I don't know that every man who ran guns was in the navy, Rachel. Stories that were passed down through the family, of course, lead us to believe that Sam was a fearless hero, one of the last and best to run the Union blockade of Wilmington. That he had a small but loyal crew and that he made a succession of trips back and forth to the port of Nassau in the Bahamas for supplies." Sam looked up and grinned. "But I suspect he may not have been above a little raiding now and again."

"Raiding?" Rachel asked.

"Capturing Union ships to seize their cargo, which would then be delivered to Southern ports, or sold in European ports. The money would then be turned over to the Confederacy. Usually the Union ship would be burned, her crew set adrift. Sometimes the ship would be impressed into the Confederate cause and given to particularly worthy members of the raiding ship. As more and more Southern ports were successfully blockaded, delivering the goods became more and more difficult, but the raiding didn't stop."

"Sort of pirating, Civil War style."

"Exactly." Sam looked at Rachel from across the vat, and added, "Looks like you just might have traded one pirate ship for another, Rachel."

Rachel laughed. "But there's not much chance of finding pirate treasure on this one."

"You never really know," Sam murmured. "Until you bring it all up, you just never really know what's down there."

"Well, if you've seen enough, Sam, perhaps you'd like to go back to the house and take a look at Trinity's diary," Norman suggested.

"Yes, I'd like that."

"Come along then." Norman waited for them at

the door, and turned the lights off once they'd stepped outside.

"How is it that you never read the diaries before?" Rachel asked as they walked to the house.

"I never knew they existed." Sam turned to Norman and asked, "Where exactly did you find them?"

"On the top shelf in the library," Norman replied. "They weren't well hidden. I suspect that anyone who'd wanted to could have read them."

"When the house was sold, weren't the contents removed by your family?" Rachel asked Sam.

"That was part of the sale agreement, I believe. Is that right, Norman? That the contents, other than Judith's personal belongings, would remain in the house?"

"Yes. I wanted to make certain that items of particular historic importance were not lost to the ages. Though Judith did, I believe, give the family the opportunity to take whatever might have been of particular sentimental value. I don't recall Judith mentioning that anyone took her up on the offer."

"As I remember, she gave us a week. I didn't receive her letter until some time after. I had been in Mexico working on one of the newly recovered Mayan wells, Daria was out of the country, and Iona was in school. I don't know what any of the cousins chose to do."

"Was there anything in particular that you might have wanted, Sam?" Norman asked as they approached the back of the house. Before Sam could respond, Norman added, "Come around to the front, why don't you? Let's make a grand entrance and see the house as it should be seen."

From the front, the house simply glowed in the setting sun, points of light shining off the windows and the old bricks giving off a rich, ruddy warmth. The scent of wisteria greeted them as they crossed the wide porch to reach the well-polished door.

"Ebony." Norman pointed to the door. "Imported from Africa and hand carved right here on Eden's End."

"It's beautiful." Rachel touched the raised relief with appreciative fingers.

"This is original," Sam noted, "but for years, it was in the barn."

"That's right. Somewhere along the line, someone wanted more modern doors. In particular, they wanted *screen doors*." Norman pronounced this as if announcing some unthinkable crime. "So this beautiful work of art was banished to the barn, and was replaced with something, I would guess, from the local hardware store."

"At least the original was preserved," Rachel pointed out. "I suppose they could have used it for firewood."

Norman looked momentarily horrified.

"Oh, look, how beautiful!" Rachel exclaimed as they entered the wide front hall. "It's just perfect!"

A wide sweep of stairs descended in a rounded curve from the second floor, where a balcony overlooked the foyer. The walls were papered in a rich red damask, the carpets over gleaming hardwood were oriental, and the furnishings were antebellum.

"Oh, my." Rachel pretended to fan herself. "I feel grossly underdressed. Why, I should be wearing a ball gown with a wide hoop skirt and a lace shawl around my shoulders."

"That could be arranged." Norman chuckled.

"It's just as I remember it, only better." Sam nodded and appeared pleased. "Of course, the wallpaper is different—I think my grandparents had a green-and-white-stripe in here—and the carpets are new, but I do recognize some of the furniture."

"When we started scraping the walls, we found many layers of paper, which I had carefully removed. The bottom layer was a handsome red. I was able to find a company that had re-created many of the patterns of the day. I was lucky to have found this one. It seems to perfectly match the scraps we were able to save of the original." Norman beamed with pride. "And much of the furniture you'll see was found in the attic. Other pieces were purchased at local antique shops and some had merely stayed in place through the years. I was able to get a feel for how the rooms looked by reading the diaries and journals and household records and viewing old photographs. I believe that were the Captain to return today, he'd feel right at home."

Stepping to one side, Norman flicked a switch and the chandelier overhead came to life, a thousand sparkling crystals in a waterfall of glass.

"This was in pieces in several boxes in the attic," Norman explained. "Fortunately, it seems the McGowans never discarded a thing. Over the years, as fashions and fortunes changed, things were replaced, but never discarded. The attic was crammed with the most unbelievable assortment of furniture and decorative items. Now, come into the parlor here . . ."

Norman led the way into a spacious room to the left of the hallway. Ornate furniture of dark wood covered in rose satin fabric sat in groupings here and there about the room to form several conversation areas. Long windows on two sides brought the twilight in.

"We used to roller-skate in here on rainy days," Sam told them. "My grandmother used to set the Christmas tree up right there."

He pointed to a space between the front windows.

"My cousin Larry broke his arm diving off that mantel when he was four." Sam walked to the windows that ran along the side wall. "My sister Daria fell through this window when she was twelve. The glass cut her face"—Sam traced along his hairline on the right side of his face from right below his ear to his temple—"and there was blood everywhere. My grandmother actually boiled a needle and a spool of thread and made tiny stitches along the side of her face to keep it together while they drove her to the nearest hospital, which was almost thirty miles away."

"Is she badly scarred?" Rachel asked.

Sam shook his head and smiled weakly, "Not nearly as badly as she could have been, if my grandmother hadn't acted so quickly. And certainly nowhere nearly as badly as Daria believes. We tell her it makes her look rakish and dangerous, but I don't think it makes her feel any better."

"Rakish and dangerous are not how most women want their faces described, Sam."

"It's really not bad. To hear Daria tell it, she's disfigured, but you have to look really close to see the scar. Most people would never know it's there."

"Sometimes it's what we see when we look into the mirror that matters most," Rachel told him. "If Daria sees the scar, in her own mind, she is scarred."

"Well, she's a very pretty woman, with or without the scar that may or may not be visible."

"Yes. Well, that explains why some of those panes of glass were replaced," Norman said. "I'd been wondering about that. Now, the dining room is this way."

The dining room was an enormous hall, the furniture gleaming rosewood, the ceiling painted with angels that flocked around the large plaster medallion that surrounded the chandelier. Painted china in several patterns was displayed from a large cabinet, and a seven-piece silver tea service held court in the center of the sideboard.

"This is all original," Sam told them. "My grandparents used this room only on Christmas, New Year's Eve and Day, my grandfather's birthday, and Easter. There's another room closer to the kitchen that they used for dining every other day of the year."

He walked to the china cupboard, and hands on his hips, inspected the contents through the glass.

"I remember some of these things. The pink and green dishes, for example. I have no idea how old they are, though."

"One hundred twelve years," Norman told him. "I had the pattern traced to the manufacturer in England."

"Amazing," Rachel exclaimed. "How could all of

this have survived the war? I thought the Union soldiers were notorious for destroying everything they could get their hands on."

"Eden's End was used as a hospital by the Union soldiers from the time of the first battle that took place right on the banks of the river until the very end of the war. The Yankee captain who commandeered the house graciously permitted Trinity to pack up her valuables and store them in the attic, and gave his promise that nothing would be touched," Sam told her. "He kept his promise."

"Even though her husband captained a blockade runner?"

"I doubt she volunteered that information."

"Actually, she passed herself off as the widow of a man who was lost at sea," Norman told them. "Ironically, that's exactly what came to pass."

"Is that in Trinity's diaries?" Rachel asked.

"Yes."

"Well, then, bring on the diaries, Norman. Maybe it's time a McGowan read of all this intrigue firsthand."

"I'll get them for you," Norman offered. "Perhaps you'd like to sit in the Captain's study to read? And I could then show Rachel to her room. Perhaps you'd like to freshen up?"

"Yes, I'd appreciate that. I still feel as if I have salt clinging to my skin and my hair."

"I'll just get Sam settled, then I'll be back to take your things upstairs for you," Norman told her, then turned to Sam. "The study is this way."

"Yes. I remember." Sam followed him out the door, pausing to whisper to Rachel as he passed,

"And it's citrus and salt air. A combination I find incredibly sexy."

"Then I'll try not to wash it all away." Rachel grinned.

"Happy reading," she called after him, her words echoing down the long hall.

11

❦

THE CORNER room that Norman had selected for Rachel was high ceilinged and papered in pink and white cabbage roses on a pale green background. A series of tall windows with deep sills overlooked the side yard, and a door in the middle of the south wall opened onto a balcony upon which a tangle of wisteria and ancient roses twisted together. The room was dominated by a handsome carved canopy bed dressed from headboard to footboard and back again in miles of pale pink silk.

"My, my." Rachel had suppressed giggle after Norman had proudly opened the door. "It's certainly . . . *antebellum*, isn't it?"

"This was Trinity's room," Norman said solemnly. "It's been authentically restored. Right down to the paintings on the walls and the perfume bottles on the dressing table."

"Trinity was quite fond of pink, wasn't she?"

"Apparently. Now, if there's nothing I can get you, I'd like to join Sam in the study."

"I'm fine, really, Norman. More than fine. Thank you,"

"Dinner will be at seven-thirty," he told her as he closed the door behind him.

"I feel like Barbie," she muttered once Norman had left. "I wonder if Sam would notice if I started calling him Ken?"

Rachel lifted a perfume bottle from the pink-swathed dressing table and sniffed. The fragrance was dense and flowery and overwhelmingly feminine.

"Why do I have this sudden urge to buy a pink sports car?" she muttered to herself. "And suck my waist in to an impossible sixteen inches?"

Rachel roamed around the room, picking up items to absently inspect, a porcelain hat pin box, a silver hairbrush that had clearly seen use over the years. Sighing, she pushed open the door to the balcony and stepped out to inhale the softest of spring breezes. The balcony was edged with a chest-high railing painted white, and she leaned her forearms upon it and gazed out upon the splendor that was Eden's End.

Even so many generations later, she could easily imagine what it must have looked like teeming with life, before history had intruded. Looking toward the setting sun, she could see the barn where Sam McGowan had once kept his livestock. There would have been other outbuildings, she thought, other barns for animals and crops. Slave quarters, for surely a plantation of this size would have had slaves. A carriage house, perhaps.

And a house for Sam's mistress, she mused, as

she looked beyond the trees to where Norman had indicated Anjelica's house had once stood, and was surprised to see that a house stood there, even now.

Rachel blinked. It couldn't possibly be the same house. Hadn't Norman said that Trinity had burned it down? She'd have to remember to ask Norman about that at dinner.

Tired, Rachel kicked off her running shoes and eased back onto the satin bed. Having been living at sea or in small hotels for the better part of the past two years, Rachel was unaccustomed to such luxury. She stood up, reluctant to muss the cool satin. Turning the bed down, she found a lightweight blanket and cotton sheets.

"That's more like it." She nodded, and laid back down, her head on one of the several pillows that lined up across the headboard.

She closed her eyes, and willed herself to catnap, Sam's face clearly in her mind as she drifted off to sleep.

Sam stood at the foot of the grand staircase and watched Rachel descend the curve of steps to the reception area below.

"I should be wearing a rose-colored satin dress with a wide hoop skirt and pantaloons. There should be violins playing and I should have gardenias in my hair, don't you think?"

Rachel hoisted her hair up in the back and stood two steps from the bottom, and struck a pose.

"Yes. That would be quite a sight." Sam grinned.

"Were you able to rest, Rachel?" Norman stepped out from the dining room doorway.

"Yes. I did," she told him. "It's been a long time since I slept in a bed like that. If ever. It's quite something."

She took Sam's outstretched arm when she reached the bottom of the steps, telling him, "It was Trinity's bed. Your great-great-grandmother obviously liked her creature comforts, Sam."

"Oh, there's no question of that. Her diaries are proof of that. Furnishings, clothing, jewelry, food—Trinity definitely had an acquisitive nature. And she only wanted the best."

They followed Norman into the dining room, where they were seated by their host at an intimate table set up in front of the fireplace.

"I hope you don't mind," Norman said, "but I thought the larger table was too formal for us this evening."

"Considering that Sam and I are dressed so casually, this is fine. If I'd known we'd be dining in so fine a room, I would have packed something a little nicer. As it was, these white slacks were the best I could do. I don't carry many clothes with me when I'm working on board."

"No need to explain." Norman held up a hand. "After all, this is a working dinner."

Norman was, as always, impeccably dressed in white linen.

Sam had changed into a blue-and-white-striped shirt, but he still wore the olive green Dockers he'd had on earlier. Rachel suspected he hadn't packed a second pair of slacks. Maybe a pair of jeans, maybe shorts, but not another pair of slacks. She'd bet on it.

Over an excellent dinner of country cured ham,

red gravy, rice, and tender fresh greens, Southern style, Sam's excitement over reading Trinity's diaries became evident.

"And look here, Rachel," he said as he passed a leather-bound journal to her. "Here she talks about how she felt upon meeting Sam McGowan for the first time."

Rachel took the book and carefully laid it upon the table, leaning slightly to her left to read aloud. " 'He has the most serious expression when he looks upon me, but his eyes, I do believe, give away his inherent humor. Eyes of a startling blue, a true blue. Suffice it to say that he is fair of face and lean of body, so unlike the others who have offered for my hand, soft of mind and body from having been waited on from the cradle. Sam McGowan is a man, I think, of action, of passion. In my life, I have known neither. He makes me think of dark things, things that are as yet unknown to me, but of which, I would wish to learn. He is a man who could take a woman, I do believe, to the dark places that lurk within, those places we suspect might exist but have never been. There are promises in his smile that no self-respecting woman would acknowledge, and yet I dream of him making such promises to me.'

"Wow! Trinity certainly wasn't shy about expressing herself, was she? Goodness," Rachel exclaimed with a self-conscious laugh, feeling the blush begin to travel from her throat to her cheeks.

Trinity's words had an almost familiar ring to them, Rachel mused. Hadn't she herself felt the same way when she'd first met Sam?

Only Trinity had been honest enough with herself to admit it.

"Rachel?" Sam touched her arm.

"What? Oh, yes." Rachel glanced back down to the diary, then looked to Norman and said, "I almost feel guilty about reading this, it's so private, and so obviously never meant for anyone else's eyes."

"I did feel a bit the voyeur," Sam acknowledged. "Particularly when she described her wedding night, but we won't make you read that out loud."

"How considerate of you." Rachel's blush deepened.

"But there is quite an interesting section here, in this one. Here, let's trade books." Sam reached out a hand and gave Rachel a second book, while taking back the first. "Now, there are others in between these two books, mostly describing the births of their children, family holidays, and the like, and while they are interesting reading, this one is truly fascinating."

Rachel glanced at the page and began to read. "'That he would even think to bring her here. Here! To Eden's End! It is an abomination to me, an insult to my family! And yet it does not appear that he will return his whore and her spawn to the rough Texas land they came from.'" Rachel looked up from the page. "Strong words. You can feel her anger, her pain, even all these years later. She must have been hurt to her core."

"And Old Sam apparently either didn't notice or didn't care." Sam nodded.

"What a guy." Rachel skimmed several pages. "It looks as if Sam flaunted his lady friend at home, and yet Trinity had to keep up appearances by pretending to the outside world not to notice. That must have eaten her up inside.

"And the situation went on for years. Here, in this one, she says, 'Sam is despondent, his whore-spawn has left Eden's End. He seems to have forgotten that he has three other sons—legally begot—but he grieves for this one. He spends his nights elsewhere—I am not so much a fool that I don't know where he goes. It is abundantly clear that he has got from me all he has wanted, and has, at least in private, made his preference clear. In public, he still accompanies me when it is dictated that he do so, but I sleep alone every night while he has made his bed elsewhere.' How sad for Trinity.

"Oh, and here, listen. 'They say there will be a war soon, that the South will have to fight to keep its precious way of life. I asked Sam if he will volunteer to fight and he merely laughed and said that if, indeed, war was to come, he would find a way to profit from it. And I do believe he would. He is a man who knows best how to exploit. Who would know this better than I?' "

Rachel shook her head as she leafed through the diary, stopping at a page near the end. "This is interesting. Listen. 'He is back, having bought his ship and paid for it with money made from Eden's End rice and cotton. He boasted yesterday after church that he will be serving the cause by running the Yankee blockades of our ports. That he has assembled a crew that will fight with him to deliver the weapons so desperately needed. He sounds so noble, even I would not suspect his motives. But I have seen this crew—they have come, one by one or in twos and threes, to Eden's End and I have had to provide shel-

ter for them. They are, it is clear, old comrades from
another time in his life, and it is a mystery to me
how he found them, but they keep on coming. By
Saturday, they will all be gone, and Sam with them.
I hope his precious ship sinks with all hands on it.' "

"This 'crew' of Sam's, as Trinity describes it,
sounds like quite a bunch, don't you think?" Sam
asked. "Notice that she doesn't refer to any of them
as sailors."

"But one would suspect that they must have some
experience, otherwise they'd be of no use to him at
sea. Trinity refers to them as being from another time
in his life. Norman, didn't you say that Sam spent
some of his early days on riverboats?"

"Yes. He probably brought on men he'd worked
with in the past. But certainly, they'd have had to
know their way around a boat."

Sam gently turned the pages of the book that lay
before him. "Now this one is later. Here, she says,
'He is back again, though I expect his visit will be a
brief one. He has come at night and has had to sneak
in through the secret passage and through the library
wall, the Union soldiers being camped outside on the
front porch. Sam has been in the library with the
door locked since two this morning, and I can only
suspect what he might be doing there. There will be
time enough to search when he leaves to go to her,
for surely he will not be spending the night under
my roof. He must know that I would drive a knife
through his heart if ever he fell asleep in my company. Easy enough, it would be, to blame it on the
Yankees, who have used Eden's End as a hospital
still, though their visits are less frequent these days.

The commanding officer has been kind, though, and has kept his promise that no harm would come to my home, even keeping a small number of soldiers here to guard it. This last I know is only to ensure that should they need it in the future, the house will be standing, but it matters not the reason, the end result being that Eden's End is protected. The commander knows that my sons have joined General Lee, but understands that they are doing what they believe to be their duty to their family. I have told him that my husband is dead, and to me, this is more truth than the lie I have lived all these years. I pray every night that God will make me an honest widow.' "

"Why would Sam sneak into this house when he knows there are Union soldiers here?" Rachel put down the book she had been holding. "That makes no sense whatsoever. That would have been a terrible risk to take."

"That's an excellent question, Rachel." Sam turned to Norman and asked, "Has anything you've found given you any clue as to why he would have done such a thing?"

"No. None." Norman shook his head.

"What on earth would he have been doing in there that would have been important enough to have risked his life?" Sam murmured.

"I've asked myself that same question many times," Norman said, "and I'm afraid I'm as much at a loss as you are."

"Let's take a look at the library after dinner, just for fun," Rachel said. "And I'd love to see that secret door."

"Unfortunately, it's still a secret, I'm afraid. I've not been able to find it," Norman told them.

"Sam, do you remember anyone in your family talking about a secret door or a secret room?" Rachel asked.

"No. Never. Though my father might know."

"Perhaps. Then again, it could simply be lost to the ages." Norman shrugged, then as if having dismissed the subject, said, "Now, if you're finished, we'll have dessert in the sitting room. Rachel?" Norman rose and held the back of Rachel's chair.

Closing the diary, Sam looked across the table at Rachel, wondering if she, too, thought it odd that Norman, so meticulous in his renovations, had so blithely dismissed Trinity's revelations about a secret passage and Old Sam's furtive visits to the library in the dead of night. But Rachel had half turned in her seat, and he could not read her face. With a sigh, Sam gathered up the fragile old books, and carried them with him to the sitting room.

Sleep would not come easily to Rachel. It could have been the coffee—she hadn't asked if it was decaffeinated, and was beginning to suspect it was not. It could be the bed, which was too soft for her taste and was not accompanied by the rocking of the ocean. Or it could be just knowing that she slept in the room once inhabited by a woman who had spent years plotting the murder of her rival and praying for her husband's demise at sea.

Then, of course, there was the matter of knowing that Sam slept in the next room, right there beyond the connecting door.

Rachel had understood perfectly Trinity's description of that first Sam as a man of action and passion, a man with startling blue eyes and promises in his smile. Those same words could have been written to describe the current-day Sam McGowan, the one who made Rachel's pulse beat faster and brought a blush to her cheeks just by looking at her. Yes, Rachel understood perfectly well why a woman like Trinity— why any woman—would barter all she had for such a man.

Must be those "dark places" I suspect he could take me to, she told herself ruefully as she turned over yet again and punched her pillow.

After another forty minutes of tossing, Rachel sat up and pushed back the blanket. Swinging sideways to dangle her legs over the side of the bed, she considered her favorite means of fighting insomnia, and realized she had few available. She had nothing with her to read, and had seen no books in the room. Of course, the library downstairs was filled with old volumes. She had visions of herself creeping down that long stairway in the dark and shivered. With her luck she'd meet Trinity on the way down.

"It wouldn't surprise me in the least to find out she was still here," Rachel grumbled. "She held on through her husband's years of infidelities and a war. Nothing I know of this woman would lead me to believe she'd go quietly."

Light from the full moon spread through the thin curtains on the French doors leading to the balcony and spilled across the carpet, beckoning Rachel outside.

Some fresh air might help, Rachel thought.

The doors were unlocked, and she pushed them open quietly and stepped into the cool evening air, far too cool, she realized immediately, for the short-sleeved cotton nightshirt she wore. There had been a woolen throw over the back of a chair, and she went back into the room to get it. Returning to the balcony, she drew deeply of the night scents, jasmine and wisteria, that flooded the balcony. She leaned over the railing slightly to touch the closed bud of a climbing rose. In another few weeks, they, too, would be blooming. The fragrance would be intoxicating. She found herself almost regretting that she wouldn't be there for it.

"Don't lean over so far." Sam's voice came from the shadows. "It's a long way down."

"Oh. Sam. You startled me." She drew the throw around her a little closer. "I guess you can't sleep, either."

"It's been months since I've slept on land. It takes some getting used to."

"I was thinking the same thing. That, and the fact that I'm feeling uneasy about sleeping in Trinity's bed."

"She's not in it with you, is she?"

"No." Rachel laughed softly. "At least, if she is, she's kept to herself."

"Knowing what we now know of Trinity, I suspect you'd know by now if there was anything to worry about."

"How do you feel about her, about all the things we read about her tonight, Sam?"

"She's still just a figure from the past, Rachel, though, granted, we know so much more about her now. She spoke of Sam using her to get her land and her money, but she herself had dangled those very things in front of him to get him to marry her in the first place. She offered them to him, freely."

"She didn't expect him to use those things to build a house for his mistress, or to outfit a ship."

"I can't think of a way to condone the mistress, but at least the ship was intended to serve the South, to help protect the home and the lifestyle she was obviously so fond of."

"It didn't sound as if Trinity needed much help in that regard." Rachel turned to face him and leaned back against the railing. "It seems to me she found a pretty effective way to protect her home on her own."

"Oh, you mean by letting the Yankees use it as a hospital? Yes, that took courage."

"And as far as the ship being intended to serve the South, I think Old Sam was in it for the adventure, don't you? Old Sam was a man who served his own interests first."

"Oh, definitely." Sam stepped out of the shadows and toward her. "And a little adventure now and then is good for the soul. But I'm having a little trouble piecing some of this together. There are some things that just aren't sitting right."

"Such as?"

"I can't figure out why Sam would have taken a chance on coming back to Eden's End when he knew there would be Union soldiers here. And Trinity had said that he'd come *again*. Meaning he'd done it before. Why would he do that? He obviously wasn't there to see Trinity. His sons weren't at home. Why would he do that?"

"I have no clue." Rachel shrugged. "Could he have been coming back to get something?"

"Maybe. Or maybe he was bringing something back here."

"Like what?"

"If we could find that secret door, maybe we could find out."

"Want to go look?"

"I already did. I couldn't find a thing."

"Maybe when the renovations were done, the workmen inadvertently closed it over."

"That's what I'm thinking is the likely explanation. But I'll tell you what really bothers me is that it doesn't seem to bother Norman. He had a real, *oh, well*, sort of attitude tonight that I thought was uncharacteristic for him, to say the least. I mean, Norman is almost obsessed with Sam McGowan—excuse me, Captain McGowan—and yet he exhibits no interest at all in the fact that the man was coming and going in the middle of the night through a secret doorway, while the woods were filled with Yankees and there was no apparent reason for him to have been coming home. It certainly wasn't to see his loving wife."

Sam had drifted across the balcony slowly as he spoke, and was now but arm's length away from Rachel, who had a sudden urge to reach out and pull him toward her. She was considering doing exactly that, when he took that last step and closed the distance between them.

"Ah, Rachel," he whispered. "You're doing it again."

"Doing what?"

"Wearing the moonlight." He reached for her and folded her into his arms.

Sam dipped his mouth to hers, brushing his lips slowly across hers once, twice, three times, Rachel's arms moving upward to draw him inside the woolen throw. He nipped at her lower lip lightly, then slowly traced the outline of her lips with his tongue until her mouth urged him in. His hands slid down the back of her soft cotton nightshirt, pulling her body closer, closer. His pulse pounding in his ears, Sam fed upon her mouth until he could barely breathe. Tracing a line from her chin to her throat with his mouth brought a soft gasp from Rachel's lips, and his hands tightened slightly, eager now for the feel of her skin. He slid the fabric up over her hips and caressed her, thighs to hips, as he probed her mouth with his seeking tongue.

For a long moment, Rachel was sure she was suffocating, then realized she was holding her breath. Sam's mouth was nibbling now along her throat, to her collarbone, and the sensations he was arousing in her were crowding out the normal reflexes such as breath. Her breath caught in her throat as his tongue traced the small well at the base of her throat, and lingered, as if tasting her skin. She leaned against the rail, pinned by the weight of his body, her head back, and invited him to feed on her mouth, on her throat, on whatever part of her body he could reach.

His hands slid upward under the shirt until they reached her breasts, and caressed the soft flesh. A soft moan escaped her lips, and she arched her back to offer more of herself, as much of herself as he would take. She raised his head from her neck and sought his mouth, wanting to taste him again, wanting to feel his tongue torture the inside of her mouth. Wanting . . . wanting . . .

"Ah, Rachel, I could lose myself in you," Sam whispered into her hair, then froze.

"Sam?" Rachel opened her eyes.

"Shhhhh." He tilted his head to one side, as if listening to something. "I think there's someone on the lawn."

"Norman?" she asked, suddenly chilled at the thought of Norman Winter watching her and Sam in what had turned out to be a very private midnight encounter.

"Go on in." Sam smoothed the throw around her shoulders and her nightshirt over her hips.

"What are you going to do?"

"I'm going to climb down the trellis and see who it is."

"It's Norman, who else could it be? There's no one else here, Sam."

"Well, then, Norman and I will have to have a little talk, then, won't we?" Sam started to hoist himself over the railing. "Host or not, he has no business spying on the guests like that."

"Are you crazy? At least take the steps." Rachel grabbed him by the arm.

"And give him a chance to come back in and sneak back to his room? Uh-uh. I'm meeting him halfway."

"Sam McGowan, you're a lunatic."

"Hold that thought, Rachel. I'll be right back."

Rachel tried to watch from the landing, but lost Sam amidst the trees that grew along one side of the fence. Thinking perhaps that she'd have a better view from the far side of the balcony, she followed the railing to the very end. Looking down, she could see a vague form below. It moved slowly across the lawn, then turned and looked up at Rachel.

It was a woman, in a long pink satin dress with a wide hoop skirt.

Rachel gasped aloud and leaned forward over the rail. Below, on the grass, the figure haughtily flipped one long end of her shawl over her shoulder, then promptly vanished into thin air.

12

"RACHEL, FOR heaven's sake, what are you doing?" Norman stood in the darkened doorway, wrapping the ties from his striped robe around his waist.

A stunned Rachel turned toward the sound of his voice, but before she could utter a word, Sam appeared at the opposite end of the balcony.

"Okay, Norman, we have to have a little talk," he was saying as he walked toward them.

It was then that Rachel realized that Norman wasn't wearing his glasses. Finally, a chance to see his eyes. She took one step forward, just as he took one step back.

"Sam. What's wrong?" Norman reached into his pocket and pulled out the dark glasses. He stepped out of the shadows as his eyes disappeared behind the frames.

Damn! Rachel thought, momentarily distracted.

"What's wrong? Spying on your guests is wrong, Norman," Sam said with characteristic calm.

"Sam, it wasn't . . ." Rachel began.

". . . and I don't know how you got back up here before I did, unless you found that secret door after all."

"Sam!" Rachel grabbed him by the arm. "It wasn't Norman."

"Excuse me." Norman folded his arms across his chest. "Who wasn't me?"

"Rachel, there's no one else here," Sam reminded her.

"I think there just might be," Rachel said softly.

"What is this all about?" Norman demanded.

"Rachel and I were . . . talking . . . outside of her room a few minutes ago. I looked over her shoulder and saw someone down on the lawn, near the trees, watching us. I assumed it was you," Sam told him.

"I assure you it was not. And there is no one else here, except for Mrs. Thurston, who sleeps like the dead."

"Close enough," Rachel told them. "It was Trinity."

Both men turned to stare at her.

"At least, that's who I think it was. She sort of . . . evaporated . . . before I could get a look at her face. Not that I know what her face looks like. But she was wearing a long pink ball gown, and we know that Trinity liked pink . . ." Rachel's voice trailed off, as she began to realize how silly she sounded.

"Rachel, are you saying you thought you saw a ghost?" Norman asked.

"Or did you see someone dressed like a woman of Trinity's time?" Sam offered what he thought would be a reasonable explanation.

"No, it was a ghost, Sam. People don't evaporate."

"I don't believe in ghosts, Rachel."

"Neither do I, Sam." Rachel sighed. "But I'm telling you what I saw."

"It had to have been some type of illusion."

Rachel rolled her eyes. "And who, might I ask, would have been able to have pulled off such an illusion? And why would anyone go to such trouble?"

"I don't know, but it makes more sense than you telling me you saw my great-great-grandmother—who's been dead for more than a hundred years—watching us from the lawn." Sam turned to Norman and asked, "You've been living here for several years, Norman. Have you seen any ghosts?"

"No, no, I haven't. Interesting that she came tonight, though, don't you think? After we'd been reading her diaries? Perhaps she'd rather we didn't." Norman appeared deep in thought.

Sam rubbed the back of his neck and sighed.

"Norman, surely you're not taking this seriously."

"Stranger things have happened, Sam," Norman told him solemnly.

"Okay. I can see I'm in the minority here. Let's finish this conversation in the morning." Sam took Rachel's arm gently. "After coffee."

"Sam, I'm telling you, I saw . . ."

"Good night again, Norman," Sam called over his shoulder.

"Rachel, would you rather I moved you to another room?" Norman asked.

Rachel stopped, considering the offer, then shook her head. "No, I didn't feel her there, Norman. I'm not afraid to sleep there."

"Let me know if you change your mind at any time." Norman paused in his doorway for a long moment, watching the couple move through the shadows. When they'd disappeared into Rachel's room—Sam no doubt would check to make certain that all was well there, as any gentleman would do—Norman stepped to the edge of the balcony and looked anxiously over the railing into the still, quiet night beyond, and wondered why she had waited until now to come back, and what she might want, now that she was here.

"Let me just look around in here." Sam preceded Rachel into her room and began to look behind the furniture and under the bed.

Opening the doors to the tall wooden wardrobe, he moved clothing this way and that, but all he got for his trouble was some dust up his nose.

"I think those old dresses could use a good dry cleaning," he said as he sneezed loudly.

"Bless you." Rachel sat upon the side of the bed. "But I imagine that cleaning them would cause them to fall apart. Sam, I don't think you're going to find Trinity—or anyone else—under the bed."

"No harm in looking."

Satisfied that there was, in fact, no one hiding in Rachel's room, Sam checked the door and found it securely locked.

"Well, I guess if you lock these doors,"—he turned on the small brass lamp that stood on the bedside table, and in its light, inspected the French doors—"I think you'll be okay."

"Sam, there's no one out there. No one except Trinity." Rachel sighed and wrapped the throw around her shoulders tightly. "And if she decided to come calling, I doubt a locked door would stop her."

"You really believe that you saw her." Sam appeared perplexed. "Rachel, I'm really surprised at you."

"And I'm really surprised at you, Sam." She drew her legs up under her. "Didn't you tell me that your mother is an anthropologist? And that as children, you accompanied your parents to sites in different parts of the world?"

"Yes."

"Then you've been exposed to other cultures all your life. I'd expect you to be more open-minded. Why can't you accept that I saw something that was, well, out of the ordinary?"

"Out of the ordinary?" Sam grinned. "You do have a way with words, Rachel." He sat on the edge of the wing chair nearest the fireplace. "Okay, we'll assume that it was Trinity. Norman said he has never seen her. Don't you think it's odd that she showed up just for you?"

"Oh, I don't think it was for me, Sam," Rachel told him. "I think it was because you're here."

"Why?"

"Maybe because you're a descendant of hers. Norman is not. It seems to me that Trinity would want, above all else, to preserve Eden's End for her children and for their children. Maybe it bothers her that her family home is no longer in the family."

"You're really taking this seriously, aren't you?"

"Yes. Yes, I am. I never saw a ghost before, Sam."

Rachel leaned back against the pillows. "Sam, did you ever dive at Bailey's Point?"

Surprised by the question, Sam responded with a hesitant, "Off the coast of Texas? Yes."

"Did you go down to the *Edgemere*?"

"Of course. That's why you dive Bailey's Point."

"Didn't you feel anything . . . unusual while you were down there?"

When Sam didn't immediately answer, Rachel knew she had him.

"That's different, Rachel. Nearly two hundred men went down on that ship."

"Tell me what you felt when you were down there, Sam."

"Rachel . . ."

"I'll tell you what I felt. I felt the eyes of one hundred and eighty-seven men watching me. I felt their panic when they realized that the ship was sinking so rapidly there was no time to react. I felt their fear and their despair and the anguish of the captain who could save neither his ship nor his crew."

Across the dimly lit room, Sam could feel her eyes on him.

"What did you feel, Sam?"

"Well, I guess I felt a lot of those same things."

"The first time I dove there, I got within ten feet of the ship and I had to turn back, the feeling of terror was so raw," she confessed. "I never told anyone that, but it's true. It scared me like nothing I've ever felt before."

They sat in silence, the ticking of the mantel clock the only sound, and it echoed slightly in the large room.

"Sam, did anyone else in your family ever see Trinity?"

"I don't know. I don't recall anyone ever talking about it. But I suppose my dad might know, if anyone mentioned it. I could ask. I'm due for a visit in a few weeks. My mom's birthday," he explained. "I can always just come right out and ask. 'So, Dad. When you were growing up at Eden's End, did your great-grandmother ever show up?'"

"You might be surprised by the answer." Rachel yawned, suddenly very tired.

"I just might be." Sam leaned back in the chair and watched her from across the room.

The soft light from the lamp played around Rachel's face like a halo. Sam knew that if he stayed in her room much longer, it wouldn't be in the chair.

He glanced at his watch. It was almost three A.M.

"I think you'll be okay, Rachel," he said quietly. "But I'll stay for a while if you like. I can sleep right here, if you're afraid to be alone."

When she did not respond, he rose quietly and walked to the bed, where she lay curled up against the massive wooden headboard, a pillow behind her head and her hands under her chin, clutching the ends of the plaid throw. She looked like a little girl who fell asleep on her parents' bed, waiting for them to come home from an evening out.

And maybe, in a way, she is, Sam thought as he gently pulled the blanket up to cover her. But that's a story for another night.

He leaned down to place a kiss on her temple, his lips lingering just a moment while he drank in her scent and recalled how his body had reacted to their closeness, how it had felt to hold her and touch her, how he had wanted her. Very quietly closing the French doors behind him, Sam returned to his room, knowing that, for him and Rachel, there would be other nights.

"Did you sleep well?" Norman asked Rachel as she entered the dining room the next morning. "All things considered, of course."

"All things considered, I did." She smiled. "Have I beaten Sam to breakfast?"

"According to Mrs. Thurston, Sam was in the kitchen seeking coffee at quite an early hour. Ruffled her feathers a little." Norman poured orange juice from a crystal pitcher into a goblet and offered it to her. "She doesn't like for anyone to step foot across that kitchen threshold. I should probably have warned Sam."

Rachel accepted the glass and studied the cut pattern before raising it to her lips. The goblet was substantial in weight and intricate of pattern. She couldn't remember ever having had her morning juice in so precious a vessel, and said so.

Norman merely smiled.

"I don't believe in locking away lovely things," he replied. "Their beauty should be appreciated, shared when possible. There's simply no point in having things if you can't look at them. Touch them."

He ran his fingers around the rim of his own glass, traced the rounded globe of crystal that formed part of the stem. It was a possessive gesture. If the glass had been a cat, Rachel thought, it would be purring.

"What would you like for breakfast?" he asked.

"Mrs. Thruston is awaiting your pleasure should you care for eggs."

"Oh, well . . ." Rachel glanced at the sideboard where a large bowl of fruit salad sat, surrounded by small plates of scones and biscuits. "I'll think I'll just have some of the fruit and a scone."

She could feel his eyes on her back as she helped herself to a small bowl of bananas, oranges, strawberries, and blueberries.

"So," she said uneasily as she sat back down at the table. "It looks as if it's going to be a beautiful day."

"Yes. It does. Though I suspect that, at sea, the bottom is still churning a bit from yesterday's storm."

"I think maybe by tomorrow we should be able to go back down."

"When do you think you'll reach the cabin?" he asked nonchalantly.

"Oh, it's hard to tell. The storm could have dumped a ton of sand back onto the wreck."

Norman seemed to blanch.

"Then again," she added, "it's totally possible that the damage to the site was minimal. If all goes well, we might be into the cabin by Sunday or Monday. Is there a rush? I thought we had until September."

"You do, of course. I was just wondering." The tips of Norman's fingers drummed silently on the ivory-colored linen cloth. "I'm anxious, naturally, having waited so long. And there is the question of how much work will be involved in cleaning and preserving the items that you find. Don't some items take months to clean?"

"Yes, but considering what we can expect to find,

I don't anticipate a problem. Keep in mind what will be on board, Norman." Rachel smiled. "Most of what's down there will most likely be made of iron, bronze, maybe some brass or copper, or lead. Covered as the ship was by sand and sediment, it's reasonable to believe that most deposits can be removed with relative ease. Like the cannon that you've already started working on."

"Good morning," Sam called from the doorway.

"Hi." Rachel turned to smile at him, and lit up his day.

"Breakfast, Sam?" Norman asked.

"I've eaten with the help," Sam said. "Though I will have another cup of Mrs. Thurston's excellent coffee."

"Were you out for a walk?" Rachel asked as Sam sat opposite her at the small table.

"Yes. And I stopped by the barn to talk to Peter, the young guy who is working on the cannons. Excellent idea to hire an archaeology student to work the vats, Norman. You're not only giving him experience, but you're ensuring that the artifacts are being carefully handled. You are to be commended for the renovations to Eden's End, Norman. Not just to the house and the barn, but to all of the outbuildings. It's remarkable, what you've done here. I admire your dedication to preserving the past. I'm sure the entire county will be thrilled once you open your museum."

"Thank you, Sam. That's very kind of you. I'm hoping that as many members of your family as can will attend the opening in September."

"I will strongly urge them to do so. I'm sure they'll

be as fascinated as I am with the thoroughness of
detail to the original that I've seen since I've been
here. Why, one would almost expect Old Sam to
come stomping in through those doors." He nodded
to the doors that stood open to the morning air at
the far end of the room.

Sam gazed around the room, as if admiring it, then
looked from one wall to the next, as if puzzled.

"Sam?" Norman asked. "Is something wrong?"

"Actually, Norman, I was looking for the old portrait of Trinity that used to hang over the fireplace
there in the corner. I thought that Rachel might want
to see her face-to-face, as it were, after last night's
little encounter. But I see that the portrait has been
replaced."

"I had it and several others sent out for renovation," Norman told him. "I expect it should be returned in time for the museum opening. In the
meantime, I replaced it with one I found in the attic."

"Is that another ancestor, Sam?" Rachel rose to inspect the painting of the dark-haired beauty that
hung over the fireplace.

"I have no idea." Sam shrugged. "But I'd suspect
it might be, if Norman found it in the attic." Sam
smiled at Rachel. "No telling what you might find
in the attic of a house like this one."

"Well, she was beautiful, whoever she was," Rachel commented.

"Yes. She was." Sam took a long sip of his coffee,
then sat the cup into the saucer and said to Rachel,
"Well, unless you have an objection, I think we
should be heading back soon."

"Heading back? To the site?" She frowned. "I was

just telling Norman before you came in that I didn't expect to be able to dive until at least tomorrow."

"I agree. But it will take us several hours to get back to the *Melrose,* and I would like to finish the sketches that I started the other night before we go back down."

Rachel stirred her coffee and tried not to look confused. Sam had completed his sketches the night before the storm. She'd seen them on board the *Shearwater* just yesterday morning.

"It's fine with me," she said without looking up. "Whenever you're ready."

"Are you sure, Sam? You've hardly had a chance to look at the cannon," Norman said.

"Oh, I've seen enough for now," Sam assured him. "Enough to know that the *Melrose* had most likely been illegally gained. I wonder what Old Sam paid for her," he mused.

"Tell me why you are convinced it was illegal," Norman prompted.

"The Confederacy was considered by the British government to be a belligerent foreign nation," Sam told him. "Maritime law prohibited the sale of warships to such nations. Fortunately for the Southern cause, there were British shipbuilders who had few scruples when it came to such matters. Their vessels could be sold clandestinely to the Confederate Navy, or to private citizens, assuming said citizens had sufficient cash."

"And since Trinity had signed the entire Prescott fortune over to Sam in order to get him to marry her, he would have had plenty of cash at his disposal," Rachel noted.

"And once he took possession of the *Melrose*, he was free on the high seas." Sam drained his coffee cup. "It's surprising, don't you think, Norman, that none of Sam's journals ever showed up."

Norman's cup hung in midair between his mouth and his saucer.

"I'm assuming, of course, that none have turned up," Sam continued. "That if they had, you would have shared them along with Trinity's."

"Of course." Norman set his cup down very carefully in the saucer. "I'd wondered about that myself. Apparently he didn't keep any."

"I would have thought he would," Sam replied. "Kept a journal, that is."

"Why is that?"

"Because it was a common practice in those days, and because his wife did." Sam grinned. "I guess part of me thinks that, knowing that his wife was leaving a written record of his sins for future generations to read, Sam would have wanted his side of the story told."

"Maybe he took them with him to sea," Rachel suggested. "Or maybe they were lost over the years. Or maybe they're still in a box under the eaves in the attic. Then again maybe they never existed at all."

"Well, I for one would have liked to have seen them, wouldn't you, Norman?"

"Oh. Yes. Absolutely." Norman nodded.

"Yes. Well, there's still a chance that they might turn up." Sam rose. "Rachel, if you've finished, why not go get your things and we'll be on our way. I'm sure that Norman has other things to attend to besides looking after guests."

Rachel placed her cup on the fine porcelain saucer, then stood up. "I didn't bring very much with me, so I'll only be a moment."

Sam watched her leave the room, then turned to Norman and said, "Family history is fascinating, isn't it? You never know what you will find."

Norman smiled in apparent agreement.

"Now, have you researched your family history as carefully as you have looked into mine?"

"Oh, yes, I've done quite a through study." Norman nodded. "And you're right, of course. You never know what you will find."

13

"WOULD YOU mind telling me what that was all about?" Rachel asked Sam as she turned to wave good-bye to Norman, who stood atop the steps of the front porch of Eden's End, clearly unhappy to be left behind to deal with his contractors while his divers returned to his wreck.

"What all what was about?"

"Don't be cute, Sam." Rachel folded her arms across her chest.

Sam smiled and looked in his rearview mirror. Norman was still standing on the porch, leaning against one of the columns, a study in white on white. Then, from the corner of one eye, Sam caught a flash of something, pale and glistening, like sunlight on satin, right there behind the dogwoods. He slowed to study the landscape, looking through first the mirrors, then the side and back windows, but there was nothing there. He paused for a long moment, considering the possibilities.

"Sam?" Rachel asked. "Why are you stopping? Did you forget something?"

"What? Oh. No. No. For a minute, I thought I saw something back by that line of dogwoods. But it must have been the way light plays through the trees." Taking one last glance behind, he accelerated, and followed the long lane to its end, where he pulled onto the highway and headed back to Dickson's Beach and the *Shearwater*.

It had to have been the light . . .

"You haven't answered my question, Sam."

"Your quest—Oh, you mean about leaving this morning?"

"Yes, about leaving this morning." Rachel shifted in her seat, annoyed. "We both agreed that we can't dive until at least tomorrow, so what's the rush to get back to the site? Which we probably won't be able to find until the *Annie G.* shows up, because the underwater beacon transponder can only be activated from the *Annie G.*"

"Great invention." Sam nodded cheerfully, referring to the device that, once attached to a part of the wreck, can be electronically activated only from the salvage vessel to relocate the sunken ship, eliminating the need for buoys or other visible markers that could aid pirate divers in locating a wreck when the salvor is away from the site.

"Sam." Rachel sighed. "Stop playing with me. I want to know why we left so abruptly this morning."

"Well, we really had no business left there. We saw what Norman had wanted us to see." Sam reached into the pocket of his lightweight jacket and searched for his sunglasses. "Ah, here they are."

"Meaning the cannon with a different name on it."

"Yes. That was the reason he gave for calling us to Eden's End." Sam craned his neck to see around the pickup truck that had pulled in front of them from a side road. Seeing no vehicles approaching from the opposite direction, he pulled into the passing lane and speeded up.

"You say that as if you think there might have been another reason."

"I have the feeling that Norman wanted me to see what he's done at Eden's End. Maybe because I'm a blood relative of Old Sam's, you know."

"Like he wanted your approval."

"Sort of. I just think he wanted me to see. And he has done a remarkable job. You would have had to have seen it before to fully appreciate what he's done. When we returned for my grandfather's funeral, we found sections of the house closed off because the roof leaks were so bad. Rooms that had been emptied of their contents, the furniture taken elsewhere so that it wouldn't be damaged by the water coming in. My grandfather just didn't have the money for the repairs, and he was too proud to let any of us know about the true state of the house. When we visited, we stayed in the areas where he stayed. None of us were surprised when Judith sold it off—except possibly my father—especially since the buyer was someone who was committed to restoring the place."

"Does it bother you that she sold so many personal things along with the house? Diaries and family china and silver, old photographs?"

"In one sense, yes. But since everything is going

to be preserved and displayed, maybe it's actually better."

"In what way?"

"Those diaries were there, in the house, all these years. I don't even know if anyone in the family knew of their existence—at least, I didn't. It took someone from outside the family to come in and go through things carefully to find them. Norman said they were right there on the library shelf, covered with dust. And yet, in all the time I spent in that house, I never even noticed them. And it certainly never occurred to me to go through my grandfather's desk to see what was in there. But Norman took the time to do that, and anything of any importance will be available to the public to see. Which is a good thing."

"Even the diary where Trinity talks about setting Anjelica's house on fire and killing the woman in her sleep?"

"Trinity didn't know that Anjelica was in there."

"Now, how would you know that?"

"Because I found this." Sam reached into his jacket pocket and removed a small leather volume. "It's another one of Trinity's diaries."

"Sam, you took this from Eden's End?" Rachel's eyebrows rose in concert. "Why did you do that?"

"Norman hid this one from me. I saw him slip it into the top drawer of the desk in the library when he thought I wasn't looking. So of course I had to go back and get it later to find out why."

"And . . . ?"

"Trinity admits she burned the house down, but says that after Sam was lost at sea, Anjelica left

Eden's End. That was when Trinity burned the house down. Not to kill her, but to make sure that she never came back, that she had nothing to come back to. Norman had to have known this, Rachel, he's read the diary. And yet he wants us to believe that Trinity deliberately murdered Anjelica. So, of course, I have to wonder why."

"And how will stealing the diary help you find out?"

"I just want to make sure that Norman doesn't destroy it," Sam said quietly. "At least, not until I can have copies made."

"Do you really think he would do that?"

"I didn't think he'd tear down the oldest section of the house, but he did."

"He said there was no way to salvage it."

"I don't know that I believe that."

"Then why would he do it? He's committed all his money and his time to restoring the plantation, Sam. Why would he deliberately destroy the remains of the old Prescott cabin?"

"I don't know. I don't know why he lied about Trinity killing Anjelica, and I don't know why he lied about Trinity's portrait being off someplace being restored. I found it in the attic covered with a sheet."

"Maybe he doesn't realize that that was the portrait you meant."

"It's the only one there was, and it was hanging over the fireplace when he took possession of the house. He had to have known exactly who it was. That brass plate identifying the subject as Trinity Prescott McGowan should have been a dead giveaway."

Rachel sat quietly, mulling it over.

"And I have to wonder why he rebuilt Anjelica's house," Sam added.

"Anjelica's house?" Rachel frowned.

"Yes. It's there, at the edge of the clearing. Right where the remains used to be."

"I could see from the balcony that there was a house beyond the trees, but I didn't know it was Anjelica's house. Are you certain it's the same house?"

"Yes. We used to play around the burned-out house when we were little, and I remember exactly where it was. The house that has been recently rebuilt is in the exact location. Strange, don't you think?"

"Maybe he rebuilt it planning to use it for a caretaker, or something." Rachel frowned.

"I don't know, Rachel. I looked through the windows. The house is furnished with what appears to be antiques, or some damn good-looking reproductions, and looks as if it's waiting for its occupants to return. I can't explain the feeling that it gave me." He shook his head.

"Sam, I'm sure it's just part of the total renovation of Eden's End in its entirety."

"The renovations of the main house are not yet complete. He hasn't even started on the big barn and the chicken house . . . it just doesn't make sense to me." He ran his fingers through his hair and it tumbled across his forehead as if in protest at having been disturbed. "It just seems odd. I can't explain it any other way."

"What do you suppose Norman will do when he realizes you took the diary?"

"Maybe he won't even think to look for it. And of course, I'll return it to the desk the next time I'm at Eden's End." Sam turned to her and grinned. "Then again, I can always claim ignorance and suggest that possibly Trinity took it back. He didn't seem at all surprised that you thought you saw her."

"I did see her," Rachel said softly. "I never thought I'd see the day when I would say that I saw a ghost, but I did see her."

"Well, it's made me curious. Curious enough that when I get back to the boat, I'm going to call my dad and see if he ever heard of anyone else seeing her."

"Are you going to tell him about Anjelica?"

"Yes. Definitely. I'm anxious to see if he's heard that story before."

"Do you doubt that it's true?"

"No. I think it's absolutely true. I think Old Sam was an arrogant, self-centered son of a bitch, and I don't think for a minute that he'd hesitate to build a house for his mistress on land owned by his wife."

"Techincally, as Norman pointed out, the land no longer belonged to his wife. It is interesting, though, to read the thoughts of someone who lived so long ago, thoughts written in her own hand." Rachel thumbed through the old book, reading a page here and there. "Oh, listen to this. 'Today I begged, in vain, for the doctors to set our Archie's leg. He fell in the stream this morning and broke at least one bone. They refused, saying that they had no time to treat slaves, freed or otherwise. I then asked for some laudanum to dull his pain, but this they refused as well. I had no choice but to sneak into the cellar to find some whiskey that Sam had hidden away. I gave the whiskey to Celia to give to Archie so that I could at least wrap his leg and hope to set the bone. He's been a good and faithful soul, he could have left me when the Yankee soldiers came, but chose to stay. I would hope that his poor leg heals straight and strong and that I have not caused him to become lame.' Archie seems to have been a former slave who stayed on to help her."

Rachel skimmed another few pages, reading as she went along.

"Oh. This is interesting. Listen, Sam." She tapped him on the arm to assure his attention. " 'He came again last night—curiously, the second time this week—and I marvel that he has been able to slip in and out of this house so many times without detection. He does not know that I know he comes here, just as he does not know that I know what he does there in the library in the dark. But I have found his secret—all remains safely hidden where he left it. To move anything would arouse his suspicions. Besides, if the Yankees found it, they would take it for their use, and I have other plans for Sam's bounty. Let him continue to add to his stash. It will, I vow, serve not him and his whore, but my sons—God keep them safe whereever they are this night!—and their sons, that future generations might profit, that Eden's End might survive. That hope is all I have left, everything else that mattered to me having been taken first by my damnable husband, and then by this damnable war.' "

Rachel looked up at Sam, her head tilted to one side, and asked, "What do you think she was referring to?"

"Read it again."

The second reading didn't seem to make things any more clear than had the first.

"What do you suppose was in Sam's 'stash'?"

"I don't have a clue, but it must have been something valuable for Old Sam to have risked his life to bring it back here." Sam shook his head.

"I wonder why he didn't take it to Anjelica's instead of here?"

"Maybe he didn't have as good a hiding place there."

"I wonder where the hiding place was," Rachel murmured, intrigued. "And I'm dying to know what it was."

"I'd be willing to bet that Norman knows."

"You think?" Rachel asked, closing the book.

"He seems to know just about everything else." Sam nodded. "But it really does tantalize, doesn't it? What could it have been? Where did it come from? And where is it now?"

They spent the rest of the trip back to Dickson's Beach speculating the answers.

Sam put the outside of his twin-engines into reverse, then kicked into neutral to give it just enough oomph to pull the bow of the *Shearwater* away from the dock. A touch of forward was all he needed to coax the inside engine into assisting. The cruiser eased away from the slip and headed toward the end of the marina where the open sea met the bay. Once beyond the buoys, he fed the throttle and headed northeast.

"Want to steer while I make lunch?" he asked after

they'd been riding the still somewhat choppy waves for close to an hour.

"Sure." She slid over to take the wheel.

"You can steer from the flybridge if you'd rather," he told her.

"I think I will. I like it up there."

"I thought that you might."

"Why's that?" Rachel stood in the doorway, about to take the steps up to the open cabin overhead.

"You just look like a woman who likes to feel the wind in her face."

"On a beautiful day like this one is turning out to be, it's a given. Sun, endless sky, endless sea. What's not to love?" She grinned and headed upstairs.

Sam smiled in her passing, then realized he'd been doing a lot of that lately, smiling for no apparent reason. Always, it seemed, when Rachel was around. There was something about her that just made him smile.

A smile from the heart, his mother used to tell them, *was the truest kind*.

That was pretty much the way Rachel made him feel, that he was smiling from his heart.

The thought reminded him that he'd wanted to call his parents. With Rachel at the wheel, the boat needed none of his attention. He reached for his phone, and dialed the number on St. Swithin's Island, wondering if anyone would be home at this hour on a Wednesday afternoon. Well, there was always the answering machine, though Sam knew perfectly well that his parents only remembered to check messages sporadically.

"Hello?" His mother picked up the phone, then his father did, too, on another extension.

"Hello?"

"Samuel, I have it," Sam heard his mother say. "Hang up."

"It might be for me," his father said. "Why should I hang up before I know who it is?"

"Actually, it's for both of you." Sam laughed.

"Oh! Sammy! Hello, son."

Sam flinched. He hadn't felt like a "Sammy" since he was six years old, but somehow the sentiment had been lost on his mother.

"Is everything all right, Sammy?" his mother asked.

"Everything is fine." Sam thought of Rachel, up on his flybridge, building the *Shearwater* through the waves. "Everything is very fine."

"How's the boat?"

"Great, Dad. Right at this moment, she's headed out to sea."

"There's someone at the door, Sammy. Just keep talking to your father," his mother said as she hung up.

"I thought you were out to sea." Sam could almost see his father frowning, his lips slightly pursed, trying to recall if somehow he'd forgotten a conversation with his son.

"I was. We had quite a storm yesterday morning, so I went inland to sit it out." Sam took a deep breath. "Actually, I was at Eden's End."

"Really?"

"Yes. We pulled a cannon up earlier in the week and Norman Winter—Dad, you remember him, I'm certain—had it brought back to Eden's End. He's bought himself some ultrasonic baths, and had them installed in the smaller of the barns. He's set up a sort of laboratory there to clean off his artifacts and ready them for display. He has an archaeological graduate student working for him part-time and actually doing the cleaning process for him."

"Excellent idea. It seems that Norman is really taking this preservation business seriously. But is it still reasonable to expect his museum to open in September?"

"Assuming that we don't get held up anywhere, Dad. Which is always a possibility, as you know. But as it looks now, we have a good shot of making it."

"Do you have good help on board? A decent crew?"

"Yes, Dad. I do. There are two other divers who were hired by Norman to assist, and they've been a big help so far, especially with the equipment. And of course, there's the salvager."

"Oh, yes. Did you remember to give him my regards?"

"If I'd seen him, I'm sure I would have."

"What is that supposed to mean? I thought you told me that Gordon Chandler was the salvager."

"His company is running the operation. Gordon himself, however, is not."

"Ah, that must have been a disappointment," his father sympathized.

"Only momentarily," Sam told him. "I've adjusted to working with his replacement. He sent someone very competent in his place."

"Good, good, son. It's important to feel good about the people you work closely with."

"Oh, I certainly feel good about it, Dad." Sam grinned as he opened the refrigerator.

"Now, what have you found so far?" his father asked.

"Just the cannon, some buttons, a couple of boxes of bullets. Intact. We really were just getting down towards the cabin when the storm came up." Sam paused momentarily, then asked, "Dad, aren't you going to ask about the renovations at Eden's End?"

"Yes, of course." Sam heard his father's short intake of breath. "How are they going?"

"He's doing a wonderful job. The plantation looks pretty much as it must have when it was first built. You'd love it, Dad. Norman wants to invite the family to come to the opening of the museum. I hope you'll be there."

"Yes. Well, we'll see."

Sam knew that this must be, in some ways, a difficult subject for his father, who had grown up at Eden's End. He had been born in the house, as had been all of his siblings. Both his mother and his father were buried on the grounds, along with countless McGowans and Prescotts who were laid to rest there. Samuel had been one of the family members who had been least supportive of Judith's decision to sell. Of course, that could have been colored by his ambivalence toward his father's wife. That his mother had been dead for almost twelve years before his father had remarried had not seemed to have mattered to Samuel. He had never accepted his father's marriage to Judith, and had not returned to Eden's

End until his father was dying. Eden's End was a sore spot for Samuel these days.

"Dad, do you remember any family stories about Trinity McGowan?" Sam asked.

"Only that she was homely and pigheaded, not unlike your sisters. The pigheaded part, not the homely. Why?"

"Norman found some of her diaries."

"Really? That's wonderful. Have you seen them?"

"Yes, actually, I read them over last night."

"Well, then, tell me. What did she write about?"

Samuel placed his hand over the receiver and called to his wife, "Margarite, my great-grandmother's diaries have been found. Sam has had a chance to read through a few."

Sam heard his mother exclaim, "Wonderful! I'm getting back on the line."

"Your mother is getting back on the line," Samuel told his son.

Sam chuckled. His mother wasn't one to miss out on news, even if it was more than a century old.

"Now you can talk. I'm back on."

"That was quick, Mom."

"This is exciting. It isn't every day one gets to hear the thoughts of a woman who lived over a hundred years ago."

"Well, to start with, Dad, you knew that Old Sam had been in the army and served with Trinity's father?"

"Yes, of course. That's how she met him. She was visiting the Colonel at some outpost . . ."

"Yes. And that she proposed to Sam, and when he

balked, she agreed to have all of the Prescott lands placed in his name if he would marry her."

"Yes, I vaguely remember that. Brazen of her, to bribe him."

"Clever of her, if you ask me," Sam's mother said, a hint of humor in her voice. "She obviously was a woman who knew what she wanted, and was willing to place all she had on the line to get it. I have to admire a woman like that."

"Well, apparently, at the time, Sam was having a relationship with a woman there in Texas, a woman named Anjelica, who was pregnant with Sam's son when Sam left her to come back to Eden's End to marry Trinity."

"Really?" Sam could almost see his father sit straight up in his chair.

"Did you not know this?"

"No. There had been rumors that had drifted down from my grandfather, about Old Sam having a bastard son, but no details that I recall. No, I don't recall having heard this story before." Samuel put his hand over the receiver as he quietly lit a match, hoping to sneak a forbidden cigar past his wife.

"Put it out, Samuel." Margarite sighed. "Go ahead, Sammy. What else did you learn?"

"Apparently after Old Sam and Trinity had had their family, he began to get an itch to see his old girlfriend again, and he made a trip to Texas to find her. That's when he found that he had a son by this woman."

"Any idea of what his name was?"

"Norman said it was Lorenzo."

"Lorenzo, eh? Interesting." Samuel took a clandestine puff of the cigar.

"Why?"

"Lawrence was Old Sam's middle name. It was also his father's name, as I recall. Go on, son." Sam puffed again, knowing his wife was glued to her telephone. He'd pay for it later, but right now, the cigar tasted mighty good.

"Well, Old Sam and Anjelica must have taken up where they'd left off. Sam built a house for her. At Eden's End."

"What?" Samuel almost choked. "Are you sure about that?"

"Positive. Remember the old burned-out shell at the edge of the woods? That was Angelica's house." Sam paused for a moment, then added, "It was Trinity who burned it down, Dad. Unfortunately, Angelica was in it at the time."

"Oh. My. That was unfortunate," his mother exclaimed. "And the boy?"

"He would have been a man by then, Mom, and long gone, I suspect, from Eden's End. I don't really know where he went, since there's no mention of him that I could see." Sam opened a package of paper plates and stacked them neatly in one of the cupboards. "But shortly after, the war broke out and Sam bought the *Melrose* with Trinity's money. The *Melrose*, by the way, started out her life as the British ship *Windemere*. Sam must have purchased her on the black market."

"That's no surprise. I suspected as much, given that he had brought his own ship to the party, so to speak." Samuel nodded to himself. "It certainly wasn't uncommon. I've heard of others who had done the same."

"Trinity's diaries also allude to Sam making clandestine trips back to Eden's End and slipping into the house via some old secret doorway."

"In the back wall, right next to the old shed room," Samuel said promptly. "We used to play there as children. Later, as teenagers, my brothers and I would sneak in and out of the house through that passageway."

"Well, apparently it's gone, now. Norman thinks that it may have been blocked off when the workmen took down the cabin."

"Removed the cabin?" Samuel's jaw dropped. "Why on earth would they have removed the cabin? Why, that was the oldest structure on the property. Whatever was Winter thinking? I thought he was a preservationist!"

"Calm down, Samuel," Margarite murmured. "I'm sure Sam asked those same questions."

"I did. Norman said there was a lot of insect damage and it couldn't be salvaged."

"I'm really shocked, son. See, I told you that Judith should not have sold the property . . ."

"Dad, Norman's done a fine job. The restoration has been beautifully done."

"The Prescott cabin had great historical significance . . ."

"I know, Dad, but it's gone. There's nothing that can be done about it."

"I'm certainly sorry to hear this. I certainly am." Samuel forgot to disguise his exhaling. Margarite graciously overlooked it. This time.

"Oh, there's the door again. I'll be back . . ."

The heels of Sam's mother's shoes clicked along the hallway to the front door, where there was some distant conversation, then the sound of heels clicking back to the telephone.

"Samuel, that was Jenny next door. She stopped at the post office and picked up a package from Daria." Margarite sounded pleased. "I'll let you open it."

"How is Daria?"

The mention of his sister's name reminded Sam that her parrot hadn't seen the light of day since late yesterday afternoon. He pulled the cloth off H.D.'s cage to find the bird swinging away quietly on his little swing.

"Daria is fine. She's having a lovely time in the desert," his mother told him.

"And what do you hear from Iona?"

"She's having the time of her life with her little shop."

"Humph," Samuel interjected into the conversation. "Up there in Philadelphia in her little flea market."

"It's hardly a flea market, Samuel. She has some lovely things for sale, Sam. She's imported a lovely line of porcelain and carpets, but the jewelry she is designing is exceptional. You really should go to see her."

"Well, it would be somewhat hard to do that right now . . ."

"That reminds me of something," Samuel said. "Margarite, I'm afraid you'll have to hang up now. I need to talk to Sam."

"He's going to tell you all about the surprise party

he's planning for me, Sammy," His mother stage-whispered into the phone. "I'll hang up and let him. Be well, dear boy. Take care of yourself."

"I will, Mom."

"Now, how the devil did she find out about that?" Samuel muttered. "Well, she's right, of course. You know her birthday is in two weeks. Is there any way you could make it, Sam? It would mean the world to her to have you here, especially with Daria out of the country and Jackson . . . well, Jackson gone."

"I'll be there, Dad," Sam promised.

Sam looked up as Rachel stuck her head into the cabin, and not seeing the small phone, asked, "What exactly are you making for lunch, anyway?"

Sam grinned and held up an unopened can of tuna fish.

"Sorry. I didn't realize you were on the phone." Rachel scooted back up the steps.

"Well, then, Dad, I'll see you in two weeks. Oh . . . and Dad, before I forget. Did anyone . . . your parents, your aunts or anyone, ever talk about seeing Trinity?" Sam asked.

"Seeing Trinity? Oh, you mean her ghost?" Samuel chuckled. "Sure. I never saw her, though my Aunt Carrie said she did once or twice. I remember the day my sister Emily nearly drowned in the pond, she said a lady in a long pink dress had reached into the water and pulled her up. Course, Emily always did have a vivid imagination, but Aunt Carrie said the woman she'd described was definitely Trinity. I only vaguely remember stories about her popping up now and then."

"Do you remember the circumstances under which Aunt Carrie saw her?" Sam asked thoughtfully.

"No, but you can ask her yourself at your mother's birthday party. She'll be here. She's eighty-five years old this year, but she's still sharp as a tack. I'm sure she'll remember." Samuel puffed more boldly on his cigar. "Did you see her, Sam?"

"No. No, I didn't."

"Well, I suppose that's good. The impression that I have is that she comes around when someone is threatened somehow, but I could be wrong. All the same, you take care, son. I'll see you in two weeks." Samuel hung up, though he would probably sit and enjoy just a few more puffs on that cigar before joining his wife in the kitchen.

On the *Shearwater*, Sam McGowan the fourth turned off his phone and set it on the counter, thinking back over his father's words. Had some threat been the cause of Trinity's appearance? Or had she perhaps been upset at the reading of her diaries, having her most private thoughts invaded by strangers? Maybe she'd been insulted that her portrait had been banned to the attic and another's hung in its place. Or was it the rebuilding of the house she'd burned to the ground that she was protesting?

And what were the chances, Sam wondered, they'd ever find out?

14

---✤---

"I'M REALLY anxious to get down to the wreck this morning," Rachel said to Hugh as she slipped her diving knife into its sheath and buckled on her weight belt. "I'm praying that the storm didn't damage the site."

"You never can tell." Hugh shrugged, "I know Norman's concerned about the delay."

"He was pretty agitated yesterday when I told him we were putting off diving for yet another day." Rachel nodded. "Explaining that the currents were just a little too strong didn't seem to make much of an impression on him."

"You want the airlift, Rachel?" Scully asked from the top deck.

"Yes. I think we'll need it," she called back.

"Well, I for one will be happy when you guys start bringing up something worth photographing. This endless footage of you swimming around the wreck really gets old after a while. At least the visibility is good. I hate it when you can't see too far ahead, you know?" Hugh shivered. "You just never know what's out there."

"I think you've watched *Jaws* a time or two too many." Rachel laughed and lowered herself into the water.

"Don't tell me you never think about it, Rachel. Sharks, barracudas . . ."

"I think about it about as often as I think of going down in a plane crash. Which is mostly when I hear about it happening to someone else. Fortunately for all of us, shark attacks are relatively rare. I only know one or two people who have been attacked, Hugh, neither of them in these waters. I've found that for the most part, sharks will keep their distance. Unless you're handing out food. Then you might have a problem."

"Maybe you've been lucky."

"Mostly, I'm cautious." She grinned and looked over her shoulder at the *Shearwater*, where Sam was just donning his air tank. Rachel waved, and he waved back.

Scully and Turk appeared with the lengths of hose for the airlift, and passed sections to Rachel to hold on to while they entered the water.

"The water's colder today," Scully muttered a rare few words.

"Well, the sun's already up, and the temperature is supposed to rise into the eighties today," Rachel said, though she knew he wouldn't bother to look at her. Scully never seemed to look at her, never addressed her directly. "We may have to shorten our dive times, though. It won't do any of us any good to get hypothermia."

"Just something else to worry about," Hugh grumbled.

"Hugh, if I didn't know better, I'd think you didn't enjoy diving," Rachel teased.

Seeing Sam approach through the waves, she slid her mask over her face and prepared to dive.

"I like it okay," he told her. "On sunny days. When it's warm and visibility is good. And the ocean is not choppy."

"Sounds like you should restrict your diving to your backyard pool," Scully told him as he went under.

"Two sentences in one day," Rachel told Hugh. "I wonder what Scully had for breakfast."

Turk laughed and followed his partner under.

"Ready, Rachel?" Sam asked from ten feet away.

"I'm there," she told him as she headed down, following the anchor line, Sam and Hugh both close behind.

Rachel made a mental note to keep an eye on Hugh. She often forgot he was there, since he didn't actively participate in the operation. She hadn't realized how nervous he was about diving. Nervous divers could be a hazard. She'd have to make certain that he didn't cause problems for himself or anyone else.

As Hugh had feared, visibility was limited, the storm having churned up sediment from the bottom. It would be a few days before the water cleared completely, but Norman would not want to hear that. With the aid of lights, they could continue to work, though conditions might be less than ideal.

Below her, the wreck appeared fuzzy, its edges indistinct, as Rachel descended. Treading water, she waited for Sam, knowing that she should not get too far ahead of him. He caught up with her, and taking the piece of hose from her hands, floated down to where Scully had already started to assemble the airlift. Passing the section of hose to Turk, Sam began his inspection of the wreck.

In spite of the storm's ferocity, the *Melrose* had fared remarkably well. It appeared that she had been tilted slightly more onto one side than she had been, but beyond that, she appeared intact. Sam turned to give a thumbs-up to Rachel, and found her waving to him from near the center of the vessel, where she was shining her light downward. Sam swam to her, curious to see what she might have found.

The doorway to the cabin stood partially open, sand wedged between it and the interior wall. An inspection of the area found that the sand wasn't as deep as they had suspected. Apparently the storm had shaken some of the sediment loose as it had rolled the vessel onto her side. Eager to see what else might have been shaken loose, Sam gestured to Turk to bring the airlift. Assuming that all went well, they'd get into that cabin today. The anticipation tingled through each of the divers. You just never knew what you would find.

It took almost two hours, but the cabin had been swept of sufficient sand to permit entry. One by one, the four divers, lights aglow, made their way past the partially opened door into the silent room.

This was the part he loved best, Sam realized, as he floated a foot above floorboards that had not been tread upon since the ship was swallowed by waves in 1864. Shining his light in first one corner, then the next, his eyes scanned the darkness searching for recognizable objects. There, against one wall, stood a desk, its drawers still tightly closed. Across the room a wooden chest had slid into a wall, the weight of it causing a crack on the side of the cabin.

Curious, Sam swam to it and tried to lift the box, but it was too large, too heavy for one man. He gestured to Scully and Turk to join him, and together the three men managed to get the trunk out of the cabin, Hugh filming every second of their struggle. Rachel raised both palms in a questioning gesture, and Sam motioned upwards.

He can't wait to see what's in that trunk, she smiled to herself as she surfaced, *and neither can I.*

"What do you suppose is in there?" she asked when she reached the back of the *Annie G.*

"Whatever it is, it's heavy and it's shifting. A good sign." Sam grinned. "Let's get it up on deck and see if we can get it to open."

Thirty minutes later, after a difficult struggle with the unwieldy load, the entire crew gathered eagerly around the wooden trunk, Sam using a mallet to strike the lock. The flat lid was raised and laid back upon the deck, revealing the chest's contents.

A collective gasp went up from the crew, then a silence.

"Are they real?" Renny asked, stepping forward to touch one of the coins.

"Yes. Yes, they're real," Sam told him.

"See, Rachel? I told you there was treasure." Renny beamed. "Pirate treasure."

"Not exactly," Sam told him. "This would most

likely have been the paymaster's chest, just like we talked about, Renny. Money that the paymaster would distribute to the men on board as their wages. Their pay."

"You mean, like Norman pays us?"

"Yes. Only in those days, they used coins like these." Sam lifted a handful to inspect. The coins were gold, all right.

That in itself offered a lot of questions. The state of the Confederacy being what it was in 1864, it was unlikely that Jefferson Davis would have had this much gold to pay the collective crews of *all* the blockade runners still in operation. How could so much have ended up on the *Melrose*?

"I think we need to call Norman." Rachel tapped Sam on the arm.

"I think that someone already has." Sam gestured toward the cabin, where Ernie was excitedly speaking with someone on the radio.

"Wow." Hugh was shaking his head. "That's going to make for some great viewing. What a sight that was, opening that lid, and then bam! Gold! Wow! I guess you guys knew that all that gold was in there, huh? I sure never expected that. Wow! All that gold . . ."

Hugh walked away, muttering.

"Do you think Norman knew?" Rachel asked Sam.

"I don't know how he could have." Sam shook his head. "How could he have known when the ship took on their payload? If that's what it was."

"How much do you think is there?"

"It's hard to tell." Sam knelt down and sifted through the coins, trying to judge how many the chest might hold. "Forty to sixty thousand dollars, maybe, in today's dollars."

"To quote Hugh, I'd say that's a 'wow.'" Rachel nodded. "Who'd have thought there'd be that much?"

"I can't explain it." Sam shook his head. "Surely, the ship would be expected to carry some sort of pay for the crew, but this just seems a little much. Curious, don't you think?"

"Hey, Rachel," Ernie called to her from the open cabin door. "Mr. Winter wants to talk to you."

"I'll just bet he does." Rachel grinned. "Come on, Sam. You want to help me give the boss the good news?"

"Nah, I'll leave that to you. I think I'll go see what washed up in Renny's basket while everyone else was struck with gold fever. How much you want to bet he's sending a case of champagne out here so that we can celebrate?"

"Champagne, huh?" she said as she turned toward the office. "Nice. A little celebration might be in order."

"Hey, Rach." Sam reached for her arm, and stopped her midstride. "I have some nice chablis on board. Not quite champagne, but a good year. I've been saving it for a special occasion. I could make us a little dinner, pour a little wine . . ."

"Do I get to make the coffee?"

"I was hoping you'd offer."

"Your deck or mine?"

"Oh, mine. Definitely. It's much more . . . private."

"I see." She nodded, as if carefully considering the offer. "I don't know, Sam. A girl could get in deep trouble on a moonlit night on the ocean, a bottle of wine, a little dinner, a little music . . ."

"I didn't mention music." Sam leaned toward her.

"I'm sure H.D. will come up with something," she whispered, adding, "I'll be over around eight," before heading toward the cabin where Norman Winter impatiently awaited speaking to her.

"You were right," Rachel told Sam as she leaned over his shoulder to see what he had dug out of the basket of debris raised by the airlift. "Norman is sending a case of champagne. Unfortunately, he is bringing it himself and expects us all to have dinner with him tonight."

Sam made a face.

"I guess this means our celebration is off."

"I'm afraid so."

"Hmmm. Well, then, I guess our dinner will have to wait for tomorrow night."

"It looks that way." She leaned closer. "What have you found?"

"Oh, a few more buttons. A few more coins. Someone's wedding ring." He passed it back to her with one hand while he sifted through the sediment in the bottom of the basket with the other.

"It's lovely," she said softly. "It's as bright and shiny as it was on the day it was made." She turned the ring over in her hand. " 'JT from KT.' Wouldn't it be something if we could track down their descendants and return this to them? If they had any descendants, that is."

"Suggest it to Norman. He might think it's a good idea. Who knows, maybe he'll even pay someone to track them down."

"You know what would be wonderful?" Rachel

leaned into Sam's back lightly. "If we found the list of crew, and got Norman to post it in newspapers across the South. Maybe some of the descendants of the men on board might come to the museum opening."

"Hmmm."

"Sam, are you listening?"

"Sure."

"Did you find something good?"

"Just the usual. There are a few buttons left, though. I think I'll save them for Renny." He looked over his shoulder, into her green eyes. "I wish we were on the *Shearwater*. Right now. I want to kiss you so badly, Rachel."

To her everlasting embarrassment, Rachel blushed.

"May I take that as an, *I want to kiss you too, Sam*?"

"Yes." She looked up at him. "Yes, I do."

"Why don't we . . ."

"Rachel! There you are! Norman's coming to see our treasure." Renny bounced out of nowhere, singing like a happy child. "We have treasure! We have treasure!"

"Yes, surprisingly, we do, after all. Now, Renny, did you take any treasure out of the basket while we were down with the ship?" Sam asked.

"Buttons," Renny told Sam. "Just like before. I'll clean them up, just like you showed me how. I like doing that, Sam. I like cleaning up the surprises that come from the sea."

"We all like those kinds of surprises. Here's a few more for you." Sam poured the buttons—concretions and all—into Renny's cupped hands. "Now, tomorrow, when we go back down, I want you to make sure to keep your eyes on the basket, Renny."

"In case gold coins come up?" Renny asked excitedly.

"Well, you never know, Renny. The *Melrose* has already proven to hold a surprise or two." Sam turned to Rachel and smiled. "I'm going to go on back to the *Shearwater* to take a shower. I guess I'll see you at dinner."

Rachel nodded and watched Sam swing himself over the rail, looking very much like a man who harbored a surprise or two of his own.

H.D. was singing a somewhat loud albeit fractured version of "Burning Love" when Sam hauled himself and his equipment onto the diving platform of the *Shearwater*. Leaving his equipment on deck, Sam stripped off his wet suit and rinsed it inside and out with fresh water from a tank he kept for the purpose, then left it on the deck to dry in the late afternoon sun. Taking his diving bag, Sam stepped into the cool of the small cabin.

"I'm a hunk of love! I'm a hunk of love! Awk!" H.D. bobbed up and down on his perch. "Kiss me quick!"

"H.D., for your sake, I hope that Daria's trip gets cut short," Sam muttered. "*Real* short."

"I'm Daria's be-u-ti-ful baby!" H.D. crowed.

Ignoring the parrot, Sam reached into the refrigerator and took out a beer, then sat down at the table. He took a few long, thoughtful drags from the bottle, reached for the diving bag, and allowed its contents to spill out across the table. With his right index finger he lined up the colored stones he'd earlier found in the basket.

Several rubies, red as blood. Sapphires as blue as the deep blue sea. Emeralds the color of Rachel's eyes, and diamonds the size of a robin's egg.

So, Great-great-granddaddy, what were you doing with these?

Sam stared at the stones, contemplating the possibilities, for the better part of an hour. He was still as stunned as when he'd lifted them from the sand in the basket, and still every bit as puzzled.

The stones were sizable, true in color and clear right through. He picked up an emerald and stared at it. He'd never seen an emerald so free of occlusions before. Just this one stone had to be worth a small fortune.

Scooping his find into his hand, he went off to find a suitable place to keep them while he showered and returned to the *Annie G.* for Norman's celebration, knowing this cache would be on his mind all night. There was simply no good reason that Sam could come up with that would explain why these stones would have been on the *Melrose*. They had to have been stolen, pure and simple. Which meant that his great-great-grandfather had been doing more than running guns, just as Sam had suspected he might have done.

Had Old Sam been doing a little pirating on the side? Nothing else would make sense.

And somehow, Sam just couldn't shake the feeling that when he finally shared this little find with his employer, Norman would not be the least bit surprised.

15

⎯⎯❦⎯⎯

Sam, in shorts and a short-sleeved sport shirt, took the dinghy to the *Annie G.* for Norman's celebration. The sight of Rachel in a simple long white cotton dress that just skimmed her body but did not cling, that showed off her tan arms but little other skin, stopped him cold. He tried really hard to remember if he'd ever seen anyone as beautiful as Rachel in that long white dress, her hair piled loosely atop her head, big, hammered-silver earrings and a tiny conch shell on a thin silver chain around her neck her only adornments, and knew he never had. She was stunning, and she took his breath away.

Damn Norman and his champagne, anyway.

"Rachel, I've never seen you in a dress before," Sam whispered in her ear as he leaned over to pile jumbo shrimp onto his plate, "and you're killing me. How can I keep my mind on Norman and his damn ship when you look like a sea nymph right out of one of my favorite fantasies?"

Rachel laughed. The knit dress was the most simple thing she owned, and she'd packed it mainly because it didn't take up much space, didn't wrinkle,
and served her well on those few occasions when
she might need to dress just a little. Besides, its high,
round neckline was modest and concealing, and it
was never her intention to call much attention to herself when she was working, particularly when she
was the only woman on the team.

"Sam, I would have thought that your fantasies
would have been wearing bikinis and serving beer
from an endless cooler," Rachel replied, trying not
to react to the fact that the caress of his warm breath
on her skin had sent a shiver from her head to her
toes.

"Well, the cooler part is pretty close, but in spite
of what you may have heard, it isn't necessarily the
clothes that make the woman." Sam could have
added that Rachel didn't need to be wearing a bikini
to cause a little sweat to break out on his upper lip,
but thought better of it, since Norman was upon
them, bearing tall fluted glasses of champagne.

"Rachel! Sam!" Norman's smiled beneficently.
"I'm delighted with what you've done today!"

"Norman, all we did was haul up what was down
there." Sam took both glasses from Norman's hands
and offered one to Rachel.

"Yes but you uncovered it. What a thrill it must
have been to open that lid for the first time and see
all that gold! A young man's fantasy come true!"

Sam winked at Rachel. "Well, Rachel and I were
just discussing fantasies."

"Oh, I'm sure we've all had the same dreams,

Sam." Norman patted him on the back. "Now, one of mine has come true. Perhaps before the operation has concluded, yours will have as well."

"I'm counting on it." Sam tilted his glass in Rachel's direction.

Rachel returned the gesture and tried to pretend she wasn't blushing.

"Now, do you think it would be all right if I permitted each member of the crew to take one coin as a sort of remembrance?"

"You own the salvage rights, Norman, you can do pretty much whatever you want with it," Rachel told him.

"Well, of course, I plan on turning most of it over to the state, though I'll keep some of it on display in my museum."

"You're going to give the coins to the state of North Carolina?" Sam was certain he hadn't heard correctly.

"Well, of course. If you're correct and the money represents wages due to the crew, it's money that belonged to the Confederacy. Not to Captain McGowan," Norman pronounced.

"I'm not certain who the money belonged to, quite frankly." Sam set his plate down on a small nearby table and leaned back against the side of the boat.

"Rachel, I thought you said you thought that the coins were the crew's wages." Norman turned to her.

"Yes, I did. It was in a trunk in the office—very possibly the paymaster's office—and we know that many of the men were paid in coinage for their service." Rachel sat in a folding chair and sipped at her champagne.

"Rachel, I seriously doubt that there were that many coins available to pay the entire Confederate Navy by 1864," Sam said quietly.

"Where else could it have come from," Norman asked, "if not the navy? Why else would it have been aboard the ship, if not to pay the crew?"

"I don't know." Sam shrugged. "But there are a number of possibilities."

"I'd like to hear them."

"Perhaps the *Melrose* had been given the task of picking up the pay for several ships."

"Sort of like a floating bank?" Rachel frowned. That wouldn't have happened. One ship would not have been entrusted with the wages for others. Why was Sam even proposing such an absurdity?

"Ah, that's certainly possible." Norman brightened. "And if, as you say, there's more money on board than would have been necessary to pay the crew of the *Melrose*, this would make sense. Yes, that's probably the explanation."

Rachel turned to Sam, about to chide him for proposing such a scenario, then allowing Norman to even consider something so unlikely, when Sam added, "Then of course there's always the possibility that the money was stolen."

Norman's raised goblet paused midway to his lips. "Whatever are you suggesting?"

"Many of the blockade runners were also engaged in raiding the Union ships, Norman, we've talked about that. It was actually quite common, especially after the Southern ports were effectively closed by the Union Navy. Keep in mind that in 1864, Wilmington was the only port that remained open. The job of the Confederate Navy was to keep food and supplies coming to the army. Agents were sent north to buy up whatever arms they could get their hands on and smuggle back."

"How could they have bought weapons in the North?" Rachel asked.

"The black market worked as efficiently then as it does now, Rachel. You could buy anything, if you had enough money. There were plenty of Northern manufacturers who didn't give a damn who paid for their goods. Profit was profit. And remember that the South sent envoys to Europe aboard blockade runners to smuggle back what they could buy. In the early days of the war, the Southern commanders had their troops salvage Union rifles from the battlefields where Northern soldiers had fallen. Of course, smuggling and salvaging only went so far. You couldn't hope to win a war that way. There had to be a more effective means of obtaining arms."

"Raiding the Union ships," Rachel said.

"Exactly. For their supplies and their weapons and whatever of value might be aboard. There were some blockade runners that were very effective as raiders. Very effective," he added for emphasis.

"And you think that Sam McGowan might have been one of them?" Rachel asked.

"It would explain the gold." Sam shrugged.

"Interesting theory." Norman nodded. "Very interesting. But I suspect that there would have been some sort of record of this, wouldn't you think? I mean, I've read about other ships that had done exactly as you say, raided the Union supply ships for their cargoes. But we know the names of those ships.

I've never seen the *Melrose* mentioned in connection with such activities. And I've read everything I could get my hands on about that ship, Sam. I would think that, had Captain McGowan been so occupied, a record would have been made someplace. I dare say I would have found it."

"Very possibly. But I suspect that many deeds go unrecorded during wartime. Who knows?" Sam drained his glass. "Maybe the answers are on the *Melrose*, Norman, a mere sixty-five feet under. And if they are, no doubt we'll find them before too long."

Norman stared at Sam for what seemed to Rachel to be an inordinate amount of time before saying, "Yes. Well, that remains to be seen. In the meantime, it would appear that dinner is about to be served. Shall we?"

Norman rose and gestured for Sam and Rachel to accompany him. With one hand on the small of her back, Sam guided Rachel to the steps leading down to the galley. When Norman stopped in the cabin to speak briefly with Ernie, Rachel turned to Sam, and in a low voice, said, "What was all that bull about? The *Melrose* being the payroll ship for the Confederate Navy, for God's sake."

Sam chuckled. "I just wanted to see how he'd react."

"Why?"

"Because Norman is hiding something, and I want to know what it is."

"How would some cockamamy story about the payroll ship help you out there?" she whispered.

"We both know that Norman has devoted a great deal of time to studying Old Sam's life, true?"

"True." Rachel nodded.

"So one would expect that, in the course of reading up about Sam and the *Melrose* and blockade running in general, one would know that it's ridiculous to even suggest that the navy would have put even a portion of its payroll on one small ship, don't you think?"

"Well, certainly it's ridiculous."

"But Norman didn't say, 'Sam, that's absurd.' No, Norman said, 'Why, sure enough, Sam, I'll bet that's why all that gold was on the *Melrose*.' And he moved right past it. Now, why would he do that?"

"I'm sure you have a theory," Rachel said dryly.

"You betcha. I think that Norman knows exactly what Old Sam was up to, and I think it serves his purpose to have us think that Sam was doing something other than what he was."

"You're losing me here, Sam." Rachel paused on the step and looked up.

"I think my great-great-grandfather was involved in something that was not recorded in any history books. And I think that Norman knows exactly what that was. I think it's something that involves a great deal more than a trunk filled with gold coins."

"You think there's something else on board?"

Sam merely nodded. It was neither the time nor the place to tell her what he'd found.

"Why?"

"Norman has sunk a great deal of money into this operation, Rachel. You'd think he'd be happy to recover a bit of it. But he's giving the coins to the state of North Carolina. He's not keeping any of it. That alone would lead me to believe there's something of even greater valuable aboard the *Melrose.*"

"That and what else, Sam?"

"Slip on over to the *Shearwater* later, and I'll show you," Sam promised as he took her arm and led her down to dinner.

It was almost one in the morning when Sam heard it, not so much a splash as a *swoosh* from the ship's stern. His first thought had been that a night-feeding bird had swooped low and snagged a midnight snack. But then there was a rustle beyond the cabin, the mere suggestion of movement, and his senses went on full alert. Hitting the save button on the laptop computer that sat before him on the bed, he closed out his work and quietly shut the lid, sliding the laptop under the bed. Slowly he stood and turned out the light, keeping to the shadows as he approached the steps leading from his stateroom to the cabin above.

A dark figure entered, pausing in the lounge area for a very long moment before continuing toward the galley.

"Right there," Sam said. "You can stop right there."

A soft gasp, then a nervous giggle.

"Sam, it's me. Rachel."

"Rachel?"

"You said come over later and you'd show me something that you thought might be on the *Melrose.* So, I'm here."

As she spoke, she pulled off the cap that covered her head, and an avalanche of auburn curls spilled out. Even from across the room, Sam swore he could smell just a hint of orange.

His mouth went dry.

"You're lucky I didn't have a gun. Or a quick fist. You scared the devil out of me, Rachel."

"I'm sorry. I thought you were serious . . ." Thoroughly embarrassed, she turned as if to leave the same way she had entered.

"I was serious. I just didn't think you'd come."

"Well, I'm here." Rachel stood stock-still, as if debating something within herself. Then, with her right hand, she began to unzip the black wet suit, from the neck straight on down. When she stepped out of the wet suit, she was wearing a very brief white bikini.

"Ah . . . Rachel . . ." Sam managed to say as he stepped toward her. "Rachel . . ."

"If you're looking for the cooler of beer, I'm afraid I didn't bring one with me," she said nervously.

"I don't need anything but you, Rachel. You—just you—are every fantasy I ever had."

"Good," she said, her voice husky now. "I want to be your fantasy. I want to be your . . ."

He gathered her into his arms, and whatever else it was that Rachel had wanted to be was forgotten in a kiss that took her breath away, along with most of her senses. His hands traveled her shoulders to her elbows, then back again, before moving to her waist. Rachel wrapped her arms around his neck and pressed closer to him.

"Kiss me again," she told him, and Sam complied, over and over, his tongue tracing the outline of her lips, then plunging into her sweet mouth.

"Rachel," Sam whispered her name between kisses, pulling her closer, closer, the small pieces of cloth between him and her body tantalizing him. She eased herself back from his embrace, and for one terrible moment he thought she was going to leave. Then she raised her hands and began to unbutton his shirt. When his shirt stood open, she ran her hands up and down his chest, as he had run his up and down her back. Leaning back against the galley counter, she pulled him with her, raising her lips to his, and seeking his mouth greedily, her hands on either side of his face drawing him down to her. Sam groaned slightly as bare skin met bare skin, and knew there was no turning back.

"Rachel," he whispered into her hair, then sighed into the softness of her exquisite neck. "Rachel."

His hands sought the roundness of her hips as his lips traced a long slow line down the center of her throat to the slight depression at the base. When his tongue traced its perimeter, she moaned low in her throat and caressed the back of his head with her fingertips. She leaned back farther, as if offering herself to him, and he gladly took, his mouth easing onto the thin fabric covering one breast. He nipped at her gently with his teeth and felt her harden beneath the triangle of cotton that was all that stood between his mouth and her skin. She released the front closure with the fingers of one hand, and urged his mouth to feast on the flesh she had exposed for him.

Nothing had ever felt so good. Nothing had ever freed her to float above and outside herself the way Sam McGowan's mouth could. Every muscle in her body tensed, and still she flooded with sensation, every inch of her saturating with it and urging him on, to give her more, begging him to let her give him more of herself. His hands slid her bikini bottom off and lifted her from her feet. The next thing she knew, Rachel was being carried down one, two, three steps, and Sam was telling her to duck, he didn't want her knocking herself out on the door. And then cool sheets as Sam lowered her to his bed, and his body covered hers. Hands caressed and stroked, his and hers, mouths sought and found, tongues teased and tickled. Heat rose and fell and rose again, and she stretched beneath him, urging him to quench the fire that he had lit in her body and that now threatened to consume her. He sought to enter, and she opened to him, hastening him in, needing to feel him inside her, rocking with the ancient rhythm, and the rise and fall of the *Shearwater*, until rhythm became rapture and rapture took them home.

They lay in still darkness, the only sound the soft lapping of the ocean kissing the sides of the boat.

"Rachel," Sam said finally, the fingers of one hand making tiny delicate circles on the side of her neck.

"Ummm?"

"That was amazing," he whispered.

"Ummm," she murmured and snuggled a little closer.

"You know, I think you seduced me. I think you came here with the intention of having your way with me."

"Ummm. And it worked." Rachel smiled, and before he could ask, told him, "I never wanted anyone the way I wanted you, Sam. It just seemed right.

Everything just seemed right, the right night, the right time."

"Everything was right. It is right." Sam pulled her closer and kissed the tip of her nose. "Definitely the right night. Absolutely the right time."

"Well, I knew you were still awake." She shifted slightly, pulling the sheet around her. "Because I saw that your cabin lights were still on."

"I was working on my laptop." Sam sat up and pounded a few pillows to plump them.

"Were you mapping the cabin? I'm afraid I forgot to sketch out the site today," she told him.

"No. Actually, I was trying to do a little research on the Internet."

"Research on what?" Rachel sat up and wrapped the sheet around her. "And how could you hook into the Internet without a phone line?"

"There's a device that you can buy that allows you to hook your laptop into your cell phone. From there you dial a number and request a manual hookup. It's a simple procedure. I was looking for information on other ships that may have gone down around the same time, in the area where the *Melrose* sank."

"Did you find any?"

"Not yet. I did find a website that listed wrecks off the Carolina coast, but I didn't see any close to the *Melrose*. Of course, the *Melrose* didn't appear on the list, either."

"Why were you looking?"

"What?"

"Why were you looking for another ship in the same place?"

Sam sucked in one corner of his mouth as if considering something more than just her question.

Finally, Sam said, "Rachel, would you please pass me that bottle of aspirin on the table next to you?"

"Oh, now he gets a headache," Rachel quipped as she leaned over and picked up the large bottle, which she handed to him.

Sam straightened out a section of sheet between them before popping the lid off the bottle and letting the contents spread across the white sheet.

"Sam, what . . ." Rachel couldn't get the words out. She sat, drop-jawed, and stared at the pile of stones. "They can't be real, Sam. Tell me they're not real."

"I think they're real, Rachel."

"Where did they come from?"

"I found them in the basket. In our excitement over the trunk, we forgot to turn off the airlift, so it just kept on sucking up sand even after we started back up with the trunk. If you remember, once we got the sand and sediment out of the cabin and saw that trunk, Scully just dropped the airlift outside the cabin."

"I'm surprised that Renny didn't find them."

"I think Renny was occupied with the trunk, like everyone else was, when these came up through the tubes."

"You didn't mention it to Norman." It was a statement, not a question.

"No."

"Are you going to?"

"Eventually, I'm going to have to. It's his operation. He owns the rights to whatever we recover from the *Melrose*. But if they weren't on the *Melrose* . . ."

"That's why you need to know if another ship went down in the same location," Rachel said thoughtfully. "But if these stones were actually on another ship . . ."

". . . would they still belong to Norman? Truthfully, I'm not sure. It certainly wouldn't be the first time that cargo from one ship had been moved by currents, by creatures, closer to another wreck site. Determining if another wreck was right there would eliminate a lot of unsavory possibilities."

"Unsavory possibilities such as . . . ?"

"Well, these sure don't look like any bullets I've ever seen." He held up a large emerald for her inspection. "Let's just say it raises a lot of possibilities."

"Ah, all that talk about Old Sam being as much a raider as a blockade runner."

"That's my first guess. He could have stolen these from another ship and was on his way back to turn them over to someone."

"Or . . . ?"

"Or he could have gotten them in other ways, most of them illegal. On the black market, for example, or through pirating. Of course, if he'd stolen them outright, he'd have had to have a market to sell them." Sam returned the stones to the bottle and snapped the lid back on.

"Sam, you could be descended from a pirate." Rachel sighed dramatically. "And to think that I thought the *True Wind* would be the more exciting operation. Maybe next time we go ashore, we could find a eye patch for you to wear. I think pirates are so sexy, Sam."

"That information could come in handy someday." He nodded. "I'll definitely put one black patch on the shopping list."

"Do you really think that Old Sam could have been a pirate?" Rachel asked.

"I think it's a real possibility."

"Do you think that Norman knows this?"

Sam nodded. "I wouldn't be surprised to find out that Norman knows a lot about Old Sam that the rest of us don't know. And I do have the distinct feeling that Norman knows he's likely to find lots more besides cannon on the *Melrose*. I think that that's why he has Hugh filming every inch of sand and every moment of every dive."

"You think he doesn't trust us?"

"I think he doesn't trust anyone. And of course, me finding these and not immediately turning them over is one good reason why he shouldn't trust me."

"Well, you're not going to keep them, are you? You just said you were going to give them to Norman."

"Well, eventually. I'm just afraid if we give them to him now, they'll disappear and we'll never know where they came from."

"How important is that, though? If they were on the *Melrose*, they belong to Norman."

"And if they weren't on the *Melrose*, they may not."

"How likely do you think it is that you'll find out?"

"I don't know, Rachel. But if my great-great-grandfather was pirating, I want to know that. I think the family deserves to know."

"Well, how would you feel about that? All these years, you've been told you're descended from a hero. How would you feel if you found out that the hero was no hero?"

"I don't know that it would make a difference to me, Rachel. But it is important to know the truth."

"Even if it changes everything you know about your family?"

"Of course."

"Sam, just suppose that Old Sam was a pirate. Just suppose that he did this more than once . . ."

"He would have had other goodies, wouldn't he . . ."

"Remember Trinity's diary? Remember she said something about finding Sam's stash . . . his bounty?"

"That could explain why he risked going back to Eden's End. Maybe he went back to hide what he stole."

"If that's true, I wonder what happened to it all . . ."

"Maybe Trinity found it and sold it to keep the plantation running after the war."

"Or maybe we're really off base and Sam came by these honestly and was taking them someplace to sell on behalf of the Confederacy," Rachel suggested. "That's as likely a scenario."

"Oh, somehow it just doesn't feel right, though. Why would he have been stashing stuff at Eden's End—if in fact that was what he was doing—if it was intended for the government?" Sam shook his head. "I can't see Old Sam going to all that trouble unless he personally was going to profit from it. I just don't, Rachel. Nothing that I know of him would lead me to believe that Sam McGowan was a virtuous or noble man, or that he was that loyal to any cause other than himself."

"I wonder if we'll ever find out the truth," Rachel mused. "Was Sam McGowan a hero or a pirate?"

Sam grinned and pulled her to him, sheet and all.

"Which do you want him to be?" he asked.

"Oh, a hero. Every woman wants a hero, Sam," she whispered.

"Then a hero Sam will be," Sam promised.

"Then again," she said as his mouth covered hers, "pirates do have a certain appeal . . ."

16

"RACHEL, WAKE UP." Sam gently stroked the shoulder of the sleeping form that nestled, curled like a child, under the flannel blanket.

"Ummm," the form murmured.

"Come up on the flybridge and watch the sun come up with me."

"Ummm." The form snuggled deeper into the pillow.

"Come on, Rach. I'll even let you make the coffee."

"Hmmm?" Rachel's eyes flew open. "What did you say?"

"I said I'd even let you—"

"No. About the sun coming up . . ."

"That usually happens at this hour of the day."

"Dawn? It's dawn?" Pulling at the sheet, Rachel gathered the cloth around her in a panic. "I have to get back to the *Annie G*. Before anyone gets up." She paused at the side of the bed. "Too late. They're up. Of course they're up. Everyone's up."

"And that's a problem because . . ." Sam, already dressed, folded his arms across his chest and looked amused.

"It's a problem because if any of them"—she pointed to the *Annie G.*—"see me coming back there from here, they'll know that I . . . that we . . ." She looked at him plaintively. "You could give me a little help here, you know."

"You don't want anyone to know that you slept here last night."

"Yes. It would not be a good thing, Sam."

"So you need to get back over there without anyone seeing you."

"Right." She tightened the sheet around her shoulders. "I'm supposed to be leading this operation. I just happen to be the only woman aboard. I don't think it's a good idea to flaunt that I've slept with the archaeologist, Sam."

"And will again, no doubt."

"Sam . . ."

"Okay. You're right. It just wouldn't be a good thing."

"It wouldn't be professional, Sam. And it would be hell for my reputation."

"I'm not arguing with you, Rachel. So, the problem is how does Rachel get from the *Shearwater* to the *Annie G.* without detection?"

"Underwater." Her eyes brightened. "I'll swim underwater to the diving platform, then just act like I had gone for a morning swim. Do you think that would work?"

"Yes, it probably would. I'm not sure I like the

idea of you being underwater alone, though." Sam frowned.

"I'll be fine." She glanced around the cabin floor.

"I guess you're looking for these." Sam held up the top and bottom of her bikini.

Rachel blushed furiously.

"Yes," she muttered, reaching for them.

"You don't need to be embarrassed, Rachel." Sam stepped toward her, his arms reaching to embrace her.

"It's not the sort of thing I do, as a general rule," she told him.

"I've no doubt about that." Sam's fingers worked to untangle the mass of curls that twisted down her back. "But I'm glad that you broke the rule this time, Rachel. And with any luck, you'll break it again, over and over, before this job is through."

Sam kissed the side of her face, then her temples, and said, "Now let's get you dressed and back onto the *Annie G.* before anyone misses you."

Still clutching the sheet around her, Rachel disappeared into the bathroom, bikini in hand, to dress, unaware that she'd already been missed, and that someone on the *Annie G.* knew exactly where she was, and even now, watched for her return.

Just before seven, Rachel quietly raised herself from the water and eased onto the diving platform on the back of the *Annie G.* She pulled off her fins, and shook her hair out of the cap. She wanted her toothbrush. She wanted her coffee. But voices from overhead told her that Hugh and Scully were about to join her, and there was no way that she could do anything at that moment other than pretend to be strapping her fins on and preparing to dive.

"Oh. Rachel. There you are," Hugh said as he hopped off the ladder. "Missed you at breakfast."

"I overslept this morning," she said without looking up, "so I decided to skip breakfast and just get ready to dive. I don't want to hold us up."

"Won't you get hungry?"

"I assure you I'll make up for it at lunch." She smiled and tried to ignore the fact that her stomach was already protesting the meal she'd missed.

"So, what do you think we'll find today?" Hugh asked anxiously. "More gold?"

"I doubt it. I doubt if there was more than one paymaster on the *Melrose*. No, I think we've had our excitement this time around. Now it'll be guns and ammo, I'm afraid."

"It sure was a thrill to see that lid flop open and all those coins, though." Hugh sighed.

"It sure was." Rachel nodded, pretending not to notice that Sam was swimming toward them leisurely.

"Morning, professor." Hugh called to Sam.

"Good morning, everyone." Sam tred water ten feet off the stern. "Looks like you're all just about ready."

"I'll just be a minute, Sam," Rachel said casually. "I just need to get my tank on."

"Take your time. The water's great this morning, by the way."

"Oh, good," Hugh said. "I hate getting into the cold water first thing in the morning."

"So do I," Rachel said.

"Well, you must have already been in," Hugh said as he strapped into his equipment, "since your suit is wet."

"I dropped one of my fins and had to go in after it," she told him, willing herself not to look at Sam, lest she grin and give herself away.

"Everyone ready down there?" Norman called from the top of the ladder as Turk, the last member of the team, came down the steps. "Rachel. There you are. We missed you at breakfast. Are you feeling well?"

"Yes. I'm fine. I just overslept."

"Oh, good. Good. Where will you be working today?"

"Pretty much the same area, don't you think, Sam?"

"Yes." He nodded. "There's a lot to remove from the office, Norman. I'd love to be able to get that desk out intact, but I'm afraid the wood is too porous to withstand a move. Besides, I don't think it will fit through the doorway, do you, Rachel?"

"No, it's unlikely. We should take down a few baskets to send up whatever's in the desk drawers, though."

"I'll have those dropped down to you," Norman told her. "Aren't you taking the airlift?"

"Probably not for another day or two," Rachel raised one hand to shield her eyes from the sun as she looked up. "We'll finish in the office first."

"Well, why not have Turk and Scully fill the baskets and send them up while you and Sam work the airlift. I'm only planning on being here through this afternoon. I'll be going back to Eden's End this evening. If there's anything wonderful to be found down there, I'd love to be here when it's raised."

"Sure, Norman," Sam said before Rachel could respond. "Send the airlift down and we'll try to finish clearing off the deck before you leave."

"Wonderful!"

For a moment, Rachel thought that Norman was going to clap his hands in excitement. She slid into the water and swam toward Sam.

"What are you doing?" she whispered when she got within two feet of him. "Why would we be working two sites at the same time?"

"Because if there is something here, I'd be interested in watching Norman's face when we bring it up." Sam grinned.

"Plus, with Turk and Scully occupied with the office, we'll just take our time sifting through the sand before it goes up the tube. I'll just turn it on low speed so that we can see what's going up the tube before it's sucked up. I want everything documented, Rachel. I don't want anything to disappear."

"You're forgetting about Big Brother." Rachel nodded toward the photographer, who had entered the water.

"We'll worry about Hugh later."

"Sam, Rachel, come get sections of hose and we'll start on down," Scully called to them.

"We're on our way." She turned her back on Sam and swam to the back of the boat, arms outstretched to grab the piece of tubing that was held out to her. "Let's get the equipment down and get busy."

"Follow me?" Rachel asked Sam as she prepared to dive.

"Anywhere," he whispered. "I'll follow you anywhere . . ."

She laughed softly, then rolled and sank beneath the water, following the anchor line to the wreck below.

Setting the airlift on low, Sam and Rachel both kneeled in the sand, keeping a careful eye on that which was being slowly churned up to pass into the end of the hose. Sand dollars, small shells, pebbles, but little else of note. Working their way down toward the stern, they cleared off most of the deck while Turk and Scully emptied the office of its movable contents. Sam and Rachel watched anxiously as basket after basket was taken to the top. Rachel was beginning to think that she and Sam should have split up this session, with one of them working in the cabin while the other worked the airlift.

"Well?" Norman asked when they finally surfaced several hours later.

"Nothing today," Sam told him. "What did Turk and Scully bring up?"

"The ship's manifest—which gratefully was in a metal box—an inkwell, several bottles. The occupant of this office fancied whiskey, it would appear," Norman told them. "Interesting items, but nothing that can compare with yesterday's findings."

"Well, that happens," Rachel reminded him as she came aboard, "especially on wrecks like this one. I wouldn't look for much else but guns from now on."

"Except for the cannon, I have yet to see any weapons."

"As soon as we get into the hold of the ship, you'll see plenty. At least, that's my guess."

"How long before you get into the Captain's quarters?" Norman asked.

"Another day or so," Sam told him, "depending on how much sand and muck are below deck. Now, let's see what Scully and Turk brought up."

Rachel knelt next to Renny on the deck, where he sat sorting the objects into categories.

"Here are pens, and here are papers," he told her. "The papers were in a box, so you can still read them."

Rachel leaned forward.

"So you can. Look, Renny, this is a list of the men on board." She began to count. "There were forty-two men on board the *Melrose*," she said, then repeated thoughtfully, "Forty-two."

"Is that a lot? Renny asked as he raised an amber-colored bottle and dried it carefully with a towel.

"Not for a ship like the *Melrose*. I would have expected there to have been more."

"Maybe some of them went home," Renny said. "Maybe they didn't like being on the water all the time."

"Do you like being on the water all the time?" she asked, thinking that perhaps Renny was projecting his own discontent onto those sailors long dead.

"Yes. I like it a lot. I didn't used to. But now that we're finding pirate treasure, I do like it. And I like it that I can row around in the dinghy. Norman said I have to wear a life thing, though."

"A life preserver, yes, that's important," she said as she looked through the odd pieces of porcelain that were being unloaded from a basket. "Aren't these pretty dishes? The pattern looks almost mod-

ern," she said of the blue and white plates that were
being laid out upon the deck.

"Sam . . . ?" She turned around to see where Sam
had gone, and found him, not unexpectedly, at the
basket into which the airlift had deposited its contents.

"Renny, I'll be right back," she told him. "Maybe
you can get the rest of the dishes cleaned up a bit
for Hugh, so that he can photograph them."

"Okay." Renny nodded enthusiastically.

"What did you find?" Rachel asked as she walked
up behind Sam. Only sheer willpower kept her from
slipping her arms around his waist and leaning her
head against his back. Later, maybe, if she could
slip out . . .

"Nothing, really. Lots of sand dollars, some pretty
shells, certainly nothing like yesterday's haul."

"That's too bad. They were sure pretty." She
smiled. "There was a ruby that would make a pretty
ring. I love rubies. I am a July baby, you know."

"Well, there sure were lots of pretty stones. I'm
wondering if there will be more."

"I think I'm going to slip on down to my cabin
and get cleaned up," she told him. "I never did get
to brush my teeth this morning, I haven't been able
to brush my hair, and I can't unzip my wet suit because I'm only wearing a bikini."

Sam laughed. "That's what you get for boarding
vessels scantily clad in the middle of the night." He
grinned. "I don't suppose it was enough to prevent
you from doing it again."

"No." She grinned back at him. "I don't suppose
it was."

*   *   *

And it wasn't, not that night, nor the next, nor the one after that.

"I'm going to have to give Norman a bit of bad news tomorrow," Sam told her several nights later as they lay in his stateroom, listening to the gentle lapping of the tide.

"What news could be worse than the news we've been giving him every day? 'Sorry, Norm, nothing but guns and ammo again today.'"

"He's getting a bit tired of hearing that, no doubt. But that's all there's been, so far, anyway. And anyone else wouldn't be surprised, you know. The *Melrose* was a gun runner, after all."

"Maybe he'll be happier once we get into Old Sam's cabin." Rachel stretched her arms and legs as far as they would go, feeling not a little like a big, lazy cat.

"It will be interesting to see what's in there, won't it? It's sort of tantalizing, knowing we're so close to Old Sam's personal things."

"So what's the bad news?"

"I'm going to have to leave for a few days. It's my mother's sixtieth birthday, and life will not be worth living if I miss her party."

"How long do you think you'll be gone?"

"Maybe three days."

"What do you suppose Norman will say when you tell him?"

"What can he say? I have to be there. I promised my father. And besides, other than the two days following the storm, this crew has worked nonstop. They're due for some time off."

Sam nuzzled the side of her face and said, "I was wondering if maybe you'd want to come with me."

"To your parents' home?" She raised both eyebrows.

"Yes."

"Where do they live?"

"St. Swithin's Island, off the coast of South Carolina, about a hundred and fifty miles down."

"Do you think your parents would mind a guest? I mean, wouldn't I be staying there . . . ?"

"Yes. Everyone will be staying there. I expect there will be quite a houseful."

Rachel lay back on the pillow and considered this. Sam was asking to take her home with him. How long had it been since a man had offered to do that?

Sophomore year in college. Darren Crane. Massapequa, Long Island. That's how long ago, she reminded herself. And that time it had barely mattered. This time, it did. More than she'd have ever anticipated. It mattered.

"I'd love to go home with you, Sam, if you think it will be all right with your parents. And assuming that Norman consents."

"Oh, it'll be fine with my parents. Of course, between now and then, I should probably prepare you to meet them, but we still have a few days for that. Right now, I think we could both do with a little sleep." Sam leaned across her and turned out the light.

"In a while, Sam," Rachel told him as she reached for him in the dark. "In a while . . ."

*   *   *

After two more days of watching nothing but rusty cannon and old muskets and rifles emerge from the deep, Norman threw up his hands and returned to Eden's End. While not happy about Sam's plan to take a few days off, Norman finally consented to giving everyone a three-day weekend, thinking that perhaps a few days away from the wreck would result in some reward for him when the crew resumed.

It was therefore Norman's luck to be inland when the Captain's cabin was located after two days of sorting through the contents of the the ship's apothecary. Sam fully anticipated that Norman would promptly return to the *Annie G.* and would suspend the previously granted holiday. Norman, not generally known for his patience, surprised everyone by announcing that he had several appointments that he could not change, and would close down the site two days earlier than planned, thereby suspending diving until the following week, when he could be on hand and Sam and Rachel would be back.

"Well, what do you think of that?" Sam mused as he and Rachel sat in the moonlight, dangling their feet off the back of the *Annie G.* "We have five whole days off."

"I can't remember the last time I had five whole days off in a row."

"Neither can I. Let's plan something special."

"We are doing something special. We're going to your parents'," Rachel reminded him.

"Something else special."

"Like what?"

"Like stopping in Wilmington and having a great dinner."

"Actually, I could do with a little shopping. I need to pick up shampoo, toothpaste, that sort of thing. Plus I've run out of books."

"What do you read?"

"Biographies, mysteries, romance . . . you name it."

"Have you read this?" Sam reached under the bed and pulled out a thick biography—unauthorized—of a well-known statesman.

"Yes. I was fascinated. Who knew that he had been involved with the black market in Eastern Europe?"

"Well, now, he's denied all that."

"Well, of course he denied it. Why would he admit to it? I was so disappointed. I'd always admired him," Rachel said. "Though it does make a great scandal, if it's true."

"I think it's true," Sam told her. "But how about this one?" He handed her a book with a dark cover adorned with a hawk just about to land on the branch of a tree.

"Kirkland Turner's new book." She reached for it. "No, I haven't read this one. Is it good?"

"Excellent. Kept me turning those pages. It's a sequel to a book he did a few years ago, but that one's out of print, so I haven't been able to find it."

"Oh, I have that one. I'll call my aunt's housekeeper and ask her to mail it to . . . oh. Where would she mail it?" Rachel frowned.

"She could mail it to my parents. That would be great. I've looked for that book for quite some time. Thank you."

"I think I'll run up and grab a bottle of water. Can I bring you one?"

"Sure, thanks."

Sam watched Rachel climb the steps to the upper deck, and his heart did a back flip inside his chest. It had never occurred to him that a man like him, who spent much of his life on the sea, would find a woman like Rachel. Unbelievable that she, too, spent so much of her time on or under the water. It was, Sam figured, a match made in heaven. Or, at the very least, at sixty-five feet down.

"Sam, could you take a few minutes and look at some photos for me?" Hugh appeared at the edge of the deck. "There's something I think you should see."

"Sure." Sam hopped up. "What do you have?"

"I don't know. These are the pictures I took today. See, here, it looks like a big shadow." Hugh held out the photos as if worried that the big shadow might bite.

Sam sat in one of the deck chairs, studying the photos.

"There definitely was something overhead when you shot these. Something very big." Sam nodded and handed the photos back.

"Here, catch," Rachel told Sam as she joined them, flipping him a bottle of spring water.

"Rachel, these are photos that I took during the dive today. There's a big shadow . . ." Hugh passed the pictures to Rachel.

"Oh, I see it, right there. Ummm, that's big, whatever it was."

"Rachel, doesn't it bother you to know that there was something really big down there with you today?"

"No." She shrugged. "Since it didn't bother us then, it's not going to bother me now."

"Well, what if it's down there again tomorrow?"

"Then we'll deal with it tomorrow."

"Don't you even care that it was there? Or that you don't know what it was?"

"Not particularly. It's probably gone now. But if you're concerned, maybe we should watch the videotape and see if it shows up on film."

"Good idea. Come on down below. There's a TV in the galley. We can run it there." Hugh led the way.

"I can't remember the last time I watched TV," Rachel said. "A little break in the routine might be fun."

"I thought you liked our routine," Sam whispered as they followed down the steps.

"I do," she replied. "But a little TV now and again never hurt anyone."

"Oh, my mother will definitely like you." Sam laughed.

"What's that supposed to mean?"

"My parents have warred over the television for as long as I can remember. When my dad was home, he wouldn't permit us to watch. He said it was unworthy of our time and did little but promote the worst in popular culture. My mother, on the other hand, sees television as a natural by-product of our technological society and adores it because it reflects popular culture."

"Your father the archaeologist and your mother the anthropologist."

"Right. She'll see you as an ally. He'll see you as

culturally depraved. We'll have a great weekend," Sam said cheerfully.

"Sure sounds like my idea of a good time," Rachel muttered as she took a cushioned seat in the comfortable galley.

"Oh, there you guys are." Hugh slid the tape into the VCR built into the TV and pushed the play button.

For several long minutes, there was little to be seen except the activity on the wreck. At the left of the screen, several divers struggled to wrap cables around a cannon to haul it up with the on-deck winch.

"That's kind of eerie," Sam said, "all vision, hardly any sound."

Rachel leaned back and pulled her feet up under her. "The wreck looks so great on film, doesn't it? Just like in the movies."

Sam grinned. "Rachel, we are in the movies. There you are, right there, in the middle of the screen. What were you doing?"

"I dropped my knife. I'd taken it out to pick at the encrustation on a pile of shot and I dropped it." She leaned back farther into the cushions and covered a yawn with her hand.

Sam leaned forward, closer to the screen, as if studying something.

"There!" Hugh jumped up and went to the TV. "There's the shadow!"

"Oh, I think it's a Manta ray," Rachel told him. "See how almost round the shape is? Looks like a big sucker, too. What do you think, Sam?"

"What? Oh. A Manta. Possibly. Hugh, run that section over again and we'll take another look." "Yes, back it up to right . . . there. There. Stop it for a second."

Sam stared at the TV as if memorizing the frame.

"Well?" Hugh asked nervously. "Is it a Manta?"

"I think it could be." Sam nodded. "As Rachel said, it's large and sort of rounded—I don't know anything else under the sea that is round like that."

"I can't believe I was underwater with a Manta." Hugh shook his head.

"Hugh, I've never known one to be dangerous," Sam told him. "And this one—if that's what it was— must have somehow drifted over from the Gulf Stream. You don't generally see them in these slightly cooler waters. But they're really nothing to worry about. Some will even let you pet them, though their underside is pretty rough, sort of like sandpaper. Rachel, did you ever hitch a ride on a Manta?"

Sam turned to find her sound asleep amid the cushions.

"Rach, wake up," he said softly. "I think you should turn in," he whispered.

"Hmmm?" she murmured.

"I said I think it's your bedtime."

Rachel stretched her arms over her head, a gesture Sam had come to know well. "I'll walk you to your cabin." Sam took her arm. "From the looks of you, I'm not so sure you'll make it down the steps alone."

"Thanks, Sam. Good night, Hugh." Rachel stumbled to her feet and headed for the hallway on Sam's arm. "But you can't come in, Sam, not into my cabin. It would not be a smart thing to do."

"You're right. I'm not coming in. I'm going back to the *Shearwater* where I will spend the night dreaming of you."

"Will you, Sam?" Rachel asked when they reached her cabin. "Will you dream about me?"

"Absolutely." Sam lowered his mouth and touched her lips softly with his own. "Now get some sleep. We'll dive a little early tomorrow since we won't be going back down for five days."

"Okay, Sam." Rachel nodded, her eyes at half-mast. "I'll see you in the morning. Sweet dreams."

Sam softly closed the door behind her, waiting until he heard the click of the lock.

"Sweet dreams, Rachel," he whispered before he walked away.

17

❧

THE COOL, silken blue of the ocean surrounded her, and for forty-five minutes Rachel knelt in the sand, picking at a solid lump of concreceous material. If they'd been in the Florida Keys, where Spanish ships had gone down three or four hundred years ago, the odds would have been good that the deposits hid a pile of silver or pewter chargers or a large stash of silver coins. Here, on the *Melrose*, it was just as likely to be iron shot or a pewter pitcher.

Having stuck faithfully to her vow to keep an eye on Hugh, she glanced up to find him hovering over the wreck in his usual spot, camera running, recording the progress of the divers. Scully and Turk were in the process of removing the remaining items from the ship's apothecary. Already that day they'd recovered a store of small medicine bottles and a mortar and pestle bearing the name of a pharmacy in the English port where the ship had been built. They'd found several cases of wine and several of ale and some remarkable crystal goblets, though it was anyone's guess why they were in the apothecary and not in the galley.

Rachel searched for Sam and found him near the bottom, working the airlift one last time before they took a few days off. She started toward him when the light from overhead was shut out. Turning upward, she saw the Manta ray, fifteen or sixteen feet across, as it swam twenty feet over Hugh's head. Using her flashlight to get Hugh's attention, she gestured to him—*Look!*—pointing above and behind him.

She signaled to Sam, who turned off the airlift and turned to watch. The creature was graceful for one so huge, and floated, like a dancer, to a silent symphony. Rachel sped upward, to get a better look. Hugh, horrified, followed her with the camera. Rachel came up under the ray, and paused as if asking permission, and when the ray swooped down lightly, Rachel raised her hands and stroked its rough underside gently, so as to neither frighten the creature nor abrade her hands. When the animal appeared to have satisfied its curiosity as well as its need for a tummy rub, it swept off as silently as it had come. A grinning Rachel turned to Hugh, who was visibly shaking in his fins.

She swam toward him, until she got close enough to see that his eyes were almost rolling around in his head. She patted him reassuringly on the back several times to let him know that it was all right, but he just continued to shake his head, as if not believing what he'd just seen. Rachel swam past him till she neared Sam, who grinned, gave up the thumbs-up, and turned the airlift back on.

Later, when they surfaced, Hugh said, "Damn! I never saw anybody do anything like that. Are you crazy, Rachel? A thing that big could have eaten you alive."

"They don't eat people, Hugh." She laughed. "And if I hadn't done it many times before, I probably wouldn't have done it today. Manta rays are really sweet creatures, Hugh, they're gentle and playful. You should see the ones off Socorro, south of Baja. They make this one look like a guppy."

Hugh made a sort of croaking sound, unconvinced that so giant a creature would possess so benign a nature.

"Rachel's right, Hugh. The Mantas are no threat. Nice going, Rach. She was a beauty." Sam had surfaced several feet behind them. He paused, then said to Rachel, "I'm going to make a stop at the *Shearwater*. I want to pick up my sketches from yesterday and bring them over so we can work on them this afternoon, then we won't have to think about them for the next few days while we're away."

"Okay." Rachel nodded. "I think I'd like to get a shower and change now, anyway. I'll meet you in the galley. If we ask him nicely, maybe Hugh will let us watch today's video."

"You're nuts, Rachel," Hugh grumbled as he scrambled to get out of the water, watching fitfully, no doubt, to make sure that the Manta was long gone. "You're really nuts."

Rachel laughed and pulled herself aboard the *Annie G.*

*   *   *

"You realize that you really freaked Hugh out yesterday," Sam said as he caught the nylon travel bag that Rachel tossed into the dinghy the next morning before stepping into it herself from the back of the *Annie G.*

"He'll get over it," she replied. "Sam, I feel so . . . *blatant.*"

"So blatantly what?" he asked.

"Just so blatantly obvious that we're going someplace together." She sat in the dingy and crossed her arms over her chest, clearly not happy over this realization. "Everyone on the *Annie G.* knows I'm going with you to your parents' for three days."

"Rach, did you really think no one would notice that we . . ." He paused, searching for the right words. ". . . have feelings for each other? We do have feelings for each other, don't we?"

She nodded slowly. She hadn't wanted to acknowledge what she felt for Sam, hadn't wanted to analyze it or put a name to it. Once she named it, she'd have to deal with it, and that was the last thing she wanted to do. It was enough to admit that there were feelings there. She wasn't entirely sure that she wanted to know how deeply they went or what they might mean or where they might lead.

"Yes," she told him softly. "I believe we do."

"Well, when people have feelings for each other, they spend time together, go places together." The muscles in Sam's arms and shoulders rippled as he rowed back to the *Shearwater.* "Sometimes they look at each other. A lot. Sometimes they smile when they look at each other. It happens all the time, Rachel. Now, me, I've found myself smiling a lot these past few weeks. Grinning for no good reason whatsoever. And I have to believe it's a good thing."

He brought the dinghy up behind the *Shearwater*.

"And you may not be aware of it, but you smile a lot more, too. It's been very, very nice, Rachel. You're a beautiful woman, but when you smile, the heavens open up."

Rachel threw her bag on the back of the *Shearwater* without comment. Sam remained in the dinghy for a long moment before getting out.

"That was a compliment, Rachel," he told her as he dragged the dinghy onto the diving platform.

"Thank you." She stood on the deck with her hands in the pockets of her white shorts. "Can I help you with the dinghy?"

"No. Thank you." He turned his back on her and proceeded to tie the dinghy to the side of the boat. "Rachel, sometimes you confuse me. A lesser man than I might not be willing to give you the benefit of the doubt and might think you are poorly mannered. I happen to know better. I know, for example, that you know when to say 'please' and 'thank you.' So, while I know better than to think that you're flatout rude, I am mystified that you tend to dismiss a compliment as if you didn't hear it."

"I just don't think of myself as . . . beautiful." She looked uncomfortable just having the word come out of her mouth.

"Why not?" He stood on the platform right in front of her so that she could not avoid looking at him. "Hasn't anyone ever told you how beautiful you are?"

She shook her head no.

"Well, that's a crime that should be punishable by something dire." He shook his head. "I guess I'll just have to make it a point to tell you every day until you start to believe it. And you should believe it, Rachel, because it's true. I know a beautiful woman when I see one."

Rachel looked awkward, as if she was about to cry. "Thank you, Sam. That's the sweetest thing anyone has ever said to me."

"You'll find I am a very sweet guy, Rachel," Sam told her as he hauled up the anchor. "Now, how does a stop in Wilmington this afternoon sound?"

"That would be great. I'd like that."

"Awk! I'm the bear! I'm a teddy bear!" H.D. called from his perch in the lounge.

"Does your sister listen to anything besides Elvis?" Rachel asked.

"Sure. Fats Domino. Chuck Berry. Buddy Holly."

"Fifties rock." Rachel nodded. "Jared is very heavy into classic rock, too."

"No, you misunderstand. Daria is stuck totally in another era. Her idea of *modern* rock is Cream. Traffic. The Drifters."

Rachel smiled, and the tension abated just a little.

"See, you're doing it again, Rachel," Sam told her as he started the cruiser's engines. "You're smiling in spite of yourself."

"Should I make some coffee?" she asked as if she hadn't heard.

"Okay."

Rachel slipped past him and went into the galley. Sam leaned back into his seat at the helm and not for the first time that week, pondered the situation.

At times—like now—Rachel seemed to make an effort to distance herself from him. Sam didn't like it, and was at a loss to explain it. At night, in Sam's bed, Rachel was passionate and sweet and, yes, loving. Once up on deck, however, a barrier seemed to come between them, one Sam could not name and could not explain.

No, Sam didn't like it at all.

Maybe over the next few days he'd figure out what caused it. Then maybe he could begin to tear it down. It hadn't taken Sam long to realize that Rachel was the perfect woman for him. Unfortunately, he wasn't sure that Rachel realized it. His goal for the week was to make it as obvious to her as it was to him. Feeling better, having an agenda if not a specific game plan, Sam began to whistle.

"Here's your coffee." Rachel appeared in the doorway. "We'll need to pick up some cream when we're in Wilmington, though. I hate this powdered stuff."

"Thanks." He gave her his biggest, most confident smile. "Here, come sit with me."

Sam leaned back to give Rachel room to pass in front of him and sit next to him on the bench.

"Sam, I've been thinking. I'm not sure that it was a good idea to leave the wreck . . ."

"Stop right there," he told her. "We're not talking about work this weekend."

"We're not?" She raised a skeptical eyebrow.

"No. We are not," he said firmly. "We're on a little vacation, you and I, and we're not going to talk about Norman or the *Melrose* or anything else related to that wreck. We're only going to talk about important things."

"Like what?"

"Like us."

"Us?"

"Us. You and me. Sam and Rachel." He nodded. "Us."

"What about us?" She eyed him curiously.

"Whatever feels right. Let's start with something nonthreatening, like what we're going to do while we're in Wilmington."

"Okay."

"What would you like to do?"

"Well, I told you I'd like to do a little shopping at the drugstore and the bookstore."

"And we'll have to make a stop at the grocery store," he added. "You know, we never have time to eat together in the morning. Over the next few days we will. Do you like breakfast cereal, or are you an eggs and toast woman?"

"Cereal, definitely. Something crunchy. With strawberries."

"Okay. Let's make a list. Look inside that compartment next to your elbow, there should be paper and a pen in there . . ."

Rachel rooted through the pile of maps until she found the unlined pad and a pen.

"Okay," Sam said. "Put cream, strawberries, and crunchy cereal on the list. And bottled water. I see you drink that a lot. And we should get some snacky thing. What do you like to snack on?"

"Popcorn. Hershey's Kisses. Honey-roasted cashews."

"Three of my favorite things. Add those." Sam nodded. "Now, we won't need any dinner stuff 'cause we'll eat out tonight, and we should reach the island by noon tomorrow."

"What's it like?" Rachel asked.

"St. Swithin's Island? Just like most of the other coastal islands. Some marsh, some swamp. Lots of beach."

"Are there other houses there?"

"Oh sure. There's a small village. My parents' house is the last house in town, right this side of the dunes."

"Isn't that precarious, having a house so close to the ocean?"

"Not as bad as you might think. For one thing, it's on the protected side of the island, and for another, the dunes are quite high there. Which is not to say that they haven't weathered a few storms over the years."

"You said they're retired, both of your parents."

"Yes. Officially, though you'd never know it. My dad is writing a book about his travels and my mother is working on a collection of nonfiction vignettes written by women from different cultures that she has collected over the years in her own travels."

"Is there a theme?"

"Yes. The theme is love."

"Love?" she asked warily. "That doesn't sound very scholarly."

"Au contraire, Ms. Chandler. My mother firmly believes that love, as it affects the daily lives of women in various cultures, is a driving force in the world today. Love between spouses, parents and children, siblings, friends, lovers . . ." He paused to look at her, then asked, "Rachel, haven't you ever been in love?"

"No."

Sam thought that perhaps her answer came too quickly, as did the sip from the coffee cup that followed it.

"Never?"

"Never that mattered."

"Rachel, love always matters. Let's leave romantic love aside for a moment, surely you love your father, your brother . . ."

"Yes, of course."

"Who else?"

"Who else do I love?" She was beginning to look annoyed.

"Yes."

"I love my Aunt Bess. She raised me. And my friend, Jill, though we only see each other once a year."

"You only see your friend once a year? Why?"

"Because she lives in London. We get together and go someplace to dive once a year."

"Who else?"

"No one else."

"None?"

She shook her head.

"How about your family?"

"We talked about my family. My father. My brother. My aunt. That's it."

"No cousins? Aunts and uncles, grandparents?"

"Nope. My grandparents are all dead. My father was an only child. And I don't really know any of my mother's family, except for Aunt Bess."

"Why not?"

"I guess because I never knew my mother."

"Rachel, I'm so sorry . . ."

She smiled, thin-lipped and terse.

"I think I'll have some more coffee." Rachel rose. "Want some?"

"Don't run, Rachel," he said softly, grabbing her arm.

"I'm not comfortable talking about myself, Sam. I never have been."

"I'm sorry, Rach. It's just natural when two people are involved that they talk about themselves, their families, things that matter to them. It's one of the ways you get to know another person."

"I know that, Sam. I am not totally inept, socially."

"No, you're not inept. But you are the most guarded person I've ever known."

"I think I'll get that coffee now. Excuse me."

Sam stood and let her pass.

When she returned, she leaned against the door-jamb and said, "I feel like I should be sketching or something. Making a list of the artifacts we brought up this week."

"We weren't going to talk about the *Melrose*, remember? We're on vacation, brief though it will be."

"Vacation is a relatively unfamiliar term to me."

"When was your last?"

"A few months ago. Jill and I took our diving vacation in Curaçao."

"When was the last nondiving vacation you took?"

"I don't remember that I ever took one where diving wasn't the focus."

"Well, how 'bout as a kid, where did you used to go?"

"We didn't go on family vacations, Sam. My mother was almost always someplace else. My father's idea of a vacation was taking Jared with him for the summer on whatever adventure he was on at the time. I stayed home with Aunt Bess and learned how to knit." Tears formed in the corners of her eyes, but she would not permit them to fall.

"Camp?" he asked.

Rachel shook her head. "My aunt was always afraid that something would happen to me. I'd get hurt. I'd catch something from the other kids. I'd get poison ivy. I'd drown. The first few times I talked Jared into getting Dad to let me come along on the boat my aunt went to church every day I was gone. Sometimes I think it's almost a blessing for her that she's been essentially senile for the past ten years— she's in her late eighties now—and doesn't realize what I do for a living."

He reached out and drew her to him. With one hand he steered the boat, with the other he held her, stroking her arm and the side of her face.

"I'm sorry," he whispered. "I'm so sorry."

"I don't mean to sound like I was brought up terribly. My aunt was kind enough in her own way, and she loved me—loves me—very much. I think she was afraid for me. Maybe she was afraid that if something happened to me, my father would take Jared and me away. I didn't realize it when I was younger, but I know now that Jared and I were all she had. I think she thought she was protecting us."

"That's very mature of you to understand that."

"It's what's fair. And my father . . ." Rachel swallowed hard. "It just never occurred to my father to include me. In anything. He would come home after being away for a few weeks or months, and at the dinner table, he'd address Jared when he talked about where he had been and what he had found. As if I wouldn't be interested. As if I didn't matter."

"Rach . . ."

"Oh, I know that I mattered, Sam. My father just didn't know how to show it or what to do with me. He lived on board ship with almost all men for most of the year, and he'd come home and there I'd be, this cute little girl all dressed in some fluffy little dress." She sighed heavily. "My aunt loved fluffy little dresses. She still does. I always looked like the poster child for those little girl beauty pageants."

"Hair all curled?" he asked.

"Just like Shirley Temple." She nodded sadly. "And crinolines. My skirts would be out to here."

"Your aunt probably thought you liked it."

"I did like it. At least, when I was four and five years old, I liked it. I loved the way the skirts swished and swirled when I turned around real fast in them. I loved my shiny black patent leather Mary Janes . . . they're shoes, in case you didn't know."

"I didn't. My sisters wore mostly sneakers. Not much call for crinolines and fancy dresses where we went."

"Your parents really took you everyplace with them?"

"Damn near. There were occasions when their schedules conflicted, and then they'd have to work it out. Sometimes Jack and I went with my dad, the girls with my mom. There were some rare times when we kids all stayed home and our grandparents would stay with us. But yes, for the most part, we were always together."

"What did you do about school?"

"We had a tutor, if we were going into someplace remote. But our parents didn't travel twelve months out of every year, you know, so sometimes we went to regular school, too."

"That must have been so much fun." She leaned back against him. "You must have so many wonderful memories of growing up."

"I hadn't thought about it in terms of memories, but yes, I suppose I do," Sam told her. "We had great times together, great holidays. My mother and father were terrific parents. They still are. A bit . . . different, both of them, but terrific parents and wonderful people."

"What do you mean, different?"

"Ah, how to explain?" Sam tapped his fingers on the steering wheel. "Beyond the fact that they are as different as night and day . . ."

"You're kidding? The way you talk about them, I had this image of them as being, well, like two peas in a pod."

"And sometimes they are." He scratched his chin. "It's just that sometimes the pod isn't quite big enough for both of them at the same time."

"I don't understand."

"They've been known to argue from time to time."

"Somehow I had this notion that your parents had a perfect marriage."

"Oh, they do." He nodded vigorously. "Absolutely, my parents are perfect for each other. They adore each other. They always have. The fact that they aren't always on the same page at the same time doesn't mean for a second that they don't love each other more than anything on the face of the earth. Even as kids, we all somehow knew that as much as they loved each one of us, neither one of them was complete without the other. They are totally devoted to each other."

"That's really lovely, Sam," Rachel said, as if the concept had never occurred to her. "That's really romantic."

"Oh, there was always plenty of romance in our house. Maybe not the garden variety, but there was romance, all right," Sam said wryly. "I guess you'll see soon enough."

"Are you sure they don't mind that you're bringing me along?"

"They're thrilled. Oh, but I think I should warn you that they're concerned about my bachelor status, so just be prepared for a lot of hints."

"Hints about what?"

"Oh, you know, what a cute and brilliant baby I was. How my cousin Larry is already on his second family and I haven't started on my first. That sort of thing."

"Oh. Well, I can handle that. I'm certainly not looking to get married. Nothing personal, of course."

"Of course." He slowed down as they approached the mouth of the Cape Fear River, watching for the channel markers. "What's wrong with marriage?"

"I just don't see where it's necessary," she answered tersely.

"Necessary? That's an odd way of looking at it."

"I've never seen a marriage that worked, Sam."

"Never?"

"Not really. Certainly not in my own family."

"Every family isn't like yours."

Rachel shrugged. "I don't know that marriage is for everyone. I don't know that it has to be."

"Rachel, have you ever been in love?"

"I think we already discussed this."

"Let's discuss it again."

"Maybe there were times when I thought I was," she admitted.

"Well?" Sam watched her face. It told him nothing.

"Well what? What happened?" She stood up and looked as if she was about to pace. "We just weren't headed in the same direction so we just . . . went on with our lives."

"You shook hands and just said 'see ya'?"

"It may have been a little more involved than that." She shrugged, even now not willing to think about how much it had hurt, when Curt, the love of her life three years ago, had left her for another woman whom he had promptly married. "How about you? Have you ever been in love?"

"Sure." He grinned. "Many times. Oh, maybe not the kind where you wake in the middle of the night and your heart just stops because she's not there"— at least not until now, he could have added—"but sure, I know what it's like to be in love."

"What happened?"

"The last time?" Sam laughed. "I made the mistake of falling in love with a woman who gets seasick. Not a good thing for a man who lives on a boat.

That relationship was, as you can imagine, doomed from the start. Since then, I've been working pretty steadily. I don't have to tell you how long you can go without even getting a chance to meet someone."

"Occupational hazard," Rachel remarked.

"Don't you ever think about where you'll be in five years?" Sam persisted. "Don't you want a home of your own, don't you want children someday?"

"I don't know if I'd know what to do with a child, Sam. I don't think I'd know how to be a mother. My mother certainly didn't."

"You're not your mother." He turned to her and took her face in his hands. "Rachel, everything that you've told me about your mother leads me to suspect that she was a selfish, immature, and unloving woman. You are none of those things. There is absolutely no reason for you to think that you would ever be like her."

"She must have been different at some time. My father must have loved her once, Sam. There must have been something about her . . ."

"Did you ever ask him?"

"What?"

"Did you ever ask him what there was about her that had made him love her?"

"No, of course not."

"Maybe you should."

"I never thought to do that. He just never talks about her at all. And besides, it was his business, Sam, his and hers. Whatever it was, it was between them."

"That's where you're wrong, Rachel. It involved

all of you. Your mother, your father, Jared. And you. That's what families are all about."

"I guess I just don't have experience with families like that, Sam. It's foreign territory to me."

Not for long, Sam thought, as Rachel abruptly rose and took both empty cups into the galley to rinse them.

Over the next several days, ready or not, Rachel would be steeped in family. Up to her ears in family.

His.

18

THE BOOKSTORE in Wilmington had a great selection of mysteries, and both Sam and Rachel stocked up with their favorites. They swung by a diving center, Rachel wanting to replace her wet suit, weeks of kneeling in the sand having made the knees a bit ragged. By the time they had finished at the grocer's and the drugstore, they were laden with bags.

"How about if we run this stuff back to the boat before dinner?" Sam asked as they stood at a busy corner. "And we need to decide where we want to eat. Do you want to get dressed up and go someplace elegant? Wilmington has several really good restaurants."

"I don't think I have any elegant clothes with me," Rachel told him. "And actually, I'm feeling a bit relaxed and casual right now."

"Relaxed and casual is fine. What do you feel like eating?"

"Seafood is always good."

"You might want to have something else tonight. We're likely to have a lot of fish over the weekend. My mother said the bass are running."

"Oh. How about pizza, then? I haven't had pizza in months."

"Which kind do you like?"

"How many kinds are there?"

"Well, there's the kind where you sit in a nice restaurant and eat with a knife and fork, and there's the kind that you pick up with your hands and the stuff runs down your chin when you bite into it."

"Yes. That kind."

"You are in luck." Sam took her hand. "I know just the place."

"Now, do you like pepperoni, mushrooms, sweet peppers . . ." Rachel said after they had seated themselves at an empty table for four in the small, brightly lit restaurant and piled their purchases on the two empty chairs.

"Yes." Sam nodded. "All of those."

"So do I."

"Then that's what we'll have." Sam rose to go up to the counter to place their order. "One large pizza with everything on it . . ."

"Except anchovies," Rachel told him. "I hate anchovies."

Sam had barely returned to the table when they heard a loud clanging from the direction of the kitchen, followed by some cursing in Italian.

"I never heard Italian spoken with a Southern accent before." Rachel leaned across the table and whispered. "It sort of loses something, don't you think?"

A crowd of teenagers, the boys sporting their best

swaggers; the girls, henna tattoos, came in and pushed three tables together, instantly raising the noise level by several decibels.

"Maybe it's not too late to get takeout," Sam told her.

"It's okay. I don't get much of an opportunity to observe teenagers anymore. There aren't too many of them at sea." Rachel watched one of the girls pop open a small round tin of lip balm, dip her index finger in, then slather her pouty lips in a pale pink frost. "Girls are just so much more self-assured than I was at that age. They fascinate me."

"Then you're in for a fascinating time this weekend," Sam assured her. "I believe my cousin April will be arriving sometime tomorrow with her sixteen-year-old twins. A good time will be had by all, I'd bet on it."

More shouting from the kitchen.

"Are you sure you don't want this pizza to go? This is not very romantic."

She opened her mouth and before she could speak, Sam said, "Don't say it."

"Don't say what?"

"Don't say that you don't need romance, Rachel. Because you do. Everyone does." Sam took her fingers and laced his own through them. "Especially you."

He raised her hand to his lips and kissed her fingertips, one by one, mindful that several of the occupants of the next table were poking each other in the ribs and snickering.

". . . and I'm going to see to it that you have all that's coming to you. Tonight, and every night that we're together. So don't even try to fight me on this, Rachel. You're long overdue."

"I'm not going to fight you, Sam. It's just a little new to me."

"Then maybe we'd better get started. It looks like we have a lot of catching up to do." Sam signaled to the waiter. "We've changed our minds. We'd like the pizza to go, please."

Rachel lay in bed long after Sam had gotten up to walk to the store at the corner to get the morning paper. *I should get up and get dressed,* she told herself, but her body felt weightless this morning. She rolled over onto one side and sighed. When Sam McGowan promised a night of romance, he delivered.

Had that really been her, Rachel Chandler, dancing on deck in the moonlight the night before, with the irresistible Sam McGowan humming one sweet ballad after another in her ear? Being swept off her feet, making love in the lounge, then in the stateroom, until the early hours of the morning? Being fed strawberries from glasses of champagne by the most incredible man she'd ever met?

How, she wondered, had she lived for so long without such beautiful moments in her life?

How could she stand it if her life never held such moments again?

"Hey, lazy!" Sam called from the galley. "Aren't you up yet?"

Rachel jumped up and grabbed her bag, then slipped into the bathroom, calling as she closed the door, "I'll just be a minute."

Sam was whistling when she came into the galley.

"The shop at the corner had some great coffee, so I bought some for both of us." He leaned over to kiss the side of her face. "How about if you fix two bowls of cereal while I get us out of the marina and into the open sea?"

"Your cereal will get soggy." She frowned.

"Don't put the milk on it yet," he whispered, kissed her cheek and headed for the helm.

Rachel took a sip of coffee before she set about preparing breakfast. There was a rustling sound from H.D.'s cage as she walked past to have breakfast with Sam on the flybridge. On her way back to the galley with the empty bowls, she reached out and pulled the cover off the cage.

"So how's the teddy bear this morning?" she asked.

"I'm all shook up!" H.D. squawked. "I'm all shook up!"

"I know exactly how you feel." Rachel laughed out loud and opened the cage, inviting the parrot onto her shoulder. "I'm a little shaken myself this morning."

"I'm feeling fine!" H.D. sang out his slightly askew version. "I'm feeling fine!"

"Yes, I'd say that pretty well sums it up." Rachel laughed. "I'm feeling pretty fine myself."

The *Shearwater* crept slowly into the marina on the western side of St. Swithin's Island, eased into the slip like a bird returning to it's nest. Rachel gathered her things and bit her bottom lip.

"Oh, come on, Rach," Sam said from the doorway. "It won't be that bad. I promise."

"I was just trying to remember if I have everything."

"You have everything you need." He stepped forward to embrace her. "And if you don't stop fidgeting, I'm going to start to think that you're nervous about meeting my family. Which is not necessarily a bad thing, now that I think about it. God knows that, collectively, they've made me nervous enough over the years."

"I'm not nervous," she assured him, but let him rock her in his arms for a moment anyway. "What about H.D.?"

"Oh. Right. The King." Sam sighed. "I suppose we should put him back into his cage and take him with us. If Daria calls, she's going to want to talk to him, and when she finds out we left him on the boat she won't be happy."

Rachel laughed and swung a bag over each of her shoulders.

"Want me to carry yours so that you can carry H.D.'s cage?" she asked.

"No, I'm fine. We only have two blocks to walk."

"It's now or never!" H.D. sang as Sam carried the cage off the boat and down the dock.

"Good morning, Mr. Hansen." Sam nodded to the elderly man three slips down.

"Morning, there, Sam." The man nodded agreeably. "Good to see you back, son."

"It's nice to be back."

Sam paused at the end of the dock, the birdcage in one hand, overnight bag in the other, waiting for Rachel, who seemed to be stopping here and there to look around, to catch up.

"It's about time you got here," a young, dark-haired woman appeared at the edge of the parking lot just as Rachel caught up with Sam. "Mom's had everyone haunting this place since eight this morning."

Sam set the cage down and wrapped his arms around the woman, kissing the side of her face with a loud smack.

"Good to see you, too, Iona." Sam gave her a quick hug then turned to Rachel to introduce her to his younger sister.

Iona pushed past him to offer her hand, saying, "You're Rachel. I'm Iona. It's a pleasure."

Iona McGowan was small-boned and slender, with lively eyes that looked straight into Rachel's and cheeks that bore a natural blush. Rachel took an immediate liking to her.

"It's good to meet you, Iona." Rachel smiled.

Sam picked up the cage and his bag.

"I understand that you and Sam are working together?" Iona asked, then paused, looking around, before putting two fingers into her mouth and whistling.

"Yes." Rachel flinched at the harsh, unexpected sound.

"Rachel's the salvager on the project I'm working on."

"There's a marriage made in heaven," Iona mumbled and whistled again. "Daphne, get over here. Damn that dog."

Iona took off down the dock in pursuit of a small black pug that had shot past them and was chasing a gull at the end of the pier.

Rachel looked at Sam blankly.

"No one's talking about marriage."

"Right," Sam agreed. "I'm sure that was just a figure of speech."

Sam just couldn't bring himself to tell her that his mother and all three of her sisters had probably talked of nothing else since he said he'd be bringing Rachel home with him. His mother had worried about him spending so much time at sea, she'd said; the family was convinced that he'd never meet a nice girl and settle down.

Well, he reasoned, up until now, that had been true. He had never given it that much thought before. To Sam, marriage meant a total, no-turning-back commitment, and while the thought didn't particularly frighten him, it was something that had always seemed to loom off in the distant and nebulous future someday. He hadn't considered that someday might come sooner than later. Of course, he hadn't planned on having Rachel walk into his life when she did, either, but now that she had, and had made a place there for herself—whether she realized it or not—Sam couldn't imagine her walking back out.

All he had to do was convince Rachel.

"Sammy!" Margarite McGowan burst through the door of the rambling clapboard house and kissed her defenseless son—his travel bag in one had, H.D.'s cage in the other—on both cheeks. "I've been watching for you."

"So Iona told me." Sam laughed. "Mom, this is . . ."

"Rachel. We've been waiting to meet you. Come

say hello to everyone." Margarite was a determined five feet three inches tall, with silver hair piled in a disorderly knot atop her head. Silver granny glasses perched at the end of her nose.

"Who's everyone?" Sam asked cautiously.

"Aunt Lillie arrived on Tuesday and Deanna came in last night. It's been a madhouse, Sam, and your father has been of no help whatsoever." Margarite turned to Rachel as she steered her toward the steps and said somewhat conspiratorially, "Samuel always has these wonderful ideas—Let's have a party!—and then promptly goes back about his business, leaving me to plan and organize everything."

"Don't let her kid you, Rachel. We all want to live long enough to see the day that my mother lets anyone plan anything without her taking over. She just has to have her little fingers in every little pot." Iona came up the walk with the little pug scooting along beside her.

"Well, someone has to be in charge, Iona. Your father certainly isn't." She turned to Rachel and said, "My husband has the attention span of a happy three-year-old. He has wonderful ideas, which he forgets about as soon as the next wonderful idea pops into his head. I don't know where he'd be without me."

"I'd be relaxing out back in the hammock between those two sweet gum trees, doing a crossword puzzle, that's where I'd be." Samuel McGowan, gray-haired like his wife, walked onto the porch, a newspaper under his arm.

If Margarite was a tornado, Samuel was a long,

easy summer afternoon. He moved as if he had all day.

"Right. In the hammock. Where you'd promptly fall asleep and roll out of the hammock into the waiting jaws of that big gator we saw out in the swamp the other day, that's where you'd be."

"Rachel, this is my dad, Samuel McGowan."

"Hello, Rachel." Samuel took her hand. "Ah, Sammy, she's a pretty one. And a salvager, Sammy tells us. I've never had the pleasure of working with a treasure hunter before, so perhaps you can tell me . . ."

"Dad." Sam's voice held a fond warning. "Don't start. Rachel is not that kind of a salvager."

"Well, tell me what a salvager does if it isn't to uncover the past and profit from it."

Sam rolled his eyes and turned to Rachel.

"I should have warned you. My father is a purist. He thinks that no one should be permitted within ten miles of any archaeological site who hasn't been blessed by a panel made up of no fewer than a dozen or two of the world's most respected—read *stuffy*—archaeologists."

"Well, then, we should have some pretty lively discussions this weekend, Dr. McGowan." Rachel grinned. "Since salvagers are often the moving force in stirring up interest in the financial community to arrange for the backing without which so many of those sites would never be accessible. And since so many sites are actually located by the salvagers in the first place . . ."

"Young lady, I can't even begin to tell you how

many sites I've seen destroyed by the uneducated, impatient . . ."

"Later, Samuel." Margarite took her husband's arm. "At least let the poor girl get into the house before forcing her to defend herself."

"I don't mind." Rachel smiled levelly at Sam's father. "I'm well able to defend my profession."

"Good. The more people Samuel has to argue with, the happier he'll be." Margarite turned to her husband with obvious satisfaction. "And Samuel, between Iona, Rachel, and April's teenagers, you should have one hell of a weekend."

It had been one hell of a weekend, though Samuel didn't have as much time to debate with his guests as he'd thought. The rest of Friday was spent greeting guests—Rachel's head was spinning at the number of aunts, uncles, and cousins that arrived. All of the children were relegated to a large dormitory on the third floor which, lined with single beds, could sleep a small army. There was constant activity in the kitchen, as it seemed the preparations for the next meal began as soon as the previous meal had been completed. Mrs. Ross, the cook and housekeeper, had more than enough willing hands to help keep things running smoothly, but by three o'clock in the afternoon, the commotion arising from so many voices chattering at once was beginning to take its toll on Rachel.

Sensing that the young woman was slightly overwhelmed, Margarite sought her out in the throng that sat on the back porch shelling peanuts for the peanut brittle that was a McGowan family favorite.

"I'm going down to the pond to see if I can find

something interesting for an arrangement for that big table in the front hallway." Margarite tapped Rachel on the shoulder. "Would you like to come with me?"

"Sure." Rachel stood up a little too quickly.

"Hip boots?" Margarite asked.

"What?"

"Do you want a pair of hip boots to wear? We may have to wade a ways into the water."

"Are you wearing them?" Rachel asked.

"No."

"Then I won't either."

"Good." Margarite appeared pleased. "Here's a bucket and a knife."

"What's the knife for?" Rachel took the equipment and fell into step with Margarite.

"To fight off the alligators."

Rachel's step faltered.

"That was a joke, Rachel," Margarite said without breaking stride.

"Oh. Good," Rachel said with relief. "I really don't like alligators."

"They can be nasty creatures, all right." Margarite nodded. "Though for the most part, they leave you alone. They scatter when they see you coming."

Rachel grimaced involuntarily. She really *did not* like alligators.

The path they followed led through a tangled grove of live oak, their ancient limbs dripping with Spanish moss. Close by, an ibis announced the presence of intruders with an agitated *hunk hunk hunk*. Up ahead, something splashed into water. Along the worn path, wild orchids grew, and off to their right, dogwoods dropped white petals onto the ground like confetti. All in all, the walk to the marsh was like a walk through a primitive landscape, and Rachel said so.

"I like it," Margarite nodded. "I'm happier here than I've been anywhere else in the world."

"Sam told me that you'd seen a lot of it."

"Oh, yes. At one time or another, we've been just about everywhere, on almost every continent. Either for Samuel's work or my own. I often wondered if it was fair to the children, dragging them along, desert to mountain to jungle." She smiled wanly. "They didn't have a very settled childhood, I'm afraid."

"Sam told me that he loved it."

"Did he now?" Margarite stopped and looked up into Rachel's face. "Through the years I've worried that perhaps they'd have been better off with a more traditional upbringing . . . ah, here we are."

The end of the path opened directly onto a wide pond of murky green upon which the afternoon sun sparkled. Along the water's edge, a profusion of water lilies floated amidst their wide green pads. Dragonflies darted across the surface and the air all but hummed with life.

"Gorgeous," Margarite sighed. "We'll have plenty for the hall and plenty to leave here to bloom."

She dipped her bucket into the water and filled it, so Rachel did the same. Then Margarite kicked off her shoes and stepped into the pond until she was thigh deep in water. Rachel visibly shivered. The bottom of the pond would be mud, and the thought of it oozing between her toes made her queasy. Margarite seemed not to notice.

"The water's not cold," Margarite turned and told her. "Actually, it's quite warm. Though if you'd rather, you can probably reach a few from right there."

"No. I'll come in," Rachel said warily, not relishing the thought of joining Margarite in the pond. But this was Sam's mother, and if she could do it, Rachel could do it. She toed off her sneakers and stepped in.

The feel of the cool mud beneath her feet sent a wave of near nausea through her. As a child, Rachel had never been permitted to play near such a place, having been cautioned against getting dirty every time she went outside to play. What, she wondered, would Aunt Bess think of the McGowans, particularly of Margarite, who at this moment was leading Rachel through a muddy swamp in search of water lilies?

"Oh, that one's perfect," Margarite told her as Rachel used her knife to cut the thick stem of a partially opened lily. "I do love these, don't you?"

She held up a fat, creamy white bud for Rachel to admire.

"They are beautiful. I'd never have thought of making an arrangement of water lilies, though."

"You might if you lived on an island." Margarite smiled. "I love the marsh and all the swampy areas. I love the wildness of it, the peace that I find back here."

"Thank you for inviting me along with you."

"Well, you looked like you were about to OD on the chatter. It gets to me at times, too, but I'm used to it. I have the distinct impression that you are not."

"I come from a very small, quiet home," Rachel

told her. "As a matter of fact, I was just wondering what my aunt—my great-aunt, actually—would say if she saw me standing in the mud."

Margarite stared at her blankly.

"What would she say?"

"Oh, I can barely imagine." Rachel laughed. "I was never allowed to play in the mud."

"Really?" Margarite looked amused. "How . . . unusual."

Rachel wiggled her toes in the ooze that ten minutes earlier she'd dreaded encountering and smiled to herself. It would not occur to Margarite that perhaps her method of child rearing had been, in its way, just as out of the ordinary as Aunt Bess's had been.

"Like it, do you?" Margarite asked.

"I'm beginning to get used to it."

Margarite laughed.

"You mentioned your aunt, but not your mother," Margarite said a few moments later, choosing her words carefully.

"My aunt raised us, my brother and me. My parents traveled a lot. My father is a salvager and spent a lot of time at sea. My mother was a concert pianist and spent a lot of time on tour." Rachel concentrated on sawing a particularly thick stem.

"You said your mother 'was' . . ."

"She died when I was eight."

"I see," Margarite said thoughtfully. It appeared that poor Rachel had shallow roots. It was no wonder that she had appeared to be adrift in the midst of the McGowan sea earlier. "Well, then, we'll try not to run you over this weekend."

"Oh, I'll be fine, Mrs. McGowan." Rachel nodded.

"I've no doubt you will be, Rachel." Margarite stopped to watch Rachel gamely step farther into the pond, the water now past her thighs, as she sought to add to her bucket of blooms. *No doubts at all.*

Later that evening, Margarite had the opportunity to see just how fine Rachel did in fact adjust to the busy household as the young woman pitched in with dishes and accepted Samuel's challenge at chess. And though she lost the game, she had played well enough to cause Samuel to rub his chin thoughtfully on more than one occasion as he contemplated the position of the chess pieces—made from water buffalo bone and picked up on his first trip to Mongolia many years before—and later challenge her to another game.

"She's lovely, Sammy," Margarite said to her son as he helped her clear dishes from one of the several round tables they'd set across the wide front porch to use for dinner that night.

"Rachel?" he asked, as if his mother could have been referring to anyone else. "Yes, she is very lovely."

"And I sense that she is very special."

"Very special." He nodded.

"I like her, Sammy." Margarite touched his arm gently. "Don't let her get away."

"I have no intention of letting her get away, Mom."

"I'm so happy to hear you say that. And I think your father likes her, too, in spite of his bluster."

"I hope so." Sam smiled and loaded plates into his arms to carry them into the kitchen. "Mom, do you

think you could finish out that game for Dad? I need
to talk to him about something, and it looks like Rachel is into her game."

"So is your father. It will take something monumental to get him away from that chess table right
now."

"Oh, it's monumental, all right." Sam nodded confidently. "He'll come."

"Really?" Margarite's eyes sparkled. "If it's something that important, perhaps you should discuss it
with both of us."

"It's business, Mom." He leaned over to peck her
fondly on the cheek. "Just some business."

"Oh," Margarite replied flatly.

"Sorry to disappoint you." Sam laughed. "I promise to consult you first on any personal matters, but
tonight, there's something I need to discuss with
Dad. Can I count on you to keep Rachel busy for
a while?"

"Of course, dear. We'll keep Rachel company, not
to worry." Margarite nodded, wondering just what
business would lead her son behind closed doors
with his father in the midst of a family gathering,
and how long it would take her to get it out of her
husband later.

19

---◆○◆---

"WANT TO go for a walk?" Sam leaned over and whispered in Rachel's ear. "You haven't seen the beach yet."

"As soon as I finish braiding Lissie's hair." Rachel smiled up at him.

Lissie, one of Sam's cousin April's twin daughters, was sporting newly braided hair, complete with small beads woven in here and there, just like her sister Tess, seated on the floor to Rachel's left, had.

"Rachel did it." Tess swung her long hair around her head so that the beads would click slightly. "Isn't it cool?"

"Cool," Sam agreed. "Very cool."

"Where'd you learn how to braid hair like that?" Sam asked later as he took her hand and led her out the front door.

"Tess had a picture from a magazine that came complete with directions. They wanted to try it."

"That was nice of you."

"I enjoyed it. It was fun."

It had been fun, in a way that Rachel didn't want to analyze too much by putting into words. Sitting there on the wide, dark green plush hassock, weaving beads into the hair of Sam's young cousins while his Great-aunt Carrie talked about growing up at Eden's End had made Rachel feel that she was a part of something easy and close and important.

"It's nice you're getting to spend so much time with your dad."

"We just had a few things to discuss, that's all." Sam's face told her nothing. "Where did you and my mother disappear to this afternoon?"

"Oh." Rachel's face brightened. "We picked water lilies."

"Out in the swamp?"

"Yes. That's where they grow."

"I hope you wore hip boots."

"No. Your mother offered them to me, but since she didn't wear them, I figured I didn't need them either."

"My mother walks a fine line sometimes between brilliancy and lunacy." Sam shook his head. "You're lucky you didn't get snake-bit."

"Snakes? There are snakes out there?" Rachel went white and clutched his hand. "She didn't tell me there were snakes."

"Well, she should have. There are cottonmouth and water moccasins in that pond." Sam ran an exasperated hand through his hair. "My mother thinks that she's invincible, you know? That nothing could ever harm her. She's been like that all her life, and there is nothing I can do or say to change her. But she shouldn't put you in a situation like that."

"To tell you the truth, I kind of liked it," Rachel said. "Of course, if I'd known about the snakes, I probably wouldn't have—I think I view snakes pretty much the way Hugh felt about that Manta ray—but I liked being out in the swamp today. There was something about walking around in the mud that made me feel . . . I don't know, *free* somehow. It's something I've never done before."

"Rachel, you walk on the bottom of the ocean."

"That's different. For one thing, I wear fins, so I'm not barefooted. And for another, the ocean generally washes you clean. I had to hose myself off when we got back up to the house today."

"You say that as if you're proud of it."

"I guess I am," she admitted. "I've never done that before."

"Never done what?"

"Never got dirty enough that I had to hose myself down before I could go into the house," she said softly.

"Are you serious?"

She nodded.

"Aunt Bess didn't like dirty kids, I take it."

"No. No, she didn't."

"I think Aunt Bess needs to spend a few weeks of quality time on St. Swithin's with my mother."

"Oh, she couldn't, Sam. She's too old and too sick. She's deaf and nearly blind. But even if she wasn't, I couldn't imagine her being like your mother. I mean, she never even had a garden. Not even a neat, tidy, well-tended, well-behaved one."

"Did she let you have pets? Did you have a bicycle?"

"No pets." Rachel appeared horrified at the thought of an animal having the run of that immaculate, antique-filled home she had grown up in. "And I wasn't allowed to have a bike until I was in high school. Aunt Bess thought it was unladylike, and besides, I might hurt myself. And of course, none of the girls in my high school rode a bike. It was just one more way that I was different from everyone else. One more thing that set me apart. I just never really fit in anywhere."

Sam put his arms around her and swayed with her slightly, left to right.

"You fit in here," he told her. "You fit in here just fine."

"I almost think I do, Sam." She rocked with him, snug in the circle of his arms. "I could almost believe that I do."

"Believe it," he said as his lips sought hers, and the thought occurred to her that whereever Sam was, was where she belonged.

The thought terrified her, and at the same time, made her whole.

"I know where there's a secluded spot just a little way down the beach," Sam whispered in her ear.

"I just love a man with a plan." She sighed.

"Oh, and I do have plans for you." He laughed softly and took her by the hand. "We'll have to stick to the boardwalk here on the dunes. We don't want to disturb the dune grass."

Ghostly white shapes flashed across their path when they stepped from the boards onto the sand.

"Ghost crabs," he told her when she jumped. "Sometimes it seems as if there are millions of them down here."

"Oh, come here often, do you?"

"Not often enough. But that could change."

They strolled down along the water's edge, slipping off their shoes to let the warm surf wash around their feet. Lights from nearby houses spread faintly across the top of the dunes, but down here, by the ocean, the only light was from the stars overhead and a half-moon. The sea kissed their ankles, and they walked close together, Rachel in the curve of his arm, just under his shoulder, where she fit so perfectly. They ambled casually through the gentle night until they rounded a sweep of dune that opened onto a sheltered cove.

"Ah, this is seclu—" Rachel began to speak, then stopped, the words catching in her throat.

Upon the sand, silhouetted in the faint moonlight, a couple danced, cheek to cheek, heart to heart, swaying to music meant for their ears only. Even from the darkened dune, Rachel recognized Sam's parents.

"I see we weren't the only ones who thought a little romance was in order tonight." Sam chuckled softly.

Rachel tugged on his hand. "Let's go before they see us."

"Oh, they won't see us," Sam said, turning to follow her all the same. "There are times when they don't seem to see anyone but each other."

They walked in silence back down the beach. When they reached the top of the boardwalk, Rachel looked back over her shoulder in the direction of the cove and told Sam, "That was one of the most beautiful things I've ever seen, the two of them just holding each other, dancing like that. It was magical, Sam." She shook her head. "To think that after all the years they've been married, to still have such magic in their lives."

"It is pretty special," Sam agreed. "But I can't remember a time when they weren't like that with each other. They might spend all day bickering back and forth, but something seems to happen between them, and whatever they were debating just seems to fade away. At least for a time."

"I don't think I'll ever forget that, Sam. I've never witnessed such a perfect moment between two people. I'm almost embarrassed that I did. But imagine loving someone like that for so long."

"Yes," Sam told her. "Yes, I can."

"Because you've grown up with people who always felt that way about each other. I grew up with parents who couldn't stand to be under the same roof at the same time."

"Oh, and I suppose that means that you have to relive their lives, Rachel. I suppose you're doomed to repeat every one of their mistakes, with each other and with their children. I suppose your life can't be different from theirs."

"I never thought it could be, Sam." She swallowed hard. "Now I'm not so sure."

"I'm encouraged by that, Rachel. I really am." His voice softened. "It scares me to think that you could believe that the type of relationship your parents had is normal. Because it isn't. A loving relationship where two people respect and cherish each other, that's what's normal. That's what's right. That's how it's meant to be. And it's not nearly as uncommon as you think."

"The concept might take a little getting used to," she told him, "but I'm trying to give it some consideration."

"Everything can't be studied in a scientific fashion, Rach. Relationships can't be dissected and you can't control what you feel in your heart. I suspect that you've tried for most of your life, but I'm asking you, just this once, to just go where this takes you, Rachel. Just be honest with yourself about what you feel and what you want. Just this once."

Rachel nodded slowly. Just this once, perhaps it wouldn't hurt . . .

They had reached the house, and even from the street could see several forms stretched across the darkened steps. A dog barked gruffly, and Iona called to him from the porch.

"Now, do you think you can take a little more McGowan shenanigans?" he asked.

"Sure. I think I'm getting used to it."

"Ah, Rachel, you're making me a happy man tonight."

"Not as happy as I thought I was going to make you."

"Day after tomorrow we'll be back on the *Shearwater*," he whispered in her ear as they walked up the uneven brick path.

"I'll make it up to you then." She broke away as Iona's pug, Daphne, jumped off the bottom step and came running toward them, wagging what tail she had.

"I'm counting on it," Rachel heard him say as she leaned down to lift the little dog.

Though barely dawn the next morning, Rachel woke in the twin bed in the room she shared with Sam's sister. Carefully sitting up and lowering her legs over the side of the bed so as not to waken Iona, sleeping in the bed nearest the window, Rachel gathered the things she needed and tiptoed into the small bathroom, where she dressed as quietly as she could. She hoped that Daphne would not bark and that H.D. would not start singing, though he'd grown somewhat subdued the night before at the sight of Margarite's two cats.

"I'm Daria's be-u-ti-ful baby boy," the parrot had announced loudly, as if warning the cats away.

Even so early in the morning, the day promised to be a warm one. Rachel pulled on shorts and a T-shirt and tied a sweatshirt around her shoulders just in case it was cool on the beach. She needed to be alone to think, and there was no place in the world but the ocean where she could clear her head.

Of course, she reminded herself, sitting on the beach isn't quite the same as diving, but today it would have to do. She slipped out the front door on quiet barefeet and followed the same path she and Sam had taken the night before.

Last night, where at low tide the ocean had lapped gently at the beach, this morning it pounded and pummeled, casting a great wash of spray with every wave. It was vital and glorious and she followed its course along the beach, picking up shells to inspect. Sharkeye and channeled whelk, coral, sand dollars,

lightning whelk, all strewn as if by a giant hand, cast
like dice across the face of the beach. This was familiar territory in a place that seemed to hold little of
what she had known in her life. The sea never
changed and it never disappointed. On a morning
like this you could walk along the water's edge anywhere in the world and feel exactly as she felt at
that moment. It calmed and soothed her, and she sat
midway up the beach inspecting the shells she had
found, dropping them absently into a tidy pile next
to her on the sand.

She leaned back upon her elbows and tried to sep-
arate herself from the situation, to examine it in a
rational fashion, a technique that she often used
when deliberating or making important decisions.
This time, however, she found that she was unable
to remove herself from the picture that came to mind
when she called up Sam's face. It seemed to be looking into her own, and no matter how hard she tried,
she could not seem to make him look away. Finally
she stopped trying, and gave in to the dialogue that
ran in her head.

On the one hand, she'd only known Sam for a
short time.

On the other, it seemed she'd known him forever.

Everything she'd ever known of love had taught
her that it couldn't be trusted, that it would, sooner
or later, bring pain and loss.

Sam had always been sure that love could be forever, that it could calm, could restore, could bring
joy, because it had been a constant in his life.

Rachel lay back on the sand and watched the
clouds change shape. An enormous monkey morphed

slowly into a mountain, a bird stretched into a snake. A train sped across the sky only to change, in time, into a giant football.

Life was full of changes. Sands shifted, tides ebbed and swelled. When Rachel had been seven, her best friend had moved away. When she was eight, her mother had died. The summer she turned ten, Jared had gone to sea with Gordon for the first time, leaving her alone in that quiet house with Aunt Bess, and Rachel had cried and cried.

"Rachel, all through your life, people will come and go," her aunt had told her then. "You can't stop them from leaving, so it's best sometimes not to care so much. It's too great a risk."

Aunt Bess had believed that. She had raised Rachel to believe it.

Maybe, just maybe, Aunt Bess had been wrong.

Rachel sat up and looked up the beach to see Sam and his mother, rods in hand, cross the sand to do a little surf fishing. Rachel watched the body language that spoke volumes of their love for each other, mother and son, and it warmed her to watch their wordless interaction. They would welcome her if she joined them, and she realized that there had been few times in her life when she'd felt like she had truly belonged. Sam's family had reached out to her with unconditional welcome, and while it frightened her on one level, at the same time it lifted her up.

She was only beginning to learn all the things that love could do, all the changes it could bring. Rachel stood and brushed the sand from the back of her shorts and walked across the beach. Sam turned and waved happily when he saw her, calling her to join them.

This time it was, she figured, clearly worth the risk.

Margarite's birthday dinner was a noisy affair. In addition to family, friends from the island poured into the house until Rachel simply could not keep track of them anymore. Mrs. Ross had enlisted a number of her cronies to prepare a buffet that would have made Martha Stewart green with envy. Fresh oysters and steamed crabs, plump pink shrimp and lobster claws, all surrounded by lemon wedges and heaped on beds of crisp green lettuce to start the feast. Next came enormous sugar-cured country hams and platters of fried chicken, oozing cholesterol and calories, and whole sea bass, stuffed with corn bread dressing and grilled to perfection. Yellow islands of butter melted atop mountains of mashed potatoes, and bowls of green beans cooked with bacon shared space with salads of fresh-picked spring greens. Just-baked biscuits were piled onto trays with hush puppies and corn bread squares.

Rachel had never in her life seen such food.

"Does your family eat like this often?" she asked Sam as she stared wide-eyed as platter after platter emerged from the kitchen.

"Sure. As long as Mrs. Ross is around, we do."

"I can't believe that none of you are grossly overweight. If I ate like this everyday, I'd weigh a ton."

"Well, my mother's theory is that you have to eat well to have enough energy to work hard. Fortunately, there's Mrs. Ross, since my mother's personal culinary triumphs have been few and far between."

Mrs. Ross was, indeed, a gift from the gods.

"You look like a happy camper," Sam noted as Rachel returned to her rocking chair on the front porch with a second helping of salad.

"Sam, this ham is incredible . . ."

"One of Mrs. Ross's specialties." Sam nodded.

". . . and the sea bass is to die for. Not that there's anything wrong with Norman's cook, but Mrs. Ross is in a class by herself. Maybe we could talk her into running away and signing on with the *Annie G.*"

"Shhhh," he whispered conspiratorially. "Don't let my mother hear you even suggest such a thing. That type of talk would be considered treasonous."

"It might be worth it."

"What did you try besides the ham and the bass?"

"Everything." She sighed happily. "I tried everything. I won't eat again till Monday, at least."

"Well, you can't skip dessert," Sam told her.

"Dessert? How could anyone even think about dessert?"

"How could you not?" He grinned. "Banana pudding, sweet potato pie, fruit salad . . ."

"Stop!" Rachel groaned. "I can feel my thighs swelling just thinking about it."

". . . not to mention homemade ice cream and birthday cake."

"I couldn't possibly." Rachel shook her head.

But she did. Vowing to run the length of the beach first thing in the morning, she sampled a bit of this and a taste of that. She toasted Margarite with champagne and nibbled on birthday cake after the birthday song had been sung and the candles blown out. Over coffee and a second round of cake—which Rachel declined, reminding Sam what the Bible had to say about gluttony—she gathered with the others in the spacious living room as presents were opened and oohed and aahed over.

As the evening wound down, old family photos made the rounds—Margarite predictably pointing out to Rachel just how adorable a baby Sam had been— and old family jokes surfaced. A wistful sadness swept the room when a photo of Iona and Jackson at their high school graduation was circulated, and everyone, it seemed, had a story to recall about the missing McGowan. Daria's absence, too, was noted, and Samuel proudly filled everyone in on her latest discovery. Rachel settled back against Sam and just soaked up every last bit of warmth and fellowship that she could absorb, content to listen to family stories that everyone else had undoubtedly heard before, though no one protested at their telling yet again.

At the sound of her name, Rachel sat up.

"Sam not only read some of Trinity's diaries, but he tells me that Rachel saw her, big as life," Samuel was saying. "Is that right, Rachel?"

"Oh. Trinity." Rachel felt her face flush, embarrassed as she was to admit to the entire McGowan clan that she had in fact seen a spirit—she decided she wouldn't refer to it as a ghost, that sounded too otherworldly for Rachel's scientific sensibilities. "Well, I saw something . . . that is, someone . . . wearing clothing of the day. It did occur to me that it could have been Trinity."

"Any chance it could have been someone dressed up in old clothing?" April asked.

"I had thought of that, but . . ." Rachel nodded, reluctant to finish the thought.

"But the 'someone' evaporated before her eyes," Sam finished it for her. "That was the word you used at the time, Rachel. 'Evaporated.' "

"Yes, well, it did seem that way at the time." Rachel's flush deepened.

"Cool," Lissie pronounced. "Rachel saw a ghost."

"Very cool," her twin nodded enthusiastically.

"So, Rachel, was Trinity as homely as everyone said she was?" Iona, Daphne curled up on her lap contentedly, asked from the far corner of the room.

Rachel hesitated. Trinity was, after all, the ancestor of many of the people crowded into the room.

"I don't recall that I noticed her appearance as much as her demeanor. She seemed to be somewhat . . ."

"Agitated. Restless," Samuel's eighty-seven-year-old Aunt Carrie said.

"Yes." Rachel turned to her. "How did you know?"

"Because I saw her myself the last time I was at Eden's End. For the reading of my brother William's will."

"Aunt Carrie, you never mentioned that." Samuel leaned forward.

"Oh, of course I didn't, Samuel." Aunt Carrie's voice rose an octave or two. " 'Poor dotty old Carrie, thinks she saw a ghost.' Ha! Do you think for a minute I was going to let you run with that one? Ha!" she repeated, then turned to Rachel and asked, "I knew instinctively it was Trinity."

Rachel nodded. "So did I. I don't know how I knew, but I did."

"Where were you?"

"On the balcony overlooking the grounds. She was down below, on the grass, looking up. She stared at me for a second, then she . . ."

". . . flipped one end of her shawl over her shoulder and disappeared," Aunt Carrie offered.

"Exactly."

"And, Sam, you didn't see her at all?" Sam's great-aunt asked.

"I saw a movement down below on the lawn, but I didn't see anyone in detail, as Rachel did." He fell silent for a minute, then added sheepishly, "Though when we were leaving, I thought I saw a flash of something, shiny and pink, among the trees on the way down the lane. I stopped the car, but it was gone."

"You didn't tell me that." Rachel turned to look at him. "Why didn't you tell me that?"

"Because I really didn't know what I saw. I'm still not sure. I'm not sure that I believe in ghosts, Rachel."

"Neither did I, Sam."

"Well, I think that the important thing is that she was seen. Though Rachel may be the first person outside the family who claims to have seen her," Aunt Carrie said. "Which is interesting in itself. Why would she show herself to Rachel?"

"Maybe she sensed that I was on her side," Rachel said softly.

"On her side?" Samuel frowned. "What are you talking about? On her side about what?"

Rachel glanced at Sam. She thought he should tell this part of the story, and he did. The tale of Old Sam and his ladylove from Texas, their illegitimate son, Trinity's involvement in Anjelica's death, the discovery of Trinity's diaries, set the room on its end.

"Now, Sam, you said you didn't believe that Trinity deliberately murdered this woman," his father said. "Why not?"

"Because I found her diary. She was anguished when she found out that Anjelica's body had been found inside the house. She apparently believed that Anjelica had left Eden's End some time earlier. She never intended for that to happen."

"Why not go get the diary, Sam, and read it to everyone?" Rachel suggested.

"That's a wonderful idea, Rachel." Margarite nodded. "I would love to hear it myself."

"I'll be right back, then," Sam told them. "Mom, ask Mrs. Ross to make another pot of coffee. I'll be back by the time it's ready."

Sam departed for the *Shearwater*, leaving aunts, uncles, and cousins sitting on the edge of their seats, anxiously awaiting his return. This was, after all, a bit of drama they'd not anticipated, and the room buzzed with expectation.

So it was as if a bomb had been dropped when Sam came back into the room twenty minutes later and announced, "It's gone. The diary is gone."

"Sam, it can't be gone." Rachel frowned. "It was on the boat two days ago when we docked. Remember, you put it behind the paneling in your stateroom with the . . ."

She paused, and met his eyes across the room. He'd put the diary and the aspirin bottle containing the jewels in a space he'd made behind the bed.

"That's gone too, Rach." Sam looked confused and

distraught. "The aspirin bottle is gone, too. And the *Shearwater* has been trashed. Paneling ripped out, carpets torn up . . ."

Rachel stared blankly, trying to comprehend what had happened.

"Was anything else taken?" Sam's mother asked. "Your laptop? Your stereo equipment? Television?"

Sam shook his head. "I have the laptop with me. Everything else is right where I left it."

"It sounds as if someone knew exactly what they were looking for," Iona said. "But who would have known that you even had it? And why would anyone want Trinity's diary, anyway? Other than a McGowan, who'd even be interested?"

In a daze, Sam went off to call the Coast Guard. His boat had been trashed and he'd been robbed. They wouldn't think the theft of the diary was significant and he sure as hell wasn't going to tell them about the contents of the aspirin bottle, but he wanted it on record that someone had trashed the *Shearwater*.

Only Sam and his father knew that the thief hadn't found the most likely object of their quest. *That* sat at this very minute on Samuel's desk in his locked study, in the same silver box that Sam had pulled from the bottom of the sea just days earlier. No one, not even Rachel, knew of its existence. So Sam had thought.

Someone, apparently, had suspected. Someone had come looking for it.

It wasn't much of a stretch to figure out who that someone was.

20

---∞---

ARMS FOLDED across her chest, Rachel leaned against the counter in the galley of the *Shearwater* and watched Sam's face as he screwed a piece of siding back onto the wall. He and his Uncle Will had spent most of the morning and the entire day before, screw drivers in hand, putting pieces of paneling back into place and cleaning up the debris left behind by the intruder. Dishes had been smashed, windows knocked out, but the instrument panel was intact, the engines still ran, and there was no damage to the hull.

"Kids out to cause havoc," the Coast Guard had pronounced.

Sam had been unable to disagree, not having decided at that moment how he was going to go about confronting the man responsible for the theft.

"Why didn't you tell them it was Norman?" Rachel said after the Coast Guard had made their report and left the boat, freeing Sam and Rachel to head back to the wreck site.

To Rachel's surprise, Sam cut the engines at the end of the channel leading out to sea, and had called her into the stateroom.

"And don't tell me that you don't think it was Norman, because we both know you do. It's obvious that he's behind this. The only question is why he would go to all that trouble for Trinity's diary. Of course, there were those jewels in the aspirin bottle, though how could he have known about them?"

"He wasn't after the diary." Sam sighed and sat on the edge of the bed. "And I don't think he came looking for the jewels in the aspirin bottle. Although he certainly wasn't about to leave them behind, once he found them."

"Then what?" Rachel asked. "What else could he have been looking for? And why didn't you tell the police?"

Sam crossed the room and lifted the blue nylon bag he'd taken to his parents' home. He unzipped the top and took out a light yellow bath towel. Setting the towel on the bed, he unwrapped it, folding back the edges to reveal a square box made entirely of gold. A crest in its center was rimmed with perfectly round red stones.

"What the hell is that?" Rachel gasped. "Where did it come from?"

"I found it buried in the sand the day you played with your Manta. When Hugh had run the video of the shadow, I thought I saw a quick glint of something—just a flash—in the sand. When we went down the next day, I went back to that spot. One corner was just slightly exposed—that's what I'd seen on the video—and it took nothing more than a quick dig to uncover it. I stuck it into my bag right before we surfaced and took it directly to the *Shearwater*."

"It's such a beautiful box, Sam." Rachel touched the red stones reverently, then smiled up at him and said, "You know I've always been partial to rubies."

"I know. You're a July baby." Sam smiled wanly. "Open the lid."

She sat cross-legged on the mattress and lifted the box onto her lap. With her thumbs she pried the lid open, not knowing what she might find, suspecting something wonderful, but not prepared in the least for what she found.

"Oh!" she gasped, her jaw nearly dropping to her knees. "Ohmigod, Sam!"

"I know." He nodded. He'd had the same reaction. As did his father, when he showed him two nights before.

"Are they real?" she asked. "Of course, they're real. They'd have to be real." She looked up at Sam. "They're really real?"

Sam nodded and lifted one of the diamonds the size of a hen's egg.

"The Tears of the Angels," he said softly.

"If they have names, they're real," Rachel muttered, still in shock.

"I wasn't sure what they were," Sam told her, lining the seven perfectly matched diamonds up across the velvet lining of the case. "I took them to my dad to see if he had any ideas. He knew right away what I had found and where they came from and when they disappeared."

"How could he know?"

"Diamonds like these—huge, perfect stones—are

the stuff legends are made of, Rachel. Who better to ask about legendary jewels than an archaeologist? I opened the box on my father's desk and he stared at them for a long time and then he said, 'My God, Sammy, you've found the Tears!' "

"Tell me," Rachel demanded.

"The rough stones had been found in India, about a hundred and forty years ago. The Vatican commissioned a gemologist to cut them into seven stones of exact size and shape. The stones were then to be mounted into the faces of seven statues of angels that had been carved by a famous Italian sculptor, Umberto Giorgio. After the stones had been cut, they were placed on a ship and sent to Bermuda, where an Italian ship was to take them to Italy and deliver them to the Vatican. The ship from India met the Italian ship as planned and reportedly turned over their cargo. The ship carrying the stones was last seen some twenty miles off Bermuda. There was some speculation that the stones never existed at all. Others said the ship disappeared in the Bermuda Triangle."

"How did they turn up on the *Melrose*?"

"An excellent question." Sam nodded. "One I intend to ask as soon as I get my hands on Norman Winter."

"He must have known the stones were on the *Melrose* when it went down," Rachel said. "But how in the world could he have known that?"

"That's question number two," Sam said calmly. "As a matter of fact, I have a whole long list of questions I'd like answered."

"Sam, I don't think we should have these stones,"

Rachel told him. "I think we should turn them over to the police."

"They belong to the Vatican, and that's where they'll be going."

"But the police need to know. What are you going to do, walk into the Vatican and say, Hi, I believe these might be yours? And in the meantime, Norman could be dangerous if he thinks you have the stones. He's already trashed your boat looking for them."

"And since he didn't find them, he's probably thinking that I don't have them."

"I still think we need to call the police. You should have told the Coast Guard."

"Technically, this is not a U.S. Coast Guard matter," he told her. "This involves the theft of antiquities. I think this is an FBI matter first, then, ultimately, Interpol."

"Then let's call them." She went into the galley and returned with the phone, which she handed to him. "Call them now, Sam."

"My dad and I called the FBI yesterday afternoon. They're already on it. An FBI agent will be meeting up with us at the wreck site. Arrangements are already being made to return the stones."

"Thank goodness. I was beginning to worry about you, Sam." She sat on the bed and wrapped her arms around him. "You know, I always thought there was something weird about Norman."

"There has to be something more than theft involved, Rachel."

"What do you mean?"

"I'm not sure I understand what's behind it, but look at the situation. Norman bought Eden's End and

has spent a fortune restoring it. If his only interest
was in finding these stones, why would he have done
that? He didn't need to buy the plantation to hunt
for the *Melrose*."

"Because it's a good front? Because he knew the
stones were on the *Melrose* and he needed to get
them, so he told the state he'd open a museum if
they let him bring the ship up?" Rachel paused and
frowned. "That sounds lame, even to me."

"Which brings us back to how did Norman know
they were on the ship?" Sam posed the question
again. "I for one can't wait to find out. And I fully
intend to find out, the minute we set foot on the
Annie G. Which by my calculations should be in
roughly another three hours."

He carefully closed the lid of the box and re-
wrapped it with the towel, then slid the box back
into the nylon bag.

"Come sit with me on the flybridge. It's a beautiful
day, Rachel. The sky is endless."

"I'm coming." She rose, her face creased, apparently in deep thought.

"But Sam . . ."

He paused in the doorway, waiting for her.

"What if it wasn't Norman?"

"What if what wasn't Norman?"

"The person who trashed the boat. It just doesn't
seem like a very *Norman* thing to do. It's just too . . .
obvious. Too blatant. Too . . . uncontrolled." She
stood in the cabin with her hands on her hips. "I'm
a very controlled person, Sam. I recognize the signs
in someone else. Norman is quite possibly the only
person I've ever met who is more controlled than I

am. In my wildest dreams, I can't imagine losing it so badly that I would do what was done to this boat. Somehow, I can't imagine Norman doing it, either."

"He could have someone working with him. Turk. Or Scully. Or Ernie. Or Hugh. Or Richmond. Rachel, it could be just about anyone on board the *Annie G.* Norman has his share of minions."

"Well, all this speculation won't get us anywhere. I think it's time to head on back to the wreck site and find out." Rachel started toward the ladder leading up to the flybridge. "Just pray that this FBI person is already there."

It was late afternoon by the time the *Shearwater* dropped anchor fifty feet from the *Annie G.*

Rachel stood on the flybridge and waved to Renny, who waved back excitedly.

"Let's take the dinghy on over and have a little chat with Norman," Sam said.

"Sounds good to me. Where are the Tears?"

"Inside the can with the coffee beans. They should be safe enough there for the time being."

"Anyone who's tasted your coffee certainly wouldn't think to look for them there."

"Very funny." Sam flipped the inflatable over the side of the cruiser. "Ladies first."

Rachel eased into the small boat, and sat, knees up, facing the sun that was dropping rapidly toward the horizon.

"Sam, I was thinking," Rachel said. "I think we should wait for the FBI agent before we confront Norman."

"I fully intended to," Sam replied as he dipped the

oars into the water and began to paddle toward the larger vessel. "The thought that Norman might have someone working with him has me concerned. One of them could be armed. Neither of us, you may have noted, is."

"I hope no one is. Guns and knives scare me. I spent years learning karate so that I could defend myself, but it's often occurred to me that karate's a poor defense if the other guy has a gun."

"You're not going to tell me that you have a black belt, are you?"

"No. Brown. I was working on it, though." Rachel leaned back against the side of the small craft and sighed. "Maybe I'll go back to it when this job is over—which could be sooner than we'd anticipated, Sam."

Rachel sat up straight, startled by the realization. "Sam, if we can prove that Norman was up to no good and he's arrested, this job will shut down."

"Most likely. At least, until the state of North Carolina decides what to do with the wreck. I guess you'll be going back to the *True Wind* with your dad and Jared."

Rachel nodded.

"Any thoughts on where you might go from here, Sam?"

"Well, some time ago I was offered a position as a staff archaeologist. I've been thinking about maybe seeing if the job's still available."

"I thought you liked freelancing."

"I did. I do. But maybe the time has come to look for something a little more stable, you know?"

"Hi, Rachel! Hi, Sam!" Renny was leaning over the

side of the *Annie G.* "I was watching for you! You're just in time for dinner! Mr. Cook the cook made sea scallops in wine! And rice pudding for dessert!"

"Two of my favorite things," Rachel called back. "We'll be there in a few. Why don't you save us seats at the table?"

"Okay! Sure! I'll do it!" Renny disappeared from the top of the railing.

"What do you suppose will happen to him if Norman goes to jail?" Rachel asked.

"I don't know."

"I've really become quite fond of him, Sam. I'd don't know where he could go," Rachel said thoughtfully. "I wonder if my dad would have a place for him. Renny knows his way around a boat and knows how to use some of the equipment. There are lots of things he could do."

"Well, just don't be too disappointed if he ends up holding you responsible for Norman's getting arrested."

"That's assuming that that's going to happen." Rachel stood as the dinghy reached the diving platform of the *Annie G.* "The bad guy doesn't always get what's coming to him, does he?"

"No, he doesn't," Sam said as he tied the dinghy up to the back of the boat. "But the last time I looked, the good guy still gets the girl."

"The good guy has already gotten the girl," she told him as she started up the ladder.

"I meant for keeps, Rachel." Sam grabbed her leg and tugged on it, stopping her momentarily from taking another step. "Not just for while this job lasts, but for keeps."

"It could happen, Sam." Rachel reached the top of the ladder and turned to look down at the man standing at its foot, and smiled. "It just could happen."

Dinner was a wary event, with Rachel eyeing every member of the crew suspiciously, weighing the possibility of their involvement with the theft from the *Shearwater*. Everyone seemed possible, but no one seemed probable. Norman, unfortunately, had yet to arrive. Rachel had been looking forward to watching how he might interact with the others. Maybe a look, a gesture, could be enough to give away the identity of his accomplice. With Norman absent, everyone else appeared to behave normally.

Rachel bit her lower lip. Somehow, she'd hoped that they'd get on board the *Annie G.* to find that the FBI had already arrested Norman and his accomplice—if in fact he had one—and that she and Sam could turn the Tears over and that would be that. She toyed with her dessert. When had anything ever been that easy?

Sam's foot pressed against hers under the table, and she looked up and met his eyes.

This had been that easy.

This had been incredibly easy.

Falling in love with Sam had been the easiest thing she'd ever done. The most important. The most inevitable. Why had she ever even thought to fight it? She couldn't remember now. The thought made her smile.

Sam leaned down and whispered, "Looks like Norman won't be showing until tomorrow. And our friend from the FBI apparently hasn't arrived yet, either. I say we go back to the *Shearwater* and spend the rest of the night talking about whatever it was that put that smile on your face."

"Sounds like a plan." She took his hand. "And you know how I love a man with a plan."

They slipped from the table discreetly and were halfway to the doorway when Renny called after her.

"Rachel, you didn't have your coffee yet."

She hesitated, then looked back at the small table where the coffeepot usually stood.

"Looks like it's going to be late tonight. I guess I'll have to wait until breakfast for my after dinner coffee." Rachel smiled. "I'll see you in the morning."

"Did you get a chance to ask Renny where Norman is?" Sam asked her as they untied the dinghy.

"He didn't know. He thought he'd be back by now. Who knows? He's probably back at Eden's End reading your great-great-grandmother's diary and using those gorgeous stones as Monopoly markers."

The sea was impossibly dark and calm, the swells so gentle that the ocean felt like an immense pillow beneath the tiny dinghy. Rachel lay back and looked up at the stars.

"Everything looks bigger out here, doesn't it?" she said softly. "The stars look bigger and brighter, the moon looks creamy gold and the ocean looks positively endless. It's so romantic, Sam."

"Ummm." Sam reached over and grabbed her leg, stroked the bare skin from her calf to her thigh, and began to whistle. "Moonlight Becomes You."

Rachel closed her eyes and hummed the melody. When had life ever been so good?

They hauled the dinghy onto the back of the *Shearwater*, and left it on deck fully inflated. Kissing eagerly in the doorway of the cabin, they failed to notice that they were not alone until they heard the sound of someone clearing his throat. They paused, midkiss, and slowly drew apart.

"I thought perhaps it best to announce myself," Norman said from the lounge, "rather than to permit you to continue to embarrass yourselves."

"How thoughtful," Sam said dryly.

In the semidarkness, Norman gestured—*It was nothing*—with both hands.

"Now, do come and join me. We have things to talk about."

"What might that be?" Sam asked as he casually entered the cabin before Rachel.

"Oh, I think you know quite well enough, Sam. Don't waste my time or try my patience by pretending otherwise."

"I suppose you're referring to your recent trashing of my boat." Sam crossed his arms over his chest. "Stealing back the diary, the little aspirin bottle . . ."

"What on earth are you talking about?" Norman snorted. "If I'd wanted the diary, I'd have had it back before you'd left Eden's End. And I'm allergic to aspirin. What would I want with yours?"

Rachel and Sam exchanged a long look.

"Norman, do you expect us to believe that you didn't have anything to do with the theft of the jewels . . ."

"What jewels?" he snapped. "You don't mean the diamonds? How could the diamonds have been stolen?"

"I'd ask my partner, if I were you." Sam nodded. "You do have a partner, don't you?"

Norman hesitated.

"Where are they, Sam?" His eyes narrowed. "Where are the Tears of the Angels? I know you have them. You're not the only one who saw that glint on the videotape. Interestingly enough, that 'spark' wasn't on the next day's film. Makes me think that someone already found them. Especially since the tape clearly shows your diving bag weighted down with something."

"You really didn't miss a thing by not diving, did you, Norman?"

"Not a thing. Where are the Tears, Sam?"

"You know, I just can't figure out how you could have possibly know about them, Norman. How could you have known that they were on the *Melrose?*" Sam rubbed his chin. "Those stones haven't been seen in roughly one hundred and forty some years. How would you have known they were on the *Melrose?*"

"He told me," Norman said simply.

" 'He'?" Rachel spoke for the first time.

"The Captain. Captain McGowan."

"Why would he tell you, Norman?" Sam asked.

"Because I'm his great-great-grandson," Norman told him. "Just like you, Sam."

"Anjelica's son . . ." Rachel said.

". . . my great-grandfather." Norman turned to Sam and said, "You may have his name, Sam. But I'm the one he's chosen."

"Chosen for what?"

"To have it all."

"You mean Eden's End?"

"Everything," Norman whispered.

"What else is there?"

"All of it," Norman repeated. "He led me to it. He wanted me to have it all. He saved it all for me."

Sam scratched the back of his head and tried to pretend that he didn't notice that Norman held a small pistol in his right hand.

"Well, now, Norman, I think you've got one hell of a story to tell. And I know that I for one would like to hear it. Mind if we sit?"

"You sit at that end of the table," Norman told him, "and keep your hands flat on the table. You"—he pointed to Rachel—"sit at this end."

Rachel stepped forward in the shadows and slid onto the bench seat at the opposite end from where Sam sat. She saw the gleam of chrome in Norman's hand and her mouth went dry.

"Start at the beginning, Norman. You know you want me to know," Sam said. "You know you want to tell me why he chose you, and not me."

"You are from the wrong one, Sam. He never loved her. The only woman he loved was Anjelica. Their son was his first son. He—Lorenzo—should have inherited Eden's End."

"Ah, Norman," Rachel piped up. "You're forgetting that Eden's End actually belonged to Trinity's family and Old Sam only . . ."

"It belonged to *Sam*. Legally. He ran it the way a plantation should have been run," Norman sneered. "Trinity was running it into the ground, what with her sneaking money to the abolitionists, running the Underground Railroad from Eden's End, helping her own slaves to escape so that the Captain couldn't sell them." Norman shook his head. "No. The plantation was meant to be *his*. He had bartered his love for Anjelica only to obtain Eden's End for the woman he loved, for their son . . ."

"It seems to me that was a choice Old Sam made strictly for himself," Rachel said. "He wanted Eden's End for himself, Norman. It wasn't until after he and Trinity had a family and he began to get bored that it even occurred to him to find Anjelica."

"That's a lie. One perpetuated no doubt by that murderous woman . . ."

"Norman, we all know that Trinity never intended to kill Anjelica. She didn't even know that anyone was in the house that night. She just wanted to make the house go away. Every time she looked at it, it reminded her that her husband . . ."

"Loved another woman. Loved another child more than he loved hers. It was all in his journals, Sam. And he left them for me to find."

"Where were they?"

"In the wall in the library. I've had them for years."

"You worked here when you were a young man . . ." Rachel recalled.

Norman nodded.

"I guess it's too much to think that it was coincidence that you ended up working at Eden's End."

Norman snorted. "It was all as he meant it to be, Sam."

"You think Old Sam led you to Eden's End?" Rachel asked.

Norman nodded. "All my mother ever talked

about when I was small was how my father's people
owned a big plantation in North Carolina. If my father had had any pride, she would say, he would
have stepped forward to claim his share. But of
course, he never did. After he died, she said it was
up to me."

The gun hand slipped just slightly, and Sam was
sorely tempted to make one quick grab for it. He
decided to ignore the temptation—at least for now.
He didn't know how good a shot Norman might be,
or how fast his reflexes were. Sam wasn't sure he
wanted to test either with Rachel smack in the
middle.

"So you came to Eden's End . . ." Rachel
prompted, trying to keep him talking.

"I walked up that long lane, and as soon as the
house came into sight, I knew that I was home. I
could feel it. I walked right up to the front door. And
just as I did, the door opened and Mr. Kelly—the
contractor who'd been hired to do some work on the
house—opened the door. His helper hadn't shown
up that day, or the day before. He figured me for a
likely replacement. He taught me the trades, carpen-
try, masonry. I worked for weeks with him, repairing
the clapboards and the windowsills outside. He told
me I'd done such a meticulous job on the windows,
that he'd put me to work inside. One of the chimneys
was crumbling, and needed repair. My job was to
carefully remove some paneling on either side of the
fireplace in the library so that the brick and mortar
could be replaced." Norman paused, as if reflecting.
"It took me a while, as one might suspect of so delicate a job, so I was alone with my task for quite some

time. Long enough to find that one of the cabinets had a false back that opened to a tunnel that led into the woods. Now, at first, I thought perhaps it was part of the Underground Railroad—until I saw what was there on the floor. Boxes of gold coins, small caskets of jewelry, things a boy like me could never even have imagined. But more important than the gold, more important than the jewels, was the Captain's journals. Finding them there like that, I knew. I knew . . ."

"Knew what?"

"That it was all just for me." Norman addressed Sam from across the room. "All the years you spent in that house, he never allowed you to know. He was saving it for me."

"So you took everything."

"Not all at once, of course. But over the next few weeks, yes, certainly. I had to take it, just as he'd intended for me to do."

"Where is it now, this treasure?" Sam asked casually.

"I sold it, piece by piece."

"How could you have done that without someone becoming suspicious?"

"There are few questions asked when you're buying or selling on the black market. I invested as I sold. Soon, I had enough to buy back Eden's End. All I had to do was wait. Sooner or later, it would be for sale, and I would buy it. It was as the Captain wanted, Sam."

"How did you know about the Tears?"

"He wrote about them in his journal. He wrote about all of his exploits, about how he had gathered together some of the men he'd fought with in the Mexican Wars to sail with him. How they met British ships in the Bahamas and picked up armaments to be delivered for the Confederacy and ran the blockades for fun."

"For fun?" Rachel's eyes widened. "Old Sam must have had a warped sense of humor if being fired upon by the Union Navy was his idea of fun."

"I'd appreciate it if you'd refer to him in more respectful terms." Norman frowned. "Anyway, yes. It was sport to him. A game. Later he would find it much more entertaining to chase the Union ships and take them."

"What did he do with them after he took them?" Sam asked.

"First they would strip them of their cargo and whatever else on board had value, and then he'd burn them."

"Burn them? But what about the crews . . ."

"I believe the expression is, Dead men tell no tales."

"He burned the ships with their crews on board?" Sam looked horrified.

"Of course," Norman replied calmly. "It was war, Sam."

"And the cargo?"

"Some sold on the black market in the Bahamas or Bermuda—the spoils split amongst the crew, of course—and some was delivered to the Southern ports that still remained open. It was helpful for him to maintain his reputation as a gun runner, of course."

"And in the meantime, he was amassing a personal

fortune in stolen goods. He was nothing more than a pirate after all, Sam," Rachel said.

"Oh, but he was a most successful one." Norman grinned. "And his booty helped to finance the renovations at Eden's End. Bought the *Annie G.* so that I could find the *Melrose*. And as we all know, the *Melrose* held something precious indeed."

"The Tears of the Angels," Sam said. "Well, since those stones had last been seen in India in 1863 when they were put onto a ship to sail to Bermuda, did he happen to tell you how they ended up on the *Melrose* a year later?"

"Of course. In port, in Bermuda, the Captain met a British sailor who'd had a bit too much to drink and was muttering something about having come from India on a ship that had something priceless aboard. The good Captain took him back to the *Melrose* where he was . . . persuaded to tell all, that his ship was to rendezvous with an Italian ship to hand over some priceless stones. The stones were to be taken to Italy, where they were to be embedded into the faces of some statues that had been commissioned by the Vatican. Well, how could the Captain have resisted? The stones were there for the taking, and so he went after them. Unfortunately, it appears that the *Melrose* went down on its way back to Eden's End. The Captain's last entry in the journal detailed his plans to go after the stones. The *Melrose* went down two weeks after that entry."

"What made you so sure that he had been able to take the stones?"

"I figured it was worth the gamble, Sam. He wrote about his plan to intercept the Italian ship around

Bermuda. If he had, and the stones were, in fact, on the *Melrose* when she went down, chances were that they'd still be there. It was worth the money I'd have to spend to bring it up. I knew if they were there, that you would find them for me. Of course, I did expect that you would turn them over to me, Sam. Seems you might have a bit of the Captain's pirate blood after all."

Sam lunged across the table, aiming for Norman's right hand. Norman reached out and, grabbing Rachel by the arm, pulled her from her seat. By the time Sam had hit the end of the table, the small gun was smack up against Rachel's right temple.

"I wish you hadn't done that, Sam. She's so pretty with her face intact. Sit down now, and it will stay that way. You don't want to be responsible for pretty Rachel losing her head." Norman chuckled at his little joke.

Sam froze, seeing the terror in Rachel's eyes. He sat back down slowly.

"Very good. Now, Sam, about the Tears . . ."

"Rachel?" a voice called from beyond the cabin. "Rachel, Mr. Cook the cook made coffee after all. I brought you some."

"Renny, stay outside," Norman called to his brother.

"Norman, I didn't know you were here. I would have brought you some, too, but I . . ." Renny crossed the deck.

"Renny, go back to the *Annie G*," Norman demanded.

"But, Norman . . ." Renny stood in the doorway, and stared for a long time.

"What are you doing to Rachel, Norman?" Renny asked in a voice quivering with fear.

"Go back out to the *Annie G.*, Renny," Norman repeated.

"Are you going to hurt Rachel, Norman?"

"Just go back out to the dinghy, and no one will get hurt, Renny," Norman said.

"Please don't hurt Rachel, Norman. She's my friend. She taught me to find treasure." Big tears began to roll down Renny's round cheeks. "I'm her buddy, Norman. I'm supposed to watch out for her."

Renny began to cry.

"Renny . . ." Norman said sternly, easing his grip on Rachel slightly, just enough for her to slam her head back as hard as she could into Norman's forehead.

In the blink of an eye, Sam dove forward for the gun still clutched in Norman's hand. Norman was no match for Sam physically. Within seconds, Sam had Norman facedown on the cabin deck, his arms pinned behind him.

"You okay, Rach?" Sam asked.

"Except for this pain in the back of my head. Damn, but Norman has a hard head, Sam."

Holding the small handgun on Norman, Sam reached behind him for the phone. Tossing it to Rachel, he said, "Call the Coast Guard."

"They're already on their way," Turk announced from the cabin door.

"You're . . ." Rachel stammered.

"FBI." Turk nodded. "We've been watching Mr. Winter for some time now. Seems he's had a lot of interesting items for sale over the past few years."

Turk leaned down and tapped Norman on the shoulder. "I saw your pal floating around behind the cruiser in his little dinghy. He was starting to get impatient waiting for you, and got a little careless. I figured now might be a good time to check out what was going on over here." He turned to Rachel. "I'm sorry that I wasn't here a little sooner. I hope you're all right."

Rachel nodded. "I'm okay. But Norman's pal. Who . . . ?"

"Hugh," Turk told them as he slipped handcuffs onto Norman's wrists.

"Hugh!" Rachel exclaimed.

"Well, I knew he was never really comfortable on a dive," Sam said. "But I never would have expected this."

As Turk pulled Norman to his feet, the dark glasses that had been the man's shield slipped off and fell to the floor.

"Allow me," Rachel said, bending to retrieve them.

She stood in front of Norman, her hands still shaking from the ordeal. His eyes, finally exposed, reminded her of a lab rat's, with their pink pupils and bloodshot whites. Rachel shivered and wordlessly slid the glasses onto his face and adjusted them slightly.

"Thank you," he said, as if they were still in the gracious dining room at Eden's End.

Rachel stepped back and looked at Turk.

"He's all yours," she said.

From across the dark night on the dark sea, the sound of a boat cutting across the waves grew louder and louder.

"Why, Mr. Winter, I do believe your ride is here. The Coast Guard will give you a ride back to shore. From there, I think the FBI will want to chat." Turk grinned. "Sam. Rachel. We'll want to talk with you."

"We'll be available," Sam assured him.

"I want my lawyer," Norman announced. "I'm a respected preservationist and I am . . ."

". . . wanted in three countries for the theft and illegal sale of antiquities. I wouldn't say anything else if I were you, Mr. Winter," Turk told him as he led him out to the deck, where Renny sat crying.

Sam stood in the open doorway of his cabin and silently watched the harrowing events of the night conclude.

Watched as Norman was walked to the diving platform.

Watched as he was helped onto the dinghy that would lead him to the Coast Guard cutter that was riding the waves at a point between the *Shearwater* and the *Annie G.*

Watched Renny collapse on the deck, wailing, as his brother disappeared into the night.

Watched as Rachel went to the small dark man and wrapped her arms around him, and rocked his restless form until his sobbing stopped.

21

❦

RACHEL LAY on her stomach across Sam's bed, oblivious to the fact that the ice pack covering most of the back of her head had slipped down to her neck. Sam leaned over and lifted the ice pack as gingerly as he could. She moaned softly in her sleep, and he eased the hair back from her temple before making a quiet ascent to the cabin level, where he dumped out the water and replenished the ice. Returning to the bedroom as quietly as he'd left, he sat on the edge of the bed and gently reapplied the ice pack to the lump that had risen on the back of her head.

"Sam?" Rachel murmured sleepily. "What time is it?"

"Almost three."

"AM or PM?"

"AM."

Sam lay down beside her and stroked her back. "How's your head?"

"Throbbing unmercifully right now."

"Well, I must say, that's one fine butt you have, Rachel."

"No doubt you are referring to my incredible head butt." She yawned. "Damn, that looks so easy when they do it on TV."

Sam laughed softly. "Well, it was a gutsy move on your part, Rachel, smacking him with your head like that."

"I only hope he's in as much pain as I am right now."

"Want some aspirin?"

"We have no aspirin. That sleazy Hugh stole the aspirin. Along with all those lovely jewels. You don't suppose he might have dropped a ruby or two on the carpet, do you?"

"Unlikely."

"Too bad. It would have been nice to have come out of this with just one little ruby ring. Who do you suppose will end up with those stones, anyway?" Rachel turned over slowly, catching the ice pack in one hand, to look up at Sam.

"I don't know." Sam shook his head. "I don't know if the true owner will ever be identified. In which case they may be turned over to the state."

"Who should rightfully split with the salvor." She struggled to sit up. "Which would be me."

"Wouldn't it be nice if it turned out that way?"

"It would. As it stands now, I have to go back to my father empty-handed." She sighed. "The fat fee we anticipated from Norman won't materialize, and I haven't even any salvage to sell."

"All things considered, I think your father will just be happy that you weren't hurt. It could easily have turned out differently, you know, if you hadn't been so quick witted."

"I was trying to think of a way to distract him, and the old head butt was the only thing I could think of. I don't know that I'd have done it if you hadn't been there to jump on Norman. Bless Renny for coming in when he did. Speaking of whom . . ."

"He's okay. Scully took him back over to the *Annie G.* Which the FBI has confiscated, by the way." Sam reached for Rachel and tucked her into the crook of his arm. "I have the feeling it will be years before this mess is sorted out."

"The wreck site will be shut down . . ."

"Yes. The FBI will seal it, which may or may not keep pirate divers from diving on the *Melrose.*"

"What do you think will happen to her? The ship?"

"Eventually, I think rights will revert totally to the state of North Carolina, and they may or may not try to bring her up."

"And Eden's End?"

"I don't know. It does belong to Norman."

"Isn't it ironic?" Rachel nestled closer. "Norman bought Eden's End with money he stole from your family."

"Who stole it from someone else," Sam noted. "And here's another irony. All these years, Old Sam was hailed as a hero, while Trinity was remembered only as a homely shrew. And here it turns out that not only was he not a hero, but he was a thief and a traitor. And when you take into consideration all the men he sent to their graves when he burned their ships, he'd probably qualify as a mass murderer, too."

"And Trinity was the real hero, after all. She was clever enough to save her family home. She was brave enough to help slaves—even her own—to escape."

"Why do you suppose she came back, that night we were at Eden's End?" Rachel asked softly. "Do you think your Aunt Carrie was right, that she was there to warn you?"

"That's anyone's guess. It could well be that the whole situation disturbed her. Her descendants moving out, and Norman, one of Anjelica's descendant's, moving in, living in her house. Not to mention the fact that he tore down the old Prescott cabin—no doubt to rid the plantation of their pesky presence. I guess that might be enough to bring one back from the dead."

"And I'll bet that Norman's trying to discredit her—branding her as a murderer when she was innocent—upset her."

"Maybe she just wanted us to know the truth. About Sam, I mean."

"Will her diary be returned to you?"

"It's being held as evidence, but it will be returned eventually. I'd really like to have that back. Then again, let's not lose sight of the fact that I lifted that from Eden's End. It really doesn't belong to me."

"I think Trinity is glad that you took it. Otherwise, you'd still think of her as a murderer. But what about the other diaries? The ones still at Eden's End?"

"I guess we'll have to wait to see what happens. I

think it's going to be a long time before the legalities are all straightened out."

"What would you like to have happen? It is your family, after all."

Sam thought it over for a long time before answering. "Oddly enough, I think I'd like to see it happen the way Norman had planned. With the museum and all. I don't know if the state will do that now, with the financial backing gone. Then again, maybe they'll end up selling it. Eden's End would make a great B and B."

"Ummm, it would. It's a lovely house, Sam."

"I wonder how my father will react to all this," he said softly. "I guess now that I'm unemployed, I'll have time to sit down and explain it all to him."

"Do you think he'll be upset?"

"At first. Then I expect he'll be intrigued by it all." Sam stretched his legs out in front of him. "I suppose you'll be going back to work on the *True Wind*."

Rachel nodded. "There's nothing left to do here. Want me to call my dad and see if he'd be interested in talking to you? He's going to need a good archaeologist on this job." Rachel leaned up and whispered in his ear, "I'll give you a real good reference."

Sam smiled. "Thanks, Rachel, but I've already made an inquiry about my next job. But first thing in the morning, we can head for Maryland and see if anything interesting has been recovered yet."

"Maybe we could spend a few days on the Outer Banks, you and me. Just the two of us."

"That's a possibility. I will need to dock someplace long enough for the insurance adjuster to look at the damage to the *Shearwater*."

"Most of it's fixed," Rachel reminded him.

"Yes, but we have all the photographs that Iona took and the police report. I don't expect a problem."

"The insurance company will probably want to go after Hugh to recover anything they pay out, since he caused the damage."

"They'll have a tough time getting anything out of him, since he'll be going away for a while for all the assistance he gave Norman. Not to mention what he did to my boat."

"You're pressing charges, then?"

"You betcha. Nobody touches my boat."

Rachel closed her eyes and raised her hands to her temples.

"Head still hurts?" Sam asked, and she nodded. "I wish I had something to give you for that."

"You know what?" She sat up. "I just remembered that I do have aspirin. I bought some when we were in Wilmington. The bottle's in my bag, Sam. It's on the floor near H.D.'s cage, if you wouldn't mind getting it for me."

"I don't mind." Sam eased off the bed so as not to disturb her, then turned the light on in the cabin. He was back in minutes with a glass of water and the unopened bottle of aspirin.

"Damn childproof lids," he muttered.

"Here, I can do it." She reached for the bottle and with the twist of her wrist, flipped the top off.

"How did you do that?" Sam frowned. "I've never seen anyone do that."

Rachel laughed and popped two white tablets into her mouth, then washed them down with water.

"You're an amazing woman, Rachel Chandler.

Head butts the villain to save the day and opens childproof caps with the flick of a wrist. I've never known anyone like you. I may just have to marry you, Rachel, to keep you from getting away."

"I'm not trying to get away, Sam," she told him. "You don't have to marry me to keep me here."

"Well, I might just want to marry you anyway, Rachel. Just because you make me smile." He took the empty glass and placed it on the small table next to the bed, then sat down and cradled her against him. "What do you think?"

"I think we need to think this over, Sam. We haven't known each other very long."

"Have you ever known anyone who makes you laugh as much as I do?"

"No, actually, I haven't."

"Makes you smile for no reason other than because I make you feel like smiling?"

She shook her head, aware that she was, at that moment, smiling just because he made her want to.

"Any man ever kiss you the way I do?"

"No, Sam. No man ever has."

"Loved you the way I do?"

"No." Rachel lay back against the pillow, her eyes half-closed.

"So what's the problem?"

"I guess I just have to think it through, Sam. There are a few things I need to work out."

"Take all the time you need, Rachel. I'm not going anywhere." He covered her with a light blanket and turned off the light, then lay down beside her, holding her hand until she fell asleep.

* * *

Gordon Chandler stood on the deck of his refitted tug, the *Albemarle,* his hands on his hips, listening to one of his divers describe what had just been found on the ocean floor. The first of the *True Wind*'s treasure, several golden goblets and an old wooden chest, were being raised at precisely that minute. Gordon only heard half of what the man said, and barely acknowledged that he'd heard at all. Under any other circumstances, the long-anticipated news would have caused his heart to pound, his palms to sweat, and that well-remembered jubilation to engulf him.

The morning's news had preceded the discovery. Everything that had happened after that was inconsequential as far as Gordon was concerned.

His daughter—his Rachel—had had a gun held to her head by a madman. A madman that he, Gordon, had sent her to work with. And no word had been heard of her—from her—since Norman Winter had been arrested by the FBI the night before.

"Gordon, someone's on the radio from CNN. Said he's a friend of yours," a curious crew member called from the cabin doorway. "He wants to know if you've talked to Rachel."

Gordon all but ran to the radio, hoping his friend had news to share with him, but he knew no more now than he'd known this morning. Rachel had seemed to disappear. He walked to the stern and looked down into the water where his divers were surfacing, hooting and hollering as they drew up a length of gold chain and scrambled to bring it on board. A laughing Jared swung over the side of the

boat and opened his diving bag as he eagerly walked
to his father.

"Hey, Dad, how'd you like to drink your celebra-
tory toast from this." His eyes shining, he presented
his father with a goblet fashioned of gold encrusted
with deep purple stones. "We thought we'd rinse it
out and fill it with some of that champ—"

Jared stopped in midsentence as his father turned
an ashen face in his direction.

"Dad, what's wrong?"

"Rachel." Gordon very clearly struggled to maintain his composure. "It was on the news . . ."

"What about Rachel?" Jared seemed to freeze.

"Norman Winter was apparently dealing antiquities on the black market. Somehow Rachel and Sam
McGowan got between him and something he
wanted. He held a gun to her head, Jared."

Jared's knees went weak.

"Dad, she isn't . . ."

"No, no. The news reports were very sketchy, but
apparently the FBI managed to disarm Norman."
Gordon swallowed hard. "The bastard held a gun to
my little girl's head, Jared, and I sent her there."

"Dad, come on, you had no way of knowing . . ."

"And even now I don't know where she is."

"Winter's boat, maybe?"

"It's already come ashore. She wasn't on it, according to my friend at CNN. They had a crew at
the dock when the *Annie G.* was brought in by the
Coast Guard. Most of the crew came back in on it or
the cutter, but Rachel wasn't on either."

"Dad, Rachel will turn up and she'll be fine. Didn't
they say she was all right?"

"No. They only said she hadn't been shot."

"That in itself is something to be grateful for. She'll be in touch soon, Dad."

"It can't be soon enough for me, Jared. I need to see her. I need to see with my own eyes that that crazy bastard didn't hurt her. You know, she did tell me that she had misgivings about him, and I ignored her."

"Dad, let it be until we get the whole story."

Gordon nodded, turning the goblet around and around in his hands without even seeing it.

"I'm sorry, son. This is such a big day for you. Finally, your ship has started to give up her secrets."

"It's a pretty hollow triumph, all things considered. It doesn't seem quite as important as I thought it would." Jared told him. "Maybe I'll call the divers in for the rest of the day. I seem to have lost my enthusiasm."

"Don't, Jared. Let them go back down. They've worked hard for this."

"I guess you're right." Jared nodded. "Dad, Rachel will come here. She knows where we are, she has to know we're worried about her."

"Then why hasn't she called? Unless the batteries are low on the phone and I didn't hear it ring. I'll change them now, just in case."

Gordon started for the cabin, and Jared called after him, "Dad, have you talked to Delia? Doesn't she know someone who used to work for the FBI?"

"No, I haven't called her. I wanted to leave the line free. But now that you mention it, that private investigator she uses from time to time was a former agent. I'll call her right now . . ."

Gordon hurried past Jared into the cabin. Through the large window, Jared could see his father look up into the sky as if in prayer. Jared added his own prayer that his sister was safe, wherever she was, and that she would let them know she was safe before too much more time had passed.

It was almost four in the afternoon when the cruiser appeared off the stern of the *Albemarle*. Jared didn't pay it much mind until it came within three hundred feet of the dive boat and continued to close. Curious, and wary that perhaps news of their find had somehow managed to leak, Jared climbed the steps to the flybridge, his binoculars in hand. Training the lenses on the cruiser that now was less than seventy-five feet from his bow and appeared to be preparing to drop anchor, Jared watched the boat ride the waves for a few long minutes before a woman appeared on board, sun glinting off her auburn hair. A man in dark green trunks and a tan shirt, a red baseball cap on his head, emerged from the cabin, and appeared to be arguing with the woman. He tossed a dinghy off the back of the cruiser and the woman got in, arms crossed over her chest as one who has allowed a concession she clearly believed to be unnecessary.

Jared broke into a wide grin and took the steps two at a time until his feet hit the deck with a thud.

"Dad!" he called into the cabin. "Come quick! It's Rachel!"

Rachel and Sam McGowan, Jared realized as the dinghy came closer.

"Hey, Rach!" Jared called from the starboard side of the tug.

She waved back enthusiastically, as did the man who rowed the dinghy.

Within minutes Rachel was climbing on board the *Albemarle,* to be swept off her feet and swung around by her brother while Sam tied the dinghy to the foot of the ladder that hung over the side of the boat.

"Rachel! We were worried sick over you," Gordon exclaimed as he folded his daughter into a bear hug. "Why didn't you call?"

"Worried?" Rachel frowned as if the thought had never occurred to her. "How could you even have known . . . ?"

"The news carried a sketchy story about Norman's ship being boarded by the FBI and the Coast Guard and Interpol and how Norman had held you and Sam at gunpoint until the FBI rescued you and arrested Norman."

"Oh, the FBI rescued us, did they?" Rachel turned to Sam, who was just climbing over the side of the boat. "Did you hear that, Sam? Dad said it's all over the news about how the FBI rescued us from Norman's clutches."

"Did they now?" Sam dropped his paddles onto the deck. "Hello, Gordon. Jared. Good to see you both."

"I can't tell you how happy we are to see you." Gordon extended one hand to shake Sam's, his other arm still around his daughter's shoulder. "Thank you for bringing her back, Sam. But really, if you'd called, we would have come to pick her up. No need for you to have gone to the trouble."

"No trouble at all, Gordon." Sam's mouth curved slightly at one corner. "It was my pleasure."

Sam and Rachel exchanged a look of amused conspiracy that, while unnoticed by Gordon, was not overlooked by Jared.

"Now, come on into the cabin out of the hot sun and tell us everything," Gordon said as he walked his daughter to the cabin. "Jared, where'd you put that goblet? I think I'm ready to celebrate now."

"Jared, Sam, are you sure you don't want to come with us?" Gordon called from Sam's dinghy.

"No, I'm anxious for Sam to take a quick look at the *True Wind*," Jared called back.

"I hate you both, you know that, don't you?" Rachel glared up from her seat in the dinghy. "There is absolutely nothing wrong with me. You are worse than a bunch of old women. Worrying about nothing. Sam wouldn't even let me swim from the *Shearwater* over to here. Dad's making me get my head x-rayed and Sam is going to get to see the wreck before I do. It's not fair."

"Rachel, only an idiot would swim—or dive—with a head injury," Gordon said calmly. "Fortunately, Sam appears to have more sense than you do."

"I don't have a head injury," she told him flatly.

"We're just going to rule that out, sweetheart. It won't take long. Assuming all is well, you can dive with the crew tomorrow. But today, we're having someone look at that lump." Gordon began to paddle toward the *Shearwater*. "Sam, thanks again for loaning me your boat to take Rachel in to Bishop's Cove."

"Don't mention it. Hurry back, Rachel." Sam

leaned against the side of the boat, then laughed when Rachel stuck her tongue out at him.

"So, Sam," Jared said as the dinghy carrying Gordon and Rachel reached the back of the *Shearwater*. "Dad tells me that you and he have been chatting back and forth by phone a lot recently. That you've been discussing the possibility of you joining Chandler and Associates."

"Yes. Yes, we have. Your father has offered me a position on several occasions. " Sam nodded. "I'm strongly considering it now."

"Good. We could use your expertise. Particularly on this job, Sam. Let's take a quick dive, and you can see what we have down there. Then we can come back up and have a beer, and I'll tell you where I think we are with the *True Wind*." Jared smiled and slapped Sam on the back. "And then you can tell me what's going on between you and my sister."

22

<hr>

"I TOLD YOU I was fine, Dad," Rachel said as they walked out of the emergency medical facility three blocks from the marina in Bishop's Cove.

"No harm in checking things out, Rachel." Gordon tucked his daughter's arm through his own, grateful for her presence there, even if it had been brought about by what could have been a disaster.

All morning long, while he had paced, awaiting news of her whereabouts, Gordon had been nagged by the thought that he and his daughter had never spent much time together. He had vowed that, given the opportunity, he'd change that.

Starting now.

Pausing at the wooden sidewalk that ran down along the pier, Gordon asked, "Can your old man take you to dinner?"

"Sure. I'd like that."

"What's your pleasure? The Bishop's Inn is a few blocks over. Or there's Captain Dan's down on the dock."

"Let's do Captain Dan's," Rachel said. "I'm not dressed for dinner at the inn."

Captain Dan's was a dock bar with wooden picnic tables and benches overlooking the pier. Across the narrow inlet the marsh curved to form a small cove where a pair of swans floated with their young. Overhead nosy gulls kept keen eyes on the dock for scraps, and upon a telephone pole, a black-crowned night heron kept its eyes on the tiny swans.

A cheery waitress led Gordon and Rachel to a table near the silent bandstand—the band having yet to arrive—and told them, "We have some killer crabs today. Blues, this big." She held her index fingers about eight inches apart. "Not counting the claws, by the way."

"Rachel?" Gordon asked.

"Sounds great."

"Bring us a dozen."

"How would you like them seasoned? We do a mild, a spicy, and an 'oh mama,' which is a particularly exciting combination of hot spices."

"I think I can handle spicy, but 'oh mama' might have to wait till the next trip. I think I've had just about all the excitement I can take for a while," Rachel told her father.

The waitress covered the entire top of their table with brown paper and handed them each a mallet. She returned in minutes with frosty mugs of beer and a basket of highly seasoned french fries.

A busboy appeared with a tray piled high with the fabled Maryland blue crabs.

"You have a dozen steamed? Spicy?" he asked.

"Yes."

The crabs were dumped unceremoniously onto the table.

"Enjoy," the young man said.

"These are incredible." Rachel licked the seasoning from her fingers. "I haven't had these since . . ."

She hesitated.

"Since when?"

"Since Sam and I visited with his parents last week on St. Swithin's Island," she said quietly.

"Oh?" Gordon's left eyebrow raised, as close as he generally came to registering surprise. "Sam took you to meet his parents?"

"It was his mother's birthday."

"I see."

The silence filtered about them as they each re-grouped to collect their thoughts. This was news Gordon hadn't expected to hear, news that Rachel hadn't planned on sharing that night. It had caught them both off-guard.

"I think I met Sam's father some years ago." Gordon cleared his throat. "Nice man."

"Very," Rachel agreed.

"So. How was it?"

"It was fine. Great. Interesting," she told him. "Sam comes from a big, close family. So many of them were there for the weekend. It was noisy and there were always about a half-dozen conversations going on at once. I walked through a muddy swamp with Sam's mother to gather water lilies, and I went surf fishing for spots and sea bass."

"Quite a change for you, I would think."

Rachel nodded.

"It was a form of culture shock at first, but I did

okay. I got used to it. I liked the McGowans. They're warm, wonderful people."

"And Sam?"

"He's pretty warm and wonderful too, Dad."

"Hmmm. Yes. I see." Gordon fumbled with his mallet, missing the claw he'd been aiming at. "So, I'm assuming that you're telling me that you and Sam . . ."

He couldn't think of the appropriate words to finish the sentence, so he just left it hanging.

"Yes."

"I see." Gordon made a second, more successful assault on the crab. "And is this serious?"

"Yes, it is. At least, I think it is."

Gordon digested this latest for a moment, then asked, "What do you mean, you *think* it's serious?"

"Daddy, Sam is the single absolute best thing that ever happened in my life."

"Are you in love with him?"

"Yes."

"Is he in love with you?"

"He says he is."

"So what's the problem?"

Rachel placed her mallet down on the messy brown paper and looked up at her father.

"It scares me to death, Dad."

"Loving Sam scares you?"

"Yes."

"Why? Is he unkind to you? Are you afraid that he'll hurt you somehow?"

"No, no, of course not. Sam would never hurt me."

"Then what?"

"What if I'm wrong, Dad? What if he's wrong?

What if we don't love each other enough? What if we stop loving each other and . . ."

"Whoa, Rachel, where is this coming from?"

Rachel swallowed hard and asked the question she knew she had to ask.

"Did you ever love Mom? Did she ever love you?"

She hadn't intended on being that blunt, but the words tumbled out and she could not stop them. If Gordon was surprised by the question, he did a damn good job of hiding it.

"Yes, Rachel, I did. I loved your mother very much."

"Did she love you?"

"I like to believe that she did. For a while, anyway."

"What happened between you, Dad? All these years, I never wanted to ask. But now I need to know. Why did you stop loving each other?"

"I guess we should have talked about this sooner, shouldn't we?" Gordon's eyes blinked back tears that he had not shed in years, and he sighed heavily. "Rachel, your mother was a beautiful woman. You have her eyes and her hair, have I ever told you that? No? Well, you do. She was lovely."

He pushed the crab shell debris around on the table with the mallet, as if needing his hands busy.

"I met Amelia when she was eighteen years old. I was twenty-six. She was a talented pianist, she could play anything by ear, though she'd never had a lesson. Her parents had never given her much encouragement, and as a result, she lacked confidence. But I thought she was very talented. For a wedding present, I arranged for piano lessons for her. Her instructor told me she was one of the most gifted pianists he'd ever seen, that she should train for a career. Amelia was astounded, but delighted. For her birthday that year, I bought her a piano."

"The Steinway."

"Yes. Well, after a time, Amelia spent her time doing little else but practicing, hour after hour, day after day. Even Jared's birth didn't seem to affect her. She started taking the train down to New York two days each week, then three, then everyday, for lessons. That's when Aunt Bess moved in, to care for Jared. Soon, she was offered an opportunity to play professionally. She'd landed an audition with an important conductor and apparently knocked him off his feet. He offered her a position on the spot, which she accepted on a temporary basis."

"Why only temporary?"

"She found out she was pregnant with you."

"Oh, I'll bet that news thrilled her." Rachel inhaled sharply. "No wonder she didn't like me."

"Rachel, it wasn't that she didn't like you, or Jared, or me. It's just that we were, more or less . . ." He tried to chose his words carefully.

"In her way," Rachel said flatly.

Gordon tried to think of something to say that could take the sting from the truth, but all he could say was, "I'm sorry, baby."

"So she just left us? I never knew she wasn't coming back."

Tears swelled in Rachel's eyes and began to run down her cheeks. Gordon reached across the table with his handkerchief and blotted the drops from her face.

"I'm sorry, baby," he repeated. "I'm sorry that she left us, and I'm sorry that I wasn't there more often for you, after she did. Lately it's occurred to me more and more just how much I let you and Jared down over the years."

"I guess you had your own hurt to deal with. I don't know that we can blame you for not wanting to be home after she left."

"Why, thank you, sweetheart, for sticking up for me, but I'm afraid that that's not a good enough reason. I'm an adult. Whatever pain I had, I should have been able to handle that without leaving my children in the care of a woman who didn't know the first thing about child rearing. And while it would be easy to blame it all on your mother's leaving, well, that simply wouldn't be fair."

"What do you mean?"

"I mean that while I was, indeed, heartbroken when your mother left, it never occurred to me to stop working. Not after Amelia and I were married, not after Jared and you were born. Salvaging was my job. Chandlers had been scrounging from the sea's floor for three generations. I wasn't about to go back to Connecticut and look for something else to do. So while it's certainly easy to blame your mother for leaving you to follow her own dreams, I don't think we can ignore the fact that I was doing the same damned thing. Oh, at the time, I didn't see it that way, of course. And somehow I always thought there'd be more time, later on. But it passes so damned quickly somehow. The years fly past so much faster than we ever intend for them to do."

Rachel reached across the table and took her father's hands.

"I never meant for you to grow up so fast, Rachel. Sometimes I still don't understand how it happened."

"No wonder you never remarried." Rachel shook her head slowly.

"What do you mean?" Gordon frowned.

"After all that, with Mom, who would want to?"

"Rachel, the only reason I never remarried was because I hadn't found a woman I loved enough to commit to, to share my life with. Until now."

"Dad, what are you saying?"

"I've been thinking about asking Delia to marry me, but I wanted to discuss it with you and Jared first. I wanted to know how you felt about it. How you felt about Delia . . ."

"Why, she's wonderful, of course." Rachel smiled. "A tad strong-willed, perhaps . . ."

Gordon laughed out loud. "Yes, I know. She can be a bit overbearing at times, but she means well, sweetheart. Delia has a big heart, and she just always wants to make everything right for the people she loves."

"I think she's charming, Dad."

"But . . . ?" Gordon sensed there was something left unsaid.

"But are you sure you want to go through all that again? Aren't you afraid?"

"Of course not. Delia is not Amelia, and besides, she's already established in her career, as I am in mine. We respect each other's professions, Rachel. It's not the same."

"How can you be sure?"

"Rachel, love never comes with a written guarantee. Sometimes you just have to trust."

"But what if you're wrong?"

"What if I'm right?"

"But didn't you think you were right when you married my mother?"

"Yes, of course. But what happened between Amelia and me has nothing to do with my relationship with Delia. And in spite of the fact that marriage between your mother and me did not work out, I wouldn't change the past, Rachel, even if I could. I have you, and your brother, and there's nothing else in this world that even comes close in importance to me. So even out of that bad situation came something wonderful. Who am I to have regrets?"

"That's very sweet, Dad."

"It's very true, Rachel."

Rachel leaned back to permit the busboy to roll up the brown paper upon which discarded crab shells and claws were piled.

"You folks finished?" he asked, and they both nodded.

"Rachel," Gordon asked after their dinner debris had been removed, "I have a feeling that this conversation is about more than your mother and me, or about Delia and me."

Rachel nodded.

"We're really talking about you and Sam, aren't we?"

She nodded again.

"Sweetheart, no one can see into the future, and Lord knows I'm not qualified to advise anyone on

their love life. But if you love Sam, then you have to
trust him. You can't forge a good relationship while
you're busy looking over your shoulder wondering
if history will repeat itself. What happened between
your mother and me is not going to happen to you.
You're much too smart to let that happen, and so is
Sam. If you want my opinion, I think he's an uncom-
monly good man. Besides being one of the brightest
young lights in his field, I trust Sam. It's one of the
reasons why I offered him a job . . ."

Rachel's head snapped up.

"You what?"

"I offered him a job. Didn't he tell you?"

"No. No, he didn't. When?"

"Rachel, I've been trying to hire Sam for years, but
he kept turning me down. Then he called a few
weeks ago and said that he'd reconsidered, and that
if there was still a position available, he'd like to
interview for it. Well, of course I wanted him to join
C and A. We agreed to meet once the job for Winter
was completed. I'm hoping to talk with him about it
tonight." Gordon drained the last of the now-warm
beer from his mug. "How would you feel about
that?"

"About working with Sam?"

Rachel thought back over the past month or so,
about the days she'd spent working alongside Sam,
of the nights she'd spent in his arms. She'd trusted
him with her life.

"Sam is wonderful to work with. I can honestly
say he's one of the best I've ever seen." She smiled
up at her father. "That's an unbiased opinion, by the

way. I recognized that in him even when I didn't like him."

"Got off to a rocky start, did you?"

"Just for a while. But Sam was smart enough to make things right." Rachel smiled, remembering. "Sam was disappointed when you weren't on the *Melrose* project, Dad, and I didn't take kindly to that."

"I'm sorry, Rachel."

"Don't be. Of course, he had every right to be disappointed. You're Gordon Chandler. And I'm . . . I'm me." She held her hand up to him to cut off his protest. "Dad, you're The Man when it comes to this stuff. I'm very good, but I'm not you. Not yet, anyway. But someday, I will be."

"I'm glad to hear you say that, sweetheart. I know that when I retire, the family business will be in the very best of hands."

Gordon signaled for the check.

"Now, let's go on back to the *Albemarle*. I have some business to discuss with our Dr. McGowan."

"You and your dad were gone a long time," Sam said when Rachel joined him on the bow of the *Albemarle*. "Is everything okay?"

"Everything is wonderful." She sat down next to him. "We had dinner at a dock bar and ate spicy crabs. My lips are still burning."

Sam leaned over and sampled the spices. "Hmmm. Lot's of Old Bay. Must have been great."

Rachel laughed.

"It was." She snuggled close to him.

"Actually, I was asking about your head."

"My head?" She shifted around until she was leaning against Sam's chest. "My head has never been better."

"Good." He eased back against the side of the boat and looked up to the stars. "It's a beautiful night, isn't it?"

"The best." She sighed. "I've come to the conclusion that nothing is more romantic than a moonlit, starlit night at sea."

"Ummm. I agree." He shifted again, and reached into his pocket for something. "Here. Give me your hand."

"Which one?"

"The left." He took her hand and slid a ring onto her middle finger, saying, "I was afraid this would be too big, but I think we can have it cut down, if you'd like to wear it on another finger."

Rachel looked down at her hand, where a cabochon ruby sat upon her finger in a twist of gold. "Oh, Sam, it's so beautiful . . ."

"We found it on the *True Wind*," Sam told her. "When Jared and I went down earlier. There it was, just lying on the sea floor."

"Did Jared see this, or did you slip it into your aspirin bottle?" She eyed him with mock suspicion.

Sam laughed. "I showed Jared. He told me it was mine. I thought I'd give it to you."

"I love it, Sam. It's the most beautiful thing I've ever seen. And you know how I've been dying for a ruby ring." Rachel turned her finger to the ship's lights. "And you know that I am . . ."

"Yes. A July baby." He kissed her fingertips, then

her chin, her nose, her mouth. "Rachel, there's something I have to tell you."

"What's that?"

"I've been talking to your dad about coming to work for Chandler and Associates."

"I know. My dad told me." She held her hand up in front of her face, still admiring her ring. "When did you decide to do that?"

"After the first night we spent together. I realized that my life would never be the same without you. You are committed to your job, as am I. But if we could work together, I figured we'd have it all."

"Why didn't you tell me?"

"Because I didn't want you to think that I was using my relationship with you to get to your father. That I had any interest in you other than the fact that I loved you."

"Do you love me, Sam?"

"Do you doubt for a minute that I do?" His arms drew her closer. "Do you doubt for a second that I always will?"

"No, Sam. I don't doubt it for a second."

"Do you love me, Rachel?"

"More than I ever expected to love anyone."

"Good. Then you'll be here waiting for me when I get out of my meeting with your dad, and we'll talk about what we're going to do with the rest of our lives."

Rachel threw her arms around Sam's neck and whispered in his ear. "I have a few really good suggestions . . ."

"You hold that thought," Sam kissed her again,

then started back toward the cabin, his softly whistled tune floating over the deck of the *Albemarle*.

"Moonlight Becomes You."

Rachel dropped a life preserver behind her back and leaned against the side of the boat.

It was all going to be just fine. She and Sam would have the sea and the stars and the moonlight to share for a long time to come. Her father had been right. Sometimes, you just have to trust.

And if ever there was a man Rachel could trust with her heart, it was Sam McGowan.